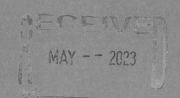

WHEN
the ANGELS
LEFT the OLD
COUNTRY

WHEN

the ANGELS

LEFT the OLD

COUNTRY

by sacha lamb

LEVINE QUERIDO

MONTCLAIR | AMSTERDAM | HOBOKEN

This is an Arthur A. Levine book
Published by Levine Querido

LQ

LEVINE QUERIDO

www.levinequerido.com • info@levinequerido.com

Levine Querido is distributed by Chronicle Books, LLC

Text copyright © 2022 by Sacha Lamb

Library of Congress Control Number: 2022931609

ISBN: 978-1-64614-176-0

Printed and bound in Canada

MIX
Paper from
responsible sources
FSC
www.fsc.org   FSC® C103567

Published October 2022

First Printing

For my grandparents. You have always wanted to know what I'm up to, even when you don't understand it.

PART I

WHEN the ANGELS LEFT the OLD COUNTRY

one

IN THE BACK CORNER of the little synagogue in the shtetl that was so small and out of the way it was only called Shtetl, there was a table where an angel and a demon had been studying Talmud together for some two hundred years. Indeed, they had been studying in that corner since before the little shul was built, and had been rather startled to look up one day and realize an entire building had sprung up around them.

Because the corner they had claimed for their own was close to the door and far from the stove, no one had ever felt it necessary to question their presence. They were always there; there was no reason to assume they would ever not be there. They showed up to study and sometimes could be seen davening in the back of the shul at minyan, too, but never when there were fewer than ten men in the room.

One of them never wore a tallis, and the other wore a tallis even during the night, folded over his back like a pair of delicate wings.

The demon's name was Ashmedai. He was not the demon king Ashmedai you may have heard of, but one of that Ashmedai's children. The demon king enjoyed an over-generous measure of self-regard and had named a great number of his children after himself. Perhaps he intended to stymie the Angel of Death. Perhaps he had trouble thinking of another name.

In any case, our Ashmedai was a very minor prince of demons, belonging to that class of creatures another people might call fairies, and we Jews know as sheydim: mischievous spirits of the earth who enjoy leading people astray. Most of those who knew him did not call him by his full name, but shrank it to fit his stature, and called him Little Ash.

Little Ash knew hardly any magic and did not even have the wings with which most adult demons fly from place to place. He had made trouble in the demons' yeshiva, where they learn their magic, and without completing his studies he had been sent to Poland, where he found he liked it better than at home, as in his father's palace other demons were always treating him like a child and telling him what to do.

The angel had been sent to Shtetl for a purpose it had now forgotten, and had stayed in Shtetl to hinder the mischievous whims of Little Ash. Like Little Ash, it resembled a human youth; unlike Little Ash, who considered himself to be male, the angel had merely chosen the shape of a man for convenience, as angels have done since the time of Abraham, Our Father. It had never had a bar mitzvah, or a bat mitzvah, or any such ceremony at all, and had never bothered to wish for one.

Its name, of course, changed according to the activity in which it was engaged. At the moment, the angel's name was Argument.

"They call it the Golden Land," said Little Ash. "All the young people are going there."

"Golden Land!" said the angel. "Ashel, I have no interest in gold. Why should I? I find gold excites the yetzer hara terribly."

"Yetzer hara, yetzer shmara," said Little Ash. "We're not talking about the evil inclination."

"*You*," said the angel, "are always talking about the evil inclination."

Little Ash slapped a hand on the table next to the open volume of Talmud. The noise was loud enough to startle the doe goat who was ruminating in the doorway, but not loud enough to startle the old men who were the only others in the shul at the moment. It was a market day, and most of the people of Shtetl had gone to a larger town nearby to earn money for their Shabbes dinners. The men would be home soon for the evening service, bringing the town gossip with them.

Little Ash had started the argument with the angel, as he usually did. Little Ash, being young and unmarried, preferred the company of young, unmarried people, because he did not understand anyone else, and he found that youth made people particularly open to his mischievous suggestions. Lately all of the people he liked best had been leaving their Shtetl. There were no jobs for Jews in Poland, everyone was saying, but in America they had jobs. In America they had all kinds of wonderful things, according to the papers and to the gossip Little Ash had heard from those whose families had sent them letters.

It was not only that America sounded exciting, although it did. It was also that Shtetl, which had always been small, was even smaller and quieter now. Little Ash was finding it harder to go about his business and was afraid that people would start to notice his presence, and then he would be banished, or else eaten up by one of the gentile demons from the towns around them, who were always throwing rocks at him and telling him to keep to his own territory. The pogroms in the east had everyone unsettled, always looking over their shoulders. Shtetl was too small to merit that kind of trouble, but if trouble ever came, it was certainly too small to survive it.

"I was already listening to whatever you were going to say," said the angel in reproach, taking Little Ash's hand and moving it farther from the sacred pages. There was dirt under the demon's fingernails, and he couldn't be trusted with books.

Little Ash slapped the table again, with the other hand. "All I'm *saying* is, if the young people are going to America, oughtn't we go with them? Who will look after them if you don't? Who will foster the yetzer tov in the Golden Land for the children of Shtetl, if not you? That's all I'm saying."

The angel, who suddenly felt as if its name were going to change today, said, "I'm sure they have rabbis in America."

This was perhaps too confident on the angel's part, but Little Ash did not have time to mock it, because at this moment there was a noise of boots being knocked clean outside, and all the old men sat up a little straighter, for the rest of the minyan had come back from the market. Little Ash, ears keen for gossip, turned around at once, and jabbed the angel with a sharp elbow when it kept its eyes on its page of Talmud.

"Look, look," he hissed. "It's Samuel the Baker—his daughter has gone to America."

The angel did not remember who either Samuel the Baker or his daughter was, and it only wanted to return to its studies, but it sighed and closed the book, knowing Little Ash wouldn't settle down until the prayers started. The men did not seem close to starting their prayers. The younger ones, who'd just come in, were explaining the news, which could take them quite a while, depending on how the weather and the prices and the road had been, and of course depending on whether anyone had run afoul of the tsar's officials, which could delay the first blessings by nearly half an hour.

"I've tried to get word through the agent," Samuel the Baker was saying. "Fishl, they call him. He promised he'd taken care of everything, but it's not like Essie not to write."

"Did you check the newspapers?" said one of the other men. "There haven't been any ships gone down, have there? God forbid."

"There was a notice her ship had come in," said Samuel. "Believe me, I was watching for it."

The worried tone of the conversation had finally caught the angel's attention. Our sages tell us that angels only understand Hebrew, the holy language, but our angel with great effort had taught itself Aramaic, in order to occupy Little Ash by reading Talmud with him. Despite many centuries of exposure to other languages, however, it had never quite been able to wrap its head, or any tongues it happened to possess, around any language that was written with vowels. The men were speaking in Yiddish, and so it did not know what they were saying. "Why are they upset?"

"Essie hasn't written back from America."

"Who is Essie?"

"The baker's daughter! You remember, she used to sit in his lap and he'd read the Talmud to her, before she became a woman and had to go do women's things. Hush, I'm listening."

It seemed from what the men were now saying that there had in fact been no word from America, and Essie's last message had been from Warsaw, which wasn't after all so far away. She'd met with the immigration agent, Reb Fishl from Krumer Street, and written her family to say she had her tickets and was to take the train to Hamburg. From there, she should have been in America already. Samuel the Baker was now trying, with the help of his friends, to make small numbers bend into the shapes of larger ones in order to convince himself that he could afford to leave his business for a day or two and go to Warsaw himself.

No one was keeping score, but if they had been, they would have been able to tell you that Little Ash hardly ever lost an argument with his friend the angel. Of course, as is the nature of these things, it usually turned out that whatever selfish, mischievous, or destructive impulses he put in the hearts of the people he encountered eventually led to new forms of selfless creation.

In this case, Little Ash had planted the idea of leaving their village in the head of the angel. When he explained to it what was happening, it took this idea and turned it around, so that it was no longer an idea to go see the world and entertain themselves, but the idea of doing a mitzvah.

"Forget America, Ashel," it said. "Tell me how we can go to Warsaw."

two

LITTLE ASH PACKED a satchel with his few belongings, and the angel packed nothing, as it owned nothing but the clothes on its back and had never needed anything more than that. For centuries it had only worn the same white caftan with which it first arrived in Shtetl, but for the occasion of their departure, Little Ash presented it with a vest, a shirt, and trousers, so that it would blend better with the population in the larger towns and cities, where its angelic appearance might draw unwanted attention from Jews and Christians alike. The angel was not used to wearing trousers, but it accepted what Little Ash told it about humans thinking it was terribly old-fashioned to wear a caftan. The angel had always accepted things Little Ash told it about humans, and about Christians, as he pretended quite convincingly to be an expert.

They caught a ride into town with an old bookseller on his cart, and from town they rode a larger cart belonging to a gentile peasant who took them to a larger town, and from that town they took a train to the city. Neither of them particularly liked the train, which seemed to them a kind of rude angel who refused to speak to either of them. The train also required tickets. These, Little Ash stole from a station attendant, and they would have made it to Warsaw for free had the angel, feeling Guilty, not compelled him to buy overpriced kosher sandwiches on the train to make up for it.

When they arrived in Warsaw, they were both feeling a bit dizzy from the motion of the train, and were made even more dizzy by the hustle and bustle of the station. The angel had changed its tallis for a plain, undyed woolen shawl that was less conspicuous among the gentiles, but it felt, once they arrived, that it need not have made the effort, and perhaps could have kept its caftan as well. No one so much as glanced at them.

While Ashmedai and the angel are standing on the platform, newly arrived in Warsaw, let us take a moment to look at them. As I mentioned, they both appeared human, for the sake of convenience, but not entirely human. Ashmedai had eyes like a cat's, with vertical pupils, and the angel had eyes like a goat's, with horizontal ones. Ashmedai had feet like a bird, which made his shoes uncomfortable, and the angel had cloven hooves, which did not bother it, because angels are too single-minded to pay attention to their own shapes. These oddities had never given either the angel or the demon any trouble from humans, for it seemed that no one over b'nei mitzvah age ever noticed these features.

As our sages tell us, cherubim have faces like children, and perhaps this angel was one of those, because its features were soft and rounded, its face beardless. It had an air of quiet serenity, like a kosher creature ruminating in the sun. Little Ash, beardless also, had sharp elbows, and the way he carried himself suggested that he was always about to go running after something. In their odd way, they were perfect matches for each other, as study partners, chevrusas, ought to be.

The most important thing to note about their appearance, however, is that they were both unmistakably Jewish. This is why when a young man detached himself from the crowd, intending to fleece these newcomers, it was a young Jewish man.

This young man's name was Yossel. That is, people called him Yossel. It was not the name his parents had given him, nor did it bear anything whatsoever in common with that name. Yossel had a number of reasons for having changed his name, but in doing so he had proven to himself and the rest of the underworld that he could forge unimpeachable documents for identities that had no history behind them at all. For Little Ash and the Shtetler angel, this was, as one might say, a godsend.

Yossel did not know, and indeed had no way of knowing, that the reason he felt compelled to speak to the angel and the demon, out of all the Jews on the platform, was that Little Ash had reached out into the crowd and plucked from the general noise of people's minds the strongest selfish desire he could find. This was one of the little demonic magics that Little Ash was able to do, something that came to demons as easily as speaking languages, and hardly counted to them as magic at all. Yossel thought he had spotted a good mark, as both Little Ash and the angel, for very different reasons, looked remarkably fresh and innocent, but it was Little Ash's gentle tug on the thread of his desire that compelled him.

In fact Yossel was the mark, and Little Ash was quite as delighted with the look of him as Yossel was with the look of Little Ash.

"How beautiful!" Little Ash said, catching hold of the angel's arm so he could point the newcomer out to it. "Look, he's guilty of more crimes than Jews have obligations!"

The angel couldn't see that sort of thing on a human's face. What it saw on Yossel's face was that he had reasons for committing his crimes, many of which were perfectly admirable. For instance, Yossel lived with a woman who was, according to her papers, his wife, and she and a woman identified by the law as her sister had, from somewhere, acquired a parcel of children. Someone had to support those children, and at least one-third of the time, that someone was Yossel.

Or, ultimately, whomever Yossel chose to fleece.

But the angel was a bit shortsighted, as angels usually are, and it tended to miss details that didn't fit into its simple, short-term view of the world. Yossel was standing in front of it, and so Yossel was whom it noticed.

"What a nice young man," it said.

"Nice indeed!" said Little Ash. "And he knows the city too."

The angel was not sure how Little Ash knew *that,* but it supposed he had reserves of demonic knowledge to which it would never have access.

Yossel being now in greeting range, the angel said, "Shalom aleichem!"

"Aleichem shalom, aleichem shalom," said Yossel, in the breathless, in-a-hurry way that city people always had. He thrust out a hand for the angel to shake, and the angel shook it. "First time in Warsaw? Looking for a meal? A minyan for prayers? A good kosher house?"

Little Ash insinuated himself between the crook and the angel, grinning up into Yossel's face. Being in the presence of the self-centered and the self-motivated always made Little Ash feel particularly lively, and he wanted to do the talking, not least because he was aware, as the angel was not, that *good kosher house* did not necessarily mean here what people claimed it meant in less wicked environs. While the angel, of course, approved of human pleasures, certain complexities of their accomplishment were beyond its understanding.

"Good afternoon!" the demon said. "Actually, we have a reference from Reb Fishl. He said that in Krumer Street they know a way to get us tickets to America."

"In Krumer Street!" said Yossel, drawing himself up

indignantly. "In Krumer Street they know nothing! It's nothing but rogues and cheats in Krumer Street!"

The angel looked down at Little Ash. If it had a name at the moment, that name might have been Concern. It did not understand the conversation, which was taking place in Yiddish, but it did not like the look of what Yossel was saying.

Little Ash liked it very much. Demons, backward creatures that they are, love nothing more than dealing with rogues and cheats. In fact, this was precisely how Little Ash made a living for himself, since the job of a small-town demon is a poorly paying one. It seemed to him that if this were the sort of person Essie had gone to for her tickets to America, then Little Ash was the right person to have come after her, and the angel could watch him do what he did best and would perhaps be very impressed with him.

"But everyone says the tickets they'll sell you in Krumer Street are the best, and the cheapest," he said, making his slit-pupiled grey eyes very big and very innocent. Little Ash had practiced his facial expressions, with the aid of a mirror, so that they projected the trust and naïveté of the greenest of pious, rural adolescents. He had also been blessed by nature with delicate bones and long eyelashes, which made him look younger than even other demons considered him to be.

"Reb Fishl, may his name be trampled in the dust, I mean no disrespect," said Yossel, "is a liar, and a dangerous man."

"Oh," said Little Ash. "Do you think so?"

"I know so!" exclaimed Yossel, throwing a hand in the air as if to chop off the reputation of Fishl from Krumer Street. "They say he's in the pocket of the police, and he's had his rivals arrested—or killed."

"But then you have to tell us where to find him!" Little Ash interrupted. "Reb Fishl was supposed to get tickets for our cousin, and we haven't heard from her at all."

"Your cousin?" Yossel asked. "Are you brothers, then?" He gave the angel a thoughtful look. Yossel was perceptive, and he was wondering if there was more to the angel than met the eye. He knew from experience that it was possible to appear one way and feel quite another, and had developed a sense for when a person was wearing not only their clothes but also their body as an ill-fitting garment. Against his own judgment, he could not help feeling somehow protective of such people, and felt uncomfortable at the thought of turning them over to Reb Fishl.

"Aren't we all brothers in Israel?" said Little Ash, who didn't care to answer questions about what he and the angel were to each other. "The point is, Essie hasn't written home, and this Fishl will know where she is."

Yossel thus began to give them directions, and then when it became clear that they didn't understand him, turned to lead them, in a state of confusion, to Krumer Street.

three

Just as in little Shtetl, many young people were leaving from other towns and cities all across the Pale. One of those cities was Belz, to the south and east of where the angel and the demon had been living. Belz, unlike Shtetl, was large enough to have a name. It also had shops, synagogues, and endless arguments between the local Hasidim and those who considered it the highest mitzvah that they should earn a larger paycheck and eat a little better.

One of the latter was a young woman named Rose Cohen, whose father owned a shop but was not good at running it. Rose's father would have been better suited to the work of a melamed, teaching Hebrew to small children, as his favorite way to pass the time was to chant Torah verses in his hoarse, not unpleasant voice to the goats as he milked them. Mendel Cohen, as he was called, had had the terrible misfortune, as a child, to be born into a secular family and, as a young man, to inherit a dry-goods store.

He had had the good fortune, however, to have had a clever daughter.

Rose, who was sixteen years old and had been told more times that she was unladylike than that she was pretty, had a head for numbers and a mouth for bargaining, and one day when she was fifteen she had read in a newspaper a published advertisement from a steamship company, which had explained with solid mathematics the practicality of going to America. This had, of course, been meant as an enticement to migrants to buy their tickets from that steamship line, but Rose had taken it as a challenge.

She would, she had decided, save up the money to take herself to America, and her best friend Dinah Pearl besides, and between the two of them they would grow rich and buy tickets for their families to come after them, and none of their younger brothers would ever have to go into the army. Of younger brothers, Dinah had a whole flock, and Rose had only the one, Motl, whose safety she kept as a priority because unlike any other boy in all of Belz, he admired her.

Not that Rose needed admiration from boys. She knew her own merit better than anyone else, as she reminded herself nearly every day, whenever someone asked her to speak more quietly or perhaps a little less, or tried to tell her it wasn't a young woman's business to be demanding the overdue payment for the sack of tobacco she'd sold them months before on credit. Never mind what anyone said; Rose knew herself to be the cleverest girl in town, and when one was the cleverest, one needn't be the prettiest.

Which was lucky, because the prettiest girl in town was Dinah, anyway.

Dinah Pearl, with the big, dark eyes of a doe and the fine, delicate hands of a seamstress fit to make the prettiest lace from the softest thread. Dinah Pearl, whose unruly tumble of younger brothers seemed always on the edge of starvation, their grandfather's reputation as a miracle worker bringing in strangely little in the way of food. Dinah, who had been Rose's best friend since the two of them had barely learned to talk, and who had never once told Rose that she was getting ahead of herself. No one in the world, in Rose's opinion, had quite so many virtues as Dinah.

It was for these reasons that she had decided she would take Dinah to America with her. Two young women together would be safer than one alone, in any case. And Dinah would never think to leave if Rose didn't push her. She was the sort of person who would be content to sit by the fire in her own little house forever, gently stirring a pot of soup while she repaired her brothers' little trousers and warmed up the water for their baths. Dinah had never once com- plained about such a life, but Rose knew it wasn't good enough. In America, Dinah could have dresses, nice dresses, for herself, that someone else had sewn, and she could buy sandwiches for her brothers instead of always eating soup, and she could go to dance halls. At least, Rose had heard that in America they had dance halls, and when she got there, she intended to take Dinah with her to confirm that it was true.

Dinah had no way to earn money for a steamship ticket, but this was no obstacle for Rose Cohen. The day after she had read that advertisement in the paper, Rose had gone out to the back of the pasture behind the Cohen house, where her father was chanting a portion of Torah under his breath as he piled green branches for the goats to nibble on.

"Papa," she said, "did you know that the account books in the shop haven't been updated since the High Holy Days?"

"Hmm?" said her father. "Oh, Rose. Is there someone in the shop?"

Mendel Cohen, as his wife was often saying, was a kind man and a good one, but his ears were no good at all.

"I've been thinking," Rose said, "that it would make sense for me to do the accounts, and we could hire Dinah to sit behind the counter, and help people measure their weights, and take the payments. I think everyone would be happier to give money to Dinah than to just about anyone in the world."

"Ah," said Mendel. This he understood, as it had something of the flavor of tzedoke, that form of financial justice that is commanded upon us in Torah. Dinah's family had nothing, and the Cohens had a shop, so should not Dinah have some part in the shop, to keep her going?

"That's my clever daughter," he said. "You do whatever you like."

Rose smiled and kissed her father's cheek, and left him

to finish his verses. She went to the shop and took out the account books, and then she went down the street to the Pearls' and told them she'd like to hire Dinah to smile at customers and make sure they found what they were looking for. And then she and Dinah went back to the shop, where Dinah sat quietly behind the counter and mended tiny pairs of trousers while Rose checked sums and made a list of delinquent payments and waited for her brother Motl to get back from cheder, so she could hire him as a messenger.

The dry-goods shop did better with Rose in charge than it had under her father's distracted leadership. People found that the shelves were restocked and cleaned more frequently, and they mostly didn't mind as much that it was harder to buy things on credit, because at least the requests for money came from the lovely, smiling mouth of Dinah Pearl, who was, after all, the sister of a truly astonishing number of hungry little boys. With Motl carrying packages, it was easier for the elders to make purchases. And Rose carefully divided the money into piles: for the shop, for Motl and their parents, for Dinah's family, for America.

America was hungry for money, and there was a whole list of expenses. Travel papers, to prove they were allowed to leave Russia and then to enter America. Steamship tickets. Train tickets, to get to the ship. Food for the journey. And a little extra, because Rose believed in being prepared.

Rose kept all the papers in the back of her father's account book, and the money she kept in the goat shed, where no one but Mendel would ever find it, and Mendel could be trusted not to touch it. He considered his daughter a genius, particularly since her efforts in the shop had allowed him to buy, once in a while, some rabbinic text for himself, for the edification of the goats while he repaired his fences.

Rose ran the shop in this way for a year, during which she also made regular visits to the Jewish Immigration Bureau, where she picked up pamphlets and newspapers to read while she sat in the back of the shop, in between doing the accounts. When there were no customers coming in the door, she would join Dinah at the counter, and the two of them dreamed together of all the things that one could do in America. Dinah was not such a hungry reader as Rose, but she liked to look at the advertisements in the newspapers and think about how in America there would be feathers for hats, and perhaps it would not be so shocking for a girl to wear a red dress in the street. Dinah was self-conscious of her taste for fashion, which seemed to her unthrifty and therefore somehow selfish, but Rose assured her every day that she had the right to a little selfishness.

And she had the right to be pretty. After all, it was her pretty face that made people so happy to visit the Cohens' shop.

"That's true," said Dinah, blushing, on one occasion when Rose mentioned this. "But, Rose, it feels awfully embarrassing to say so."

"Everyone in the world has talents," said Rose. "You shouldn't be ashamed that you're the loveliest girl in the Pale of Settlement."

"Oh, Rose," said Dinah.

Dinah found herself saying "Oh, Rose" about a hundred times a week. Rose had always been the wild one, which was what Dinah loved most about her, but at the same time, it was a little frightening. Dinah was not as sure as Rose was that it would be a wonderful adventure to cross an ocean and leave everything behind. Dinah, after all, had more brothers than Rose did, and was perhaps a little more attached to them. Rose's brother Motl was only a few years younger than herself, not so little that Rose had cared for him his whole life, and besides, he was at an age where boys become terribly rude to their sisters if they aren't watched closely.

Another reason for Dinah's worries, as she sat and chatted with Rose about the life the two of them would have across the sea, was that among the people who had been visiting the Cohens' shop in hopes of glimpsing Dinah's face, there was one young man whose face she found she liked just as much as he liked hers.

She tried not to bring him up too frequently in conversation, because Rose, perhaps out of some unconscious resentment toward her irresponsible father, had a habit of dismissing at once the merit of any young man who seemed likely to become a Torah scholar. And the boy Dinah loved was not only likely, but certain, to become a scholar, as he was a disciple of one of the Hasidic rebbes on their end of town, an old man with a bad leg and a reputation for working miracles.

Dinah's life had not had enough miracles in it, and when

she looked at this young man she saw in his eyes the suggestion that she, herself, was also a miracle.

Rose also looked at her this way. But Dinah had not noticed.

four

LITTLE ASH EXPLAINED the situation to the angel in Aramaic as Yossel led them away from the train station. Unlike angels, demons are quite gifted with languages, although Little Ash, for reasons known only to himself, had adopted a Yiddish accent in all languages, around the time of the false messiah, in the reign of Tsar Alexis Mikhailovich.

The angel used a certain vague sense of superiority to excuse to itself its failure to communicate with humans. What did anyone need to speak of, it sometimes thought, that could not be said in holy words? Nevertheless, it also considered itself too generous to be annoyed by Little Ash's accent or by the demon's insistence on speaking in modern jargon while in public. It now realized that not speaking in modern jargon might be a problem, if it wished to speak to modern people, to find Essie and bring her home to her worried family—which is what it thought they had come to do, having half forgotten that she was meant to be on the other side of an ocean.

"So he is helping us," it said now. "Because he is a good Jew."

"He certainly is," said Little Ash. "He is helping us find the man who sold Essie her papers for America."

"I don't understand all this paper," said the angel. Angels are easily distracted, and it was feeling thoughtful as it squinted at the advertisements and playbills that were pasted to the walls of the nearby buildings. The angel could remember a time when one hardly ever saw paper. As far as it could remember, that had been practically yesterday. It could not read any alphabet other than the Hebrew one, and was particularly fascinated with the advertisements in gentile writing. Had it not known that if it lost sight of Little Ash it might forget its purpose in coming to Warsaw, it might have stopped to puzzle over the illustrations.

Little Ash was not particularly interested in angelic ruminations. Keeping half an eye on the angel, just in case it should wander off, he took a couple of quick steps to catch up with Yossel.

"You said you can do better than Reb Fishl. Do you get a lot of business for America these days?" he asked.

"Oh, America, Canada, Cuba," said Yossel, waving a hand with a worldly air. "I know all the Americas."

"Is it true what they say, that all the young people forget the Commandments in America?" Little Ash's eyes were shining. The angel, had it been paying the least bit of attention, might have chided him for sounding so hopeful.

Yossel, who was himself, by most definitions, a young person, and who had forgotten any number of Commandments, glanced back at the angel. It seemed to him that the quieter of his two new clients might be the sort of person who disapproved of forgetting Commandments. Should he say no?

"Don't worry," said Little Ash. "My friend speaks only the holy language; you can be honest."

"Only!" Yossel was impressed, despite himself. "Now that's what they call a pious Jew."

"They say in America they have dance halls on every corner," said Little Ash. Although he considered himself something of a radical, he liked to read the Orthodox papers, because he found they detailed a great deal more misbehavior than the others. Socialists, and so forth, seemed to find more good in the hearts of humankind than did the pious writers, and so it was to the conservatives that Little Ash turned when he wanted to feel a dose of optimism.

Yossel would have liked to tell tall tales, but, with the specter of his rival Reb Fishl hanging over him, he felt compelled to deliver a measure of honesty. "In Warsaw, too, they have dance halls," he said, a little reluctantly.

The demon looked down at his feet, which were, as usual, feeling a bit sore from walking on the earth. Perhaps if the streets of America were paved with gold, as the wilder storytellers liked to claim, he wouldn't have such trouble, but he had a suspicion that those stories were entirely invented.

"In any case," Little Ash said, "I imagine America isn't *less* sinful than Poland."

"Oh, no," Yossel agreed. He wasn't sure what Little Ash was trying to imply. "I imagine not. I suppose . . ." Yossel tended to save his creativity for his forgeries, and not for meditations on the nature of the world, but he stretched his mind as best he could. "I suppose in the end, the whole world is more or less full of sin."

For the next minute or so, all three were quiet. Yossel and Little Ash were contemplating the forger's philosophy of the world. The angel was contemplating an advertisement for tooth-whitening powder, the wording of which had stretched the limits of the Hebrew alphabet as far as Little Ash's questions about morality had stretched the mind of Yossel the forger.

"Well, in any case," said Yossel, "you'll want to find me again as soon as you've heard from Reb Fishl about your cousin. Don't stay by him a minute longer than you must. He eats shtetl Jews alive, Reb Fishl. You must understand."

Little Ash simply smiled. He had no intention of being eaten alive. Yossel, seeing the smile on what he mistakenly thought was an innocent face, felt terribly uncomfortable, and was glad when they came to the corner of a street with a sharp twist in it like a broken bone.

"Since it's Friday night," he said, "I suppose he'll be at the synagogue. I've heard he does business there."

"Business!" said Little Ash, still smiling. He turned to the angel and said, "We are going to a synagogue."

"Oh," said the angel, and blinked at him, confused. It usually had to argue Little Ash around to attending prayers, and was not sure why he looked so pleased with himself.

"It's just down that way," said Yossel, pointing. He was not the sort of Jew who went to the synagogue, whether to do business or otherwise, and in any case he did not wish to show his face in Krumer Street, where he had on occasion been threatened with having his nose kicked in. Nor did he wish to see the poor, naive village boys, Little Ash and the angel, have their noses kicked in. He was already backing away from them, taking small steps.

Neither of them paid him much attention. The angel had caught the scent of the approaching Sabbath in the air, and Little Ash, like a terrier, had caught the scent of a rat.

Inside the little synagogue on Krumer Street, it was quite crowded and quite loud. It seemed a good portion of the Jewish Quarter had come here this evening, most of them for gossip rather than prayer. A good number of the people in the room were liars and schnorrers and cheats, this being one of those poor neighborhoods in which the quickest way to fill one's mouth, and indeed often the only way, was to become a liar and a cheat. The tsar's laws had only made this more true, and business in Krumer Street was busy indeed. Little Ash, even with his keen eyes and ears, could scarcely keep track of all the sins and violations going on around him.

The angel was oblivious to this. Its name was now Maariv, as its thoughts turned without conscious effort to the evening prayers. It could see only holiness in a synagogue and was quite unaware that to many of the men surrounding it, God was a distant and untrustworthy ruler, hardly more beloved than the tsar himself. Even before the prayer leader began his chanting, the angel Maariv was focused on its task, already singing praises in a tone inaudible to human ears which, nevertheless, produced in everyone who felt it a strange sense that everything around them was both more real and more miraculous than it had previously been.

Little Ash, meanwhile, glanced around and surreptitiously removed his shoes, which after a day of travel were beginning to hurt him terribly. Should the angel notice, he had an excuse prepared. While in the palace of his father Ashmedai for Yom Kippur, he would explain, his brother, also called Ashmedai, but Ash-*kutty* for short as he lived in India, had told everyone that in his shul in Chendamangalam they did not wear shoes to worship.

Little Ash felt this would be an excellent excuse, and he was a bit disappointed when the angel, otherwise engaged, declined to notice him at all.

Thus having made himself more comfortable, and with his study partner paying him no attention, the demon looked around the room with interest. Little Ash liked being among people. He never ceased to be amazed at their capacity for hopping the fences around the Torah and trampling the Commandments beneath their feet. While the angel's inaudible singing made even the motes of dust which fell from the ceiling seem as precious as jewels in the crown of the tsarina, may her name be erased, Little Ash's hungry eyes counted a minyan of hypocrites, another of scoundrels, and several minyans' worth of broken promises.

The angel, unhindered by the pace of the congregation, had already reached its Amidah halfway through the service, while the rest were only starting on the Kaddish that marked the beginning. This would cause no trouble, however, because the Amidah of angels is, in their homeland, ceaseless and endless, and even in exile it could last them a long time.

Little Ash tucked one foot behind the other knee, and thus fulfilling the tradition of praying on a single foot, continued not to actually pray. One face in particular on the other side of the room had caught his attention. This face would put on a pious attitude when that would profit it, but only then. This was someone who, in his heart, held no regard for anything of benefit to anyone but himself.

The person Little Ash was looking at, a veritable well of wickedness, was quite tall for a Jew, and well muscled, with a rather attractive, healthy face. However, to the eyes of a demon, all of his handsomeness was wasted, as little creatures seemed to crawl over his skin like ants—creatures which, upon closer inspection, would prove to be built of little tangles of Hebrew letters that detailed all of his sins. To the eyes of a demon, these sins revealed all of the lives this man had destroyed to get to where he was, which was, incidentally, quite a comfortable place.

He had in fact, Little Ash noticed with interest, not just destroyed lives through the usual disregard for any and all of the 613 Commandments, but had even destroyed a number of them directly, by disregarding the Sixth.

The Sixth Commandment, as you know, once broken, cannot be unbroken or forgiven. Little Ash was aware that the man he was looking at knew this, and had, all the same, contrived to disobey this Commandment on more than one occasion.

Anyone who had looked at Little Ash in that moment could have been forgiven for thinking his eyes were purely black. He had, like a cat spotting a mouse, focused so intensely on his target that his irises had entirely been swallowed up by his pupils. Though other demons saw Little Ash as rather pitiful, as his lack of talent for magic made him rather less dangerous than most of his kind, he still knew suitable prey when he saw it, and he was not afraid to go hunting.

The mouse, or, I should say, the murderer, was called Reb Fishl the Silk Merchant.

five

REB FISHL, ALTHOUGH he did not know it, had just solved a problem for the demon. Little Ash was not thinking of Essie, as it was not in his habit to think of others. He was merely thinking of the problem of how to get himself, and the angel, to America, a goal he had not given up.

To get to America one needed papers, which would need to be forged as neither of them had a legal identity; then they had to go to Germany, and from Germany board a ship, and after the ship, Ellis Island. The angel, like all angels, required no more sustenance than the Presence of God's Holiness, but Little Ash needed to eat, or else he could starve and die, as a human would. As he thought himself too excellent to be wasted by dying, he therefore needed at least one meal daily. So there was food, which the angel would insist he pay for honestly. And everyone knew that to get out of Russia a Jew often needed to bribe the officials at the border.

In short, even had there been no Essie, Little Ash needed more money than he had, and Reb Fishl had more money than Little Ash had, and they would, in a way, be helping each other. Reb Fishl would help the demon get to America, and Little Ash would help the murderer remember his Commandments.

Maariv, the angel, beside him, had reached the three-hundred-and-sixtieth of its eighteen blessings and would still be praying for a while. Satisfied for the moment working through the details of a plan in his head as he would untangle the meaning of a sentence in Talmud, Little Ash looked away from Reb Fishl and took the chance to enumerate some blessings of his own.

When the leader opened up the ark for the Aleinu prayer, Little Ash slipped out from between the standing men and climbed the narrow steps at the back of the room. These led to a women's gallery that looked ready to collapse at any moment, having been affixed to the interior wall by an indifferent carpenter long enough ago that the steps were worn smooth, although how any woman dared place her weight on them was anyone's guess. The carpenter would have served the community better by building the mechitzeh to divide male from female on solid ground, Little Ash thought, but it served his own purposes at the moment because he wanted to be closer to the rafters.

No one noticed Little Ash, and indeed, even had there been women in the women's gallery that day, which there were not, they would not have seen anything amiss if they had looked at him. He had remembered Essie on the way up the stairs and now wore what he recalled of her shape. Little Ash's most reliable magic, aside from plucking the selfish thoughts out of human heads for his own perusal and amusement, was the ability to change his shape to make himself less conspicuous. Even this was limited: he remained the same size no matter how much he might try to make himself taller. Fortunately, however, at the moment he did not need to be taller, and only wanted to be sure that no one should look up and suspect him of impropriety.

The reason Little Ash wanted to be closer to the rafters is that the congregation's sinful ghosts, who had been released from Gehinnom for the Day of Rest, were up there, clinging to the high parts of the room. A ghost is a creature that tends to grasp whatever surface it can find, as an infant will try to grasp any object it is given. Because ghosts are very light, they have a tendency to float upward on currents of warm air. They clustered, therefore, in the rafters, which was just as well, because there wouldn't have been room for them down below, the shul, as I have said, being quite crowded.

Most demons do not speak to ghosts. They consider ghosts to be rather beneath them, as demons are, albeit in a sideways, backward, or upside-down way, lower orders of B'nei Elohim, and ghosts are merely remnants of the children of Abraham. Our Father, while of course an eminent ancestor, does not quite measure up, in the opinion of most demons, and ghosts tend to be preoccupied with a very limited set of concerns, none of which demons, with their superior talents in magic, can put to much use.

Little Ash, however, considered himself a socialist, and it was without qualm that he chose to lower himself, metaphorically if not physically, to the prospect of a conversation with these unfortunates. He was looking for the souls of those Reb Fishl had killed. He hoped Essie was not among them, but Little Ash had some experience with murderers and had found on many occasions that the names of their victims disquieted them. The more details he could discover about their deaths, the more he could rely on words to do his work for him, and the less he would need to rely on miracles, or, worse still, on physical confrontation.

Little Ash's scanty magic was no good for fighting. As for winning arguments by the strength of his arm, let us not humiliate him with details, but only note that, of the two divine creatures from Shtetl, the angel could have thrown a more respectable punch if sufficiently provoked. Cleverness, therefore, was Ash's best weapon.

As the demon had expected, there was a knot of little ghosts, huddled together like bats, on the thickest rafter-beam in the middle of the room. He leaned somewhat precariously over the balcony railing and hissed, to get their attention. The ghosts rustled and squeaked in consternation. They had not been expecting anyone to address them, for the very good reason that no one ever had.

They really were a lot like bats. Little Ash supposed it had something to do with habitat. Perhaps, being stuck to the ceiling, they found they couldn't help but develop leathery wings to complement their little grasping fingers, or else it was some deep, ancestral memory that caused humans to lose their shapes and change to something more like other mammals when they died.

"Sholem aleichem, ghosts," said the demon. "Is there someone among you called Essie, the baker's daughter, from a shtetl that doesn't have a name? And which of you has a grudge against Reb Fishl down there, the tall one from Krumer Street?"

He had been expecting a response of some kind, but he was quite startled when all of the ghosts began to shout at once.

The angel had been approaching four thousand blessings in the Shemoneh Esreh, and had not noticed that Little Ash was no longer standing beside it. When the ghosts began to speak, however, it found itself transformed, with inconvenient suddenness, from Maariv to Startled. Blinking at the space where it expected the demon to be, it realized that he was not there, and then it saw, also, that he had left his shoes behind. Only after noting these facts did the angel think to wonder what it was that had startled it in the first place.

Oh, yes. It must be that, in addition to the gossip of living humans who had concluded their last Kaddish and were catching each other up on the vital news of the last twelve hours, there was now a second layer of conversation in the shul. On that layer, there was a great deal of shouting.

The angel could not, at first, make out any of the details, but with the wisdom of experience it assumed that Little Ash must somehow be responsible. Which meant, in a way, that the angel itself was responsible.

It put away its prayer book, picked up its chevrusa's shoes, and went to see what was happening.

six

ROSE AND DINAH had been saving for America for one
year, from New Year to New Year, and then for another six
months into the spring again after Dinah had to scrape
together to help pay for her grandfather, the Lame Rebbe
of Belz, to travel to America and see his daughter, Dinah's
aunt, who was getting married and needed his blessing. Now
Passover had passed over, and Rose, sitting with her pocket
notebook in the goat paddock, found herself underlining a
number she had calculated herself out of all the newspapers
and pamphlets she had read.

She had the money for America.

They could buy tickets and leave whenever they
wanted.

She sat for quite some time, staring at the number. She
found it very difficult to believe that her plan had really

worked, but the weight of the cashbox she kept hidden in the hay was quite convincing. She had everything else she needed—papers for herself and for Dinah, an extra quilt so she wouldn't be cold on the journey, even a new pair of boots so she wouldn't have to buy them in America. Yet she felt as if there must be something she had missed. Something so enormous that it would make everything she had done mean nothing at all.

All of her lists added up. There couldn't be anything. What could there possibly be?

She did the calculations again, just in case, and came up with the same answer. Then she sat in silence, trying to compose the perfect speech to give Dinah to explain that it was time to move forward, until Mendel Cohen came in with the goats, and one of the does came over to Rose and ripped the page of numbers out of her notebook to chew on.

"Ah," said Mendel quietly. "She is hungry for knowledge."

"Papa," said Rose, in a faraway, shocked voice, "we have enough for tickets."

For a long moment, Mendel said nothing. It seemed he found it no easier to believe than Rose had.

Finally, he said, "That's my Rose. Blessed be the God who gives men daughters."

For some reason this made Rose burst into tears, and she jumped up to give her father a hug. Her tears brought tears to his eyes in turn, and they stood there for several minutes, hugging each other and crying, before Mendel suggested they ought to go back to the house and let Rose's mother, and little Motl, know that Rose would soon be in America, and they would soon be rich.

Rose's mother, Penina, cooked a chicken soup with dumplings to celebrate, as if it were Shabbes, making enough so that the Pearls could come over and eat with the Cohens. Rose helped her knead the dough, excusing her reluctance to talk to Dinah by the thought that she ought to present the news with real ceremony. The way one would announce an engagement, almost. She ought to have a beautiful speech to give. Dinah deserved only the most beautiful things. Details, numbers, boring things—those were all for Rose to take care of so that Dinah didn't have to.

Besides, she was terribly nervous, and pummeling the dough helped her feel less like a bird trapped in a basket, fluttering pointlessly at the walls. She was a grown woman, she told herself, and a grown woman ought to act dignified. If she ran over to Dinah's house at once, she knew she would slam her way through the front door and find herself screaming in her most high-pitched tones, jumping up and down, and possibly even crying. She wanted to present a more responsible picture to the Pearls, in case Dinah's mother worried about sending Dinah to America with only Rose for company. Dinah's mother, as much as Dinah, needed to believe that Rose could keep her daughter safe. After all, they had heard hardly anything from Dinah's aunt in that country, and the last letter from the rebbe had come from Warsaw, where he had stopped to meet some colleagues before taking the train to Hamburg. No one would say it, but god forbid it was possible he had become ill on the journey, or lost, or the great holiness of his person had not protected him from such mundane and worldly things as government officials and thieves. Who knew what evils Rose and Dinah, as young women alone, could expect.

"Sweetheart, those are ready," said Penina gently, lifting Rose's hands away from the table. "If you keep battering them, the dumplings will be too heavy. Go talk to Dinah. At least tell her we'll be feeding them tonight, so she doesn't have to cook."

"Oh," said Rose. "Yes, of course. Yes."

But should she dress up? She should certainly not go in her flour-dusted dress, with straw from the goat shed still clinging to her hems. She ought to dress in her Shabbes best, as long as they were having a Shabbes feast.

Motl was in their little attic room, reading one of Rose's newspapers instead of the Mishnah he was supposed to be studying.

"Get out, get out, get out!" said Rose, flapping a hand at him as she dipped the other in the washbasin to clean her face. "Go read in the goat house. Papa will help you with your Mishnah."

"I don't want Papa to help me with Mishnah," said Motl,

who was sometimes, in Rose's opinion, a terribly inconvenient person. "I'm reading about America."

"Well, I'm going to be leaving for America any day now, so I need to change!"

"Why do you need to change to go to America? You're just changing because you want Dinah to see you looking pretty."

Rose frowned at her reflection in the washbasin. Her hair was terribly frizzy from doing chores, and her cheeks were red from excitement, or perhaps from the unaccountably embarrassing feeling of knowing that Motl's words struck a chord inside her.

"Why would Dinah care what I look like?" she snapped. "If you don't go to the goat house, I'll tell Mama you're not studying."

Motl made a face at her and slunk away down the stairs, taking not his Mishnah but the newspaper with him. Perhaps he would teach the goats about the Golden Land in between their lessons from Mendel.

Rose changed into her Shabbes dress and rebraided her hair, then sat with her water-cooled hands on her cheeks until they stopped feeling so hot. She wanted to run to Dinah's house at top speed, but she would restrain herself. Running was childish, and she was, as she had reminded herself a hundred times today, a grown woman, about to make the biggest announcement of her life, to the most important person in it.

She should be as dignified as the Queen of the Sabbath.

"You look like a regular princess," her mother said when she came back into the kitchen. Penina had suffered a great deal of gossip from the other women in town about her daughter's willfulness, but in her heart she could find only pride for Rose and her mathematics and the good head she had on her shoulders.

"I'll be back in no time," said Rose. "I'm sure Dinah and her mother will want to help with dinner."

She measured her steps very carefully as she walked down the street, pretending that she had something balanced on top of her head to maintain her dignity and, she hoped, to prevent anyone from noticing that she had dressed herself up as if it were a holiday. She didn't want the gossips to announce her news to the whole world before she had the chance to do it herself. She was, in fact, so intent on maintaining her stance of regal aloofness that she almost didn't notice Dinah running up to her from the other direction, until the other girl threw her arms around her and shouted, "Rosie, oh, Rose! I have the most wonderful news to tell you!"

Rose stumbled back, startled. How could Dinah possibly have known already? Mendel and the goats could hardly have told her. Had Motl run over to tell her, as revenge for being kicked out of his room? "News?"

"Rose!" Dinah took her by the shoulders and beamed into her eyes. Rose had never seen her so happy: she seemed to glow with an inner light, as if she would have lit the whole street had it not been the middle of the day. "It's all thanks to you—oh, it's wonderful. I never thought this would happen!"

"Of course," said Rose, baffled. "Did your grandfather write?"

"Oh, but it's all worth it," said Dinah, not hearing her. "It's all been worth it! I never thought he would ask me. I'm so excited I can hardly stand!"

This seemed to be true, as she threw herself into Rose's arms and leaned her head on Rose's shoulder. Dinah's hair smelled of flowers—she dressed it with rose oil, which she brewed for herself from her own garden.

Rose stood motionless and shocked. Ordinarily, there was a thrill to holding onto Dinah, a sense that a part of herself that had been separated from the rest was returning to its proper place. But something was wrong today. A piece that didn't fit.

"You thought . . . he?" Rose asked, hesitantly.

"Saul Lehman!" said Dinah. "His father agreed, he said, his father agreed because I have a dowry now, from the shop-minding! So it's all thanks to you, Reyzele. It would never have happened without you. I'm so happy."

She let out a little, delighted sob into the shoulder of Rose's Shabbes dress.

"Saul Lehman?" Rose repeated, feeling incredibly stupid.

"Saul Lehman! I know!" Dinah said, as if there were something the two of them had agreed on, regarding Saul Lehman. But there was not. It took Rose a moment to remember who he even was—the young man who was always hovering around the store with a little prayer book in his pocket, mumbling bits of Hasidic wisdom over the counter whenever he saw an opening to try and start a conversation with Dinah, at a safe distance, with at least one witness to ensure there was no misconduct underway.

Rose had always assumed that the only agreements she and Dinah had, regarding Saul Lehman, were that he was very annoying, and didn't spend enough money, and always forced them to calculate change for him when he did spend, because he had no head for numbers whatsoever.

His father, Rose vaguely recalled, was well-off. And people admired Saul because he was sure to be a rabbi and perhaps become famous for his mystical acts; he had followed Dinah's grandfather around like a duckling since they were all children. But Rose had never much paid attention to that. She had decided, privately, that a husband whose greatest skills lived in a world above our own was hardly a husband at all. After all, the rebbe's great wisdom had fed none of his grandchildren.

Dinah should not have to be the one, in her marriage, to worry about details.

"Saul Lehman proposed to you?" Rose asked. She tried very hard to sound as excited as Dinah clearly was, but it was impossible. Her throat was dry, and her voice sounded choked.

"Saul Lehman proposed!" Dinah confirmed. "To me! Because you helped me!"

This had not been part of the plan.

seven

THE ANGEL HAD no trouble recognizing Little Ash, even when, as now, he had drawn himself a veil of illusions which swapped his tzitzis for long skirts and his sidelocks for pigtails. Of course, it helped that he wasn't wearing any shoes, and that, like the wicked creature he was, he was sitting on a stack of women's prayer books written in Yiddish.

"What are you doing?" said the angel. Unlike Little Ash, it had not changed itself at all. The angel, neither male nor female, simply did not think to worry that its trousers, in the women's gallery, could be seen as a transgression. "You're always making so much *noise*. You really don't need to."

The demon gave it an incredulous look. He knew it did not have the magic of seeing ghosts. Nevertheless, he couldn't help feeling wounded.

"Maybe it's a matter of pikuach nefesh," he said. He found the primacy of saving lives to be quite a useful argument whenever he was breaking the Law in front of his study partner.

"It can't be," said the angel. "Stand up, won't you?"

Little Ash stayed where he was. If he stood up, he knew, the angel would be so busy kissing and apologizing to the disrespected prayer books that it wouldn't listen to anything he, or the ghosts, had to say. "All right, so it isn't pikuach nefesh, exactly. The lives in question are lost already. But it *is* something."

"What?" said the angel. It blinked its eyes, suddenly, and looked around. "Not Essie? From our shtetl?"

Little Ash was quite interested to observe the look in its eyes as it changed its purpose in that moment. There was a sharpness there he did not think he had seen before. Almost the sort of sharpness he admired on himself in a mirror. He wondered what the name of this angel was.

"Not Essie, don't worry. I looked, and she isn't here. No one here has heard of her. But I have found someone we were looking for," said Little Ash, and pointed over the edge of the gallery. "Take a look at that slippery specimen. The tall one."

The angel took a look. It looked for a very long time, turning its head this way and that.

"I see," it said, at long last. "Yes, I think you may be right."

Little Ash, at this remark, checked surreptitiously over his shoulder for the messiah. Not seeing him, however, the demon stood up and shook out his skirts. "If I'm right, then I have work to do."

The angel glanced reluctantly toward the Torah ark. "But it's Shabbat."

Little Ash folded his arms and tilted his head, inspecting once again the angel's face. "Is it?" He wanted to see how far that strange sharpness in his partner's eyes would carry them. "Is it still Shabbes and I can't work if we consider that Essie, from our shtetl, could be in trouble?"

"Are you quite certain she is not here?"

"You don't trust me? Oh, never mind, don't give me that look. Here, I'll show you."

With this, Little Ash performed a strange ritual. He tugged a hair from his head so that tears came to his eyes, and these tears he picked up on his index finger. Then, telling the angel to stand still, Little Ash swiped his own tears over its lashes. With a couple of blinks the angel found itself looking at a whole flock of strange creatures, with eyes like lamps, and long fingers, clinging to the rafters.

"Don't worry about having my wickedness stuck to you," said Little Ash cheerfully. "It will wear off after a while."

"What does Essie look like?" said the angel, who saw that there were a few young women among the ghosts, but then realized it still did not quite know who Essie was.

"She wears spectacles."

None of the ghosts wore spectacles. With another blink the angel realized that what resembled fur on their bodies was really strings of Hebrew letters, and those letters, if you were clever enough to read them, spelled out the life story of each ghost, albeit with an emphasis on its sins, since the tears in the angel's eyes were a demon's tears. But none of the ghosts had come from a little shtetl without any name, and so Little Ash had, against his own habits, been telling the truth.

"She could still be in a great deal of trouble," said Little Ash. "Reb Fishl killed five or ten of these people, and the rest have terrible grudges against him."

The ghosts had explained that Reb Fishl the Silk Merchant was in the habit of swindling emigrants out of all their belongings and then leaving them, helpless, to the mercy of the streets of Warsaw or, sometimes, to even worse fates. Reb Fishl was also, as the whole kehilleh was aware, on good terms with the police, which made him not only the most dastardly sort of criminal but also, of course, practically a traitor to the Jewish People. Sometimes he sent an emigrant along their way to Hamburg with ship tickets, but rumor among those who had not been sent so far was that even these were not destined for the work they thought they would have in America, and what's more, one of the ghosts had seen in Fishl's apartment a box full of letters intended for his clients' families, which he would never deliver.

In short, Essie's father had been right to worry.

Krumer Street had grown dark by the time the angel and the demon left the synagogue. Little Ash led the way, following an instinct as strong as the one that told the angel what its name should be. They went down the crooked alley and around a corner, out of the crowds until there was no one left on the street but themselves and the scrawny, suspicious dogs that crouched in the shadows. The angel, less used to such places than Little Ash, began to feel quite uncomfortable and was about to ask its partner if he were sure he knew where he was going when they came upon a pool of sickly yellow lamplight. There Reb Fishl was outside a tenement that he owned, smoking a cigarette and frowning up and down the street as if he were waiting for someone.

Well, thought Little Ash, someone has come to meet you.

"This is demon business," he told the angel. "You might not like to watch it."

"I might not like if you go alone and don't come back," said the angel, though it did not feel as brave as it tried to sound. "And I don't trust you to remember it's Essie you're here for."

"I remember!" said Little Ash, offended. "She's from *my* shtetl."

"Very well then," said the angel. "What do we now?"

"We talk to him." Little Ash much preferred talking to other things he could have done, such as putting a curse on Reb Fishl (which would not be reliable, as he knew only child's curses and half of them were nothing more than doggerel) or fighting him. Talking to demons tended to make people uncomfortable, and even without knowing it was a demon who spoke, Fishl might be put off guard by having the names of a few of his victims recited to him on a dark night when the street was empty.

Little Ash had not, however, counted on the angel's reaction to his words, which was to simply step forward and approach Reb Fishl to begin a conversation, as if he were not dangerous at all, and as if it expected such a man of the world to be able to speak with it in its own Holy Tongue. Its decisive movement forced Little Ash to hurry in order to arrive in the lamplight first.

The angel, approaching, seemed to Reb Fishl a sheepish young Hasid, with long, curling sidelocks and worried eyebrows. Little Ash was glaring, and so he classified the demon, not incorrectly, as a nuisance.

"Can I help you, gentlemen?" he said, keeping his eyes mostly on Little Ash. Reb Fishl was not overly concerned. It seemed to him clear that if this little jumped-up yeshiva-bokher thought he was going to pick a fight with Reb Fishl and win, then he deserved to be taught a lesson.

Little Ash grinned. He, also, was thinking that someone would learn a lesson from this confrontation. "We have business for you from someone. Maybe you'll know the name? Motl the Cobbler, olov hasholem."

"May he rest in peace," Reb Fishl repeated automatically, though he was extremely displeased to hear Little Ash mention Motl the Cobbler. Fishl had not expected to hear this name, possibly ever again. He thought he had quite successfully buried all of Motl the Cobbler, his name included.

Surely, this newcomer could not possibly know anything about Motl the Cobbler.

"I don't know any Motl," he said, lying so blatantly that even the angel saw it.

"Oh, I'm so sorry," said Little Ash. "Of course I meant the old rebbe, Menachem ben Yakov, the one with the limp, from Belz, olov hasholem to him also."

Reb Fishl stared at Little Ash. Little Ash put his hands in his pockets, adopting a pose of deliberate nonchalance, and gazed evenly back. The angel watched them both in fascination. Little Ash's confidence was, to the angel, one of creation's most puzzling miracles.

Reb Fishl, meanwhile, was thinking that he had been sent some idiot children by a relative who thought they knew something, and now his perfectly peaceful Friday night, not to mention the meeting he'd been expecting with a police officer with whom he had a mutual agreement, was about to be ruined by the need to hide a couple of bodies. He'd done it before, of course, but it was so inconvenient, the Jewish neighborhoods being packed to the gills with gossips. All these village Jews writing half-literate letters to him, demanding to know the whereabouts of their daughters, their husbands, their sons. Sending brainless louts to try and teach him a lesson, as if he weren't far wiser than them, a real macher with his hands in more than one pie and connections, even, in America. It was tedious.

"Come in off the street, won't you, boys?" said Reb Fishl, affecting an attitude of geniality. "We can have a cup of tea and find out what it is you're asking after, hmm?"

"Please," said Little Ash. On his way in the door, he

kissed the mezuzah, which was left from a previous, more kosher resident. The angel was rather startled by this. Little Ash had a habit of walking past mezuzahs without any acknowledgment that they were there, and the angel had had to talk down many a mezuzah in their Shtetl from barring entry to him entirely.

Reb Fishl brought them not to any kind of place to have tea, but to a storeroom off the back which had, conveniently for him, a lock on the door. The angel was surprised to be locked in a storeroom with a murderer; Little Ash was not.

"I know what you've done," the demon said. "I can keep naming names, if you'd like. I think I've got a minyan, even. Enough to say Kaddish for you, Reb Fishl, but I don't think they will. If you don't want the whole world to know, I'd like to ask about Essie, please. A girl around sixteen? She wears spectacles, a real modern girl. You were supposed to send her on her way to America, and you've not buried her yet— so where have you put her?"

Reb Fishl saw no reason to be afraid of his visitors. First, Little Ash was, in fact, not very big. Second, the angel looked like it had no idea what was happening. Third, there was the lock on the door.

Also, Reb Fishl had a gun in his pocket, which he now took out and pointed at them.

"Who cares what you know?" he said. "It's easy enough to shoot you before you can tell another soul."

"Go ahead," said Little Ash, without so much as blinking.

The angel, now staring at the gun, an object it had never seen up close before, said nothing. It still, even in the presence of a weapon, did not speak Yiddish.

"Why don't you tell me who sent you," said Reb Fishl to Little Ash. "Is it really for some silly chit from a nothing village? Or are you working for someone else?"

Little Ash tilted his head to the side and said nothing.

Reb Fishl, whatever else may be said of him, was not stupid. He had noticed that at all times since entering the house, Little Ash had kept himself between the angel and Fishl. Taking this into account, Reb Fishl now adjusted his aim. "Go ahead and talk, or I shoot him first."

Little Ash did blink this time, but perhaps only because his eyes were beginning to dry out. "You'll really wish you hadn't."

Reb Fishl had not gotten to be the wealthiest Jew in Krumer Street by arguing with upstart adolescents. Rather than repeat his threat, he simply pulled the trigger. The angel's body hit the wall behind it with the terrible crack of an unprotected skull making direct contact with a solid surface. This sound, almost as loud as the gunshot, seemed somehow even more deadly.

At this, Little Ashmedai moved very swiftly.

One moment he was standing at bay by the angel, and

the next he was toe-to-toe with Reb Fishl, what duelists would call inside his guard—too close, ironically, to be touched. Too quick to be stopped, the demon reached up with both hands to Reb Fishl's face, plunged two fingers into each of his eye sockets, and seemed to draw a shining something out of them, in the form of a long silver thread.

This was Fishl's soul, which Little Ash crumpled up, rolled into a ball the size of an olive, and swallowed.

"Ashel!" said the reproachful voice of the angel, as Reb Fishl's suddenly empty body crumpled to the ground.

The angel was sitting up, entirely unhurt. As it turned out, Little Ash was better at bluffing than Reb Fishl had supposed. He would have had better luck had he shot the demon, because Little Ash, even with a soul to eat afterward, would have found it less convenient to dig an iron ball out of his insides than the angel had found it to simply wish the ball away. It had, admittedly, been startled, but the angel was often startled, and found it no great hardship.

"If it makes you feel better, his soul is dry as matzeh," said Little Ash, coughing and pounding his chest like a penitent chanting the Ashamnu. "I didn't enjoy that at all. Anyway, he wanted to hurt you."

"It isn't more important just because it was me," said the angel. It was thinking of the people Fishl had killed, whose bodies were not, as the angel's was, disposable. It was also wondering if its chevrusa had intended to get himself shot, and, if so, why he'd seemed to be enjoying himself so much. "You can't think that."

"Yes, I can." Little Ash crouched down to check Reb Fishl's pockets, first cleaning his fingers on the man's trousers to make sure he had not stained them with blood while dragging Fishl's soul from his head.

"You said you were going to talk! You hardly talked at all. And you only said 'Essie' one time, so don't tell me he's explained it all to you, because I won't believe you."

Little Ash rolled his eyes. "He lives two doors down, in the second-floor apartment. We'll take a look in there and see what he's got for us."

The angel hesitated a moment. "I suppose someone ought to watch over his body," it said, thinking of the Law, and of tradition.

"Why?" said Little Ash, not unreasonably. "The demons already got him. Come on, you. We should be gone already. Unless you want I should eat the police?"

The angel neither wanted to see the police eaten, nor, indeed, to see the police at all. Saying only a quick blessing on the name of the True Judge, it followed Little Ash back into the street and up to Reb Fishl's apartment.

Here, the angel, who had so recently scolded Little Ash for holding its own life in higher esteem than a human being's, now found it had more in common with Reb Fishl than it had thought. In his rooms, Fishl had quite a collection of objects that did not belong to him, and among these was a tattered, well-used set of the Talmud, which the sinful one, may his name be erased, had thrown haphazardly onto the floor as he searched its owner's trunk for something more saleable.

This, the angel thought, was a sin worthy of months in purifying fire.

Perhaps some of Little Ash's selfishness had rubbed off on it. It should have been more concerned about the people Fishl had killed. It certainly should have been more concerned about the girl from its village whose well-being had drawn it here. But, after all, it had not met the strangers and barely knew Essie, and these books, it could see clearly.

While Little Ash searched the room, the angel carefully packed the volumes back into their case, kissing each one and whispering blessings. It seemed to see something in the corner of its eyes as it did so, but dismissed this as a side effect of Little Ash's charm for seeing ghosts, and so ignored it.

Little Ash meanwhile turned up several stacks of money, including even a small number of American dollars, cleverly hidden about the room. These he stuffed into his pockets. He then found the box of letters which some of the ghosts had described. Sorting through it he found quite a number of distressing stories. He then found a letter addressed to Samuel the Baker, under his proper name of Samuel Singer, and tore it open.

"Essie is already in America," he said.

The angel looked up, shaken out of the daze of settling the holy books in their case. "What's that?"

"Essie is in America," said Little Ash. "She has a job there but she's written to her father that she can't send money yet because she has to pay a debt first, back to Reb Fishl. The passage was more expensive than she thought, and she had to borrow from him, and then she borrowed more from his friend in America, the *shop boss.*"

The last two words he said in English, savoring their exotic taste a bit. He wanted very much to know what kind of creature was a shop boss.

"Here's even a photograph," said Little Ash, showing the angel a small print of a girl in a neat shirtwaist, with her dark hair braided around her head and a pair of spectacles that did not quite manage to blur the brightness of her clever eyes. "She looks a real revolutionary. I remember now; I liked her, she was a troublemaker."

The angel was thinking. Little Ash could see its thoughts, almost, with the skill of long practice. He knew it was thinking that they had agreed only to come to Warsaw and then go home, and yet—

"To rescue Essie from her debts would be a mitzvah," said the demon, slyly. "She needs help and there is no one in America to help her."

The angel looked at him. "You are very wicked to say so without feeling it in your heart," it said. It could read Little Ash's thoughts just as easily as he could read its own.

"Reb Fishl was a very wicked soul," said Little Ash. "Whatever friend of his this *shop boss* is, how do we know she isn't in terrible danger? Or god forbid she should be dead, and her family can't say Kaddish for her. We can't let one of our own people become a wandering spirit. What if she came home as a dybbuk and spread bad luck in our study house?"

"You don't really think she could have died?" said the angel, horrified.

Little Ash realized he had gone too far in his imagining. Looking from his partner's face to the photograph of Essie, he suddenly wished he hadn't said any of it; it felt like tempting the evil eye.

"It's only that the world is very dangerous," he said. "You can't be certain of anything."

He did not feel as triumphant as he had expected he would when the angel nodded its head decisively and asked, "Then how do we get to America?"

eight

REB FISHL FROM THE GRAVE was able to do one final
favor for the divine creatures from Shtetl. As part of his
business in swindling emigrants and collecting their debts,
he also sold forged papers, the templates for which he kept
stacked in a locked box next to the box of letters. Little Ash
had broken both locks with his pocketknife, and having
found the papers, he sorted through for ones that could
describe the angel and himself—not so difficult, with such
numbers of young people leaving for America—and filled
in the last few details on his own, inventing for each of
them a name out of his own head. He then stuffed Essie's
letters along with the rest into his satchel, in case he should
need them later, and handed the angel its new identity
documents, which it looked over and then handed back,
being unable to read the Yiddish vowels.

"I do not know what it says."

"It says you're my cousin," said Little Ash, quite pleased with himself. "And your name is Uriel Federman. See here, your eyes are brown and you're a man. Like a human person. And you're a Jew, of course."

The angel took the papers back. The rest of the letters it did not understand, but Uriel at least was written as it would be in Hebrew. It was not sure how it felt about having such a thing as a name attached to itself. A single, solid name, that is, written in the letters with which the whole world was once written. There was something about the alef at the beginning that made it feel a little dizzy. You never quite knew what was going on with an alef.

"Does one have to be a man to be a human person?" it asked, settling on an easier question to consider. Little Ash and the angel had discussed, on occasion, the difference between its feelings and his when it came to looking like the boys who studied at the yeshiva rather than the girls who milked the goats and ran the markets. It was a subject which troubled the angel much more than it troubled the demon.

Little Ash laughed. "You've met women; you know one doesn't have to be a man. It's only that you look like a man. Or anyway, how people expect a man to look."

Little Ash truly believed that he was the same sort of creature as boys, albeit of a superior variety, being a demon and therefore knowing things that human boys did not. The angel, however, merely found it convenient to wear a shape in which one could easily study the holy books. Inside itself, it felt closer in kinship to the books themselves, or to the sorts of things an angel might be tasked to look after, like sunlight and rain. Little Ash understood by the angel's question that it had some hesitation about being incorrectly defined by the identity document, and he supposed it was a reasonable enough fear to have, if you were used to being what the Universe told you to be instead of choosing for yourself.

"This isn't real; it's just paper." He shook it, to demonstrate. "Mine says my name is Asher Klein. And that I'm sixteen years old. One doesn't need to be sixteen years old to be a person either."

"I see," said the angel, but it persisted in feeling uncomfortable for as long as it held the papers with the name Uriel Federman in its hands, and so it had to give them back to Little Ash, who hid them, along with Reb Fishl's dollars, in a secret pocket he'd sewn into his tallis katan.

"Done. We can stay here, and take the train after Shabbat, if you insist on resting?"

The angel of course insisted on resting. Its rest, however, was not very restful, because it was troubled by what it had seen since arriving in Warsaw, and disturbed by the thought of a young woman from their shtetl in danger so far away and all alone, and also it kept thinking that it had seen someone from the corner of its eye. Little Ash had never figured out the trick of sleeping, though most demons do it; the angel usually slept quite contentedly and deeply by shedding its body like a jacket, leaving the flesh behind as a lifeless shell while it drifted in the space between the letters of the Universe, where angels rest while they are nameless.

Tonight it found it was unable to shed itself, and while Little Ash lay in Reb Fishl's bed with his aching feet propped up on the wall above his head, the angel sat on the floor and looked again through the little trunk full of Talmud. The books were printed very small, so that a traveler could take with him the whole of the text, and they had been carefully handled before Fishl found them, but still showed signs of being used. The angel could feel that these books were beloved. Their owner would not have left them if he could have helped it.

Tucked between a couple of the volumes it found some correspondence, on which it puzzled out an odd string of Hebrew letters which seemed to spell *AMERIKE*. The owner of these books, it decided, had been going to America, and Fishl had stopped him. It would be a mitzvah, therefore, to bring the books where they were meant to go, and if the angel could not find the rightful owner, then, if nothing else, it could read them; it knew that we are commanded that books should be read. Perhaps Little Ash would read aloud the whole of the letter when he was awake, the angel thought. It did not realize that Little Ash wasn't sleeping, only running schemes through his head over and over and tossing them about like dice, to see them from every angle.

At the bottom of the trunk it found the owner's tallis, smelling of the packet of cloves someone had tucked between the folds, and a woolen sweater, knit thick, in which the angel's fingers could feel the love of a daughter twisted alongside the threads. A woman had given the garment to her father to keep him warm on his journey, because he was elderly and he was frail, and she respected his wisdom in some things, but part of her feared that he was making the wrong decision in crossing the sea.

The angel folded the sweater carefully and put it away, blinking its own tears from its eyes. Perhaps Little Ash had been right about America. They needed angels there. And angels on the way, as well.

Thus the two divine creatures passed an uneasy Shabbes, and both were glad to board the first train to the west on Sunday morning. Little Ash was carrying steamship tickets and money he'd stolen from Reb Fishl, and the angel was carrying the old man's trunk, with the sweater and the books and the heavy burden of love inside it. Little Ash didn't question it about its new luggage. He assumed it merely wanted to read the books.

PART II

HAMBURG

nine

O N THE DOCKS at Hamburg was a young woman who was also going to America. I should say, rather, that many young women were going to America, but among them was Rose Cohen, who had recently suffered the betrayal of discovering that Dinah was not only engaged but had given up on leaving home entirely.

Rose had shouted at her, screamed at some trees in the forest, screamed at the goats and Motl and her father, cried for three days, and then decided that she had never liked Dinah anyway and that Dinah, may she live to a hundred and twenty, could go hang.

Rose packed up and left Belz by herself, standing tall and confident and glaring at everyone she met, so that even the customs officials, who were used to rather more nervous and worried customers, were intimidated by her and hardly even asked her for a bribe. She was, therefore, determined to stay as angry at Dinah as possible, for as long as possible, because it seemed to be working out quite well for her.

It was this aspect of Rose Cohen's character which caught the attention of Little Ashmedai Shtetler, just arriving with his counterpart the angel on the same dock, to take the same ship, and having been directed to the same area to wait. The person inspecting their tickets had asked Little Ash where his sister was, based on what it said on Reb Fishl's paperwork, and without blinking he had responded that she had gone ahead. Thus the two impostor creatures had been sent to the place where families were waiting for steerage boarding. Little Ash was not terribly concerned about the deception, while the angel had been reminded that its name was supposed to be Uriel Federman, and this had made it feel queasy again, so it had not asked Little Ash what he and the steamship agent were discussing.

"What a shining evil impulse she has," the demon said now, his eyes also shining as he looked at Rose.

At sixteen, Rose was a tall girl with a great pile of curly red hair, and so her evil impulse was not what most people noticed. She was seated on top of her traveling case, so that no one should steal it, and she was glaring at everyone around her, so that she would not start to cry again. She had found that any relaxation of the muscles in her face inevitably led her back to crying. Feeling very alone while the steamship agents asked her if she had recently had fevers and glanced at her appearance to be sure she wasn't tubercular, she had wished for a friend to hold her hand and then despised herself for the weakness. Subsequently she had scowled so fiercely at anyone who came close that no one had spoken to her at all.

"She's going to America to earn money for her little sibling and for her family," said the angel, following Little Ash's gaze. "A woman of valor."

"So angry, yet," said Little Ash. "I love a grudge. Do you think if I spoke to her, she would bite me?"

The angel considered this carefully. It had never seen a human bite someone for approaching incautiously, but, it supposed, it was not always watching Little Ash, and perhaps he had been bitten before. If it removed itself far enough to look at him with objectivity, it was aware that its friend could be very annoying.

"I think she would be right to bite you," it said at last. "You only want to talk to her so you can aggravate her. That's not fair of you. She is in a terribly aggravating place already."

This remark distracted Little Ash from trying to read Rose Cohen's personal history in her eyes without getting close enough to be seen himself. He looked at the angel and realized it was, itself, aggravated.

"This is a wicked place," the angel said, sensing his concern. "I don't like it."

"Do you want we should sit closer to the water?" said Little Ash, almost entirely missing the point.

The angel shook its head. The docks smelled of fish, the odor having a strange and unfamiliar effect on its insides, and whenever it closed its eyes it only saw the letters to spell Uriel, frustratingly obtuse in their intended meaning, as if each letter somehow represented an entire task. It was not even sure, at the moment, of its own name, and wanted very much to be Comfort, or some such compassionate thing, as they were surrounded by wailing infants and frustrated mothers—but it could not quite grasp the intention, and so just sat, feeling uncomfortable.

At some point, as she carefully directed her glare at each person on the docks in turn, Rose became aware of Little Ash staring back at her. The two creatures, who seemed to be Jewish men not too much older than herself, were both sitting on a single suitcase which, though she did not know this, and would not have realized it even if she had seen the angel carrying it, contained a set of the Talmud and a daughter's love. Angels being slightly holier than volumes of Mishnah, there was no disrespect in the angel sitting on its books; as for Little Ash, he had been complaining terribly about the pain in his hips from limping about on his birdlike feet, and the angel had decided that in an emergency, it could allow him not to sit on the ground.

The livelier of the two of them kept sneaking looks at her. He seemed to like what he was looking at, which began to irritate her very much. She was starting to quite enjoy being irritated with him, and had even begun to contemplate going over to slap the delight right off his face, but then she saw the way that he tugged on one of his companion's peyes to get the fellow's attention and whisper in his ear.

The closeness of this gesture reminded her, painfully, of Dinah, and how close the two of them had been, and no longer were, and how Dinah was married and she might never see her again.

Close enough to kiss, Rose thought, and then she thought, what am I thinking? How stupid. She had been thinking about kissing a lot since Dinah got married, and the thoughts confused her terribly.

Anyway, maybe the stranger didn't want to flirt with her, after all. Maybe it was only that he had noticed she was Jewish. That wouldn't be so bad.

It wasn't that she was lonely, she told herself, sternly. It was only that it would be so much more practical to travel with companions.

Rose Cohen stood up, picked up her suitcase, and marched, with purpose, over to the angel and the demon.

"Sholem aleichem, miss," said Little Ash. "Can we help you with something?"

He said this very innocently, Rose thought, for someone who had so obviously been wanting to talk to her already. Rose didn't mind at all how blatantly Little Ash pretended to be something he was not, so long as he either did not turn it against her or she had a chance to fight him over it—an equally appealing option.

"You've been staring at me," Rose said, dropping her case and sitting herself down on it with an air of finality. "And I thought, if you must stare, you ought to do it from up close."

"Staring?" said Little Ash, eyes wide. He turned to the angel and said something Rose didn't quite catch. Had she known Aramaic, she might have heard, She says I was staring.

The angel gave him a look that said, You were, and all of us know it.

Little Ash rolled his eyes and turned back to Rose.

"I'm called Little Ash," he said. "And this is Uriel, I suppose."

Rose didn't bother to be puzzled by the phrasing of this introduction. She was only happy to be speaking Yiddish, and with someone she did not, at the moment, have any reason to argue with. "Rose Cohen," she said. "From Belz."

Little Ash did not explain where he and the angel had come from, as it struck him, just now, as a little embarrassing that they had come from nearly nowhere at all. He supposed it would be more impressive to tell her he had come from Babylon and the angel, perhaps, from the Garden of Eden. But this would only confuse her, or else she would think he was lying, and Little Ash always felt very frustrated when, on the rare occasions he told the truth, people chose not to believe him.

"Are you brothers?" Rose asked, mistaking a certain similarity of body language for a similarity in appearance, as people often do. Some strange part of her hoped they weren't, for reasons she could not name.

"Our papers say we're cousins, but that's a lie," said Little Ash, blithely. "We're chevrusas. We've been together for a very long time. You wouldn't believe how long. Don't worry it doesn't talk to you," he added, observing that Rose was looking, puzzled, in the angel's direction. "It's terrible at Yiddish."

Rose assumed the odd word choice was some artifact of whatever out-of-the-way corner of the Pale these two had come from, and she used up all her tact on not commenting. Thus run out of politeness, she said, "How can you be terrible at the mother tongue?"

"From having no mother," Little Ash suggested, and laughed at his own joke. He had quite a loud laugh, a bit like a hyena's, although Rose had never heard of a hyena and so could not have understood just how much Little Ash sounded like one of those shifty creatures. "Anyway, it's never given us any trouble. I do all the talking when we go among people."

Had the angel been paying any attention, and had it understood him, it might have disagreed with the assertion that Little Ash taking charge had never led to trouble, but luckily it was not even listening. It was singing one of its silent songs of praise, this one a sort of angelic Hashkiveinu, a prayer with the tune of a lullaby, to the crying babies, but mostly, for once, to itself. This, it felt, was not enough, but it was what the angel could do.

Rose, based on a minute of conversation with Little Ash and no words exchanged with the angel, decided that Little Ash needed watching, but Uriel she could probably trust, even if she could not speak to it. Why she felt so certain of this, she couldn't say, but Rose had a tendency to believe things so hard that they became true, which was why it had stung so badly when Dinah betrayed her.

In any case, the angel's round, vacant, Hasidic face made her feel quite comfortable, even as she was aware that Little Ash still had rather a hungry look in his eyes. He couldn't be so bad, she thought, if this was the kind of friend he had. And she could use someone to watch her back. She had heard stories.

"Would you like some dried fish?" she asked. "It's terrible, but it was all I could find that was kosher."

"You should eat something; it's kosher," said Little Ash, to the angel. He was thinking this was most likely what a human would have done in this situation. The angel didn't need to eat, of course, but maybe the warmth of Rose's hospitality would make it feel better about whatever was bothering it. To Rose, he said, "I quite like fish, no matter what shape it's in."

Little Ash, compelled by the angel to keep kosher as much as possible, which meant, in part, eating human food rather than human souls, had spent some of Reb Fishl's money on boiled eggs and potatoes and a bit of black bread. The three had quite a pleasant meal together, and then the angel sang Grace After Meals under its breath and Little Ash joined in, although, Rose thought, he seemed to be singing more to his friend than to the Universe in general. After a minute or two, she joined them as well, finding that the songs seemed to fill up some deep well of loneliness inside her that she had been denying for weeks.

Rose thought, incorrectly, that they both sang better than she did, and assumed, also incorrectly, that they must have learned it at yeshiva. The angel, meanwhile, listening to the sound of her voice as she *lai-lai-lai*ed her way through words she didn't quite have memorized, decided that Rose, like the books in its suitcase, was a treasure who had been mistreated by the world, and whose safe delivery to America must be its purpose here in Hamburg.

Little Ash, noticing that the angel seemed in a better mood, wondered if he ought to be worried that it had acted so human as to be upset when it hadn't eaten, and decided that as soon as they reached America he would bury the papers for Uriel Federman, just in case.

ten

THE ANGEL LIKED the ship even less than it had liked the docks. First of all, Rose Cohen, who had never been on the water before, got seasick immediately, as did a good number of the people surrounding them. Then Little Ash, contrary as always, got very excited to be on the water, and the angel had to catch hold of his collar to keep him from leaning dangerously far over the railing to admire the way the ship churned up the waves. And then the angel realized that, perhaps as a consequence of trying to pay attention to two companions at once, it was feeling quite sick itself.

"I need to lie down," said Rose, managing to sound authoritative even though she was sitting on her suitcase with her head in her hands and elbows on her knees, trying queasily to steady herself.

"Not down below, you don't," said Little Ash, quite cheerfully. His mother was a water demon, employed in the business of sometimes ambushing women at the mikveh and infecting them with madness to punish their husbands for thoughtless behavior. With such a mother's blood in his veins, he felt quite invigorated by the damp air and the scent of the ocean. "The air is fresh out here. Down there everyone will be sick."

Rose glanced up for long enough to fix him with a baleful look.

"What an ayin horeh, a real evil eye that one has," he said to the angel, with satisfaction.

"I need to lie down," said the angel. It was now holding onto Little Ash not so much to keep him falling off the ship as to hold itself up. This was a new experience, and one it was not enjoying at all.

Little Ash looked at his counterpart, and then he looked at Rose Cohen. Both had a pale, unhealthy appearance, and both were looking at him as if he had wronged them merely by being comfortable.

"What am I now, the nursemaid?" he said, disgusted.

"You're the one who's going to carry my suitcase," said Rose.

Down below it was, as Little Ash had expected, a real Gehinnom. The steerage deck was divided more or less in two, with a gap down the middle where the boilers were. One side of the ship was meant for men, and the other for women, but Rose's and Little Ash's and the angel's tickets were for the subsection of the deck intended for families traveling together, and so Rose and the angel were able to install themselves in bunks one on top of the other, while Little Ash arranged their luggage as a sort of barrier between them and the innumerable small children who, released from the anxious control of parents on the docks, were now racing to and fro with wild abandon and making friends.

Now, he supposed, he had to watch Rose and the angel, just because they were both fussy and he, Little Ash, was a reasonable person. The angel crawled into its bunk and immediately went to sleep, as Little Ash had expected it to. This left him sitting next to what, to anyone else, would have appeared to be a corpse, and underneath Rose, who was treating her own nausea by whispering strings of curses. Little Ash was quite impressed with these, Rose having a great deal of creativity and a talent at wordplay, which would have impressed the ancient rabbis.

"You'll dry yourself out with all that talking," he told her. "And I won't get up to bring you water."

"You will," she said.

"I said I won't. Why would I?"

"Because if you don't, your friend will be disappointed in you." She was thinking of Dinah again. Rose was getting quite tired of how constantly she thought of Dinah, when she had been determined, on leaving home, to forget her entirely. It must be the seasickness, she thought, taking all the fight out of her.

"So it will be disappointed," said Little Ash, looking down at the angel. He didn't mind sharing a bed with it; even if it had been present in its body, he would have had no compunctions about sprawling all over it, and since it wasn't there, it certainly couldn't stop him from putting his limbs wherever he pleased. Even if it didn't have a pulse or working lungs it still, at least, smelled like the angel, the scent of sheepskin and ink, like a Torah scroll. It was a warm, heymish scent that Little Ash had come to find very soothing. Still, he wished that, since the angel had gone to the trouble of learning to pretend it was asleep, it could also have learned to breathe while genuinely sleeping.

"I don't mind if it's disappointed," he said. "It happens quite a lot."

Rose leaned over the side of her bunk to fix him, once again, with her evil eye. "You do mind. I've seen you looking at him. It's very annoying."

Little Ash had no idea what this meant, and so for once he said nothing.

"Did Uriel want to go to America?" Rose asked.

He looked down at the angel's face again. "It could have said no, if it didn't."

"Then how did you get him to say yes?" said Rose, who still had not quite caught on that Little Ash was using *it* on purpose.

Little Ash was rather confused, because he felt as if Rose was accusing him of something, but he had no idea what that could be. With unaccustomed honesty, therefore, he said, "I don't know."

"Well then. You're useless," said Rose, with enough conviction that even self-satisfied Little Ash almost believed her. She threw herself down on her back and covered her eyes with one forearm. "Be quiet, and let me sleep."

Little Ash sat for a minute, puzzled and waiting for Rose to explain herself, but she didn't. Finally he realized she had, in fact, fallen asleep.

He covered the angel with a blanket, so it would be less obvious that it wasn't breathing, and went to find some water for when Rose woke up.

With both of his companions asleep, Little Ash decided it was time to find out just what his partner the angel had been carrying around with it since Warsaw. He was not in the least surprised to find the case was full of books. That was very like the angel. No wonder when it pestered him to study, its volumes had looked more tattered than usual. It was using real ones, made by humans, and not the ones made from its own inner fire, which worked all right for studying as long as the angel was there to hold them, but which never left its hands.

Little Ash considered human-made books superior to angelic books, because with a human-made book he could read ahead behind his study partner's back and have more time to think of arguments. The angel was more patient with him than his brothers or his teachers ever had been in the land of demons, but he liked to look clever whenever he could. He therefore conceded reluctantly that a trunk full of books was not a bad companion for an ocean voyage, even if it was not as exciting as a dormant golem, or a heap of treasure, or any of the other secret things one might keep in one's luggage.

In the trunk he found the letters that had caused the angel to decide the books should go to America. Of course it is a sin to read a letter meant for someone else, but the angel wasn't awake to remind him of that, and he would have ignored it anyway. Little Ash, being able to read Yiddish much better than the angel, found that the letters were from the daughter of the old Belzer Rebbe, whose ghost he had encountered in the shul in Warsaw. This daughter lived in New York. She wanted her father to come to America, as she was to be married. She had sent him tickets, through Reb Fishl, from her boss in New York who was called Mr. Boaz.

"I suppose you want us to bring these to her," Little Ash said, to the empty husk of the angel.

The angel, of course, being elsewhere, didn't say anything.

"I don't see why you always have to make me responsible

for people," Little Ash grumbled, carefully packing up the letters. "It's not what I was intended for. I didn't even really intend to care about Essie, and now I suppose we'll have to find her and pay all her debts, and bring our whole shtetl to America with us, in the end."

Still, he supposed, he had come up with the excuse of Essie, so perhaps it was his fault. It was only that he had not wanted the angel to know he was frightened of the changes in the shtetl, and had heard whispers of angry peasants stomping through some of the Jewish villages to take out their frustration with new laws and bad harvests, and he didn't want the angel to see such things if they ever came to Shtetl.

What on earth had Rose been talking about? he wondered. What did it matter *why* the angel said yes, as long as it *had* said yes? They were going to America now, no matter what the reason.

What a vexing person, the demon thought. What did she have to go and ask me all those questions for? I'm not supposed to worry about other people's feelings. I'm not supposed to worry at all.

It was tempting to go through her suitcase, too, and read her letters, and find out what was behind that bright spark of anger that had delighted him so much when he'd first seen her, but he was a little afraid if he reached into her space she might snap off his hand, like one of the crocodiles of Egypt.

He would get her to talk about it sometime, anyway. They

were going to be on this ship for an awfully long while, whether you counted it in human time, or in the length of time it would take a creature like Little Ash to get bored of sitting by himself.

eleven

WHEN ROSE WOKE UP, Little Ash was sprawled across his bunk, using the angel as a bookrest for the volume of Talmud from which they'd been doing their daily readings.

"Sleeps like a rock, this one," he said, thumping his chevrusa's chest with a fist. It made a hollow sound, but Uriel seemed undisturbed. Rose, who had not slept well at all, was terribly jealous.

It seemed to her that it was awfully dark for reading. Little Ash had excellent night vision and hadn't noticed this. He was trying to concentrate very hard on what he was reading, partly so that he could think of a better argument than the angel when it woke up, and partly because otherwise he thought he might crawl out of his own skin from boredom.

In the shadows there seemed to be something very wrong with Little Ash's bare feet. Rose, blinking in confusion, decided the seasickness must have made her feverish.

Little Ash closed his book and watched her with shining eyes, his chin propped on the angel's rib cage. "Did you know an old rebbe in Belz, with a limp, and a daughter in America?"

"Why?" said Rose, startled. That was Dinah's grandfather; she had nearly forgotten about him in the whirlwind of Dinah's wedding and leaving for Hamburg and being irritated with Hasidim in general and Saul in particular. "He went to Warsaw for some business. Did you meet him there?"

"In a manner of speaking."

"I don't know him *well*," Rose said, not wanting to air too much private business to someone who, after all, she had just met, yet tempted terribly to spread the wickedest gossip she could think of. "He had some followers."

Little Ash, reading her face with his demon eyes, could tell that she counted at least one of those followers as an enemy. This delighted him, as he couldn't think of any reason a girl so young should have enemies. "What kind of followers?"

"I don't know," said Rose, dismissively. "Men, I suppose."

"Oh, those," said Little Ash.

"I went to one of their weddings," said Rose, giving in. "The rebbe was gone by then. We supposed he had made it to America. Anyway, the wedding was terrible."

"Why, what happened? Was it a cholera wedding? I quite like those."

Rose gave Little Ash a look of disgust. Whatever was he talking about? "My best friend got married, is what happened."

Little Ash blinked. Why one's best friend getting married should be terrible, he wasn't sure. It seemed generally that humans were in favor of that sort of thing. But then, as his closest friend was just as inhuman as himself, he supposed he didn't have to worry about it happening to him. The angel went around with a tallis, when normally only married people wore them, so he didn't suppose it was looking to marry anyone.

"Do you know what sort of thing is a *shop boss*?" he asked.

Rose, who had been preparing herself to enumerate to him the sins of Dinah Pearl, was taken aback by this change of subject. "Why should I know?" she demanded.

"You seem like a clever person," said Little Ash. "Why shouldn't you?"

This surprised her as well, because it generally seemed to bother people when she was clever, but Little Ash clearly meant it as a compliment.

"Well, I don't know," she said. "Anyway, the wedding."

"The wedding," said the demon.

"I don't know what Dinah *sees* in him, first of all," said Rose, starting, despite the words, in the middle of the story. "He's awfully stuck-up, just because he thinks himself educated, and that, when he can't even calculate the change for a loaf of bread if anyone ever manages to send him on an errand. I suppose Dinah thinks it's all right to do all the business herself and be in charge of the house, but the way he lectures, how can she put up with that? If I were marrying

Dinah—if I were a man, of course—I should think it was part of my duty to make sure she knew that I could help her with it all. I wouldn't come home and ignore all her good efforts just to hear myself discoursing. I'd sing her the Eishet Chayil every night just because it's true, and not because it's a *duty*. He treats everything like that! Like he's doing it because someone else told him to! I really can't stand him. Do you know he asked me what color are her eyes? And them married already. Hadn't he ever looked at her? I mean, she's the most beautiful girl in our town—that is, everyone says so—how could he look away? Oh, it makes me want to scream. I think he really wanted to marry her grandfather, with all that!"

"I wouldn't scream, if I were you," said Little Ash, who was quite enjoying this narration. "I count six sleeping babies close enough to throw a rock at. Not that I *would* throw a rock at a baby," he added, out of habit, as the angel often misunderstood him when he was being figurative.

"Life is all right for you," Rose said. "Being a man. You'll never have to get married and even if you did, you'd have a wife."

Little Ash gave this some thought. "I don't think I would."

"Well, what else would you have? And I suppose you have sisters in America or Warsaw or somewhere, working to support you."

"No," said Little Ash. "It's brothers, only. The only girls in my family are cousins."

Demons are born able to speak, and to understand certain things about themselves as infants that humans do not. The demon king Ashmedai, over the course of several centuries of the Babylonian Exile, had taken two hundred and fifty bird-footed babies from their mothers' arms, looked into their little slit-pupiled eyes, and asked if they wanted a son's bris or a daughter's blessing. Each time the infant had asked for a bris.

The two-hundred-and-fiftieth time this happened, the king had sighed in frustration, and the newborn creature, sensing that its father somehow disapproved of it, had twisted around in his arms and bitten him quite viciously. At this, King Ashmedai decided he had had enough children. The infant who bit him grew up to be Ashmedai Shtetler, but Little Ash did not know this about himself.

"I don't think my father has figured out how to make daughters," he said.

"Stupid of him," said Rose. "Anyway, my point is, Dinah shouldn't ever have gotten married, and if she really had to, it should have been to someone with a lot more to recommend him."

"Did you tell her so?"

"Of course I did! And she told me I didn't understand. Can you believe it? I understand better than she does."

Little Ash was about to say he was sure that was true, when the angel gasped awake and sat up, coughing, almost knocking him and his book out of the bed.

"Maariv," it said, catching him. This simple statement

it meant as clarification of its own identity, in case he wasn't paying attention: the sun was close to setting outside of their shut-in steerage deck, and it was time for the evening service.

"Go find a minyan of old men, why don't you," said Little Ash. "There must be one around here somewhere."

"Must there?" The angel peered very closely into his eyes, looking for deception. "Because you said in America I would have to encourage them to pray, so why should there be a minyan on the way to America?"

"I don't know; you found the books of a rabbi on his way to America, so maybe I was wrong." Little Ash held up the book he had been reading. "Anyway, I'm talking to Rose."

Rose was watching them as she drank the water Little Ash had brought for her. She had no idea what shtetl they'd come from, but she was quite impressed with the incomprehensibility of their Yiddish, which was, of course, actually Aramaic. Perhaps, she thought, they were Litvaks: everyone said the Jews in Lithuania, for all their modern scholarly pretensions, didn't speak properly, and she was sure she remembered something odd about the way they used pronouns, in particular, which she assumed would explain Little Ash's insistence on referring to Uriel as something other than a *him*.

"I'm being told I have to pray," Little Ash informed her, switching over to words she understood. "Feel free to be angry we're abandoning you. If you tell me we're being rude, it might make me not go."

"Be considerate to your friend, you wretch," said Rose. "After you dragged him all the way to this pit of demons! I'm going to find dinner, and if you're nice enough to Uriel maybe I'll bring some of that disgusting fish for you."

Little Ash had to admit this was a nice bargain. He could not, however, be convinced to put his shoes back on, even when the angel suggested hopefully that there might even be Kabbalists on the ship, since this vessel in particular seemed a veritable Ark of Noah, holding in its belly all the beasts of the world. Little Ash, feeling contrary, informed it that the Kabbalists could come and get him if they liked, and so they both went barefoot. No one had ever noticed anything amiss about the angel's cloven feet; they seemed, even to the unusually observant Rose, merely a neatly buttoned pair of little, polished boots.

The angel's instincts, unerring as always, led them through a labyrinth of suitcases and cradles and human legs until they found, up on the open deck, a little circle of elderly Jews, with some middle-aged ones around the edge, smoking cigarettes and counting for the minyan without particularly being involved in the minyan. This was a relief to Little Ash, who felt the observant Jews on the ship might be able to tell him more than Rose about the murdered Belzer Rebbe, and thus about Reb Fishl and Mr. Boaz, information that would circle back to Essie. Rose's story, although very interesting, had nevertheless been entirely irrelevant to the mystery he was trying to solve.

The angel ignored the fact that Little Ash was hanging back at the edge of the group to gossip. Having a clear purpose again, even if only for the short time it took to daven a weekday evening service, made it feel much better, indeed so much better that it forgot it had been seasick entirely. The rhythm of prayer it found soothing. Also soothing? The way the old men erroneously complimented it for being such a dedicated young person in these days of iniquity, although perhaps, as a modest creature, it shouldn't have been pleased at the praise.

The angel was thinking of its mission to find Essie. It had generally relied on its instincts for this kind of thing, as it had relied on its instincts for the less complex, but no less important, mission of saying Kaddish and some blessings. Little Ash was the one who got caught up in details, and made what humans would recognize as plans. The angel simply expected that its mission would be fulfilled until, eventually, it was.

Little Ash was always telling it this was an inefficient way to do business, but the angel felt *doing business* was a terrible, demonic way to describe the feeling of being needed. It wasn't doing business. It was being a mitzvah. The demon was too caught up in being Little Ash to quite understand what was so satisfying about that.

My name, the angel insisted to itself, is Rescue. I am finding Essie. I know what my task is, and I am my task.

Rescue had no reason to begin feeling seasick again as soon as the prayer service was over.

They found Rose up near the bow, with the promised fish for Little Ash, and more potatoes, and her water jug full of hot tea. She was watching the sunset and feeling a bit less disgusted with the entirety of the Universe than she had been when they first got on board.

"How were your prayers?" she asked the angel politely, in the careful, slightly overloud tone of one trying to make oneself understood to a foreigner without actually changing languages.

"They were prayers," said Little Ash, who had no business saying so, as he hadn't paid any attention. For all he knew, the whole minyan could have converted to Christianity on the spot, while he was getting frustratingly useless information from the men he'd spoken to, all of whom had conflicting opinions on what it was like to work in America, in a *shop*.

"You're very kind," the angel told Rose, accepting a potato from her. It, too, spoke carefully, as if the barrier of language could be surpassed merely by being very deliberate. In this case, as it happened, Rose had no trouble understanding what was meant, as gratitude shone from every line of the angel's face.

Little Ash rolled his eyes. All this being nice. Were they going to torment him like this for the whole journey?

"I suppose I'll have to ask the crew," he said, aloud but to himself, as neither Rose nor the angel was paying attention to him. "Or else wait until America. I suppose in America they know what all the parts of America are like."

"What are you talking about?" said Rose. "No one is listening to you."

"I suppose you have relatives you're going to?" said Little Ash. "Where are they?"

"I have a cousin in Hester Street, in New York City," said Rose, feeling quite proud of this. She had read a lot about New York City, and had rather got the impression that it was not anything so boring as a New Jerusalem, but actually an improvement on all Jerusalems. "She said she can get me a job in the dress factories."

"Practical of you," said Little Ash. "Are you good at sewing?"

"I'm a born genius," said Rose, who had, the last time she touched a sewing machine, immediately broken it. "What about you? I suppose you have some scheme or other."

"Me?" said Little Ash. "I'm going there to make sure they forget the mitzvahs in America. And this one is going to make sure they don't," he added, putting a hand on top of the angel's head. "That's how I convinced it. Because if I went alone, I would cause too much trouble. If that answers your question from before."

It did not. Rose glared at him, thinking he was making fun of her. "That's no help at all. I did try that on Dinah, and it didn't work one bit."

"Well then," said Little Ash. "Maybe you were too good for her. If she were at all responsible that argument should have worked. I've used it a hundred times and it always has for me."

This thought struck Rose as so contrary to what she had been thinking for all the time since Dinah had announced her engagement, she had to chew it over, along with her boiled potatoes, in silence, while Little Ash summarized for the angel the reading he had done today, and the angel, in response, told him he had gotten nearly everything wrong.

twelve

ROSE WOKE UP in the morning with enough room in her heart to start a letter to her family, to be posted when, keynehore, she arrived safely in America. The angel and Little Ash were sleeping, or so she thought, and so tangled together in the small space that belonged to them, it made her ache with loneliness.

She sat on the angel's trunk, where there was more light than in her bed, and contemplated for a long time how to start the letter. If she told her family she should be safe on the journey because she had met a nice young man and a Little Ash, they would get very excited for all the wrong reasons. Finally, she settled on telling them she had already made friends, who could eat meals with her and watch her back, and omitted any further details so her family could assume the friends were female. She then stretched the contents of the letter considerably by asking after the health of everyone in the family by name, and then after the health of everyone on their street, pointedly leaving Dinah and her new husband off the list. She considered adding that she had heard some news of the old rebbe, but then realized that Little Ash had really not told her anything about him at all, and so left it out.

Thus satisfied that she had fulfilled her duty of respecting her mother and father, she put her writing things away and just sat, looking around at the crowded steerage deck. All of these people, she supposed, were feeling the same emotions as she was, except perhaps for the part about Dinah. Everyone here was excited and nervous and lonely and, unfortunately, still a little seasick. She supposed if she had made two friends already, it wouldn't be so hard to make more. Perhaps she could watch someone's baby, as she did at home, by recruiting Little Ash, in place of her little brother Motl, to do it for her. At the very least she could fetch some water and empty some buckets. It was already beginning to smell in steerage, and she hated to think she'd have to breathe the smell of sickness for two weeks.

She reached over and jabbed Little Ash in the shoulder with her finger. He opened one bright eye, seeming not asleep at all, as indeed he hadn't been, and glared at her.

"Make sure no one steals my belongings," she said. "I'm going for a walk."

"If they try, I'll eat them," he said, and closed his eye again. Rose took this as an exaggeration, which it wasn't, and as a promise to do as she asked, which it was. Lacing up her boots, she chose a direction, and started looking either for a friend or, in the worst case, for a mother who would tell her something she ought to do to make herself useful.

Little Ash, while pretending to be asleep, had been listening, in the way of demons, to the music of selfish desires that filled the steerage deck. Most were little things, things that even the angel would agree fell under the category of choosing life for oneself, like the wish to eat something more exciting than boiled potatoes. Some were more dangerous, the kind of things Little Ash liked to keep an eye on in case he should have the opportunity to punish someone who had done something entirely unforgivable, which was always exciting but hardly ever happened, humans having such an infinite capacity for self-correction. He had eaten Reb Fishl, and now he expected he would be restricted to human food for another century.

There were not, the angel would have been glad to hear, any murderers on board, and although there were, among the gentile passengers, a fair share of anti-Semites, none of them had an army at their back, and Little Ash was sure that should any kind of conflict break out, his people would, for once, be perfectly capable of defending themselves.

If the angel had been awake, he would have suggested this to it as a possible miracle, but it was not awake.

Uriel Federman, he thought. I suppose I made it seasick by accident somehow, giving it a name. Perhaps being a Light of God is difficult when you're in a dank box on the ocean. I should never have told Rose that's what it was called. Or told her it was called Sholem, or something; that would calm it down some.

"Wake up," he whispered in the angel's ear, and then, "Uri, uri, shir dabeiri, k'vod Adonai alayich niglah." Awake and sing: the Eternal's glory dawns upon you: the same line of Lecha Dodi that he had been thinking of since the angel got its new name, though this *uri* was spelled with an ayin, instead of the angel's alef.

The glory of Adonai not being evident in the steerage deck, the angel ignored him.

Rose, having been buffeted from Jewish mother to Jewish mother along the deck like a piece of driftwood with two good hands, eventually found herself up above, trying to clean porridge out of the bottom of someone's cooking pot with the aid of a bucket of saltwater and a rag she had bullied off of a sailor who spoke only enough Yiddish to know when he was being threatened. She had forgotten whose pot it was but supposed if she waited long enough, one of the seemingly infinite number of knee-high Jewish children on the ship would come find her and accuse her of having stolen it.

She was quite enjoying herself, though her hands were freezing and her knees could have done without the hardness of the deck. She had been so out of sorts since Dinah got married, going through the motions of leaving Belz and getting to Hamburg without paying attention to them, that she had forgotten how it felt to really accomplish something, even a task so small as scrubbing a pot until it was perfectly clean.

A dreadful number of the steerage passengers were seasick, and she worried that if they weren't given water and food they'd all be feverish by the time they arrived in America, and they'd be sent back. It didn't help that the ship's kitchens had provided mainly herrings and potatoes for kosher food. She'd spoken to a steward who insisted there was nothing like a pickled herring for seasickness, but she'd also helped more than one person in the steerage deck who definitively disagreed.

Rose, without realizing it, was doing exactly as she always did: forming in her head a list of steps she would have to take to accomplish a nearly impossible goal. This was to see every person from the family deck safely through Ellis Island and into America.

If what it took was scrubbing a thousand pots, at least it was hard to remember what Saul Lehman's hateful face looked like while she was thinking instead about her chapped knuckles and how lucky she was to have a strong stomach.

✧ ✧ ✧

The angel finally woke up to pray Shacharit, without a minyan this time, as it was feeling rather in the mood to be quiet and only talk to Little Ash so that it wouldn't have to feel sorry for not understanding the mother tongue of all the other passengers. Little Ash obligingly prayed along, but when it made to lie down on the bunk again he stopped it.

"If you go back to sleep, I'm going to toss your body overboard and make you swim to America," he said.

"Why?" said the angel.

"Because I'm bored," the demon said. He leaned over to open the trunk full of Talmud and pulled out the letters from the rebbe's daughter. "Did you read these? This is another woman who's in debt to Reb Fishl and his friends. It's a *shop boss* in America who sends him his tickets, and at every step I suppose they take a little more money. I've read in the newspapers that you can get tickets for cheaper than she sent to her father, but her *boss* said it was safer if she went by Fishl. It says with these tickets you'll always pass the health inspections, but the men at the minyan said it isn't true and that you're always inspected if you're in steerage. You cause me an awful lot of trouble, did you know that? If I weren't thinking of our Essie and our people I'd have respect for such scammers."

The angel had not, as far as it knew, ever been any kind of Trouble. It was only that Little Ash liked to complain. "You should not respect them," it said. "They are enemies to the people of Israel."

"Well," said Little Ash, darkly, "I used to think so was I."

✧ ✧ ✧

Little Ash and the angel stood with their heads together over their Gemara, puzzling over a point of grammar neither of them understood at all. They had, for centuries, been solving these kinds of problems either by arguing about it until one of them gave up and decided the other was right, or by the angel seeking out a human scholar to ask about it.

Now Little Ash's wild assertions had given the angel the enjoyable name of Passionate Disagreement, which made it feel very much itself again after two days of feeling quite out of sorts.

When Rose came down the stairs, it was also very glad to see how finding a task with which to distract herself had helped Rose overcome her seasickness. It seemed to the angel, who was attuned to such things, that a new light had sparked somehow in Rose's soul.

"Rose has lost some aggravation," it whispered to Little Ash.

"Yes, I've noticed," said Little Ash. "Poor Rose was the victim of a terrible betrayal, did I tell you? Oh, no, I suppose I didn't, because you had abandoned me."

"I was only sleeping," said the angel. "Don't be ridiculous. It is a natural phenomenon. Humans do it much more often."

"Well, I don't, and it's boring without you."

"It's only that this ship makes me so tired," said the angel, apologetically. "There are so many people and so many things. It is difficult to grasp what I should be doing."

"Keeping me company, is what," said Little Ash, and waved his hands toward the satchel in which he was keeping the letters he'd stolen from Reb Fishl. "And, I suppose, seeing what we can find in those letters, to tell us what we need to do in America."

"Oh, I wish we were in America already," said the angel, which made Little Ash frown, because his partner was very rarely impatient. Angels tend toward equanimity in the timing of things, whereas demons are always in a rush. He supposed it was being packed in the hold like sardines. The atmosphere was having terrible effects on nearly everyone.

To distract the angel from its misery, he turned to Rose. "What's got you looking so cheerful?"

"The grandmother of the family down at the end of our row has a bit of a cough, and I've been sent to make her some tea," said Rose. Nursing was not precisely her area of expertise, the need for a gentle bedside manner being somewhat superfluous in her eyes, but she had helped her father with the goats enough times that she understood the very basics of medicine, and it was good to feel a solid plan under her feet, if not solid ground. Besides, the grandmother, whose name was Rivke, had not seemed like the type who needed much in the way of coddling; she had cracked a joke about her own frailty that made her son-in-law look even more seasick. "Who is that? Is that your sister?"

Rose was pointing to the photograph of Essie, which was on top of a stack of letters next to the angel on the bed, left from before they began their Gemara lesson. Rose found herself hoping very much that the girl in the portrait was not the fiancée of either the angel or Little Ash. If she had to hear about another impending marriage, she thought she'd be queasy all over again, and what's more she didn't want to share a bunk for the whole journey with any starry-eyed, lovesick boys.

"Oh, that's Essie," said Little Ash. "She's not our sister, but she is from our village, and we're supposed to find her in America."

He did not elaborate, and so Rose assumed he meant that Essie would be finding jobs for the two of them. She picked up the photograph and put it quickly down again, so as not to seem overly curious. Something about the freckled face and bright eyes of the girl in the picture made her feel as if she ought not to be looking, but the impression of thick braids dark as ravens' wings lingered even after she turned away. "She's quite pretty, isn't she?"

"Is she?" Little Ash cocked his head, and then showed the photograph to the angel and asked it, in Aramaic, if it thought Essie was pretty. The angel said it thought probably so. By the time this exchange was finished Rose felt quite thoroughly embarrassed and had to hurry away to fetch tea for Grandmother Rivke before Little Ash could find something to tease her about.

thirteen

Despite Little Ash's pestering, the angel had used up its energy and felt unwell again, and so the demon left it behind to go talk to some sailors and see what gossip he could gather, whether to do with Reb Fishl or simply to do with America and its golden streets. The angel lay in its bunk with its shawl over its head, feeling quite thoroughly terrible. It supposed there must be angels of ships, and oceans, and traveling, and all manner of other things, and it would have been simple to be one of those angels, but instead it felt torn in a hundred directions, quite an uncomfortable feeling for a creature who was used to having one thought at once and forgetting half the thoughts the moment they'd gone through its head.

It was, of course, the Angel of Shtetl. It had to be that angel, because it was also Rescuing Essie, who was from that little village. It was, then, also a Messenger, bringing the old rebbe's books to America so his daughter could know what had happened to him and could say Kaddish.

And, in a way that it could not quite explain as fulfilling an angelic mission, it was also the Angel Who Was Friends with Little Ash. Not only the Angel Who Kept Him from Causing Trouble, but, as the incident with Reb Fishl had proven, also the Angel Who Helped Him Cause Trouble. This single feeling, drawing it forward, almost made it more uncomfortable than all the rest combined. An angel and a demon were not supposed to be the sort of partners that worked together.

But it had said yes to him, and here it was. Its head hurt.

With a groan, it rolled over onto its side, and as it did so it saw that someone was sitting by the bed, on the trunk full of Talmud. This was quite startling, as it had not heard anyone arrive, and what's more, the person in question was neither Rose nor Little Ash. The angel quickly sat up, afraid this was some ship's official come to tell it something it would not understand, and was even more startled when the figure spoke in the Holy Tongue.

"Shalom aleichem, Holy Messenger," he said.

The angel blinked. The visitor was an old man, bearded, with wispy peyot. He was wearing lumpy knit socks in the same yarn as the sweater at the bottom of the trunk, and something about the way he sat reminded the angel of Little Ash—which it realized must be because he sat as if his legs were hurting him.

It was the murdered Rebbe of Belz.

"Aleichem shalom," said the angel, having no better response. It blinked a few times to try and clear its eyes, but the rebbe remained where he was, perfectly visible.

"You are having a dream, my friend," he said, when the angel could not find words. "You've fallen asleep, as humans do. I wished to speak to you before, but your companion's charm wore off—it was only child's magic, the kind of magic old wives teach. I thought it strange."

The angel had never had a dream before and was quite upset. It didn't think it was supposed to be dreaming. "I can't be asleep like a human! I don't know how. I only know how to pretend."

"You are learning new things," said the rebbe. "That's what a journey is for. Hush, now. It's all right."

This he said because the angel had started to cry. The rebbe reached over and laid his hand on its shoulder, a little awkwardly as if he didn't know what sort of comfort to offer. Though he had been very old and learned, he had never before seen an angel with his own eyes, and had not realized they could weep in the manner of people who have become overwhelmed by the world and have no other feelings left.

"Are you well?" the rebbe asked.

The angel covered its face with its hands, and shrank back under its shawl. How did anyone continue to learn new things while keeping ahold of the old ones? If it became an Angel of Dreams, it could lose Little Ash forever—no, not Little Ash, but Essie, the mission of helping Essie and her family—no, *yes* Little Ash. It did not want to forget about Little Ash, and suddenly it felt very unfair that it might need to if it found a new task while he was away, spending time however demons spent it.

How did humans do it? How did they hold so many thoughts in their heads at once? How did they manage to love themselves and their families, and also have enemies, and go from place to place learning?

"My dear," said the rebbe, "do not forget to take a breath."

The angel took a breath. The sound of a silent breath is the sound of the letter alef, it thought. Where have I seen an alef?

How did humans do this?

Silly. Its second breath was half a laugh and half a sob. Of course, of course, it was so simple. Little Ash would laugh.

"Are you all right?" said the rebbe again.

"Yes," said Uriel, lifting its head. "Yes, thank you. I'm fine."

"Ah," said the rebbe, who was after all very wise, and what's more, was dead, and could see things the living could not. "I see you've found a name. That's good. I think you will need it."

"Why will I need a name?" Uriel asked. It could feel its soul stretching out to reach for the farthest corners of a new self, the expansiveness of a name both exhilarating and frightening, like standing at the edge of a cliff. "Why do you think I will need a name, I mean?"

"It was kind of you to bring my books with you from Warsaw," said the rebbe. "I am glad they won't be left to molder in that sinner's home. But it will not be enough. If my daughters cannot say Kaddish for me, Holy One, I will lose myself and become a wandering dybbuk. I can't stand the thought of it. I've seen what happens to souls like that, lost souls who can't find the gates of the Other World. They spread misfortune wherever they go, and their instincts draw them to the ones they loved in life, even if they try to fight it. I have two daughters, and one of my daughters has a daughter of her own and many sons. She can scarcely afford to feed them all, even now. How will she live if I, her own father, forget who I am and bring my bad luck to her doorstep? No, I cannot bear to think of it."

"It sounds very terrible," Uriel agreed. "But I don't understand what it has to do with my name, at all."

"I need to cling to you," said the rebbe. "As an ibbur, a benevolent possession, until we've crossed the sea. I can't travel so far on my own, and I can't hold onto something so light and changeable as an angel. Your soul is like a soap bubble, beautiful and fragile, until you encase it in a name. The touch of my hands would destroy you."

"But—" Uriel looked around. They were still on the ship, it seemed, only the ship was empty. They were alone. Not even Little Ash was in the bed with Uriel, where he ought to have been. The emptiness of the steerage deck went on forever, as far as it could see. "But I didn't have a name before, even after I started dreaming."

"You had a name," said the rebbe. "You simply did not know what it was. How does it feel?"

"I don't know," said Uriel. "How should it feel?"

The rebbe shook his head. "I can't answer that for you. Only tell me, please, if you will let me hold onto you until you reach America, so that I can see Malke, my eldest, and she can say my Kaddish. I was meant to join her there. My little Malkele . . . I remember holding her when she was born. Her little hands. Her crying—ach, she was a loud one, my girl! Some nights I had to hold her on my own shoulder as I read the Mishnah, so her mother, may her memory be a blessing, could get a moment of rest. We never thought she'd grow so strong."

His eyes had gone soft and distant as he lost himself in the memories. Uriel could see the love glowing in the rebbe's heart, a warm light that threw the rest of him into shadow.

"There is no one else I can ask," the old man said. "Will you help me, Uriel?"

fourteen

ROSE HAD SPENT her afternoon tracking down a ship's steward who could be bullied into giving her a better mix of tea for Rivke, the grandmother from down the row in steerage, whose chest was a little congested with the damp of the ocean. The steward she found only spoke German, and she only spoke Yiddish, but she was so determined that before she was finished she even got him to add a little honey to the pot, and she returned to her own bunk around dinnertime feeling greatly satisfied.

Little Ash was absent, but Uriel was there, reading some letters. Rose greeted it automatically with a cheerful "Good evening," and was just starting to think how unfortunate it was that Uriel had never managed to speak to her when it responded with a "Good evening" of its own, in perfect Yiddish.

"Oh!" said Rose, startled. "I thought your friend said you didn't speak. How silly, I suppose he was joking."

"Yes," said Uriel, who actually hadn't been sure if it spoke Yiddish or not, but was pleased to find that it could. "He is very silly."

Since waking from its strange dream of the rebbe's ghost, it had, on the ghost's request, picked up the letters from inside his trunk, and found that it could read them. The contents were full of words it still didn't know, describing things it had never seen, but it understood enough to be rather concerned. The rebbe's daughter in America was in the same terrible state as Essie, it seemed, tricked into debts that she hadn't expected, so that it was difficult to pay for her father's passage and more difficult still to think about tickets for her sister, who had more children than the angel had been able to keep straight from names alone.

Yet more troubling, the rebbe had told it the exact date he had died, and it had determined that the period of the first thirty days after his death would end soon after their ship arrived in America. There would be very little time to spare in finding the rebbe's daughter before his ghost became unable to understand whether his messages had passed on to her and whether she would be trapped in debt forever.

Uriel remembered everything Little Ash had told it about America, and felt almost annoyed with him for not explaining that there were sorrows there, just like in the Old Country. He had made it sound like going to America would be an adventure, a game almost. If he'd only said how difficult it could be for those who had left their lives behind, perhaps the angel would have been inclined to listen to him sooner, and then it would have known to read newspapers and understand words like *sweatshop* and *loan interest*, and then it could understand its own purpose and not feel so lost about things.

"What are those letters?" Rose asked, wanting to make conversation now that she knew Little Ash had been teasing her. "Are they from family? I was writing to my family, earlier. They'll be glad to know I've made it to America, so I intend to send something to them as soon as I arrive."

"That's very good of you," said Uriel, thinking of Samuel the Baker and the rest of Essie's family, and how they didn't know what had happened to her because her letters never arrived. "They're letters about someone that I need to find in America. I have a message from her father, of blessed memory, that I have to give to her in New York City."

The name *New York* it pronounced a little doubtfully, being unfamiliar with the sound of it and still a little uneasy with letters used as vowels.

"Well, at least New York is easy to find," Rose joked. "Does it say where in New York?"

Uriel, uncertain, handed the letters to her, and she flipped through them quickly at first, looking for an address, and then slowed down, beginning to frown. Some of the letters were signed from Malke Pearl.

Wasn't Dinah's aunt named Malke?

"You have to find Malke Pearl?" she said, a little more urgently than she'd intended. "Not Malke Pearl from Belz?"

"I suppose so," said Uriel. "Her father was from Belz."

"The old rebbe? The one—your friend asked me about him!" she remembered suddenly. "You know Dinah's grandfather? What happened to him? Are you saying he's not in America? What's he been doing all this time?"

Uriel was taken aback by the quick flurry of questions. It suddenly thought maybe it should not have shared the letters, since after all it did not have a good explanation for why it was carrying them. It was not good at lying, or even at telling half-truths, but some instinct told it that it should not immediately admit that it had run across the old man's ghost after his murder and then unwittingly taken part in the death of his murderer. It was still blinking at her, tongue-tied, when Little Ash returned from whatever wicked business he'd been about, carrying a plate of potatoes and herrings.

"What's going on?" he said. "Why are you shouting? The whole ship knows your business now."

"How did you get these letters?!" cried Rose, shaking them in his face. "Are you her grandfather's students? Is that it? Does he know what sort of suffering his family has been through, with no word from him?! I suppose he had some wise reason not to write? The angels told him not to, maybe? And she had no choice but to go and get married, because they used the money for her tickets to send him to America! And you're saying he never even got there in the end?"

Little Ash was not really listening to her as he squinted at the pages, trying to see what they were. When he identified them as belonging to the rebbe, he said, "I thought you said you hardly knew that old man."

"Well, I'd rather I didn't!" said Rose, in a huff.

"Don't be too unfair to him," said the demon. "He's been dead for weeks."

"Ashel," said the angel, reproachfully. It was aware now that the rebbe might be listening to their conversation, and it wished its friend could make a good impression and not be rude and callous. But then, demons were often so.

"Dead?" said Rose, some of the fight going out of her, as her resolve not to care about Dinah anymore withered under this news.

"Dead," said Little Ash. "Why don't you sit down? I've brought our supper."

"Oh, I despise herrings," said Rose, but she sat down anyway.

Little Ash, the practiced liar, was just preparing to tell an entirely harmless story about how he and the angel came into possession of the rebbe's letters—intending to lean heavily on the pious appearance of his partner—when Uriel spoke up.

"Ashel, I need to tell you something."

It said this in Yiddish, to catch his attention more quickly. This quite derailed Little Ash's train of thought, as he had never heard it speak that language before, and never heard of an angel that could.

"It's very important," it said, when he simply stared at it for a moment. It looked at Rose, and added apologetically, "Also, it is private."

Rose felt unaccountably snubbed by this. She'd barely known Uriel a day, but had correctly divined that it did not keep many secrets. It was also a rather poor moment for sharing confidences, she thought. News of Dinah's grandfather, contrary to her previous determined indifference, now seemed to her of the utmost urgency.

Uriel and Little Ash, unaware of this, put their heads together so that the angel could relay its news in a whisper. "The rebbe's ghost is here," it said.

Little Ash blinked. "No it isn't. I would have seen him."

"He is! I talked to him while I was dreaming."

"Dreaming?" said Little Ash, horrified. This was the second unprecedented revelation from the angel in as many minutes, and he found it deeply disturbing. He'd thought while it was seasick and dozing he could leave it alone safely, but it had apparently used the time to behave even more strangely. "You mean like humans dream, in your sleep?"

"Yes!" said Uriel, very excited. "I was dreaming just like a human, and the rebbe even told me the secret—while you're asleep, you have to keep breathing. I'll show you, tonight. It isn't only pretending; it's real sleep. And did you hear me speak Yiddish? I can do so many new things! It's so easy— would you like to hear the trick? I had to do it because there were so many thoughts at once, but it's so much easier now, and look—" It held out its arm and pinched the wrist, where the veins were close to the skin. Together they watched the skin turn red. "Look, I even have blood, like a person!"

Little Ash was staring at it now in open horror. He had quite lost the thread of what it was telling him, but he knew he did not like what he heard.

"It's all because I have a name!" the angel finished, delighted. "The name you gave me—it works like I'm a human!"

Their conversation was taking place in Aramaic, this being the only way to truly guarantee privacy in such a crowded place as a steerage deck, but the expressions on their faces made it clear enough to Rose that Uriel was telling a story that Little Ash did not like.

As she picked listlessly at the plate of potatoes, she tried to guess what they were discussing. Perhaps they really were students of the rebbe, but he had given them some terrible task to do? Or it was a task that women weren't meant to hear about? Or, worse, what if they had something to do with his death? Suddenly she felt quite suspicious of the two of them. After all, what did she know about them, really? And hadn't Little Ash admitted outright that their papers were lies? She hadn't thought much of it then, because she'd heard stories before of people who had to tell a few little lies to skirt the strictness of rules meant to keep Jews in their place—but what if she ought to have been suspicious after all?

"What do you mean, you have a name like a human?" Little Ash was saying. "What do you need a human name for?"

"I had too many thoughts in my head," said Uriel. "But that isn't important! Ashel, the rebbe has asked if we will take him to his daughter. I can carry him as an ibbur, an invited spirit, since I have a name for him to hold onto—that way, he can hear her say Kaddish. It is a mitzvah."

Little Ash narrowed his eyes, searching the rafters over their heads for a glimpse of any clinging ghost. "You can't do that. You can't trust ghosts like that, murdered ghosts. They hardly know themselves."

"He is not dangerous. He said he won't forget himself until it's been thirty days, and we have time."

"He *said*!" Little Ash didn't believe it for a second. He'd seen people possessed by dybbuks, once or twice. They tended to become feverish and paranoid, forgetting where they were and often lashing out violently in panic. It was not a pleasant thing. "I told you, you can't trust *ghosts*."

Uriel stiffened. It had expected Little Ash to be pleased about its new name, and curious, like he usually was. Now it found him hostile and dismissive, and it couldn't help feeling betrayed. He was supposed to be its partner, its support. "Well, the rebbe said I can't trust demons. What do you say to that?"

"I say he can show his face to me and tell me so himself!"

"I'm sorry. I told him you're not like how one would imagine a demon at all, only—"

"What's that supposed to mean?" said Little Ash, bristling.

The rebbe's letters were still sitting on top of his trunk. Rose put aside her dinner plate and picked them up again. Evidently the rebbe's daughter, that is to say, Dinah's aunt Malke, was a thorough sort of person, because she had written dates at the top of each message, and so it was not difficult to sort them into the correct order.

Dearest Tate, the first letter began, *all my love to you and the family. I hope little Yakov is finished cutting his teeth by now! I have made it to America. The shop is very busy and they have me working six days of the week. I hope you will forgive me that one day is Shabbes, but it is the way in this country. There was a mix-up with the tickets but Mr. Boaz says it's all right, he will take it from my paycheck and send it to Warsaw himself, so I needn't even make the calculations. Well, you'd best believe I am making them all the same! I don't mind him taking the trouble to send the money, as it's terribly complicated to figure out how, but if he takes a cent more than he can explain, I'll know about it and I won't take it lying down. With all blessings, from your daughter, Malke.*

Rose was pleased to see that Dinah's aunt was sensible. She supposed one had to be both sensible and brave in order to cross the ocean alone, and as a woman no less. Malke hadn't been married yet when she left—everyone was a little worried she'd end up an old maid.

"Ashel, I wish you wouldn't be upset with me," said Uriel.

"Well, I wish you wouldn't keep doing things you didn't tell me about!" Little Ash snapped. "What if you can die now? You don't understand how it works being able to die. What if you fall asleep and you don't wake up? You just told me you needed someone *else* to say you should be breathing!

If you have blood in your veins, you can bleed, did you think of that? You can't be responsible for being a human—you're not even a responsible angel, and at least as an angel I know if you get shot you'll just look at me with your big, sad cow eyes like it's my fault someone shot you somehow!"

By this point he had become quite upset, and his shouting was drawing attention. A couple of voices called out for the argument to stop, because they were trying to rest. A few other neighbors were simply watching, glad of a distraction. Among them was Rose's friend Grandmother Rivke, who was feeling much improved after her dinner of honeyed tea and pickled herrings, and had come to return to Rose the teapot.

"Save your quarreling for later in the voyage, my dears," she said now, in the sort of voice that manages, without being at all loud, to cut through an argument. "We've two weeks to build up steam, yet."

Little Ash snapped his mouth shut and glared around for the interruption. He had quite forgotten that he and the angel were not alone. Now, seeing they had an audience, he felt a little silly, which far from calming him made him so angry he leapt to his feet and stalked away in the direction of the upper deck.

Uriel sat where it was, unmoving. Its eyes, whether or not they could be described as cow eyes, were indeed very sad.

"What was that about?" said Rose, in a sort of stage whisper.

"I don't know," said Uriel. "He is being very horrible."

It didn't seem to want to say anything more, so Rose allowed herself to be distracted by Rivke, who'd invited herself to sit down on Rose's trunk, now that Little Ash had left the spot empty. Having got her breath back a bit, the old lady turned out to be desperate for a bit of gossip, and started telling the two of them about a time when she had to deliver breech twins for the girl down the road, and the girl had shouted so hard it nearly took the roof down and her husband had been afraid she was possessed by demons.

Uriel listened and nodded as if the story were very important, and Rose watched its face, quite unable to find there any sign that its reasons for having Malke Pearl's letters were sinister. Still. It never paid to be too trusting. She ought to follow Malke's advice, and do her own calculations.

fifteen

Little Ash crept back to the steerage deck later that night, when he hoped that the majority of human passengers had fallen asleep. Enough of them were that he was no longer being watched, but he wasn't terribly pleased to find that the angel also appeared to be sleeping, its chest rising and falling in the gentle rhythm of breath.

So it really was now sleeping in the way that humans slept. He did not like this at all. He thought perhaps he had been too harsh in saying it was not responsible, but after all, where would it be without him? It would have wandered off and become a sunbeam long ago.

He sat on the edge of the bunk and checked the angel's pulse. It had never had one before, but now it did. He did not know what to make of this. Could it really be that giving it a name had turned it human? He'd never heard of such a thing, but it was possible. The name was written in Hebrew letters, after all. He'd even joked to himself that he should have named it something more suited to being at sea. But he hadn't thought it could change so much, so quickly.

The Belzer Rebbe had a reputation for miracle working. Had he worked some change on the angel to make it easier for himself to possess it as an invited spirit? Little Ash did not see how that would be necessary, and it worried him. He did not trust the rebbe's intentions to be as simple and straightforward as they seemed.

And if the angel had changed itself, he did not understand why, which meant that he would not be able to see further changes coming. What if, in finding new parts of itself, it discovered a part that felt toward demons as the rebbe did, unwilling to look at Little Ash except as an example of an immutable demonic nature?

Little Ash had, for most of his life, thought that he approved of changes. He didn't like things sitting still. He got bored easily.

Now he realized there were things in the world that he'd assumed never *would* change, and somehow he had been relying on them not to.

It made him very uncomfortable indeed.

Uriel woke up as it usually did, when it was time to pray the morning blessings, but it woke without the usual strangeness of returning to its body. Instead there was the strangeness of a body that had stayed inhabited while sleeping—a shoulder that ached because it had been lying on its side, and a foot that had gone numb because Little Ash was lying too close next to it and it had not been able to move without kicking him.

How wonderful, it thought, feeling the blood start to move again through its body in the ways that meant *awake*. Suddenly it understood, in a way it previously had not, why humans said so many blessings for waking up in the morning. Even Little Ash had admitted that if one fell asleep, one could stay asleep forever—that is, by dying without knowing it—and so of course it was a miracle to be awake.

It wanted to rouse its partner and tell him these things, but it stopped itself at the last moment. He would not want to hear it. He was angry that it had made itself more human. The angel carefully extracted itself from the bunk, jostling Little Ash as little as possible, and discovered that it was cold. The full, deep roundness of a human name made room for so many sensations. It shivered as it ran its hand down its arm, expecting to find tfillin there, as it always did in the morning when it was about to pray.

There were no tfillin.

There always had been before. It had not had to think about it. Tfillin were made of holy letters, and so was an angel. As it could simply think of wanting a book and have a book, so it had always simply thought of the trappings of prayer and found itself dressed.

Suddenly panicked, it looked around for its shawl and saw that Little Ash had opened his eyes and was glaring at it. It was not unused to his glaring, which was an expression he found many uses for, but this morning the glare was particularly wounding. He ought to have been looking at it with concern, as a friend would do.

Little Ash had not really been sleeping. He had simply been lying next to the angel with his eyes shut, grinding his teeth and feeling stupid. This did not predispose him to placing a look of concern on his face.

"Where is my—" Uriel made a helpless gesture toward its shoulders.

Little Ash had been lying on the folded tallis, more or less using it as a pillow. He sat up now and handed it over. He watched the angel wrap itself in its shawl and begin its prayers with what looked like more than the usual urgency. It occurred to him that it had not prayed the evening service the night before. It had slept through the sunset hours.

At least its voice sounded the same, he supposed. It used the same melodies it always had. That was something, anyway. It was still itself, whatever *itself* was, and its personality had not been eaten by the rebbe's spirit.

"We never did tell Rose how we know that old rebbe," he said, when Uriel was done with praying. The remark was offered carefully, skirting as close to an apology as Little Ash could make himself go. Demons are not used to feeling that they've done wrong, much less apologizing. Little Ash himself would never have thought to do it, had he not lived elbow-to-elbow with an angel for centuries.

"We should tell her we saw him in Warsaw," said Uriel. "It is true that we did."

It had been thinking about this while it prayed, and feeling a little guilty for how delicious it was to be able to think of something else while it prayed. It supposed this must be how Little Ash felt all the time, in which case, no wonder he was so smug.

"And?" said Little Ash. "I don't suppose you've learned to lie, as well. I think we probably should lie to her. She won't like to hear that anyone was murdered, and anyway, we met him after he was, so what then? We tell her it's a ghost we met? She won't believe us."

"I know," said Uriel. "I know, we have to lie. I do not like it. But I had thought of it."

"We'll just say he was sick, and passed his things on to us," said Little Ash. "That's hardly a lie at all. I suppose he did tell you to take those things?"

"At first he didn't. But it seemed right, and when he spoke to me he said I should use them, so the books shouldn't be lonely."

"Well, then," said Little Ash, with a hint of cruel sarcasm. "What choice do we have? Since it's a mitzvah."

When Rose woke up, Little Ash was sitting cross-legged on the rebbe's trunk, darning his socks. His birdlike claws were always wearing holes in them, no matter how thick a thread he used, and then his shoes would give him blisters.

With all the traveling he and the angel had done lately, his feet had begun to hurt him quite a lot, and so he left aside the possibility that anyone in the steerage deck would notice the strangeness of his feet, and he set to work. Several small children had paused in their running about to watch him and whisper to each other, but he was not much concerned with this. In his experience, small children were easy to bribe, as long as you could find candy somewhere.

Rose was tired enough as she first sat up that it did seem to her there was something odd about Little Ash's appearance for a moment, but once she had rubbed the sleep from her eyes she forgot it at once.

"You've missed breakfast," he said, noticing that she was awake and braiding her hair. "I think Uriel saved you something. But it went up on deck, to breathe some air."

Breathing air sounded like a splendid idea to Rose. The steerage deck had not improved in its odor overnight. Besides, she had a feeling it would be easier to get the truth from Uriel than from Little Ash, and she intended not to let either of them throw her off their scent a second time without answering how, precisely, they knew Dinah's grandfather.

"You're quite fast at knitting," she remarked. "I don't suppose you're good at sewing as well? I could use some practice."

Little Ash squinted up at her. He had an inconveniently good memory. "I thought you said you were a born genius for sewing."

"Well, even genius has to be nurtured," said Rose, tossing her braid over her shoulder and starting to climb down from the bunk. "Besides, aren't you from Warsaw? You can show me all the Warsaw fashions."

Little Ash shrugged. He was not, of course, from the city, and had not noticed any of the fashions, being occupied with the pursuit of Reb Fishl. Nevertheless he supposed he ought to try and be nice, for the sake of not rousing suspicion. "If you like."

"Good," said Rose. "Then you'll teach me later. I'm going to find my breakfast."

Uriel, feeling cold and sure it would be colder on deck, had dug the rebbe's knit sweater from the bottom of his trunk. Little Ash, watching, had asked if it was stealing and, being still in a needling sort of mood, had said that if it were he'd feel more respect for it, and it had found itself so irritated with him that it ended their conversation there and then. This was what it meant by breathing air.

The angel had found itself a perch quite near the bow, where sea spray fell upon its head but it could not smell the ship or the misery of the sick passengers below, and there it sat with one of the rebbe's volumes. It was studying the laws of building a public enclosure, which were nearly all geometry and had very little to remind it either of how little it understood the modern world or of how annoying Little

Ash could sometimes be. It also liked the simplicity of a topic that had nothing to do with lying. Little Ash had made it promise to rehearse their lies for Rose, and this made it feel seasick once again, because a rehearsed wickedness felt much worse than a wickedness one fell into as if by accident.

It was reading for the fifth time an opinion of Rav when Rose arrived. She was looking flustered and annoyed, as it had taken her a considerable time to find someone on the deck who could direct her toward a boy with big eyes and long curly sidelocks who looked doomed to be a rabbi, as Rose had described the angel. She had thought she had a great deal of goodwill toward Uriel, but, given that she hadn't had breakfast before traipsing up and down the ship, she was now applying to it some of the irritation engendered in her by Dinah's husband.

"There you are!" she exclaimed, sitting herself down without asking for permission. "What have you done with my breakfast?"

"Oh," said Uriel. It had opened its mouth to start telling her all about the rebbe from Belz, forgetting that there were pleasantries to exchange first, and so it was rather thrown off course by the interruption. However, its new human name proved expansive enough to accommodate both thoughts. "Here, it was in my pocket."

It handed her a smoked-herring sandwich, wrapped in waxed paper. This Little Ash had prepared for Rose that morning, claiming that he knew better than the angel what food should taste like. He had gone on to explain that if they fed her, Rose, like a stray cat, would be better disposed toward them.

Rose unwrapped her sandwich and started to eat it. She was hungry enough that she almost didn't mind the herring.

Uriel had not eaten its own breakfast. Angels subsist primarily on the honey-sweet essence of holiness that is created when a human performs an act of goodness, and holiness has very little in common with the steerage food on a steam liner. As it watched Rose eat, however, it found an unfamiliar feeling growing in its insides and suddenly began to be dizzy again.

"Is that your stomach growling?" said Rose. She paused and looked at the uneaten half of her breakfast. She didn't want to give it up, yet instincts built up by years of taking care of Motl and all the little Pearl boys made it quite difficult for her not to share. "Would you . . . did you have your own breakfast?"

Uriel blinked at her, touched an uncertain hand to its middle, and then reached into its pocket for a baked potato, which Little Ash had given it so it could pretend to eat in front of people, which, he'd said, would be very important in the close quarters of steerage. It had not bothered to eat the potato, because it had not thought there was anything to what he was saying, but maybe a human name required human sustenance to keep it attached to one's body.

In fact, when it bit into the potato, it found it had never tasted anything so nice.

"I suppose you'd like to ask about the rebbe, who was your friend's family?" it said, cautiously, when they'd both finished eating and Rose was looking less like she might snap. "Unless Ashel told you already."

The angel was very much hoping he had but was not at all surprised to find that he hadn't.

"He's my friend Dinah's grandfather," said Rose, feeling a bit hypocritical as she'd sworn off her friendship with Dinah forever—but if she were to send word home of the lost grandfather, surely Dinah would see. See what, she wasn't sure, but certainly see something. "Are you a student of his? Where is he now?"

"We met him in Warsaw," said Uriel carefully. "But he was very sick. He did not have time to make it to America. He wanted us to bring a message to his daughter in New York City. And . . . there was a very wicked person named Fishl, from Krumer Street, who is charging too much for tickets to America, and then you have to pay him back or he won't send your letters home."

This last part Little Ash had told it to leave out, because it was no one's business, but it seemed to Uriel that, on the contrary, everyone should be aware of the wickedness of Reb Fishl, in case there was a chance they too were caught up in it.

"You see, the same happened to Essie," it went on. "Essie, the baker's daughter, from our shtetl, who went to America. We wanted to find her in Warsaw, but she went already."

"Is that the girl in the photograph?" said Rose, very interested. She recognized the story of the expensive tickets from Malke's letters, but it gave her a much more immediate shock to hear of a girl her own age ensnared in such a matter. What if her own tickets, too, were false somehow? She had worked too hard for them to face turning back if something went wrong, and she couldn't afford to do as Malke had and pay extra fees or, god forbid, ask for money from her family still at home. She was sure those unexpected extras were what had caused the delay in her and Dinah's own plans, the crack through which Saul Lehman had crept in between them.

"Yes, the photograph," said Uriel, remembering. "Her father is very worried about her."

"I suppose she's my age," said Rose. "And not married yet?"

The angel shook its head. In truth, it didn't know much about Essie, but it was sure she wasn't married. Her father was always talking about his family in shul, instead of studying; Uriel would remember if there had been such a simcha as a wedding. It and Little Ash always attended weddings in the shtetl, besides, because demons are naturally drawn to try and cause trouble at weddings and the angel, of course, had to make sure that he couldn't.

"She isn't married," it said, reaching for anything it could say. "She's very clever, I think. She used to always study with her father, before she became a woman."

Rose scoffed at this, unable to suppress the reaction. Uriel didn't know what it meant, and so was not hurt by the rudeness.

"In any case," it said, "we were the only ones who could go to find Essie, and so we are going."

"Oh!" said Rose, remembering that Little Ash had implied his friend was less eager to leave home than he had been, and that he hadn't answered when she asked how he'd convinced it. How silly, she thought, it's quite a noble reason when you think of it. "So you're on a rescue mission, of sorts!"

"Yes," said the angel. "I suppose we are."

Then so am I, thought Rose. I'll help rescue Dinah's aunt, and then Dinah will be grateful to me and sorry she didn't come with me, and then she'll want to be in America too.

How perfect it all seemed, suddenly!

She liked the idea of this adventure so much, it hardly occurred to her to be sorry so many people had been caught in Fishl's trap to begin with.

sixteen

LITTLE ASH, IN THE MEANTIME, was digging through the rebbe's trunk, out of spite. He had been unable to glimpse the old man's ghost again no matter how he tried, and though he always had a harder time keeping track of righteous spirits, he was sure his inability to see the rebbe was because the ghost had rejected him on the basis of his demonic nature.

In turn, since he had a demonic nature, he could not trust that the rebbe meant well and that, even if he did mean well, he would not bring harm to the angel anyway. Little Ash was better aware of the world's sorrows than his partner was, and it was his opinion that in this matter it was better to be ignorant, at least if one had so gentle a heart as the angel. So, with a sense of resentment, he searched the rebbe's belongings for a way to stop the ghost from sharing unwelcome thoughts with the angel and laying burdens on its innocent soul.

He did not find much with which to work any sort of demonic charm, or to turn the angel against its new friend by revealing hitherto unsuspected sins. Despite Rose's animosity toward his disciple, Saul Lehman, the rebbe was not so terrible a person. He disapproved of well-educated women, but in this he was in line with many others in the world. The rebbe, like the angel, seemed to have lived most of his life with his head in the clouds and his mouth full of holy words, and so looking at his things rather made the skin on Little Ash's hands itch, and an uncomfortable feeling grew within him as he read the letters and traced the story of the old man's journey.

The rebbe's daughter, Malke, had gone to America because there were no jobs and no money and no husbands to be had at home. It was the same for many who had left Shtetl recently. She had also gone because she was afraid of pogroms, since there were whispers of them more and more, and the family was all women and small boys, the rebbe aside. It seemed his sons-in-law had not been blessed with long lives.

Little Ash hated to admit that the reasons for leaving were familiar. The rebbe and himself, different as they were, had been pushed by the same force toward the ocean.

"What is the world coming to," he said aloud to himself, disgusted. He put everything back in the trunk and scrubbed his hands on his trousers, then jumped up and began pacing as if something had stung him and he had to walk off the poison. The confinement of the steerage deck was no good for creatures like Little Ash, who had to be constantly moving. He did not like the air in there either, as the rest of the passengers began to settle into the slow misery of weeks of seasick passage. There was a sense of futility beginning to spread through everyone's souls, the sort of dullness which could allow more serious sickness to enter.

On his fifth turn back toward their bunks, he stopped. The rebbe's ghost was sitting on top of his trunk, looking stronger than he had back at the shul, shaped less like a bat and more like a human being.

"Ashmedai," the rebbe said, inclining his head.

"What do you want?" Little Ash snapped.

"What do you suppose I want?" said the rebbe. "You were handling my belongings. I do not want you to steal them."

"I don't want to steal from you! I want you not to steal from *me*."

The rebbe straightened the fringes of his ghostly tzitzis. "What do you imagine I would steal from you, wicked one?"

"My *friend*," said Little Ash. "I don't know what you want from it—if you really just want it to bring you to America and that's all, or if you're thinking of something more, or if you even know what you want, but keep your hands off it."

"It has agreed, from the goodness of its own heart, that it will carry me to America," said the rebbe. "That is all there is to it. I cannot cross an ocean on my own."

Little Ash glared at him. "If you hurt it, I will drag you out and tear you to pieces. I know how to exorcise a dybbuk. They teach us the rituals in our yeshiva."

"I am not a dybbuk," said the rebbe. "But even if I were, could you really perform an exorcism? I saw that child's charm you used in Warsaw. Do you really know the Names you would need?"

Little Ash choked on his answer. He was tempted to leap on the rebbe and shake him, like a dog with a rat, until the old man's head should spin. But before he could make any move, Grandmother Rivke from down the row of bunks suddenly appeared at his elbow, leaning her weight on him as if they were fast friends. "Young man," she said. "My whole family is puking, and I need a hand to get myself on deck. Won't you do me a mitzvah?"

Little Ash suppressed an instinct to hiss and swipe at her. He did not want to helpful, but he did want very much to go on deck. The rebbe had disappeared again, and Little Ash didn't like to think of him watching, invisibly.

Besides, there was a little spark of wickedness in the old woman's eyes, as if she knew she was imposing and didn't mind at all. He couldn't help but respect the brazenness.

"If you like," he said, and gave the rebbe's trunk a little kick as he turned away.

Grandmother Rivke turned out to be more in need of gossip than fresh air. She first explained to Little Ash what felt like, to him, her entire life story, ending with the circumstances of her heading to America in the company of her daughter and more small children than the demon had been able to keep track of.

"My son-in-law didn't want me to come," she explained as they climbed toward the upper deck, where if they were lucky they could get a glimpse of sunlight between the clouds. Little Ash was limping in his lumpy socks and old boots, and Rivke on her elderly feet, which made their progress slow. "He said there was no money, and besides, America is a young person's country, it's not a country for old women—what would an old wife like me do in America? Everyone runs fast there, he said, and if you can't move fast there's no use for you. Well, Deborah wasn't having that, but still, there was the money, wasn't there."

"There's always the money," agreed Little Ash. "You always need it and can't ever find it. Unless you find a rich man and kill him."

Rivke laughed uproariously at this joke, which of course was not a joke at all. "Well, we hadn't any rich men handy, or at least not at first, but then we did find one. You know how it is when they ask you in America if you have a job waiting?"

"Of course I know," said Little Ash. "I read it in the newspapers. You have to say you don't have a job yet, but you'll be quick to find one. If you have one already they don't let you in."

"Exactly," said Rivke. "But you want the promise of a job, all the same. Or anyway, my son-in-law wanted the promise of a job for Deborah, and finally we found an agent who would give her an advance, to pay for my ticket also."

Little Ash had not been fully listening to her story, being not much interested in the details of her daughter's struggles, but at this his ears perked up. "You did? What agent was that?"

"I forget the name exactly." The old woman thought for a moment. "Krum-fish, or something like that, if I remember."

"Reb Fishl, from Warsaw Krumer Street?" said Little Ash.

"Do you know him?"

"Yes, he sold me and my cousin our tickets," said the demon, easily. "But he was a bit crooked, Fishl. He tried to cheat us a bit. You'd better look out for what this job will be for your daughter."

"How kind of you, how kind of you to be concerned," said Rivke. "And you with chicken feet, yet. I thought I'd have to be putting the evil eye on you, my dear."

This caused Little Ash to stop in his tracks, earning a curse from another passenger who was trying to get by them in the narrow passageway. Preoccupied with the ghost of the rebbe, and that entity's distrust of demons, Little Ash had quite forgotten that anyone else might notice anything strange about him.

He was considering the possibility of tossing Rivke overboard without being seen when she laughed again and patted his elbow. "Never mind, now. As long as you haven't come along to spread pestilence in steerage, I'll leave you to your own business. I had a fine friendship with one of your kind, a long time ago. She got me out of my first marriage—the stories I could tell you about my first husband! May he rest in peace."

She added a wink which suggested that her husband was not resting peacefully at all.

Little Ash, tilting his head, inspected her more carefully than he had done before, taking a second read of the small number of sins that crept through the air around her. He saw only the kinds of transgression that he approved of, and besides, he didn't feel any malice from her like he'd felt from Reb Fishl. She was simply, like many of the criminals he knew at home in the Pale of Settlement, a human who believed that rules must sometimes be broken for the sake of happiness. There was a hint of the witch about her, but wherever there was a patriarch who felt threatened there was always a hint of the witch about old women.

"All right," he said. "Well, I wouldn't know how to spread a pestilence. I'm only going to America, like everyone. So if you leave me to my business, I won't pluck out your soul in the night and eat your heart."

Rivke smiled and gave him another affectionate pat. "In that case, I think we'll get along very nicely. Asher, wasn't it? That's an auspicious name. And with your cousin, you're Asher and Uriel—*joyful*, and *light of God*. You're bringing good fortune with you."

Little Ash doubted that very much.

Grandmother Rivke was pleased to find Rose on the deck, as she had decided Rose was a reliable and practical young woman after her own mold, and she was determined to pass on her wisdom to the captive audience represented by such a shipmate. Rose, in fact, enjoyed Rivke's monologue about possible remedies for the seasickness that was plaguing most of their fellow passengers. Rose had some experience with medicine for goats, but less with medicine for people, and was interested to hear Rivke explain the experience she'd gleaned from years of midwifing—a combination of Holy Names, herbs, and appealing to gentile spirits or demons in the gravest emergencies.

Uriel and Little Ash were thus left to themselves.

"I have told Rose about our rescue mission," Uriel told Little Ash. "And also, I have to tell you something very important, but you mustn't be angry with me."

Little Ash scowled. He did not like the sound of such a preface. "Is it to do with that old man who won't speak to demons?"

"I'm sure you wouldn't like to speak with him," said Uriel, trying for consolation. "He speaks in blessings. You would find him very tedious."

"Oh, just get to the point," said Little Ash. He felt a bit less out of sorts in the fresh air, with salty sea spray hitting his face and the wind threatening to tug his cap off his head, but all the same he didn't know if the rebbe were listening, and did not want to admit before an invisible witness that the angel, who of course also spoke in blessings, had never seemed tedious at all. "What's your very important thing to tell me?"

"The rebbe needed me to carry him as an ibbur to get to America," said Uriel. "If I don't, he'll lose himself and become a dybbuk, and bring bad luck to his family."

"Yes. I know that."

"But you don't know that I think while he is holding onto me I can't use my magic like an angel would. I couldn't lay tfillin this morning like I always do. And you see, I'm reading a real human book. Please don't be upset."

This last, it added in a futile attempt to change the expression on Little Ash's face, which had settled into a scowl completely.

"It is the right thing to do," Uriel said, when the demon merely clenched his jaw shut and said nothing.

"The right thing to do!" Little Ash scoffed. "And you must always do the right thing, oh yes. Because you're an angel! Because you're the perfect example of what you're supposed to be! I see, I see."

"How is it any different from helping Essie?" Uriel protested. "We are already going to America for a mitzvah."

"Essie is from *our* shtetl."

Uriel could see how this made a difference to Little Ash, but it could not bring itself to think that he had a point. "The rebbe has no one else."

"He's a rebbe. His students will pray for him."

"They won't know! Not in time. He has barely two weeks

left before his thirty days are over, and no one even knows he is dead."

"And that!" Little Ash exclaimed. "You've taken on a ghost who'll become a dybbuk as soon as we get to America? What happens to you then? Do you know what happens when a dybbuk grabs ahold of you? It's bad luck everywhere. You've never had bad luck in your life; you don't even know how to imagine what it looks like. It could kill you."

"But this is why I need you," said Uriel. It felt uncomfortably as if he had a point, and so it spoke in rather a small voice, thinking that perhaps it ought to have thought a little harder about what it was doing. "You understand bad luck; you will be able to help me."

"You!" Little Ash stamped his foot on the deck. "You're always getting me in trouble!"

This seemed to the angel like absolute nonsense.

PART III

AMERICA

seventeen

DESPITE LITTLE ASH'S OBJECTIONS, there was nothing to be done about the rebbe or the name: both were attached quite firmly to the angel, and it had no intention of shedding them. The rebbe refused to show himself to Little Ash, having no trust in the demon's goodwill toward him, and Little Ash refused to give any assurance of goodwill in return.

Uriel was thus uncomfortably caught between the two. Unused to having such an extended argument with Little Ash, it retreated into solitary study, learning Holy Names from the rebbe with which, he said, it would be able to work small miracles. It was not, however, a natural talent at this, being accustomed to working small miracles without any thought, and the only name with which it was able to perform any act of creation was its own name, Uriel; using this, if it concentrated very hard, it could create a little spark in the palm of its hand, or warm up a cup of tea, or cause a golden glow to emanate from the posts of its bunk bed, which allowed it to read its human books in the gloom.

Little Ash meanwhile spent more time with Grandmother Rivke and Rose, nurturing Rose's lack of natural talent as a seamstress. A consultation between the demon and the grandmother resulted in the idea that Rose should make herself a new shirtwaist for America, one with a modern cut like the German girls they'd seen in Hamburg, who looked very sophisticated.

When Little Ash first took out his book of needles to test Rose on her stitching, Rose was instead distracted by a set of lockpicks, which he kept in the needle book. She'd never seen such tools before and was very interested in their operation, so when she became frustrated with sewing they'd switch to locking and unlocking the rebbe's trunk with the picks. Rose therefore felt she was becoming very daring and adventurous.

The voyage to America took another two weeks, during which time seasickness gradually waned and was replaced by sniffles and coughs and the other small illnesses that came from being stacked atop each other in the airless steerage. Rose fought off a cough by sheer stubbornness, and Grandmother Rivke likewise. After that the old woman, pleased to have company, dragged Rose back and forth across the steerage deck, pestering anyone who was still sick with a mixture of medicine, hot compresses, and amulets. The last thing anyone wanted was to be turned back at Ellis Island for any of the diseases which the gatekeepers of America classified as "loathsome."

Little Ash had been counting on the angel and himself to be healthy, as neither of them had ever been sick before, but his confidence was shaken terribly by Uriel's new tendency to sleep long hours of the day and the vagueness of its answers when he asked how it was feeling.

The angel would have been happy to tell Little Ash more details, including how its study of Holy Names made it understand why Little Ash had so much trouble casting his demon magic. But he'd snapped at the angel and told it to go talk to its new best friend if it was learning so much from him. It therefore decided that he did not want to talk to it about the rebbe, and so it declined to explain that most of the time when it was sleeping, the old man was telling it stories about his family and his students in Belz, recounting his own life over and over in an attempt to keep himself together.

At the end of the two weeks, they found themselves in the crowded main hall of the Ellis Island immigration center, sitting on their luggage and waiting to be inspected and let into the country. The angel had its arm looped through Little Ash's suspenders in a gesture of apparent companionship that was actually intended to keep him in his seat, as he had already showed a distressing inclination to disappear and be found outside, taking another look at the lady with the torch or gossiping with the sailors smoking their cigarettes on the pier. The angel was very concerned that if it let Little Ash out of its sight again for even a moment, its name of Uriel Federman or his of Asher Klein would be called, and it would miss them in the cacophony of different languages that echoed off the high, vaulted ceiling of the hall.

Little Ash meanwhile was doing his usual accounting of sins and evil urges in the crowd, and he had noticed, also, signs that told him there were other demons present, most of them more powerful than himself. If the other demons were Jewish, then chances were that they were his brothers, whom he did not wish to see, especially not when he was in the company of an angel. If the other demons were not Jewish, the prospects were even worse. At least Jewish demons had basic respect for Little Ash's father's name. Unlike angels, demons can choose what to believe. Christian demons answered to their own authority, a demon king of some kind whose name Little Ash could not quite remember. Perhaps at one time Jewish and Christian demons had been one and the same, but some centuries before Little Ash was born, a group of demons had broken away from Ashmedai's court, declared their belief in an incarnate messiah, and gone on to invent all sorts of strange practices. The worst of these, in Little Ash's opinion, was their habit of teasing him specifically. Or anyway, the village demons in Poland had always teased him, and he saw no reason they shouldn't do so in America just the same.

There are, of course, also demons who are neither Jewish nor Christian—there are as many kinds of demons as there are humans on this earth—but Little Ash, being rather sheltered, did not know this.

"Will you stop?" said Rose, who was sitting on the trunk with the two divine creatures and kept getting jostled by Little Ash's fidgeting. She was trying to memorize the English phrases in a bilingual pamphlet from America's National Council of Jewish Women that had been handed to her by a charity worker who'd then disappeared in the crowd. This pamphlet purported to contain every detail she, as a young girl more or less on her own, would need to know in order to make it through customs and into America. Knowing none of this English out of context, she had no choice but to memorize it from the phonetic Yiddish letters on the page, which required all of her concentration.

"I'll speak your English for you," said Little Ash, who up until now had never shown any signs of knowing that language.

"You won't," said Rose. "I don't trust you. Anyway, I mean to be very independent in America. How can I do that if I can't even get my own self into the country?"

The angel, feeling queasy, tugged on Little Ash's suspenders until he finally sat down.

"Plenty of my kind in here," he remarked. "Not a lot of yours."

"I'm sorry?" said the angel. From its perspective it seemed there were an awful lot of its kind in the room, its kind, at the moment, being living things who were not enjoying themselves at all and would like to be elsewhere.

"There are demons here," said Little Ash, and added, "Nothing to worry about. I suppose they're just here for the same reason we are."

He did not want the angel questioning him because he himself was feeling doubtful. He had spent every night on the steerage deck watching the angel breathe in its sleep, ready to shake it awake if it showed any signs of not breathing anymore or coming down with the sort of sickness people got when they had human names. He had, therefore, had quite a lot of time alone during which to decide he was terribly homesick. He missed the quiet, and the market days, and the angel always finding him on Friday nights to make sure he wasn't alone on the Sabbath.

It wasn't that they hadn't been together on the ship. They had, in fact, been in closer physical proximity, for more of the time, than they used to be in their shtetl, when not so engrossed in their studies and arguments that they stayed in the shul for days on end. But, on the ship, there had always been someone else around, and sometimes that *someone else* was just Uriel Federman, behaving in ways Little Ash hadn't anticipated.

Not that he disliked Uriel. He should not, he supposed, be upset by the angel having a new name, which had happened many times. It was only that he worried that somewhere inside of Uriel was an angel being forced into a shape it didn't want. Had he imposed on his friend an identity it didn't ask for by giving it papers, or had the rebbe imposed that identity for his own purposes? It seemed happy enough to talk to the ghost—but the rebbe hadn't shown himself to Little Ash again, and this made it difficult for the demon to trust his motives.

The angel was not aware of any of this. It would have been perfectly happy to get along well with Little Ash, and argue with him as usual, only he had been acting strange and skittish since it introduced itself as Uriel, and it had erroneously concluded that the best cure for this would be to avoid him.

I should note that they were far from alone in being unsettled by the voyage from Europe to America, but, being the sheltered creatures that they were, they were completely unaware that their troubles were perfectly ordinary and would be quite easy to set aside. They had not even asked Rose Cohen for help, which was unfortunate, because she had quite a lot of opinions on the subject of broken friendships.

Little Ash had now been sitting still for half a minute, which was the limit of his patience. He stood up again, intending to take another look around for other Jewish demons, but just as he was doing so, someone called the angel's name from the front. That is, they called for Uriel Federman. Little Ash and Uriel shared an anxious look before the same voice called also for Asher Klein. The possibility that they would be forced to separate had been plaguing both of them since they'd arrived.

"Good luck," said Rose, in an approximation of English, this being a phrase she'd picked up not from the immigration pamphlet, but from her cousin's letters. Rose's cousin had marked her own success in America by peppering a steadily increasing number of English phrases into her correspondence. "I'll find you again at the ferry."

"Good luck?" said Little Ash, in Yiddish. "Keep your luck; you need it more than we do."

With this impolite and discouraging farewell, he took off toward the desk he'd been called to, dragging the angel after him.

eighteen

PERHAPS ROSE DID KEEP her luck, but Little Ash should not have told her to, because at the podium where they had to answer questions about themselves and hope nothing they said was wrong, the official shuffled through his papers and then said they would have to separate.

"Why?" demanded Little Ash, who had been doing most of the talking, as usual. It occurred to him belatedly that perhaps he had talked too much, and robbed the angel of its chance to prove it was a capable person, worthy of entering the great nation of the United States—not some sort of degenerate riffraff, as the newspapers back home had told him Americans considered many of the Eastern-European Jewish sort to be. "Why can't we stay together? We're family."

He grabbed the angel's hand as he said so, and then hastily dropped it, as he didn't wish to frighten his friend by showing that he was worried.

"You're marked for further inspection," said the official. He seemed quite bored, as if the reasons for his decisions interested him very little.

"Me only?" said Little Ash. This he had not expected.

"You said you're Asher Klein." The official reached over to hand the angel its papers. "You, you're clear. You go that way. Asher Klein, you need to see the doctor. You go that way."

Little Ash quickly explained to the angel that it would have to go ahead and wait for him. He took some money from his secret pocket, and a needle, and pinned the money to the inside of the angel's vest, so that it shouldn't be stopped again by any immigration officials without being able to at least show them it was not destitute.

"I'll follow you in no time at all," he said. "Anyway, you have your rebbe to keep you company."

The rebbe was crouched on Uriel's shoulder, taking the shape of some small, furred ancestral creature in the daylight, rather than his own human shape that he wore in dreams. Although he had no love for demons, he did understand some of the dangers of Ellis Island, and so he gave the angel's shoulder a reassuring pat with his little clawed hand as Little Ash walked away.

Uriel went toward the ferry, throwing nervous glances over its shoulder, and Little Ash was made to sit, alone and empty-handed, in a little room, waiting for a doctor to come listen to his lungs and peel back his eyelids with a buttonhook and whatever other horrors they considered necessary to prove someone healthy. He told himself that since he'd never been sick a day in his life, he was not worried. Yet he was worried, and his worries came true.

The doctor, when he came, was another demon.

Little Ash had been sitting down, because they'd told him to sit and he'd chosen to obey them for the sake of his feet, but he got up at once at the sight of the gentile demon. He had not thought the idea of other demons was so terrible when they had been equals, but an immigration doctor was certainly not an equal. And he had Little Ash cornered, as the doctor was standing in front of the door, and the room was very small.

"Where's my cousin?" Little Ash demanded. This seemed to him the sort of question a human would ask when separated from family, and besides, he was afraid of what another demon would make of the angel. Little Ash's father bragged of being an angel himself, once. But he had also told his sons that long ago demons grew their power by devouring angels, before God gave the covenant to humans, and angels and demons had to agree to curb their tempers with a covenant of their own. There was a lot of magic in an angel, if you were strong enough to swallow it.

Little Ash was quite certain gentile demons didn't obey any covenants.

"Which one is your cousin?" said the doctor. He sounded as bored as the other official, and before Little Ash could even answer, he waved a hand as if to send the question away. "It doesn't matter. You're the only one of your kind in here today. Name?"

"What's my kind?" said Little Ash, sharply, rather than answering the question.

"Jewish goblins, or whatever you call yourself. We were all starting to think you were too clever to come here. I haven't seen one in quite some time."

Little Ash was very good at hiding how nervous he was. He had, after all, had quite a long time to practice. But this remark from the gentile demon made him very nervous indeed. It had not occurred to him that they would have demons *working* at Ellis Island, and now that he saw they did, he felt very stupid. He had assumed they would have dangerous demons inside America, but the borders of America he had failed to consider. All that time spent planning, and he hadn't thought of something very important.

At least if this doctor hadn't seen any other Jewish demons, he might not have seen a Jewish angel either. Perhaps the angel, under its new human name, could pass for ordinary. There was a chance, then, that Little Ash was in this alone, which was the way he preferred to be when he was in trouble. If one were in trouble alone, one needn't worry about dignity, and could fight tooth and nail like a wild animal, and never be told it wasn't civilized.

The doctor seemed to be making notes; on what, it wasn't clear. "Your name?" he repeated, without looking up.

"Asher Klein," said Little Ash. He was trying to think very fast. Usually, when he found himself in the company of other demons, he preferred to leave as quickly as possible, without talking to them. If he couldn't do that, he'd fight them. But he needed this doctor to let him through, and the only chance he had for that was to be cooperative.

Little Ash hated being cooperative.

"I'm here with my cousin," he said, the standard human answer. "We're going to live with family. We came to work."

"And what makes you think I want you to work in my country?" said the doctor, looking up at last and fixing Little Ash with a curiously empty stare. "A foreign, un-Christian creature like you? Do you think we want America's foundations to sink in the muck? Do you think we just open our gates wide for criminals and carriers of disease?"

Little Ash curled his hands into fists at his sides and forced himself to stand still. Clearly the answer was no, the gates were not open for him, but he didn't see why it should be this demon's business if Little Ash was a criminal. A demon ought to approve of criminals, in his opinion.

But perhaps stopping people at the island when they'd already endured the Atlantic Ocean and all its troubles caused enough pain to make up for it. Christian demons, he'd noticed, seemed to like nothing quite as much as they liked pain.

"I'm not carrying diseases," Little Ash said. "And I'm not going to do anything to America's foundations. I'm here to make sure my people get taken care of. You should be glad; it means you don't have to take care of them."

"You Jews," said the goyish demon, laughing. "No spine. That's defect enough, but I'm sure I can find more if I keep looking at you. Take off your shoes."

Little Ash didn't move. He knew he should do as he was told and hope it would be enough. But he had never been an optimist, and Ellis Island was not a place to become one. "Why? You've seen my feet already. If you're going to tell them I've got diseases, you can just make it up; you don't have to look at me at all."

The doctor took a step toward him, lifting his hand, and Little Ash ducked away instinctively. He didn't know how gentile demons took people's souls. Usually, when he encountered them, they kept things simple, and only hit him, without any magic. But he didn't want the doctor to touch his face.

Little Ash moved fast, but the doctor was faster. He caught Little Ash by the collar and pinned him in place, against the wall, as easily as if he were trapping a kitten to trim its claws.

"That's right, I don't have to look at you," he said. "All I need to do is tell them a reason you should be deported, and it's back to Europe with you. Go on and tell me it's not fair. Tell me how much that family you claim to have will suffer. Maybe if you can make the story interesting enough, I'll send in a human doctor who'll see nothing strange about you at all. Wouldn't that be nice?"

"What do you want?" said Little Ash. "Am I supposed to bribe you? Or cry, maybe? It won't happen. I'm not afraid of you."

But when the doctor lifted his free hand toward his face again, Little Ash flinched and shut his eyes. Even the confidence of a demon has limits.

In his hand, the doctor now had a buttonhook. The use to which this tool was put by ordinary, human doctors on Ellis Island was a source of enough fear for any immigrant, but Little Ash had reason to be afraid that it would be the end of him. The doctor turned up Little Ash's eyelid, and he stopped breathing entirely, frozen in place and unable to think of a plan for escape, of anything else he could say to bluff at being capable. The doctor's face was very close to his own, and he could not look away. The doctor's eyes, pale as ice chips, looked into his for a long time, and he could feel that gaze scraping along the surface of his soul, sharp and merciless.

Then, suddenly, the buttonhook withdrew. The doctor patted his cheek and let go of him. Little Ash slumped bonelessly against the wall.

"You poor thing, you have hardly any magic at all, don't you? Not even worth eating! No hard feelings, Asher. I'm just keeping my country safe and healthy. Go back to Europe and make something of yourself back where you belong."

With this he made a mark in chalk on Little Ash's coat, and went out, with his notes and his chalk. Little Ash stayed where he was, with his eyes closed, until he heard the footsteps of a clerk, who'd come to collect him. He was still trying his very hardest to come up with a plan, but all he could think was that he was glad Uriel, despite its ibbur, had been marked clear.

✧ ✧ ✧

Rose's luck, as it happened, was no better than Little Ash's. The official she spoke to turned out to speak Yiddish, and so her efforts with the English phrases were not needed, but all the same, after what felt like a half-hour interview, checking and rechecking the details of her papers, the man put a stamp at the bottom of her ticket and informed her that she could not leave Ellis Island.

"Excuse me?" said Rose, drawing herself up to be taller. This was not the first time she'd had to defend herself to a bureaucrat, and she believed that her practice in the game had given her a rare talent. Yet she could not think of anything she had done wrong. She had dollars in her pocket, to prove she would not be a burden on charity. She had a cousin to whom she was going. She had her papers, and her health. "Why can I not go? I answered all of your questions."

"Can't let you go on your own," said the official. "Sorry, miss. It just isn't safe."

"Why not?" said Rose sharply. "I never heard there was anything dangerous about America. I thought the streets were paved with gold here," she added, only because she was tired and irritated.

The official laughed weakly at the mockery. "Well, that's not quite true. And it is a beautiful country! But you have to understand, miss, there are dangers—in the world in general."

"Which dangers are we speaking of?" said Rose.

"There are unscrupulous folks who look out for girls like

you," said the official. "You know. Young, alone, and pretty. You'll have to wait for a relative to come take you from the island. I'm truly sorry you didn't prepare for this, but there's nothing I can do for you."

Rose disliked very much being told she was pretty under these circumstances. She also resented the implication that she couldn't recognize danger when she saw it. "I'm only going to my cousin, direct. I have her address here! I'm not wandering around; I won't get lost."

The official gave her what she judged to be a rather condescending smile. "New York is very big, Miss Cohen."

"And I can't find one trustworthy person in New York?" said Rose. "How difficult can it be?"

"Uncle Sam does not want you to be hurt," said the official, and pushed her papers back across his little desk to her. "Next!"

Rose would have liked to keep arguing, but the tide of immigrants behind her was too strong; she felt she might be run over if she held up the line any longer. She was pushed, therefore, out of the hall and down a hallway to another large room, jam-packed with people.

Where the main hall had been crowded with a multitude of emotions, this room seemed to hold only one. There was weeping all around her. Even some burly laborers, men whom she would have thought any country would be glad to have, if only to chew them up and spit them out as the tsar's army did—even they had tears in their eyes. But the mass of people, she saw, were not so strong-looking. There were elders, and little children, and women on their own like Rose. A man from the ship whom she recognized, who was missing part of a hand. A few who might be nearsighted or hard of hearing or whose way of moving had caught the wrong sort of attention.

And crouched on the floor next to one of the packed benches was Little Ash, chewing his fingernail and staring blankly at the dirty tile floor. Rose marched over to him and instinctively slapped his hand away from his face, as she used to do to Motl when he gnawed his nails during Torah lessons.

"What's happened to us?" Rose demanded, more for the sake of sharing her complaint than because she needed an answer. Of course she understood what had happened to her: she was a girl, and so the only thing that mattered was that she was pretty and presumed helpless. She was not sure on what pretext Little Ash had been stopped.

"I don't know what happened to you," said the demon, sullenly. "As for me, I've got the affect of a criminal."

"What?"

"Not only that, but any number of excuses," said Little Ash. "What are you doing here?"

"They won't let me leave without a chaperone," said Rose.

Little Ash made a disgusted noise in his throat. "But they will let you leave?"

"I suppose so—if I can get my cousin, or someone, to chaperone me. She's always working, though, from the sound of it. How can she afford to come walk me home? Like I'm a little child. And you? What do you need to do, to get into America?"

Little Ash frowned at the tiles again.

"They *will* let you in?" Rose prompted.

"Oh, they'll let me in," said Little Ash. "One way or another, they'll let me in."

nineteen

URIEL SAT ON ITS TRUNK, fidgeting with its tzitzis. It had been waiting for what felt like a very long time, and it was starting to feel a tug on its soul, the tug of an angelic task. *It's time to go to the rebbe's daughter.*

Once, that tug would not have been a simple thought. It would have been the angel's entire existence. It would not have sat, worried and waiting, missing a ferry and then another ferry. It would simply have gone on, to the address from Malke's letters, and forgotten there was ever such a person as Little Ashmedai Shtetler, the demon.

It had given itself a name, and with the name it was able to resist the pull of a mitzvah. The feeling was not pleasant, but there was a sort of freedom in its unpleasantness. Like pressing on a bruise.

The rebbe clung to its shoulder. The last few days on the

ship, he had been shrinking, his shape even in dreams tending more toward the ancestral-creature form he took in daylight. He was now scarcely larger than a mouse, tucked into the folds of the angel's tallis, and his feet burnt its skin like ice, even through the fabric of its clothes. "Uriel," he said. "Uriel, we must go. We must go. My daughter is waiting."

"They took him away," said the angel. "He isn't coming."

"That's right, he isn't coming—but they let you through. Stand up, now, my dear, open your eyes."

The angel shook its head. It was trying to piece together the steps of a task that was not its intended task. The path to the rebbe's daughter was so clear it could almost feel itself completing the task, but the path to Little Ash was littered with complications. It did not speak English. It did not understand the rules of America. It was overwhelmed by the crowds. It did not know whom to ask, and what the question ought to be.

But it would not turn its back on him.

Its answer arrived in the person of Rose, marching out of the main building with an expression of deep irritation on her face. The angel jumped up to greet her, and both of them forgot themselves so thoroughly in their relief to see familiar faces that they threw their arms around each other as if they were family.

"What took so long?" Uriel asked. "Have you seen Ashel? I don't understand what is happening."

"He told me to come and find you and tell you to go to New York by yourself," said Rose. "He explicitly said you should not come back in the building! What nonsense is he talking? I told him he ought to come with me and say good-bye his own self, but he wouldn't have it."

Uriel frowned. It thought it understood Little Ash fairly well, and this was how he behaved when he was doing something dangerous—"demon business," he would call it. But what could be dangerous about a building full of confused and tired humans?

"We've been stopped," Rose went on. "They said I can't leave the island without a relative, and he's been—well, they're saying he's liable to be a public charge, but no one understands what it means, except it seems to be an awful lot of the people they're not letting go to the mainland. Ashel said you can give a message to my cousin for me. And he said you shouldn't worry, he'll fix it himself, only I don't know how he plans to do that, because I heard someone say if you're a public charge they send you right back with no way to change it. Anyway, he says it doesn't matter, he knows a way, and you're the only one of us who can find Bluma. Can you do it for me? Please? I know you'd rather stay with your friend, but—after all, they didn't stop *you*."

She said all this in quite a rush, trying to get every detail without forgetting anything, and it took Uriel a moment to process it all, but at the end it understood. Little Ash was behaving as Little Ash always did, and refusing to ask for help in a situation where he clearly needed it. Rose, less stubborn and more practical, was asking for help even though she had no guarantee that Uriel could, or would, give it.

"Where does your cousin live?" it asked. It could feel a way to perform two good deeds and at the same time try to find the help Little Ash refused to ask for. The rebbe's daughter had been in America for some time; she would understand the words Rose and Uriel did not.

"She lives in Hester Street," said Rose. She dug through her pockets and handed over the scrap of paper on which she'd written her cousin's address, so she could show it to the officials and prove she had somewhere to go in America. "Here it is. You'll be all right on your own? Tell her I sent you, and I'm sure she'll find you a place to stay the night, if you don't have one. And I'll take care of Ashel for you, don't worry. When you come back, I'll have explained to him that he's being ridiculous."

"Thank you," said Uriel. It thought it felt a little of the luck of angels in the piece of paper with the address on it. Hester Street was the same street where the rebbe's daughter lived. It must be meant to go to Hester Street after all—and accepting the task was a great relief after a long, confusing day. "I will be back, and I will bring your cousin."

"Good," said Rose. "Good. Now, don't miss the ferry."

As Little Ash looked carefully at each detainee in turn, he could see signs of illness, and the occasional twisted limb or blind eye, and one or two sins that might have caught the eye of a gatekeeping demon. These were the ones judged not worthy of this new country, and Little Ash was with them, a broken thing instead of a person, a threat to the very foundations of America—foundations which he could not have located on a map and the existence of which he had been entirely unaware. He'd read the newspapers and known America was trying to keep certain people out, but his mind had skimmed over the possibility that this would affect him or the angel in any way. After all, he was healthy. Perhaps he couldn't walk entirely straight, but it had never stopped him from doing as he liked, except when there were miracle-working rabbis about.

And gentile demon doctors, it seemed. It had been a very long time since Little Ash had felt so ashamed of having only the barest drops of magic. He had left yeshiva and his father's palace to get away from that feeling; he had spent centuries in a little village with only one synagogue, his only super-natural companion an angel, to get away from that feeling. He had forgotten just how much he hated it.

He felt, as he had not felt in a long time, like being clever would not be enough.

While Rose was away giving Uriel their messages, Grand-mother Rivke came in, her usually smiling face dejected and her steps less lively than usual. Seeing Little Ash where he sat on top of Rose's luggage, she came over and sat next to him without waiting for an invitation.

"You!" Rivke said. "What did they say about you, sheyfele?

You're so young, and you run about so quickly; what could they possibly find fault with?"

"The doctor didn't like me," said Little Ash. "I should have expected, maybe. I didn't like him either. Specifically he didn't like my feet. You should be careful."

Rivke gave this some thought. "You're saying he was one of your kind?"

"No, not *my* kind, something vicious." He wouldn't have shared any details, but after all, Rivke knew what he was— and he felt terribly hollow, in a way that he usually cured by finding an argument to start with the angel. Talking was all he could think to do. "I couldn't see his sins on him, but he smelled like death. I don't think it's safe for anyone to be staying here."

"Everyone is afraid this room means sending back," said Rivke. "I didn't understand their explanation. My family had to go without me. My doctor was the ordinary kind, but he made quite a face when he put that little thing to my chest to hear my lungs working, and he wrote something on my coat about it. I told him I'm perfectly capable and haven't had a cough in days, but he wouldn't hear it—or maybe the interpreter didn't bother to tell him what I was saying. What will my daughter do without me? She's gone to the ferry with that nothing husband of hers, and she said she'll be back as soon as she can, to get me, but I don't trust that he won't slip a dollar to the doctors and have them ship me back to Russia in a suitcase."

Little Ash was certain being shipped back in a suitcase

was what the doctor intended for him. He'd read, with difficulty, what had been scribbled on his papers, and it said that his criminal affect and evidently poor physical development rendered him liable to become a public charge—his demon's skill with languages stretched far enough to interpret this as a lot of words to say he was trouble.

But how could he go back, alone, to a village everyone was leaving? And what would the angel do without Little Ash to speak its English?

"Be strong, sheyfele," said Rivke, squeezing his shoulder with a bony hand. "God will provide for us."

Little Ash didn't like Rivke telling him to rely on God. She seemed hollowed out, as if her soul were hiding somewhere far away. As if all the doctors here were demons, or else even the human ones could reach inside a person and pluck out their humanity.

"Something will happen, God or not," he said. "I won't go back to Poland without Uriel, and I won't let it go back either."

Rivke just nodded.

Little Ash could see the same wish in the eyes of everyone in the room. No one there had left Europe without a very good reason, and none had anything worth going back to.

Rivke had survived trials before, and now she pulled herself back together and reached into her basket of knitting. "Here, you, help me untangle this yarn. I might as well work on something while they make us sit."

Little Ash had never wished to be anything but a demon.

He had always quite enjoyed being selfish and a little cruel and mostly causing trouble, but he felt, now, that it would have been better if he were the sort of creature who knew how to fix things. Uriel, he was sure, could have done something to make the room more comfortable, even if only by singing one of its silent, soothing psalms. He could only look around the room and see how sapped was everyone's yetzer horeh, despair draining away even the smallest of selfish wishes until even the desire to drink a hot cup of tea was weak and out of reach. Uriel would have said this room was a wicked place, and even as he wished the angel were by his side, he thought that at least it was not here to feel how sad this room of sick people was.

If he had to be a demon, he should at least be the sort of demon who could summon a magnificent feast with a snap of his fingers, and hypnotize all of these people into forgetting their obligations, so that by forgetting they had lost their families they would forget to miss them. But he was not. He was the sort of demon who closed his eyes and tried to hide while someone more powerful told him he was not worth the effort to dispose of.

Little Ash had never felt so human, and he disliked it intensely.

twenty

URIEL KEPT LOOKING around as it boarded the ferry into the city, feeling as if it had only imagined that Little Ash was not beside it. This must be how he felt when the angel forgot who it was and wandered off after a stray cat or a lost child in the street. No wonder he was so tense all the time.

"You must hurry," said the rebbe, clinging to its shoulder. "Find Malke, find my daughter. And you'd best put your tallis away, among so many gentiles. You don't want to attract the wrong sort of attention."

Uriel, looking around, saw that indeed there were a great deal more people dressed in the modern styles of America than otherwise, although there were some women in colorful embroideries and men in peasants' clothes. Everyone was in considerably better spirits on this ferry, to the real New York City, than they had been on the ferries to Ellis Island at the start of the day. Still, it saw an ashy film in the air around some people that gave it the feeling they might not have the best intentions toward those around them.

This unsettled the angel, as it was used to seeing only the holiness in people. Perhaps its eyes were tired. It hadn't been able to close its eyes and rest in a long time, and rest was more necessary since leaving quiet little Shtetl.

Tired and worried, the angel replaced its shawl with the rebbe's knitted sweater. It double-checked that the money was still pinned inside its vest, and sat on its trunk to study the addresses of the rebbe's daughter Malke and Rose's cousin Bluma, so that it should not get lost. On its shoulder, the rebbe kept up a constant whispering, in the unintelligible language of a decaying ghost.

The angel, knowing no other cities, had imagined New York as the Jewish Quarter of Warsaw. At first it supposed Hester Street would be like the streets in its shtetl, and then it corrected itself that this was a city, and Hester Street would be like Krumer Street.

Hester Street was like ten Krumer Streets all crowded together. It was a marketplace, nearly the width of the street packed with stalls and the sounds of buyers and sellers shouting. Nearly everyone was speaking Yiddish, yet the words had an alien cast even with Uriel's new mastery of the mother tongue, and everyone seemed to be shouting at the top of their voices. It was jostled from side to side as it tried to find the house number of the rebbe's daughter, so that it could deliver to her the trunk of books it was dragging and be free then to worry about Little Ash and Rose. New Yorkers did not seem to believe in asking if one was lost, nor were they easily stopped to ask for directions.

The angel had gone to the markets with Little Ash once or twice. It had not liked them, and it had decided that whatever wickedness the demon wanted to conduct in markets would be the business of the angels of markets. As Uriel, it was not quite so spun around, but it still felt itself pulled in so many directions that it almost started to weep.

"There!" said the rebbe, his little ghost-claws pricking its shoulder as he stood up to point. "That bookshop! Her man is from a family with a bookshop."

Uriel saw it, too, after a moment of confusion as it tried to look past hurrying people in brimmed hats. The name was in Hebrew letters, with the added vowels of Yiddish, declaring it SHULMAN'S BOOKS, and in the window additional letters declared Shulman a purveyor of the finest Jewish things. This was a great relief to Uriel. It knew Jewish things. It did not know New York, but it knew books. The shop looked invitingly empty.

Indeed, when they got to the door, the shop was closed.

"Knock!" the rebbe urged. "Knock for your life—for mine, for the sake of my soul, knock!"

He was standing almost on Uriel's head, pulling its hair in his excitement, losing himself faster now than he had been on the ship, as if the promise of his daughter's proximity had released some need to keep himself together. Uriel put down the trunk and gently tugged him off of its head so that he should not tear its scalp. Holding him in one hand it knocked on the door, and then on the glass of the window, with urgency.

There was no one inside—at least, not in the shop itself. But the shop was only one level of the building. Uriel felt rude enough already from tapping on the glass, but when no one responded it bit its lip and looked around for another door, or a stair to the upper apartments. Little Ash would look for another way in, and if no one answered he would simply go in through a window, or something like that. The angel told itself it must act like Little Ash if it hoped to get anywhere in New York. This much was already clear.

There was a door to the side, but no one answered that one either. Telling itself that a human name, like a human person, must contain the capacity for wickedness, and then telling itself for reinforcement that it was in the process of performing a good deed anyway, the angel squared its shoulders and tested the lock. It was open, and behind the door was a steep set of stairs.

"Yes!" whispered the rebbe, gasping like a dying man. "Yes, we are nearly home."

Dragging the trunk full of Talmud, the angel climbed the stairs. There was a hall at the top which was cluttered with the sort of things houses fill up with when people live in them for a while—some buckets, an old broom not quite worn enough to throw out, several pairs of boots. There were two apartments on the second floor, off this hall, but it seemed both were being used as one, because the doors were open to both and there was a kettle on the stove on one side, and the sound of a small child splashing in a tin tub came from the other, along with a female voice singing a folk song in Yiddish.

"Hello?" Uriel called. "Hello, I am looking for Malke, the rebbe's daughter."

The girl stopped singing and, after a bit more splashing, she emerged from the apartment with a toddler, wrapped in a towel, on her arm. The baby looked tired, as if bathing had been a great ordeal, and watched Uriel with sleepy eyes while the girl spoke. "Malke is my sister-in-law, but she's out. Why, look at you! A real greenhorn, and a Hasid, yet! I've seen a hundred greenhorns with that glaze in their eyes, but not so many pious Jews." She laughed at this. "Have you come from Malke's father? She told us he's a real miracle worker. Mind you, we have miracle workers here in New York, and I've never seen them actually do a thing to help anyone. But Malke said they have them real in the Old Country. I'm Freidy, by the way. Who are you?"

She stuck out her hand for Uriel to shake, which caused the angel some consternation, because it realized it looked like a male yeshiva student, a species of creature that would never shake the hand of a bold American girl—but it did not like to think that just *looking* like a boy meant it had to be one. It would prefer to erase that line from its identity papers.

Why must humans make things so confusing? it thought.

Before it could decide what to do, Freidy dropped her hand. She didn't seem too offended, merely using the hand to pick up a corner of towel and scrub a stray drop of water from the sleepy toddler's neck. "Malke's at the strike meeting," she said, cheerfully, "but you can come in for a cup of tea if you like. We've got some raisin buns, I think. If you're new in New York I'm sure you're hungry. Everyone who gets here first thing off the ship seems awfully hungry. Do they not feed you?"

"Herrings and potatoes," said Uriel. It wondered what a human would add to this. The food had tasted miraculous on its tongue, but that was because it had never eaten food while having a name before, and it had not realized that food was so flavorful.

The rebbe whispered, "Tell her you did not like it. She will expect that."

"I did not like it," said Uriel. "It was tiresome."

"Herrings and potatoes!" exclaimed Freidy. "Tiresome is how it sounds."

She led the way into the other side of the apartment, where she deposited the child on a bed in the corner and gestured to a table that had clearly been combined from two others and a couple of crates, as if to accommodate a large family. On the wall a shawl was slipping off the frame of a mirror, covering half the glass as if someone had forgotten to remove it after a funeral.

"I'm sorry," said Uriel, acting as mouthpiece for the rebbe's ghost again. "But what did you say about a strike meeting?"

"Malke's gone along with everyone," said Freidy. "Even though she gets so tired, with the baby. They didn't let me go with them because they said it's too dangerous, since I'm so young—but I'm not that much younger than most of the other girls, and they're all getting into scraps with the police and everything, so I don't see why I can't."

"Baby?" Uriel repeated. The rebbe had become very excited at this, and was pulling at its hair again, but it could not reach up to move him without Freidy noticing. "Malke is having a baby?"

"That's right, and it should be soon, she's so big. It will be good to have a celebration in this house, I'll tell you that. I'm sorry, were you her brother? She never said she had brothers. Did you say you were her father's student?"

It hadn't, but it nodded.

"And do you know about the factory? No?"

Uriel shook its head. It was beginning to see that it knew very little.

"Well, it's Mr. Boaz's factory; they're striking. Oh, the tea!"

She turned to the stove and moved the kettle over the fire, then tripped around the kitchen collecting raisin buns on a plate, and a little pot of jam and a knife, while she continued explaining. "Mr. Boaz owns the factory, and he owns half the tenements on this block as well—including this one. So my father is helping with the strike, even though he doesn't work for him like that; we're paying him the rent, and all the rest of us are at the factory together, even Malke."

"Thank you for explaining," Uriel said to Freidy. She was sitting now with an expectant expression, so it took one of the raisin buns and took a bite. This seemed to satisfy her; she immediately reached for a bun herself, smearing it with generous amounts of jam. "I wonder if I can ask you something else. My friends are stuck at Ellis Island. I don't know how to help one of them, but the other one said all she needs is for her relative to come and take her. Do you know Bluma Cohen? She lives here."

It handed over the slip with Bluma's address, but it seemed this wasn't necessary, as before she'd even read it Freidy was talking again. "Of course I know Bluma! She works for Mr. Boaz too! We're both piecers, so she doesn't sit too far from me—we can talk during work; she's very nice, Bluma. All the girls like her very much. She's never condescending, even if you're younger, like me. She'll be at the meeting today, I suppose, with everyone. I'll take you to see her later, if you like!"

"That's very kind of you."

"Oh, it's only right. It must be so difficult to be stopped at the island; I don't know what I would do if that happened to me. But I was born here so I've never been."

"Will this meeting be over soon?" Uriel asked. The

shoulder the rebbe had been clinging to was now numb from the strength and chill of his grip. He must be very close to losing himself entirely, and to judge by the covered mirror and their debts to Reb Fishl's colleague Mr. Boaz, this family did not need more bad luck.

"Oh, soon enough, I suppose," said Freidy. "They've been gone for ages and ages."

In fact it was not much longer before they heard steps on the stairs, and the toddler woke from his nap to leap up and run into the hallway, calling greetings to the rest of the Shulman family.

"Malke, you've got a guest!" Freidy shouted, as a heavily pregnant young woman climbed to the top of the stairs. Uriel could see some of the rebbe in Malke's face, but even if it had not, it would have known her at once, for the rebbe leapt from its shoulder and ran to her. A young man with solemn dark eyes and a neatly trimmed beard was supporting her by her elbow, though he looked scarcely less tired than she was, and the handful of brothers who followed after him equally so.

Malke seemed concerned to see her young sister-in-law in conversation with a stranger. "Who's this, Freidy?"

"It's all right," said Freidy. "I'm not making any sort of mischief; it's just a student of your father's, from the Old Country."

At this, the expression of exhaustion cleared instantly from Malke's eyes. Uriel saw the rebbe clinging to her dress, tugging at it and trying to draw her attention, with no result.

"From my father?" she said, sharply. "What happened? Is he all right?"

Uriel looked from the tiny, ghostly scrap of the rebbe back to Malke's face. It hated to bring bad news, especially to a woman who was pregnant and tired and whose new family had troubles of their own. But the rebbe was scarcely human at all anymore; the first thirty days after his death would be over soon. He had no time to wait.

"I'm very sorry," it said. "Your father, may his memory be a blessing, wasn't able to leave Warsaw. I've come to bring you his books."

twenty-one

URIEL HAD WANTED to return to Ellis Island as soon as its message was delivered, but it had not counted on being a human guest, who could not simply slip away to the next task. It had to tell Malke everything it could about her father, and show her his belongings, and try its best to comfort her. She wept over the sweater, and then told Uriel to keep it, in thanks for bringing her the books and the letters. It wondered if the rebbe had whispered this in her ear, but it could no longer see him.

Malke then had to tell her husband Izzy, about the rebbe, how he had fallen ill in Poland and wouldn't be coming to visit, and they needed to gather a minyan for his Kaddish. So Izzy went back out and collected his father and three brothers old enough to count, and Uriel was volunteered as the rebbe's student—hoping that the Universe would not object to its being counted—and the youngest brother except for the toddler ran out to gather a handful of others from the neighborhood. And then there was a mourning meal as it got dark, and Izzy and Malke speaking to each other in whispers.

"Bad luck," one of the men whispered when they were done praying and were on their way out. Only Uriel, sitting on the rebbe's trunk by the door, heard him say it. "Another death so soon."

Uriel still saw no sign of the rebbe, and realized that with the books delivered and the Kaddish said, he had no more reason to stay. He must have gone on, as intended.

He had not told it goodbye.

He wasn't going to help it find Little Ash again and bring him out of Ellis Island. Uriel was alone.

The clerks had come at last and sorted the detainees into men and women, and brought them to the rooms where they were meant to stay until they were put on a boat, either back to Europe or into the city. Very little explanation had been given, and certainly no one had said anything so helpful as how long they should expect to wait if they weren't able to have a hearing the next day. It seemed hoping to get into America was like waiting for the messiah, an activity to which only the most faithful could dedicate any energy.

Rose and Rivke stuck together, joining ten other women

in a room of stacked bunks, three atop each other with scarcely enough room to lie down between them. There were more elderly women than bunks that were easy to climb into, and so Rose found herself helping everyone get into bed, giving them little encouraging speeches as she did.

She herself was not feeling so encouraged, as she'd heard a rumor that a female relative was just as suspicious as a girl on her own—the procurers, it seemed, liked to hire respectable-looking widows to kidnap girls from the island. Even if Uriel found Bluma, would Rose be allowed to go with her? But as usual, she felt there was no point in worrying about anything she couldn't plan for. If she couldn't leave with Bluma, she'd find another way. She would not allow herself to be sent back to Belz with nothing to show for it. In Belz there was only Dinah, who didn't need her. In America there was a job which would pay for Motl to leave the Pale and not be conscripted, and there was also Essie, whose sparkling eyes sometimes danced in Rose's head unbidden. She supposed it was the idea of a girl so much like herself, who'd found worse trouble even after she got to New York.

"I'm sure your cousin will come," Rivke reassured her, when they were lying down and the women were murmuring comfort to one another around the room. A baby was crying somewhere down the hallway: there had been a few mothers without husbands among the detained.

"And your lungs will clear up in no time at all," said Rose. "If they let me into your hearing I'll tell them. You're not sick in the least. I'll tell them it took you only a day to shrug off the seasickness when all the healthy young men were still crying in their cots."

Rivke laughed, the laugh turning into a cough for a moment. A couple of other coughs echoed it around the room.

"They would have put me in the hospital, if they really thought I was sick," said Rivke. "God willing, we'll all be out of here in the morning."

Rose didn't care if God was willing or not. She'd find a way to get past him if he wasn't.

If Little Ash had never figured out how to sleep in a place so quiet and peaceful as his shtetl, he certainly would not discover the secret in the little room, hardly better than a jail cell, in which he had been told to rest in a hammock stacked up on top of two others. It was even more cramped than the ship.

He sat up, instead, with his back to the wall and eyes wide open, making the same wild, improbable plans that always served as dreams for him, rejecting each idea almost as soon as it came to him. Although he would not have admitted it to anyone, there was a desperate quality to his thoughts as he sat there, separated from everything and everyone that was familiar to him.

The emotion Little Ash was feeling is called loneliness, but he did not recognize it. He had been born into a family in which his siblings numbered in the hundreds, and demons having no need to mature at any set pace, he had stayed in his father's palace and in cheder for many centuries. When at last he became a bar mitzvah and left the palace of demons, he had been alone only for a short time before he met the angel; they had scarcely been separated since, and never by force.

Not knowing what emotion it was that so plagued him, Little Ash was puzzled when he found himself thinking of his father. The demon king did not have many notable talents as a parent, but there was a game he had played, many centuries ago when he had a flock of sons in cheder, where in shul on the holidays they would all try to fit beneath his wings, as many as could do so without a fight breaking out. What Little Ash found himself remembering now, to his own confusion, was what it had felt like to be trapped not by human laws he did not understand, but by a warm, solid mass of living creatures who shared his history and his name, all of them clinging to one another in the shadow of King Ashmedai's feathers, while somewhere outside of the circle a chazzan's voice was raised in prayer.

The angel had not been detained, and he ought to be glad, but he was not, now that he was alone. He had written papers to get it into America, and into America it got, obedient creature. Now who, in America, would watch it sleep, and make sure it was all right? And who would watch Little Ash?

No one, it seemed.

In the Lower East Side apartment of the Shulman family, Uriel also was awake. Its gracious hosts had no space for it on a bed, as Izzy and Malke shared one and little Shuli and Freidy the other of the two in their apartment, the rest of the Shulmans sleeping on the other side of the hall. They had given it a thick quilt to sleep on, in the warm spot by the stove, next to Freidy and Shuli's bed; propriety had to be forgotten, sometimes, in small dwellings. It found, however, that it was too preoccupied for sleeping. Worried for its chevrusa, it seemed to have forgotten all of the rebbe's helpful advice on the nature of sleep.

Angels do not naturally form familial relationships. Typically, their identities are too self-contained and too fluid. The strangeness Uriel felt in the absence of Little Ash was, therefore, quite puzzling. Never having been forcibly separated from him before, it had not realized how much the separation would feel like a loss, not merely of a partner, but in fact of a part of itself. As if, without the demon, it had lost one of its senses, or a limb, though it did not think in such human terms as these.

It sat on its knees on the quilt, with its hands folded in its lap and head bowed, quite motionless enough to be mistaken for the empty body of an angel asleep, except that it was still breathing. Every part of itself not required for that necessary activity was turned toward the purpose of rescuing Little Ash, and of course Rose. From the start it had not liked that place, or any other one of the checkpoints it had encountered since leaving its shtetl. Checkpoints it knew for an injustice; Ellis Island was an injustice. As an angel, it told itself that its purpose now must be correction, the redressing of balance in the world, the repair of broken vessels. It had seen injustice and it must fix things.

But this was only a guess. What it felt much more strongly was that, as Uriel, its purpose was to find Little Ash again, and be sure he had asked no one to shoot him, and had not gotten shot.

It is not good for a creature of earth to be alone, Uriel thought, and in the dark apartment it blinked in astonishment at the realization that it, itself, was also a creature of earth. It was breathing, it had felt hunger until it ate, and it found that it could not quite remember how it was that it had left its body when it slept. Even if it had wanted to, it had entirely forgotten the mechanism. Uriel, it seemed, could no longer exist without its body, as the other angels were able to do.

I will have to tell Ashel, it thought. And made a silent note of this, in letters of fire on the inside of its own head: another new thing it had discovered about the nature of Uriel Federman. No revelation of itself would be complete until Little Ash also was made aware of it.

twenty-two

IN THE MORNING, Malke and Uriel were the last ones to wake up at the Shulman apartment, and everyone else had gone to the factory, so the angel could not ask Freidy to show it where Bluma lived.

"Let's go down to the bookshop," Malke said, taking the teapot and two cups. "With the news from my father, I nearly forgot you were here. I'd like to talk to you."

Uriel followed, looking carefully around in case the ghostly rebbe was accompanying his daughter, but he was not. Malke set the teapot on the shop counter and stood leaning on her elbows to drink, with a whispered blessing. Uriel repeated it and took a sip of tea itself.

"Is there anything we can do for you, to thank you for being a messenger?" Malke asked. "Other than keeping the sweater—that's hardly enough. Do you need help finding family? Do you *have* family in New York?"

"There is something." Uriel did not like to ask for help—after all, as an angel it should have known exactly how to accomplish its tasks, and had the magic it needed for them at its fingertips. But it was no longer sure that it was an angel. "I need to find my friend's cousin, to bring her out of Ellis Island, and Freidy promised to take me. But my chevrusa also was stopped, and I don't know how to help him. They said he can't come into America because he won't be able to work. But he can; I don't know why they would stop him."

It wished it could have talked to Little Ash. Why did he have to be so stubborn? If it had been able to speak to him, it could have learned more details. The angel felt that it was telling Malke hardly anything, but that was all it knew, except for the creeping feeling that there was something dangerous Little Ash did not want it to confront.

Malke thought about the question for a while. "Sometimes, they just stop you. There are rules, but you can't rely on them to be the same day-to-day. Some of the doctors just don't like us—Jews, I mean. But you can appeal it. You might try to get help. There's a rabbi uptown who helps people sometimes; he helped one of Izzy's brothers get through, and he gave us some charity when Dvorah, that is, Mrs. Shulman, died, may she rest in peace. You might speak to him."

"A rabbi," said Uriel. This sounded promising. A rabbi could tell it what to do about Little Ash, surely. "Yes, I would like to talk to a rabbi."

"Rabbi Wolf, he's called." Malke looked around for a slip

of paper, and started to write directions. "You'll have to take the elevated train—you know what that is?"

Uriel of course had no idea, and so the rest of their conversation was about elevated trains, and technology, and how to get uptown. When it was time for Malke to open the bookshop, Uriel took her hand-drawn map and went back out into the hustle and bustle of Hester Street.

Uriel was relieved to find that the elevated train was just a railway, albeit a railway that ran over the top of busy streets. It considered itself an expert on railways, after taking one to Warsaw and another from Warsaw to Hamburg. It paid for the ride with Reb Fishl's American money, feeling very grown-up and human, and squeezed itself into the crowd in the car. Malke had told it to count stops if it couldn't hear the conductor announce them in English, and this advice proved helpful, as it therefore had something to concentrate on that wasn't the shrieking and clattering of rails, or the way the high buildings flew by outside, or the scents of smoke and sweat and soap from the people around it. It could feel little flutters at the edges of its head that would have called it to a new task if it hadn't had its name, and the counting, to hold onto. It could have become an Angel of Messenger Boys, or an Angel of Maids Riding Uptown for Work, or god forbid an Angel of the Aggravation people felt every time more travelers squeezed into the car than left it at a stop.

When it got off the train at last, it was in a place that looked entirely unlike the Lower East Side, as if it had traveled not merely to a different part of the same city, but to a different place entirely. The world outside the study hall in Shtetl was turning out to be much bigger and more complicated than it had realized; this looked more like the fairy-tale America Little Ash had tried to tempt it with, back in the shtetl. Since arriving at Ellis Island it had decided that that America did not exist, but maybe in *uptown* it did. Still, the streets weren't paved in gold, and once in a while as well-dressed people walked by they would give it a sour look, and some of them seemed to have little soot-covered creatures running after them like mice, which disappeared if the angel ever looked directly at them. It wished the rebbe had come with it, so he could explain what those were.

Malke's directions were good enough that when it came to a building with a soaring, stained glass—decorated front, it understood that this was a synagogue, though it looked nothing like the synagogue in Shtetl, or the one in Krumer Street with the rafters full of ghosts. This synagogue indeed did not seem to have any ghosts in its rafters, though Uriel checked for them. The angel's hooves echoed on the floor of the lofty, airy interior of the building, which was empty of living creatures too. Where were the old men who never seemed to stop studying? Where were the little children? Here, there were only stiff wooden benches, and golden decorations, and quite a lot of sunlight to show off the silently drifting motes of dust that seemed to be the only occupants. The Torah ark soared over its head in splendor, stopping the angel for a moment in its tracks. It was astonished to find itself feeling shabby, in the clothes Little Ash had hand-sewn for it, and Malke's own knitted sweater. The Torah ark seemed to scold it for not being a holier creature.

It quickly blinked and looked away. Toward the back of the sanctuary there was another, smaller door which offered an escape from the judgmental gaze of the ark. Behind the smaller door was a corridor in which Uriel immediately felt more comfortable because it was more cramped, and darker, and it smelled of books and candle wax, missing only the scent of goats to make it a proper beys-midrash like they had at home. Here it found yet a third door, with a bronze plaque on it. Recognizing the look of an office, from seeing officials' offices in Hamburg, it went over and knocked.

"Come in," someone called in English.

An elderly man with a neatly trimmed beard sat behind an elaborately carved wooden desk, surrounded on all sides by volumes of Talmud and other important books. A silver-headed cane leaned against one side of the desk, and the man was wearing very shiny golden spectacles. He did not look, to the angel, like a rabbi. He looked much more like a wealthy, modern gentleman.

The look he gave it was not sour, like the looks of the people in the street, but he did look perplexed, as if he were not used to taking visitors who looked like Uriel. It wondered which part of its appearance was puzzling him. Unless he knew it was an angel?

"May I help you?" he said, in a tone of voice that suggested he might not want to know the answer. He had been writing when Uriel came in, and he carefully put down his pen, but he did not put the paper aside.

"Are you the rabbi?" said Uriel, timidly. It wasn't used to knowing more than one language; it could hear that it spoke with an accent inflected by its familiarity with the Holy Tongue, but it was not sure how Little Ash managed the twisting of the mouth that made him speak like a native in whatever language he pleased.

"I am."

"I was told you might help. Malke Shulman from Hester Street said you helped a relative of hers, and my—relatives—have been stopped at Ellis Island."

"Ah." Rabbi Wolf thought about this for a moment, then sighed and gestured for Uriel to sit down. When it did, he said, "What has happened? I hope the Shulmans have not suffered another loss. The family is honest enough, and it was terrible what happened to poor Mrs. Shulman."

"I have one friend who could not leave the island because she is a woman, and she is alone," said Uriel. "They said she could leave if a relative came to get her. This is all right. She has a relative. But my cousin they stopped because . . . I don't know why they stopped him, only they said he couldn't work in America."

"I'm very sorry to hear it," said the rabbi. "Your cousin,

is he sick? Has he had some illness, or perhaps he is not very strong?"

This seemed to Uriel a strange way to characterize Little Ash. He seemed very strong from its perspective. He never seemed overwhelmed by the world, the way it often was.

"I don't think so." It gestured to the rabbi's cane. "Only, his feet hurt him sometimes."

And he is a demon, it thought. Could that be why? But who would have known?

"I'm afraid this is the law," said the rabbi. "If a newcomer is liable to become a burden on charity in America, they must go home to where there is more support."

"But there is no support," said Uriel doubtfully. "Anyway, he came all the way here."

"You understand, it is terrible that we cannot bring in every charitable case from the whole of the world," said the rabbi. "It is a great misfortune that life is so difficult for Jews like yourself, in the Russian Empire and elsewhere. But America cannot solve the world's problems. It is better that some of you stay home, and work hard in your homelands to improve your lot. Otherwise, America would be overwhelmed and would sink beneath the weight of charity. I have helped a few cases, here and there, it's true. But there are hundreds of thousands of miserable people pouring through Ellis Island every year, and I cannot help them all. Rest assured that the temple gives all it can to philanthropic causes in the Lower East Side, and Europe, and Palestine. I can give you a bit of money, if you like, to help your cousin along. But if he has been excluded, then he has been excluded."

The thought of a rabbi with money had not occurred to Uriel previously. Nor had it realized that an offer of money could feel so like an insult. "But he is here to help someone," it protested. "We came to help someone, and I can't do it alone—Ashel is a good person, in his own way."

"It is a pity," said the rabbi. "All the same, there is only so much I can do. If our American Jewish community were to drown in poverty imported from abroad, who then would be a beacon of hope for the diaspora?"

Uriel looked down at its hands. It felt unaccountably ashamed. It had expected to speak to this man and immediately have the help that it needed. It had wanted, it realized, to hand the question of what to do to someone else.

There was no one else. It must drag Little Ash off the island with its own two hands.

"Thank you, rabbi," it said. "I will accept your money. And then I will leave you alone."

twenty-three

LITTLE ASH, ON ELLIS ISLAND, had come up with no better plan for his own future than to track down the demon
doctor, find some way to make him disappear forever, and
use his one reliable bit of magical talent to make a human
doctor look at him again and find nothing wrong whatsoever. In terms of the number of steps involved, this was quite
a simple plan, which ought to have made it quite appealing.
They could not bar him entry to America for being a demon
if they were not aware that he was a demon.

He could even, perhaps, extend the illusion beyond
himself, if the doctor were particularly weak-willed or
exhausted, and persuade them that there was nothing wrong
with Grandmother Rivke, or that Rose had the chaperone
they wanted her to have. It seemed to Little Ash that all the
human doctors on Ellis Island were, in fact, exhausted, and

they ought to be easy marks, if he could only get the one demon out of the way first.

Little Ash's plan, in short, was perfect, except that he could not execute any of the later steps without having done the first.

Of the first step, he was terrified.

Because he did not sleep, Little Ash was not terribly familiar with the experience of having nightmares. Like diseases, nightmares were close relations to sheydim like himself, and so he was familiar with them in concept, much as he was familiar with loneliness in concept. But, as with the loneliness he had felt the night before and been unable to identify, he had been unable to figure out why, whenever he shut his eyes, he found himself imagining that the demon doctor had hold of him again and was about to put a button-hook in his eye, not to check under the lid for infection and not for inspection of his magical potential, but to drag out his soul from behind the eyeball.

If he kept his eyes shut for long enough, he could imagine all of it, watching from outside himself until his soul had been eaten and there was nothing left of him but a body to be tossed away in some corner of the island even more miserable than the rest, and no one to tell the angel what had happened.

This was why he had kept his eyes open all night, hardly blinking, watching the door for intruders and feeling the pace of his heartbeat pick up each time a guard or doctor came around with their lantern to check that no one had either run away or died since their last round of patrols. It was distressingly easy to convince himself that he had not imagined the scene at all, but actually watched it, and he must now be a ghost like those poor deluded creatures on the ceiling of the shul in Warsaw, too confused by his own death to realize he could be elsewhere.

He was therefore quite relieved, against his own will, when, having been brought back to the miserable waiting room to eat an equally miserable breakfast of milk and oatmeal, he found Rose and Rivke, and they saw him in return and spoke to him as if he were not a ghost at all.

"Do you think it's even kosher?" Rose asked, poking at her oatmeal with a spoon as Little Ash sat down beside her. The porridge barely deserved the dignity of being placed in a bowl, even a chipped, cheap bowl like the one Rose had. It had only just come out of the pot, and was already congealed.

"Kosher by virtue of being the only food there is," said Rivke, who was eating hers as heartily as if it had been a bowl of potatoes and cream. She seemed to have recovered a bit with her night of sleep. "How they expect anyone to be healthy on this, I don't know."

"Have you seen a goyish doctor with very pale eyes?" Little Ash asked. "A tall one."

"I've seen more goyish doctors than you can count, my dear," said Rivke. "Kept waking me up in the night, wandering around with their lanterns like a pack of demons."

"I need the specific doctor." Little Ash looked around,

searching for signs of magic, and saw nothing, only the same heavy air of disappointment that had so oppressed him the day before in the room where they'd been made to wait.

"Why?" said Rose. "Is that the one who said you look like a criminal?"

"Just because," said Little Ash, not in the mood to recruit any co-conspirators. Perhaps, he thought, he could cause some kind of trouble, and they might send for a doctor. If he pretended to be very upset, maybe. Or perhaps he could cause any type of trouble at all, and the one demon doctor would come after him. After all, the man had known to come check on Little Ash the day before. He must have been able to see that there was another demon, from farther away than Little Ash could see. Could Christians see through walls? It seemed like the sort of irritating thing they would be able to do.

Rivke reached over and tapped his knuckles with her spoon, making him jump. "You need to eat," she said, sternly.

"I really don't," said Little Ash. He was not in the mood to be told what to do by even one more person, no matter what their intentions were. There was a nurse, or some kind of other official, over by the doorway, speaking with one of the kitchen staff. If he went and talked to that nurse, he was sure he could come up with something. If he could get in a room alone with the doctor again, this time he would be ready.

He couldn't make himself get up from the table.

Rose had been watching him very closely. Now she said, "You're shivering. Are you actually sick?"

Before Little Ash could reply, she reached over and put the back of her hand to his forehead, checking for fever.

"Eat your breakfast," she said. "You're warm. They'll never let you leave if you get sick—and then where will poor Uriel be?"

Little Ash slapped her hand away, startled and bristling. "You eat your own breakfast, damn you."

"If you don't want to eat, then go talk to that nurse over there, and get Grandmother Rivke some hot tea with honey," said Rose, digging her spoon into the suspicious oatmeal. "Get some for yourself as well. And if you do see that doctor you're looking for, put something cold on your head first!"

Rivke was watching Little Ash with a calculating expression. "This doctor," she said. "What sort of doctor is he? Not an ordinary type?"

"A demon," said Little Ash, not caring if Rose thought it odd. She'd probably think he meant it metaphorically, anyway. As he looked around the room, he realized he didn't see any of the other demons from the waiting hall the day before. He was the only one. There had been a handful of others, waiting. If the doctor hadn't detained them—and wouldn't let them into the country—then where had they gone?

He had a terrible feeling that he knew exactly what had happened.

✧ ✧ ✧

Rose's cousin Bluma had left a message with Malke, at the bookshop, which was waiting when Uriel got back. Bluma said that she couldn't take a day off to visit Ellis Island because the factory bosses wouldn't allow it. This, of course, was part of the reason everyone was plotting to strike. Today was Friday; she would be able to go to Rose on Sunday only. She'd written a letter it could take to Ellis Island explaining the situation, so it could show the officials and maybe they'd let Rose go, but her accompanying message implied she had very little faith in this method.

After the rabbi's unhelpful response, Uriel could not find the energy to mind. It was already going to get Little Ash, so it might as well get Rose, too, and then they could all spend Shabbes in New York City, where the streets were paved with gold.

Somewhere tucked away in the letters of its name, it had found bitterness and sarcasm.

"I will go and find them," Uriel told Malke. "I will find a way to help them."

Malke sighed and nodded. She knew there was little to be done without hearings before a Board of Special Inquiry, which could take weeks and weren't guaranteed to go well. She had seen any number of cases where someone's friends and relatives couldn't get into the country or had to stay at the island until they recovered from illness they'd picked up on the ship. And of course she felt the heartbreak of her own father's death, and her own separation from her sister and niece and nephews.

"They like it better when you have more letters," she said. "Go to the *Women's Council House*, down the street. See if they will send a letter with you, to prove that Bluma is real. They know her there."

Uriel already felt exhausted by walking up and down all over New York, but it did agree with the Ellis Island officials when it came to the power of letters. It tucked Bluma's message carefully into its vest and followed Malke's directions down the street to the Council House, a place that Malke had named in English in the midst of her Yiddish sentences. This Council House belonged to the same National Council of Jewish Women that had provided Rose with her English phrase book on Ellis Island, and Uriel found it to be a clean, bright, and airy building with its door propped open in welcoming fashion. When it kissed the mezuzah, it sensed that this was a comforting place, overall, but had seen its fair share of strife also.

As it stepped over the threshold, a woman in a nurse's apron stuck her head out from the room on the right and said, "May I help you? No unaccompanied young men upstairs, please."

Uriel declined to inform her that it was neither young, in absolute terms, nor a man at all. "I need a letter for Ellis Island. Mrs. Malke Shulman sent me, from the bookshop."

"Oh!" The nurse's face opened up at this. "What sort of letter?"

"A friend has been stopped because she is a girl alone." This seemed to be a familiar problem. The woman invited Uriel into her little office, where three desks and a medicine cabinet were already squeezed in. One of the women at the other desks turned out to be a social worker, and at Uriel's request she filled in a form with Rose's name and Bluma's address, with an assurance that Rose would be well taken care of.

"Good luck to you," she said, handing it over. "Oh. And welcome to America."

Uriel tucked this second letter into its vest and went back out into the street. If it were truly welcome to America, it thought, it should not have needed to go back and forth so many times.

twenty-four

LITTLE ASH HAD NOT INTENDED for his plan to include Rose, but when he tried to slip unobtrusively out of the waiting room, she followed him.

"Where are you going? To find that doctor?"

"Yes," he said. "And you'd best sit here and wait for your cousin to come take you off the island, or else you'll miss her and be trapped forever."

"I don't like sitting, and I don't like waiting," said Rose. "Where are you going to look?"

They were on the main part of the island; there was a second set of buildings where the sickest passengers were sent to be looked after by nurses who Little Ash hoped had less malice in their hearts than the demon doctor. Little Ash had thought he would pretend he was simply wandering around, and go to the hospital, where he thought he could sniff out another demon without much trouble. The detainees weren't really supposed to wander about unsupervised, but the main thing was keeping them from getting on the ferries if they weren't allowed. He didn't think that anyone would pay him much attention. He could put on his most innocent face and pass for young enough to be engaged in childish mischief, if need be.

He did not want to tell Rose any of this, but she had caught hold of his sleeve to keep him in place, and she had very strong fingers.

He let out an irritated breath. "I'm going to the hospital. And you shouldn't come, because I'm going to cause trouble, and the doctor's very dangerous."

"All right. So you shouldn't go alone."

"Yes, I should. You don't understand."

"Then explain!"

Little Ash looked her in the eyes. For a moment Rose saw something in his face that she hadn't seen before, and she blinked in surprise. He had intended for the look to frighten her and make her let go, but it didn't work at all. Instead, she narrowed her own eyes.

"What is going on?" she hissed. "There's something strange. And don't think you can foist me off with some story about how I'm a girl and I'm too fragile and sensitive for whatever you're doing, because I could beat you in a fight."

"Fine. You want the truth? Have the truth. The doctor is a monster, and I think he's killed a few of the other immigrants—and if he changes his mind about me, he'll kill me too. And you're a human being, so you're much easier to kill, so go away."

"What, he's like a werewolf?" said Rose, incredulous. She liked telling frightening stories to Motl, to make him look over his shoulder if he had to visit the outhouse at night, but she had never personally put much stock in them. Still, she'd seen something in Little Ash's face. He didn't seem as if he were lying. He still looked frightened, and she'd come to know him well enough on the ship to be sure that wasn't something he liked people to notice. Plus the more she looked at him, the less she could deny that his eyes were very strange, like the eyes of some nocturnal creature. It made her head hurt, as if she were staring at something her eyes didn't want to focus on.

"Werewolves are stories for children," said Little Ash. "But yes."

"And you're going to hunt the werewolf? What makes you think he won't chew you up and spit you out, then? What if that whole hospital is full of werewolves? Don't be ridiculous. If you go sneaking off on your own, how will I tell Uriel where to find your body when he gets back?"

"When *it* gets back," said Little Ash. "You can tell it I've died doing a mitzvah."

"Stupid," said Rose. "You aren't going to die, because I'm going with you, so we can be smart about this. Why does a werewolf doctor want to kill you?"

"You're incredibly annoying," said Little Ash. "I told you he isn't a werewolf, and he'll want to kill me because I'm the only one who knows what he is. But if you insist on making a scene about it, then fine, you can be my lookout. Stand outside whatever room we're in and scream for your life on my signal, how's that?"

"Better," said Rose. "I'm not bad at screaming. The trick is to pretend there's a fire—or start one, if you have to."

Little Ash was done arguing. If Rose decided to set fire to a hospital, he decided, it would not be on his head. He turned away from her, looking down at the ground for the traces of the doctor's footsteps that would be visible only to another demon. Rose followed, watching him pause occasionally to crouch down and stare more closely at the floor, occasionally even sniffing the air.

Little Ash's demon instinct led them—dodging the occasional immigration official—to a door around the back of the hospital, which opened to a set of stairs going downward. He was not surprised that the doctor would be in a place like this. He had been in this situation many times before. They liked to do their work out of the way, where it was often difficult to hear cries for help. At least the petty types of sinners Little Ash was used to.

Before, though, he'd always dealt with humans. Other demons were not his business. He could socialize with other Jewish demons when they were around, although when they were his brothers he generally preferred not to. But he knew hardly anything at all about Christian demons and their magic. He couldn't be certain if the doctor had weaknesses. Little Ash would have liked to think the doctor was similarly ignorant of Jewish demons' ways, but he was not an optimist, and in any case, he'd felt the scraping sensation of the doctor's gaze turning his soul inside out. The doctor had seen what the ghost of the Belzer Rebbe had also seen: Little Ash hardly counted as a demon at all.

The proof of this, he supposed, was that as he looked down the stairs and inhaled the damp, decaying scent that came up from below, he found it reassuring to think he had someone at his back, even if that someone was only a human girl who was too bold for her own good.

"He's down here somewhere," he said. "I don't think you should follow me."

"I don't like the look of this," said Rose.

"This is my job," Little Ash told her. "This is what I do. So there's no need to fret over me like an old mother hen."

This he said expressly so that she would be offended and do the thing least like a mother hen. It worked just as intended, because she crossed her arms, planted her feet firmly, and glared at him.

"Fine, then. Scream when you need my help," she said.

"If I don't come back," said Little Ash, "say Uriel's name thirty-six times fast, and maybe you'll be granted a miracle."

He shut the door behind him, and just so Rose couldn't come running if he did scream, he locked it, leaving himself alone in the dark.

Alone, that is, until he saw the ghosts.

✧ ✧ ✧

Uriel arrived for the second time at Ellis Island, aboard a ferry packed with relatives eager to pick up their newly arrived family members, every one of them excited for reunions that were sometimes not as happy as expected. With its newfound skill in English, it was able to explain perfectly well to a clerk whom it was looking for, and show off Bluma's letter, but that clerk handed it off to another clerk, and that one to a third, and the third one brought it to the waiting room where the detainees were cooling their heels while the Board of Special Inquiry worked through its day's list. In the waiting room, Uriel did not find Rose, and it did not find Little Ash.

It did find Grandmother Rivke, sitting and waiting by herself. She'd been given some notes by yet another clerk, which she did not understand, and she was counting stitches in her knitting with the same determination that Uriel had brought to counting stops on the elevated train, as if her life nearly depended on the count.

Seeing her, Uriel felt the air leave its lungs, and it swayed on its feet. It felt in its bones that it was meant to stay by her. The path unfolded in front of its mind's eye. Rivke would have her hearing soon. She would have trouble with the translator's Yiddish, which was a different dialect from her own. She did not know that it wasn't her cough that had stopped her, but the suggestion that her son-in-law would not support her. She needed Uriel to speak her English.

Not Uriel, that is, but the angel.

The Universe was calling on it to leave its name behind.

It ought to allow itself to be the Angel of Rescuing the Captives, using its English and its luck and the way people looked at it and felt they ought to be their best selves in order to please it. This was what any angel would do in these circumstances; this was the mission it was meant to undertake in this moment, the open space in the Universe where it could tuck itself neatly and complete a picture of goodness.

But it did not want to do those things. It wanted to be Uriel, and it wanted to find Little Ash.

"Here," it said. "Here. The officials are worried you don't have enough money. This is from a rabbi, in uptown." It dug out from its pocket not only what Rabbi Wolf had given it, but the whole of the money Little Ash had given it from Reb Fishl. It was not sure what the value of it all was, but it was better than nothing. "I need to find—I need to go. I'm sorry."

It did not wait for Rivke to say anything. It had to leave the room before the wrongness of what it was doing tore it to pieces.

"Wait!" Rivke called, though Uriel was already running. "My dear! They went toward the hospital!"

On Ellis Island, sometimes people died. The immigrant processing center was not, of course, intended to be a place where people died, but after all, it was also a hospital, and people arrived there from having been on ships, and ships were full of sickness. Sometimes people died, and their ghosts, it seemed, had gathered under the hospital, clinging to the low, damp ceilings. There were more of them than Little Ash would have thought. Hundreds, though it was hard to tell in the low light, even with the excellent night vision of a cat-eyed sheyd.

They were whispering in all the languages of the earth, or at any rate, all the languages of those parts of the earth that skirted the Atlantic Ocean and the Mediterranean Sea. Most of them were simply lost and lonely, wishing for someone to remember and mourn them, or for relatives to come and claim their bodies—the sad, inevitable wishes of the forgotten dead. But some of them, Little Ash heard, his ears tuned always for scandal, were like the ghosts in the little shul in Warsaw, thirsty for revenge.

Some of them, the doctor had killed on purpose. Drinking the sparks of life out of them, touching them with hands they had hoped, but had not really thought, were intended to heal them.

Little Ash bent down and took off his shoes. It gave him a moment to think. This was his last chance to turn back. His mother was a water demon; he could simply jump into the harbor and swim ashore in New York City, and everyone would think that he had drowned. Or he could go back to Poland and work his way back through a different immigration station. Chicago, Cuba—he could go anywhere he liked. He ought to run, really. It was the selfish thing to do, and demons are not meant to be selfless.

But the angel was in New York, and how would he face

the angel if he did not chase down the killer who lurked behind America's gate?

"Can you help me?" he whispered to the nearest of the vengeful ghosts, as he tucked his socks into his empty boots. "I'll help you get your revenge if you'll lend me some magic."

At once he was met with a clamor of enthusiasm. All of the ghosts, not only the murdered ones, were excited to be spoken to, to be acknowledged. They were excited to have something to do.

There is only a very little spark of life inside a ghost. Just a whisper of it, which, if turned to substance in the hands of a demon, would not even make up the bulk of an olive.

But there were a lot of ghosts on Ellis Island.

The ghosts told Little Ash that he would find the doctor at the other end of the cellar, in the part that really was used as a morgue. The doctor had a handful of bodies down there, they said. Ones he'd brought down after the ships came yesterday, strange ones that hadn't been sick and had left no ghosts behind them.

The other demons he'd seen while waiting for processing, Little Ash supposed. Even with the borrowed magic of the ghosts to warm him, he shivered. How lucky he had been that the doctor had found him beneath concern.

Now that he had the ghosts at his back and knew the doctor for a murderer, it was easier to ignore the fear. He could stop thinking and follow his instincts, instead of trying to make plans with not enough information and no resources.

He found it much easier to move forward when he wasn't thinking.

twenty-five

THE DOCTOR WAS WAITING for him, as Little Ash had expected he would be. It would have been too much to hope for the element of surprise, even if the doctor weren't listening to the excited, rustling whispers of the ghosts. Anyone who could pluck every demon out of the crowd in the immigrant processing center and check on each of them individually, letting none through, would have to be alert to threats, even threats as small as Little Ash.

There were, indeed, a handful of bodies in the room: five of them, five empty bodies that had once been demons—Czech and Italian and Irish, some of them belonging to religions Little Ash had never heard of—demons Little Ash didn't know and perhaps wouldn't have talked to on the street, but with whom he now had something in common. Demons who had been more powerful than himself, and had died for it. Demons who had lived among humans, died, and left no ghosts among the ghosts of the humans they'd died with. How lonely. How sad, to die for no reason and leave nothing behind.

"I thought I was giving you a second chance," the doctor said, amused. He was leaning on one of the tables, his hand next to an uncovered corpse, as casually as if Little Ash had come upon him in his dining room instead of a dank and ice-cold basement under the Ellis Island hospital. "I thought to myself: this one's just a child, you're above this, just let him go. A good act, I thought. A bit of a sacrifice."

"You'll need more repentance than that," Little Ash said, "to get yourself back in the world's good graces."

"Lucky for me that I have no interest in redemption, then," said the doctor. "I've found myself a place in the world, and I intend to enjoy it for as long as possible. I meant to give you a bit of good advice, telling you to go back to Europe where you belong. You could have found a place, yourself, if you weren't so intent on causing trouble. Some muddy little village where you could cackle over the petty squabbles of your people."

Little Ash could have told him that merely walking into a room hardly counted as causing trouble. He had not told everyone on the island about the soul-stealing doctor. He had, in fact, only told Rose, who had barely seemed to believe him. He had stirred up the ghosts, yes. But the doctor didn't seem to notice the ghosts, some of whom, now, were creeping up under the table next to him. Perhaps, satisfied with his place in the world and with no thoughts to spare for repentance, he was not *able* to see them.

"I know where I belong," Little Ash said, taking a step to the side, so the table was between them. "I know where you belong, too, and it's not here at all. Here you're just making things worse for everyone. I don't know how it is in your religion, but in mine we don't play with people just to watch them suffering."

This was not really true. There were Jewish demons, too, who had no interest in the ultimate results of their troublemaking. But Little Ash had not been in a community of demons for a long time and had allowed himself to re-arrange the rules so that they pleased him better.

When the doctor stepped forward, the ghosts beneath the table grabbed him with ten small, grasping hands, giv-ing Little Ash time to duck away. The doctor stopped, con-fused, and looked around, but it seemed he really couldn't see the ghosts, and he brushed clumsily at the places where their claws had caught him, frowning.

Here, now, was Little Ash's element of surprise. He ducked underneath the table, coming up behind the doc-tor, but the demon was quicker to react than Reb Fishl had been, and as close as Little Ash had come, his fingers swiped harmlessly across the doctor's face. The doctor was off-balance already from trying to brush away the ghosts, and now he fell, Little Ash landing on top of him. The ghosts were still scurrying around like spiders, grabbing at what-ever part of the doctor they could find, which, now that he was on the floor, included his face. It seemed he could feel them, if not see them, because he swatted at the ones that got close to his eyes, and they disintegrated into nothing at his touch.

Little Ash reached again for the doctor's face, but the doctor caught him by the wrist, wrenching him to the side so strongly that his head smacked into the leg of the table. The doctor had the advantage of weight, and now he was angry, the emotion rising off him as searing cold, burning any ghosts who tried to touch him, and burning Little Ash's wrist where the doctor still squeezed it in a grip like iron. Little Ash clawed at him a third time with his free hand, and the doctor jerked his head back to avoid it, caught Little Ash by the collar, and slammed his head against the floor.

The ghosts were shouting very loudly now, enough to be heard over the ringing in Little Ash's ears as he tried to pry the doctor's fingers off his wrist. The doctor had him pinned, a knee on his chest. Little Ash was afraid that as soon as the magic he'd borrowed from the ghosts was used up, the doctor's anger might be enough to freeze him from the inside out, and his vision had blurred from hitting his head. He could no longer feel his left hand, the one the doctor was holding, and he struck blindly at the doctor's face with the other, but it was slapped aside. The doctor pressed his knee harder against Little Ash's chest, and there was a snap of bones, a taste of blood in his mouth as he bit down on his own tongue from the pain.

He had been so close, but now the doctor had a hand

free again, and Little Ash couldn't shift his weight, and the ghosts were hanging back, afraid to come any closer.

The doctor lifted his hand toward Little Ash's face. He felt the brush of a touch on his cheek and shut his eyes, clenching his jaw tight. Most demons would draw the soul out from the mouth, rather than the eyes as Little Ash liked to do. Perhaps, Little Ash thought, he could bite the man's fingers, and if not, at least Rose would let Uriel know where he'd gone. Before the doctor could catch hold of his soul, however, someone spoke, very loudly, in an authoritative English. Little Ash had never heard that voice speak English before, yet some part of him was always listening for it, and so he could not mistake it for the voice of anyone else.

"Let *go* of him," said Uriel.

Rose had struggled for a minute, jabbing at the lock with a hairpin to no effect, before cursing herself for an idiot and going to find another way into the hospital basement. On her way around the front of the building she had run into the angel, who was by now so agitated it was nearly in tears.

"I know where he is," said Rose, before it could speak. "Only we need to find another staircase, because he locked me out! Come on, act like you know what we're doing."

She gripped it by the hand and marched into the hospital, managing by force of will to look as if she belonged there. There were a couple of nurses in the hallway, but none paid Rose and Uriel much attention as the two of them checked doors until they found the one they needed.

"Ashel is down there with a doctor," said Rose. "He said the doctor is a werewolf who wants to kill him."

"Then I have to find him," said Uriel. "You stay here; it isn't safe."

It ran down the stairs without waiting for her reply. Rose clicked her tongue in disapproval. Why did they think she would simply stand around waiting?

Instead, she looked for something she could use as a weapon.

Uriel had only just come into the room, but angels and demons, when they want to, can move as quickly as thoughts, and the doctor had no time to react before it stepped forward and swung Little Ash's boots into his face. The doctor fell back, spluttering and lifting his hands to his nose, which Uriel had hit quite hard. The angel dropped Little Ash's shoes and grabbed the doctor's collar, lifting its hand to his eyes as it had seen demons do to each other, and as it had seen Little Ash do to Reb Fishl.

It wasn't quite sure how this procedure was supposed to work, but, as it turned out, it did not need to know the details. The doctor had hidden himself in the basement morgue for a reason, that being he preferred the cold and the dark, and tried to stay out of the sunlight when he could.

Uriel had broken out of its angelic path, but part of it was still a Flame of God, full of righteous anger. The magic blazing under its skin was much more powerful than even it had known. Its touch hurt the goyish demon much more than sunlight, burning through him so that it scorched him at his very heart. Little Ash, still lying on the floor, felt something pass over him like the shock wave that precedes an explosion, and the clammy basement room seemed suddenly to fill with heat. It occurred to him, in a way it never had before, that his friend was an angel, and an angel was a dangerous thing.

The doctor did not even have time to struggle before he seemed to melt away behind his own eyes, like ice into a puddle on a summer morning, until there was nothing left but a heavy, empty body, which Uriel dropped, startled, to the floor.

For a moment, no one spoke. The little ghosts crept forward, hesitantly, to prod the doctor's body and check for any signs of life, but they were silent. Little Ash sat up, carefully, taking shallow breaths and counting places he felt pain. His left hand wouldn't move, and like most demons, he preferred that hand over the other. He would have to heal that first, but there wouldn't be much magic left over for his broken ribs. He had borrowed as much as he could from the ghosts, and he had used nearly all of it, and for what? He had done nothing. He felt an unfamiliar, oppressive feeling weighing him down as he looked at the handful of ghosts who were left. Perhaps it was enough, for them, to have their vengeance. But Little Ash did not feel that he, himself, had done enough.

This feeling is called *responsibility*, and it is not a comfortable feeling for a creature like Little Ash to have.

While its study partner was engaged in knitting the tendons of his hand together again, Uriel simply stood where it was, shocked into a strange stillness. It stared at the demon it had just killed without even quite knowing it had intended to do so. It, too, had felt the shock wave, but behind that wave of energy there had been a terrible nothingness. Uriel lifted its hands and looked at its blistered palms, scorched from within by a power it did not know it had. There was a ringing in its head, as if some great voice had stopped crying out. The voice that always told it where it was needed next. It was now receiving no instructions, and it could not even remember what to do with its own limbs. Where once there had been the endless singing of the Universe, now there was nothing but emptiness. Rejecting its last task had changed its nature entirely. All its life there had been someone holding it with the tenderness of an attentive parent, and now, suddenly, there was no one. It had run away from those sheltering hands when it came here to kill the doctor, and now it was alone.

"I didn't know you spoke *English*," said Little Ash, at last. Aside from the word *English*, though, he said it in Aramaic.

"I needed to, so I did," said Uriel. It had been holding its hands before its face as if it had forgotten it had them, but now it seemed to remember, and scrubbed them on its trousers, rather frantically. "Ashel, I think we had better go."

"I'd love to," said Little Ash. "I'd love nothing more than to leave this place and never ever come back. But we ought to bring Rose with us; I left her upstairs."

Uriel had forgotten about Rose, but at that moment she came into the room, rather out of breath and carrying a curtain rod.

She stopped in her tracks at the sight of the bodies on the tables, and the doctor on the floor. For a moment they thought she would scream, but then she merely took a quick breath and squared her shoulders.

"So, you didn't die," she said to Little Ash.

"I suppose not," said Little Ash, flexing the wrist and fingers of his left hand to make sure they were working.

Uriel was relieved to see that, other than a troubled knot between his eyebrows, Little Ash seemed unchanged. Whatever it had done to the doctor, Little Ash had not been hurt by it. It bent down to help him to his feet with its hands under his arms, but the movement jostled his still-broken ribs, and he shoved it away with an inarticulate howl of pain.

"Don't touch me," he hissed. "So, we have Rose. If anyone sees me they'll stop me from leaving. Get me a skirt or something."

Uriel stepped away. It didn't like Little Ash quiet, and it certainly didn't like him too hurt to complain about it in words, as he usually did. It would have preferred to look at his injuries itself, to see what it could do to help, but the tone of his voice made it hesitate to come too close. Instead, it glanced around for some way to disguise him, and saw only the doctor's victims laid out on their slabs. Did Little Ash want to borrow a dress from a corpse?

Rose had heard him, too, and was quicker to react than Uriel. Holding herself a little stiffly, so as to control the scream that was in fact building inside her, she put aside her curtain rod and stepped over to one of the morgue tables. One should treat the dead with respect, but it was too late for that. Borrowing a skirt from one of the bodies was an awkward business, but she was able to do it without leaving the girl uncovered. After a moment's thought, she took the doctor's coat from a hook on the wall and covered the body with that as well.

Little Ash put his boots back on, moving slowly so as not to jostle either his ribs or his head, which was still rattling. The ghosts, he noticed, had all gone away. It seemed there was nothing keeping them any longer. He decided to have Kaddish said for them anyway, to rid himself of the awkward weight which seemed to drag on all his limbs whenever he tried to move them.

He got to his feet and Rose presented him with the skirt. Little Ash put it on without changing his own face as he usually did, and as he had done in the synagogue in Warsaw. He had no magic left to do it.

"Are you all right?" Uriel asked cautiously, seeing this.

"Are you?" Little Ash snapped.

This question was so difficult to answer, it decided not to answer at all, and it merely completed his disguise for him by taking off its shawl and putting it over his head, which Little Ash halfheartedly complained made him look like a greenhorn, but at least hid his face a little, and his short hair.

Really, he liked the weight of it, and the way, if he turned his head just a bit to the side, he could smell the angel's Torah-scroll scent in the fabric. The sight of it burning the doctor to nothing with only its bare hands had shaken him more than he would like to admit, but there was some re-assurance in knowing that it was, nevertheless, still his partner.

"We should go," said Rose. "Right now. Or else I will start screaming and never be able to stop."

twenty-six

NO ONE STOPPED THEM as they left the basement, and the ghosts, and the corpses. No one seemed to notice them at all, until they got back to the room where Uriel had left Rivke for her hearing, and found her there with her papers newly stamped for America.

"The money you gave me," she said to Uriel. "They were reassured by it. My son-in-law will have to take me now: I'm a wealthy woman."

She tossed her head back and laughed, for a moment looking years younger.

"Oh!" said Rose, remembering suddenly that the world was not only full of dark basements and demons, but also mundane obstacles. "Uriel, did you find my cousin?"

"No," said Uriel. "That is, she couldn't come. I can speak English now, like a real American, and I have documents.

Everyone said the officials like these very much, the documents."

Little Ash was surprised to hear it speak so confidently. It had been so strange on the ship, seeming not entirely present, that he had been very worried it was losing hold of itself and would go to pieces in America without him by its side. Instead it seemed somehow to have made itself stronger.

Rose could perhaps have felt frightened to be approaching an immigration official on the arm of someone she had just helped to handle a corpse. But the air in the morgue had felt sinister in a way she had never imagined, and she could not bring herself to be afraid of Uriel, who felt solid and warm and real at her side.

She might scream later. Just to be rid of the feeling. But for now, she wanted to be as far from Ellis Island as possible.

"I was told I could go if I had a relative with me," Rose told the clerk they had managed to corner. "My cousin couldn't come, because of her bosses, but look, I have letters."

The clerk looked her over, then looked at Uriel. It seemed to him that this was a regular greenhorn of the type who were always falling victim to scams and illnesses—more likely that than a procurer, but still. You never knew what schemes these people would come up with. "Show me the letters."

Rose showed him the letters from Bluma and the Council of Jewish Women, and he read them over very slowly, looking from the letters to Rose's own papers and back, checking each line against the others as if to root out any deception or inconsistency.

"You must let her go," said Uriel, when it seemed the man was hesitating. "You see, this Women's Council has said she will bring nothing evil to your America. She is only one girl, with a family."

"And who are you?" the official said, giving it another once-over, also taking in Little Ash and Rivke standing behind them, Rivke leaning on the demon's arm as if he were one of her own grandchildren.

"We are family," said Uriel.

"Married?"

"No, not married." It had prepared this story on its way back to the island, using Little Ash's technique for their identity papers as a base. "Cousins, only."

"I've got everything I need to get in," Rose insisted. "See, I have twenty American dollars. I have my health. I'm not going alone. I have a place to live, yet."

The official finally took out his stamp and stamped her papers. "Welcome to America, Miss Cohen."

Welcome to America!

They boarded the ferry in a mood of celebration, Uriel and Little Ash and Rose, and Grandmother Rivke with one of her older grandchildren, who'd been sent up from the Lower East Side to check on her and was astonished to find her grandmother ready to come home, and with fifty dollars in her pocket. Reb Fishl's stock of American dollars had been more generous than Uriel realized.

While Rivke was relating her story to her granddaughter, Rose turned to Little Ash and Uriel. "Now that that's over, are you going to explain what happened? Are you some sort of miracle workers? Is that what Dinah's grandfather does in his yeshiva, hunts monsters? Is that why she thinks Saul is so amazing? Why wouldn't she have told me if she had a secret like that!"

She was ready to be very displeased with Dinah, but Little Ash said, "Actually, we lied about being that rebbe's students. We aren't, at all."

"I think I was," said Uriel. "On the ship, only. He taught me how to keep breathing in my sleep."

"Yes, well." Little Ash didn't have the energy to feel resentful toward the rebbe. "All the same. I don't know if he did miracles or not, but he has nothing to do with anything."

"What, then?" said Rose.

"Like we told you, we're looking for Essie, from our shtetl. Her father couldn't afford to go to Warsaw to find out what happened to her, so we went. And we found out that she was in America, but her letters back were being stopped, and someone called Fishl was extorting money from her. The same happened to your Dinah's grandfather, only he died in Warsaw, so Uriel took his things to bring to his daughter, since we were looking for Essie anyway."

"That doesn't explain anything at all!" Rose protested. "I don't know how you killed that doctor, and Ashel, I saw your feet when you took your boots off, and they looked very strange."

"Oh, you noticed?" Little Ash supposed that in the midst of confronting something so unusual as a murderous doctor, Rose must have forgotten to ignore his feet as adult humans usually did. Or perhaps she was simply cleverer than most. He liked Rose, so he decided it must be cleverness. "Yes, I'm a wicked demon, very dangerous to your soul."

Rose sniffed. "You don't seem dangerous."

Little Ash, in fact, didn't feel very dangerous either. His ribs hurt. He was trying to think of something to say that wouldn't reveal just how sullen he felt—the sullenness seemed unworthy of him, and uncomfortably close to childishness—but Uriel spoke before he could.

"He is more dangerous than you might think. He killed Reb Fishl and ate his soul."

"Really? How does one eat a soul?"

"He plucked it out through his eyes and swallowed it," said Uriel. "I tried to do it to the doctor, but I don't know how." It looked down at its hands, rubbing one thumb over the blisters. "Honestly, I don't know what happened."

"Are you both demons, then?" said Rose. "Are there demons everywhere? Even here in America? Somehow I thought it . . . I don't know. It seems awfully *Old Country* to be a demon. Doesn't it?"

"What do you know about America," said Little Ash. "You're just as Old Country as anyone."

At the Shulmans' bookshop in Hester Street, they found Rose's cousin Bluma helping Freidy and Malke prepare dinner, which was especially luxurious as it was Shabbes evening and Malke had, with optimism, told the girls to prepare as if they knew Rose was coming, as a sort of charm to ensure her success. Malke, rather than allow the news of her father's death to weigh her down with despair, had chosen to treat Rose's arrival and that of Uriel and Little Ash as a homecoming to be celebrated as she would have celebrated the rebbe's own arrival.

"Reyzele!" Bluma exclaimed, putting down the cloth with which she had been dusting the holiday plates and running to hug her cousin. "You've gotten so tall, so beautiful! Oh, I'm so glad they let you off the island. I felt so guilty! But the bosses at the factory don't let us go until the very last minute, even though the owner is Jewish himself— and everyone says he goes out gambling on Fridays, and leaves his wife at home alone. And he calls himself a mensch! But here you are, my darling cousin! A woman already! Look at you!"

Despite her assertion that Rose had grown up, Bluma couldn't resist pinching her cheek, then kissing it, and then pulled on her hair for good measure, as if she simply couldn't contain herself. Bluma had been in America for two years, during which time Rose had gone from a gangly fourteen-year-old to indeed a more settled image of herself, and besides, she was wearing the new dress she'd made on the ship, with Little Ash's tweaks to the tailoring, which made her look particularly sophisticated.

"Uriel pretended to be a relative for me," said Rose. "The man at the island didn't seem to care so much. It's all right, I'm all right! I was hardly there for any time at all."

Uriel introduced Little Ash to Malke. After they had left the ferry, the demon had removed his disguise and now looked like himself again. For Malke's benefit they pretended that Little Ash, like Uriel, had been a student of her father's, which meant that he, too, was subjected to kisses on the cheek, these ones born of gratitude.

"I wish my father had been able to see the baby," she said. "But thank you for bringing his books. The case smells like him—it almost seems as if I can feel him in the room. As if he were sitting at this table, studying, while I cooked this afternoon. I tell you, for the first time I felt so at home here . . ."

She trailed off, lost in her thoughts. Little Ash drew Uriel aside and whispered to it, "Is the ghost still here? He won't show himself to me."

"I haven't seen him," Uriel whispered back. "Not since they said Kaddish yesterday. But why should he be here for me? He is with his daughter now."

Little Ash noticed something odd about how it said this, as if it did not entirely believe its own words. He didn't bother to ask about it, as he was glad to know the rebbe was not watching and judging him unseen. Little Ash did not much care about the rebbe's reunion with his daughter, and only cared that Uriel would now, he hoped, have more time for him. He wanted to ask it what had really happened to the doctor, and how on earth it had managed to burn its hands, and whether it wanted him to bury its identity papers so it could go back to being normal.

Uriel, for its part, would very much have liked to answer all of Little Ash's questions, and also to ask him what foolishness possessed him to go after the doctor by himself, but they were constrained by the rules of hospitality to enjoy their Shabbes dinner in the home of the Shulmans, so all it did was squeeze his hand before Malke's husband came in and they had to go around introducing themselves again.

twenty-seven

As the Shulmans and Bluma worked at Mr. Boaz's factory, and Malke and her husband's family were all in debt to Mr. Boaz, much of the conversation over dinner was about their plans for a strike against him.

"It didn't use to be like this," Issak Shulman said. He'd been explaining to the newcomers that his mother had contracted a sickness of her lungs, a tailor's cough, and Mr. Boaz had refused to let her rest without losing her job. She'd gotten sicker and sicker until she died, and then the whole family had been kept from mourning. There was something of the righteous warrior in Isaak's character, and he had taken on a leading role in the strike planning in hopes that he could win for the workers the right to rest. Only once this goal was accomplished could any of them stop to grieve their mother, and now, Malke's father, lost across the sea. While Isaak told the tale, his father, the widower, kept his head bent over the table. He had a long beard and sidelocks, and a quiet manner that reminded Rose of her own father, the absent-minded scholar.

"This Boaz is everywhere," Little Ash whispered to Uriel. "Essie works for him too."

Uriel had been listening carefully, trying to untangle what exactly was meant by *strike*. Such things were not entirely uncommon in the Pale, of course, but Uriel, having never left its small village, was not familiar with them and supposed they were an American phenomenon. Now that Little Ash had reminded it of Essie, it realized it only needed to understand one thing: that Mr. Boaz was wicked and should be given the chance to mend his ways. Perhaps he needed a push, as from an angel, or a shove, as from a demon like Little Ash. Either way, this was the mission that had brought them to America, and even if it did not hear the voice of the Universe in its head to tell it so, it knew that going after Mr. Boaz was the right thing to do.

It was surprised to find that it was more pleased than lonely at the thought of deciding the right thing for itself.

"Do you know an Essie, Esther Singer?" Little Ash asked the table at large. "She is from our village. She used the same emigration agent that Malke used, and I think she works for Mr. Boaz also."

"Esther Singer?" Bluma exchanged looks with Freidy. "She's not a seamstress."

"No," Little Ash agreed. "I didn't think she would be. She was always with her father, in the books, learning. Until she got too old to be in the study hall, and then I think she started reading newspapers and things."

"Is she that girl . . ." said Freidy. "You remember? The girl who does the books, up at his house—she came to the factory once, only."

"Oh! She was pretty—with spectacles?" said Bluma.

"Yes," said Rose. "Yes, they showed me a picture of her, on the ship."

"She does have spectacles," Little Ash agreed.

"She works up at his house," said Freidy. "Uptown—he's very rich, you know."

Little Ash and Uriel exchanged glances. They would have to find a way into Mr. Boaz's house.

"She didn't seem very happy when she came by," said Freidy. "She was looking at the account books. She looked tired."

"Who wouldn't be tired, trying to chase Mr. Boaz's money," said Bluma scornfully. "Every cent he squeezes out of us, he throws away on cards the night after."

"A girl accountant?" said Rose, very interested.

"I suppose she's cheaper than a man," said Bluma. "We all are."

"Show us her picture," said Malke. "If we see it, maybe we'll know her. She could have come into the bookshop."

Little Ash got up to look for Essie's letters in his satchel, which was sitting by the rebbe's trunk against the wall. Uriel, meanwhile, was staring at the Shabbes candles and wondering if it ought to feel more uncomfortable with all of this un-Shabbesdik talk. Should they not be singing psalms? But on the other hand, should they not try to find Essie as quickly as possible, in case she was unwell?

Malke and Isaak considered the photograph at length and finally agreed that they thought Essie had come into the bookshop before, but they hadn't seen her in some time.

"She used to read the revolutionary pamphlets," said Isaak. "I always remember who buys those, because my father doesn't want me stocking so many—but it's what people want, you know, they don't want a Chumash! Here, if you want to find her, since you're landsmen, why not look for her tomorrow at the Cafe Krakow? It's down on the corner, and all the revolutionaries like to drink their coffee there."

Little Ash's eyes lit up at this. He liked very much the sound of drinking coffee with revolutionaries, and on the Sabbath no less. He'd been feeling very sour toward America since the doctor first cornered him, but this brought him back a spark of his own self. He looked at Uriel and found that it was watching him.

"Morning services, first," it said.

"To hell with morning services!" said Little Ash, because this was what the angel should expect from him. "I have been a prisoner—why should my first morning of freedom be spent in services!"

"Because," said Uriel, "that way you will remember who it was that saved you."

Practically speaking, Uriel was the one who'd saved him.

✧ ✧ ✧

The little shul Uriel found on Hester Street the next morning was simply a shop front converted by the addition of curtains across the front windows and a handcrafted Torah ark on the back wall. The women's section consisted of a corner blocked off with a row of chairs, which were easily removed when it became clear that no women would be in attendance. Little Ash and Uriel took their habitual spot near the door, as they always used to do in Poland, and Uriel relaxed at the familiarity of the prayers and melodies and the crowd of old men who filled the room. Where Rabbi Wolf's uptown synagogue had made Uriel feel small and shabby, in this one it felt like itself again, happy to enumerate the world's blessings to itself and to the Universe while Little Ash stood on one foot next to it, looking around curiously and not praying, just like himself.

Little Ash noted that this shul had only a couple of ghosts, none of them particularly active, most nearly ready to fade away. Otherwise he saw only the petty sins and squabbles of ordinary people, not too good and not too bad, who worked hard but still gave their Saturday mornings to performing a mitzvah. Many of them were tired, some almost falling asleep on their feet, but there was no sign of wickedness of the kind that would catch his attention. Thus he, too, was able to relax, and took comfort in the sound of Uriel whispering its prayers beside him, with its shawl over its head.

The two of them left the shul in a better mood than they had had going in, and Uriel even agreed that it would be better to find Essie sooner rather than later, even if it meant going, on Shabbes, to a cafe, a place where it knew Little Ash would be tempted to cause trouble and spend money. The cafe was only a few doors down from the shul, and where the shul had a little knot of older men with their heads covered outside, sharing their gossip, the cafe had a knot of younger people—mostly men, still, but with a woman or two among them—standing outside smoking cigarettes and sharing gossip of their own. In fact, the angel was rather relieved at what it saw there, as this seemed to be in its own way a gathering for study.

"I thought this place would be more wicked," it whispered to Little Ash as they went inside. "But I don't see those little creatures that run around where people are unkind."

"The creeping beasts?" said Little Ash, surprised. "The sins that run around like insects? You can see those? I thought you could only see the hidden holiness in things."

"I don't know," said Uriel. "I mean, I started seeing them on the ship, I think. Only I didn't realize until yesterday, at Ellis Island, that that doctor's morgue was full of them."

Little Ash frowned. "On the ship?"

"After I spoke to the rebbe, I think . . ." It tried to remember, and could not. "Certainly not before we saw Reb Fishl. I don't remember seeing them by him. I thought I should ask you about them, only I forgot."

"You shouldn't be seeing those," said Little Ash. "Those are for demons. Must be my fault, because I put my tears in your eyes—but that was supposed to wear off."

"The rebbe said it did," said Uriel, doubtfully. It was not sure it should bring up that conversation with the rebbe, recalling that it had also said the wrong thing to or about Little Ash and had offended him. "I could only see him because he taught me another way to do it, with Holy Names. And I don't like that way. It makes me very tired."

"Of course my charm wore off," said Little Ash. He was somewhat relieved to think that if something strange was going on with his friend, it was not because he'd done his magic wrong. "But then why can you see them?"

Their speculation was interrupted, at that moment, by Rose, who had not attended morning services but had decided to find her friends at Cafe Krakow once services were over. She was determined that they should not leave her out of whatever plan they had to rescue the mysterious Essie, girl accountant, with the freckles that, from looking at the photograph again the night before, Rose had confirmed were very fetching. She also was not sure if Mr. Boaz was secretly a werewolf, or vampire, or some such creature like the doctor on Ellis Island, and if he was, she wanted to know about it. Rose believed in having information.

"Well?" she said, appearing at Little Ash's elbow. "Have you found Essie yet?"

"We haven't asked," said Uriel.

"I've never been in a revolutionary cafe before," said Rose. "I wonder what my family would think. I suppose they'd be a bit worried."

She wished she could tell Dinah, and quickly suppressed

it. She could imagine all too vividly the look on Dinah's face. The secret thrill that went through her imagining Dinah being equal parts frightened and impressed by Rose's boldness was too much like admitting that she missed Dinah after all.

"Uriel has never been in a revolutionary cafe before either," said Little Ash. "Look at you both, you'll be ungreened in no time."

"And look at you, a greenhorn also!" said Rose. "Excuse me!"

This was addressed to the nearest table of young gentlemen, who were having a heated discussion over a Yiddish newspaper and several cups of coffee each. They were surprised to be interrupted by a girl, and there was a quick discussion between the group before one agreed to be the representative and spoke up.

"Yes, comrade miss?"

"I'm looking for someone. She's called Esther Singer, or Essie, and she's from . . ." She looked over her shoulder at Little Ash.

"She's from a very small village in Poland," said Little Ash. "No one will have heard of it. We're looking for her, for her family."

There was a second round of discussion, and then the spokesman said, "Actually, it's been a while since anyone saw Essie. That is, we know Essie! We know Essie very well! Only, she hasn't been in for a while."

"She works at Mr. Boaz's house," said another from the group. "Uptown."

"He's very rich," said the spokesman. "May his name be cast into the dust."

There was general approval around the table at the curse.

"Do you all work for him too?" Rose asked. "My cousin works at his factory. Only she had to work today, even though it's Shabbes."

"Oh no, we don't work for him at all. He won't have our kind in his factory. We're rabble-rousers."

"Oh, right."

"Why does Essie work for him, then?" said Little Ash. "If she's your kind also?"

There was some argument over this, and then the spokesman said, "We don't know. She didn't talk about it much."

It soon transpired that none of them had asked Essie many questions, or indeed given much thought to her at all since they'd seen her last, which could have been two weeks ago or could have been a month ago. Rose and Little Ash were beginning to be quite exasperated with them when Uriel gently took them each by an elbow and led them away.

"We know that Essie used to come here," it said. "And she used to come to the bookshop. She has not come to either place in some time. She works at Mr. Boaz's house. So we must find Mr. Boaz's house, and see if Essie is there."

"We, you and me," said Little Ash. "Not we, three of us. Don't tell Rose what we're doing—we'll never get rid of her now!"

"You weren't getting rid of me anyway," said Rose. "How do you plan to approach a girl you don't know and talk to her out of nowhere? She'll talk to me, because I'm also a girl!"

"I can be a girl," said Little Ash, disgruntled. "Besides, it's dangerous."

"Oh, 'dangerous,' 'dangerous,' you keep saying this. It seems to me that coming to America is dangerous, and I'm here already. Bluma was supposed to get me a job at that factory, so I'm already involved. Shouldn't I take things into my own hands if I want to get my labor's worth to send home to my family?"

"She is right," said Uriel. "Ashel, I think it is good to have help."

"Fine, fine," said Little Ash. "Since I'm outnumbered."

twenty-eight

THE END OF THE SATURDAY workday at Boaz Brothers Fine Garments saw Little Ash, Rose, and Uriel waiting outside of the factory, in as inconspicuous a fashion as they could, to see if the *shop boss* Mr. Boaz would reveal himself, and lead them to his home. No one in the neighborhood had managed to tell them where it was in any greater detail than "uptown," and so they had resorted to this method. Uriel had put away its shawl for safekeeping, and Little Ash had given it his cap so that it could tuck away its long sidelocks and keep its head covered without being so obviously a greenhorn. To Rose, he had given his knife, which was longer and sharper than an ordinary pocketknife and, he told her, probably a better weapon than a curtain rod, if it came to that.

The Boaz Brothers factory was one of a stack of textile

factories in a ten-story building just on the edge of the Jewish neighborhood. Boaz Brothers occupied the second and third floors, and the staircases were kept locked during the day, so that no one should wander out with fabric in their pockets or take breaks when they hadn't been told to. This standard practice applied to all of the factories in the building, and so it was easy to keep an eye on who was coming out at the end of the day, as they all came by the same path and at the same time. Little Ash and Uriel took one corner of the building and Rose the other, placing themselves so that they could see the doors without immediately being noticed. Rose in particular did not want to be distracted by conversation with Bluma: she didn't want her cousin to know what she was up to, as sensible Bluma would surely both stop her and tell her parents.

The workers came out at the end of the day with an air of relief, despite their exhaustion. Knots of girls chatted together, excited for a night at the dance halls after sitting all day at the machines, their legs turning to stone. The burly men who wielded the great cutting knives lit cigarettes on their way down the street, some of them discussing a passage of Talmud as they passed by Uriel and Little Ash, and some others talking about their plans for the strike, and how they'd heard some of the other factories were planning strikes as well. It seemed New York was a land of discontentment.

Mr. Boaz did not emerge until most of the workers had already gone, and his arrival was preceded by a shiny automobile, which pulled up in front of the factory.

"Silly of us," said Little Ash, "watching so close all this time, as if he'd go home on his own two feet. But if he leaves in that, I don't know how we'll chase him."

It turned out he did not need to worry about running after a motor vehicle. Mr. Boaz came out, dressed in a pin-striped suit and wearing a mustache like a Christian. He did not get into the automobile, but instead handed a paper-wrapped package through the window and spoke briefly to the driver before waving him off. The car pulled away, slowed by the progress of pedestrians who didn't much care about getting out of the way. Mr. Boaz, hands in pockets, turned in another direction and headed toward the Bowery.

"He'll pass by Rose," said Little Ash. "We should follow."

Mr. Boaz was not alert to being followed, but even if he had been, they were not terribly conspicuous on the street. Tonight was the night before most workers' single day off, and the young people were ready to enjoy themselves as much as they could before their feet gave way beneath them. Little Ash, Rose, and Uriel, looking like three greenhorns just escaped from their day at the tailors' shop, fit well into the crowd headed for the Chinese restaurants and the dance halls.

"Dancing!" said Little Ash with triumph, when Boaz's destination became clear. It was a gaudy, gilt-fronted build-ing like a theater, with the sounds of cheerful talk and fid-dle music spilling into the street.

"Dancing," repeated Rose. "My father's heart would

tremble! Oh, how I wish Dinah could be here," she added wistfully, speaking more to herself than her friends. She had dreamed so often of seeing Dinah, free of responsibility, indulging in the small, cheerful wickedness of young girls alone.

"This is one of the dens of iniquity they foster in America," said Little Ash to Uriel, a gleeful look on his face. "Do you dare step over the threshold?"

"If you are with me," said Uriel, declining to take the bait.

Indeed, the angel found it was more curious than anything else. The people outside the dance hall looked more happy than iniquitous. There were a few little scuttling sins here and there, but not as many as it had seen on the streets uptown. Perhaps the warm golden light from the windows was making them harder to see.

"I'm sure there's worse wickedness inside," said Little Ash. He, too, was watching the sins, a little frown on his face. "If that Boaz went in. Did you see the thing clinging onto him?"

"No," Uriel admitted. "Was it something terrible?"

"Some sort of dybbuk," said Little Ash. "With its fingers half-sunk into his flesh. He's called down some curse on himself, that Boaz."

There was a vicious light in his eyes. Little Ash enjoyed curses cast on sinful people. They gave him a way in, an excuse to behave as terribly as he liked. If he could swallow Mr. Boaz's soul, he thought, he'd feel much better about himself. He'd forget the scrape of the Ellis Island doctor's scrutiny on the surface of his soul.

"Well?" said Rose. "I came here to America to be wild, and here's a place where people are wild—why are we standing around outside?"

It was not traditional for girls to pay their own way into a dance hall, but Rose had all that was left of Uriel's American money, so she paid the nickel for each of them and they went inside. It was not immediately clear where Mr. Boaz had gone. The dance hall was crowded and bright, loud with music and laughter, so that Uriel had to reach for Little Ash's sleeve in order not to lose him.

The dance hall was, by the standards of New York City, not as rich or elegant a place as it appeared to one young woman and two magical creatures who had lived most of their lives in little towns. Belz and Shtetl lacked such things as electric lights and places that existed for dancing only. The dance hall had been decorated in the manner of a theater, with gold paint on the plaster-molded walls, and plenty of lights, which were intended to give the impression of great luxury to those who paid their nickel to come in at the end of a long day of work. Little Ash, if he had bothered to remember the palace of his father Ashmedai, might have recognized that this place was not really so gilded and decorated as that, but he was never one to judge a place for cheapness and gaudiness when he could see that it was full of people chasing, without restraint, after things that gave them pleasure. Besides, he liked the music very much.

Uriel had no way of understanding what was cheap and what was expensive when it came to lights and gilding and such things as that. It was simply astonished by the sight of so many young people packed close and full of happiness. The young people of Shtetl were never so great in number, and even the most joyous simcha in that little village never glittered and glowed like the dance hall seemed to do. It could tell, from looking, that some of the people in the dance hall were there with the intention of committing sin, but it did not want to scold anyone tonight. It looked at Little Ash, and the way his eyes were shining, and realized more than anything it wanted to dance with him.

Rose was equally delighted by the gold paint and the lights, and the number of pretty girls in bright dresses and hats who whirled about the room. Wouldn't it be nice to have Dinah with her, so they could join those girls! Or if not Dinah, perhaps Essie. From what the factory girls had said, it seemed Essie wasn't seen in places like this. Did she have no friends to go with? Rose had not made girl friends yet either. They could fill the space for each other.

"I told you it was a Golden Land," said Little Ash. He scraped a bit of gold paint off the wall and held his hand up in front of Uriel's face. "You see?"

"They all look very happy," said Uriel. "But there must be some unhappiness here, or that Mr. Boaz would not have come."

"Where is he, anyway?" said Rose. "He's too old for this place!"

"There." Little Ash pointed to a door at the back of the room. "Let's see what's in the back."

Little Ash led Uriel by the hand toward the back of the room, Rose close behind them. They threaded their way through the groups of young men and women who were waiting at the edges of the room to catch one another's eyes, or gossiping, or in the case of a few, making little illegal transactions under their breaths. Little Ash was quite at home in places like this, but Uriel gazed around with wide eyes, fascinated by everything. Rose walked with her best appearance of confidence, but kept close on the others' heels.

There was a man leaning against the frame of the door at the back, scowling under his hat and looking about in a way that made Little Ash draw to a halt before they were noticed. There was a little counter that sold drinks nearby, and the demon suddenly drew Uriel aside, as if he had intended to buy it a treat the whole time.

"He's guarding something," he hissed, grabbing for Rose's sleeve as she veered off course. "Pretend we aren't interested, and keep your ears open to hear what it is."

The drinks counter sold schnapps and lemonade and that new wonder, carbonated soft drinks, which Little Ash had tried once when he was exploring the larger towns in Poland. He wrangled another handful of nickels from Rose and sent Uriel to purchase ginger beer, as Uriel now spoke English but Little Ash did not trust its ability to eavesdrop on a frowning gangster in the midst of the crowd. He and Rose stood by the wall while the angel waited in line.

"You're being noticed in that dress," the demon said, in part so that Rose might give him the credit he deserved for his help in tailoring it, and partly to look natural. "A real modern lady you look in it."

"Thank you, I suppose," said Rose. She glanced around to see if he was telling the truth. "Who's noticed me?"

"That boy with the mustache, over there," said Little Ash.

Rose looked, and made a face. "No, thank you."

"If he comes over to ask for a dance, you want I should stamp on his ankles?"

"I can tell him no for myself, actually."

"Of course you can—I gave you a knife."

Uriel came back with three cold bottles of ginger beer. It should be noted that the angel was getting as much attention as Rose was. It had a beautiful face; it could have danced with anyone, if it liked. But it did not notice. Little Ash noticed, and said nothing, because it grieved him that they had no time for dancing.

"Try this," he said instead, opening Uriel's bottle for it. "It's like nothing you've ever had before; you'll learn something."

"What is it? What blessing do I make?"

"I don't know; spices, I suppose."

Uriel obediently took a sip, and found that the drink was very strange and seemed somehow alive, which alarmed it terribly, until Little Ash broke out laughing at the look on its face, and it realized he was teasing it.

"It's bubbles, you see?" he said, as it massaged the bridge

of its nose to try and get rid of the sensation. "I don't know how they make it do that. Isn't it interesting?"

"I think it is very horrible," said Uriel, which made Little Ash laugh harder. "Ashel, you dreadful creature. You knew I wouldn't like it!"

"No I didn't," Little Ash insisted, taking the bottle back though he'd set his own unopened one on the floor by his feet. He took a drink himself, as if to prove that ginger beer was not poison. "I thought you would appreciate the miracle."

"You're a wicked, awful thing," said Uriel, fondly. "Show me something that is better to drink."

Little Ash obligingly brought it over to the counter and bought it a lemonade, which it liked very much, and a schnapps, which it liked less at the first taste but then felt compelled to taste again. Rose finished her ginger beer and Uriel drank another glass of schnapps while they waited for a sign of anything happening in the back room.

Soon the angel found that its cheeks were growing warm, and everything looked softer than it had before. When it lifted its hands and cupped Little Ash's face in them, it found that his cheeks also were soft, but cooler than its own. It almost wanted to press their two faces together, to see if his cool skin would feel soothing. Little Ash's eyelashes cast a shadow that hid the bruises under his eyes, and with the bright lights, Uriel could see the galaxy of his freckles. This face it knew better than its own, because it only ever saw its own face by accident, and Little Ash's face it was always either looking at, or searching for. It wanted to tell him everything that had ever happened, in its whole existence, and why every single thing it was telling him had led to them both being here, and why that was a miracle.

"Ashel," Uriel said. "Will you dance with me?"

Little Ash could not avoid the question, since Uriel was holding his head between its hands and gazing at him from mere inches away. Still, this was a modern place, and in modern places, Little Ash knew, men and women danced together, not demons in trousers and angels in trousers. Girls danced with one another often enough. But no one thought they really meant it, the way girls meant it when they danced with boys. Little Ash knew better, but it was the appearance that mattered, in places like this, where everyone knew everyone else and gossip spread faster than fire.

He didn't want to say no, and found himself tongue-tied. At that moment Rose, who was feeling a bit left out, jostled Uriel by the shoulder.

"There's no time for dancing. Look what's happening."

Someone had approached the guard at the back door. Little Ash immediately pulled away from Uriel's hands and tilted his head to listen. The newcomer was young but rough-looking, a gentile with a swaggering look. He spoke briefly to the guard, then the guard nodded and opened the door to let the man in. They had a glimpse of a staircase leading upward before the door was shut again.

"He said he's here to talk to Boaz," said Little Ash, whose

ears were keener than the others'. "You two stay here and follow Boaz if he comes out. I'm going to listen in."

He didn't wait for them to acknowledge the instructions, only handed his ginger beer to Rose and took off toward the main entrance. Rose and Uriel, left behind, looked at each other in concern. Neither of them had great confidence that Little Ash wouldn't get himself in trouble on his own.

In fact he had taken off so quickly because he knew this, and did not wish to waste time explaining to them that he was very good at sneaking and spying.

twenty-nine

OUTSIDE THE DANCE HALL, it had begun to rain, and the crowd had thinned out as people sought shelter. Little Ash slipped into the alley, passing by a few couples who had come to whisper together and kiss in the darkness. There were no lookouts on the fire escape. It seemed Mr. Boaz, and whichever colleagues he was meeting, had not thought anyone would bother with this level of scrutiny.

Little Ash crept up the rusting iron steps, careful not to let his boots clatter on the grating. There was a light in one of the second-floor windows, and if he crawled on hands and knees he could crouch outside without being seen. The window was shut, but it was loose in its frame, poorly sealed. And the men in the room were not being overly cautious. Mr. Boaz, in fact, was upset, and speaking quite loudly.

"You don't understand!" he was saying as Little Ash pressed himself against the damp bricks. "There simply isn't any money; there won't be more money for weeks yet. They're planning a strike against me, do you know that? If you ask me how much harder can I push, I can't push any harder."

"So throw them all out and hire greenhorns," said the gentile. "Greenhorns don't know how to ask for a better wage."

"These days you can't trust a greenhorn not to know things," Boaz snapped.

"Throw out the Jews, then. It's you people that start all these strikes, and troubles, and complain and complain that you're not getting your due. I'm not getting *my* due, Solly, and I'm fed up with it."

"If I can't cook the books so my brother doesn't notice, there will be no money, ever," said Boaz. "It's wait, and get the money, or ruin everything. It's that simple!"

"Seems to me you live in a nice house, have a nice life," said the other. "Maybe it's time you start making sacrifices."

"Sacrifices! How dare you? You're nothing but a thug; you have no right to speak to me like this!"

Little Ash, had he been consulted, would have strongly advised Mr. Boaz not to talk that way. The other man in the room was crawling with sins of violence, such that to a demon's eyes his real face was almost obscured. This man would not live a long time, even if Little Ash were to leave him to his own devices. Another demon would get him, or his own sins would devour him. He was not the sort of person to be intimidated by threats delivered with a hysterical edge and without the backup of a weapon.

"I'm a thug—you're a dirty coward," said the stranger.

"I'd watch your back from now on. Unless you get me that money. Then you apologize, and we can call it even. If you don't come up with it by the end of the week, I'll start taking it, one way or another. Let's say half by your daughter's birthday. Half by next Sunday night. Or you'll regret it."

For a moment it seemed this would be the end of the conversation, and Little Ash started to move away from the window, but then Mr. Boaz called out, "Wait! Wait. I can get you the money—only, you have to help me break the strike. There's one of the men, the cutters. A ringleader. Isaak Shulman. If something . . . if you . . . well." He coughed uncomfortably. "That is, Mr. Sullivan, if Isaak Shulman were not around, I believe the strike would fall to pieces."

Little Ash slipped on the wet iron, his knee banging against a rail, and the conversation went silent. The demon did not wait for them to call out, or to see him. He leapt for the stairs and ran.

Rose and Uriel had been watching the guard at the door, expecting that eventually Mr. Boaz would come out and they could follow him and hope Little Ash caught up. Instead, someone must have shouted from behind the door, because the guard suddenly turned to open it and ran for the stairs, slamming it behind him.

Rose looked at Uriel. "Do we follow him?"

Uriel would have followed if it had been alone. But it was not used to being careful; as an angel, it had been immortal. It was, however, used to protecting others, and it had enough sense to know that Rose could die if anyone on the second floor had a gun like Reb Fishl.

"We can't follow," it said. "We should go. We should find Ashel."

They ran into him in the street outside, but he shoved them immediately back into the dance hall.

"We are pretending nothing strange is going on!" he hissed, grabbing Rose's hands and pulling her onto the dance floor. At the moment, the band was playing a lively and somewhat scandalous jig, which luckily disguised how out of breath the sheyd was from sprinting through the alley.

"What?" Uriel tried to stick close to the two of them, jostling other dancers with its lack of grace. A couple of strangers called advice, thinking it was trying to follow the steps without a partner, but it did not hear them. "Ashel, what is happening?"

"Several things are happening, and all of them are dangerous. For now, we're dancing. They'll be looking in the street for who was eavesdropping out back; they won't look in here."

"Some sort of a spy you are!" exclaimed Rose, who was rather irritated at having her hands gripped so tightly, and also irritated that Little Ash knew the steps better than she did. "Why did you let yourself be noticed?"

"You wouldn't have done better," said Little Ash. "Not in skirts."

Rose was about to suggest that the comparison was unfair and she would be a fine spy in trousers, but at that moment the back door opened and the guard and Mr. Boaz came through, both looking in a terrible temper. Rose, Uriel, and Little Ash all stopped talking and tried to keep an eye on them without losing track of the movement of the dancing. The guard was looking around as if, contrary to what Little Ash had said, he was still considering it possible that the eavesdropper was in the building.

"Stupid!" Rose hissed suddenly. "You're wet from the rain."

"Can you disguise yourself?" Uriel asked. "With your magic?"

Little Ash made a face. He had not wanted to admit it, but all of his efforts were going toward healing himself still, leaving nothing over for clever tricks. "Not at the moment, no."

There wasn't much else they could do to make him less conspicuous. Uriel took off its borrowed cap and put it on Little Ash's head, and Rose turned him so that he should be hidden by her body. Still, they all held their breaths until Boaz and his guard had gone out into the street.

"Now we follow," said Little Ash. "On the way I'll explain to you what happened. We have to tell your rebbe's daughter her family is in danger," he added to Uriel.

"Dinah's aunt?" Rose exclaimed. "Why?"

"Hush, hush." Little Ash was pulling them toward the door again. "Voices down—we're spying, remember."

They were hindered by the same crowd that had hidden them, and when they got out to the street, Boaz and his door guard were nearly turning a corner. The three spies hurried after them, Little Ash glancing around to check that Mr. Sullivan, Boaz's gentile accomplice or enemy from upstairs, was not watching for them.

"Boaz owes someone money," he explained under his breath as they followed their quarries north. "He needs to pay it back by the end of the week—something about a birthday—and he doesn't have enough to pay the man, so he's going to try and break the strike. Malke's husband, in particular."

Uriel looked over at him in concern. Little Ash had his hand pressed to his side and was gasping as he spoke. The angel had not known he was still injured from his fight with the doctor. It hesitated to ask if he was all right, when he'd been so irritable about it trying to help him on the island.

"We have to tell Isaak to be careful," said Rose. "Malke's just learned that her father died, may he rest in peace! We can't let her husband be hurt as well."

"I think they're all in danger," said Little Ash. "Anyone who's tangled up in Boaz and Sullivan and Fishl's scheme. Essie too."

They followed Boaz and the door guard north for about a mile, by the end of which Little Ash was limping, and even Rose's boots were beginning to pinch her. Mr. Boaz lived in a house finer than the wealthiest shopkeeper's home in Shtetl—a house with an iron fence, and its own garden, across from a park with trees in it. Rose, being from a larger shtetl, was less impressed than Uriel, and Little Ash declined to be impressed at all, instead taking in details of the layout with a housebreaker's eye. Mr. Boaz opened the front door to a spill of warm lamplight, and he seemed to argue for a minute with the man who'd come with him from the dance hall, pointing him away from the house. The surly man then went around the side, as if to use a servants' entrance. There did not seem to be any more guards about, but Little Ash estimated that there would be at least two more servants, along with Boaz's family.

The street was lit well enough that they didn't go too close to the house. Instead they stopped at a corner, where Little Ash leaned against the wall of the park to catch his breath.

"You two should go back and tell the Shulmans to keep their eyes open," he said, after a minute or two. "I'll stay here and watch. I'll come back in the morning with a plan."

"I don't see why you should be the one to make the plan, all by yourself," said Rose. "Why don't you slow down and stop rushing from place to place for a moment? We might see something you don't."

"Why should you wait by yourself?" Uriel added. "What if something happens?"

"A kapores the both of you," said Little Ash. "We don't all three need to stand here in the rain!"

"I won't leave you alone," said the angel stubbornly.

"And I can't go back by myself, because I'm a lady," said Rose, crossing her arms.

Little Ash glared at her, and she tilted her chin up to return his gaze with defiance.

"We are friends," said Uriel. "We will look after one another. In any case, humans sleep at night. What will you see if you stay and watch? It would be better to go back and rest. Then we will be better at thinking."

Little Ash had wanted them to leave him behind precisely so that he could rest before walking another mile back to the Lower East Side, but he saw that he was outnumbered. He sighed and pushed himself off of the wall he'd been leaning on.

"Fine. We'll come back in the morning and try to find Essie then. In the meantime, you . . . Do you want to bury your identity papers?"

Uriel blinked at him, startled. The question seemed to it to have come from nowhere. "Do I want to what?"

"To go back to being, you know, yourself."

"But I am myself."

"No, you're not; you told me you're seeing creeping beasts. And you've had the same name for weeks. The rebbe's gone now. Why keep it?"

Rose looked from one to the other, confused. She felt as if suddenly she had become unable to understand their dialect, though they were still speaking Yiddish.

"I'm burying mine," said Little Ash. "I'm tired of Asher Klein, and anyway he's not allowed in America, so his papers won't do me any good. If you bury yours, you can stop being Uriel Federman and you won't have to worry about things."

"But I like being Uriel Federman," said Uriel. "It is like being an angel but also a person. I can do whatever I like! Did you know that? I had a task on Ellis Island and I didn't do it; I did what I wanted. Just like you always do. It's just like being a human!"

Little Ash frowned. "Humans get sick and they die," he said in Aramaic.

"So? I will not do that."

"That's not something you can just *decide*. It happens to them all the time, when they're not expecting it. You've seen—your friend the rebbe didn't know he was going to die when he went to Warsaw, and he knew more than most humans do."

"It's true," Uriel admitted. "But I don't care. I like having a name. I feel bigger this way. Or . . . there is *more* of me, somehow."

"Hello!" Rose flicked Little Ash's ear with her finger. "If you're arguing about our plan, do it so I know what you're saying!"

The demon swatted her hand away and turned toward the park. "Fine, fine," he said in Yiddish. "We weren't arguing anyway."

"Where are we going? That isn't the way home."

"He needs to bury his papers," Uriel explained as they followed. "I do not understand why. It is just one of his ideas."

Little Ash was secretly hoping that throwing away his human name would make him feel better and perhaps let him shed the weakness he'd felt since being detained. In the park, he found a tree whose roots offered a sheltered spot to dig, and Rose and Uriel waited under the branches while he dug a hole and covered his identity papers in mud. When he was finished, he sat for a moment, waiting to feel more powerful, but sensed no change. Some things could not be undone with the simple, childish magic Little Ash knew how to perform.

"You really don't want to be free of yours?" he asked Uriel at last. "Even though it says you're a man?"

Uriel shook its head. "I have not been paying attention to that part of the paper, Ashel. I do not think it is about my papers at all. I only wanted to have a name, and it was the first name I thought of, because you gave it to me."

"Oh."

"I'm freezing," said Rose. "Are we finished sitting in the mud? I need a pot of coffee and a knish. And *sleep*."

"Yes," Uriel agreed. "I need sleep also. Please, Ashel. Don't be so worried about it. It's really all right."

The angel held out its hand to Little Ash, who took it, and they turned toward the Lower East Side, retracing their steps back home.

thirty

IN THE MORNING, Rose and Uriel and Little Ash met at Cafe Krakow, where the loudly argumentative atmosphere offered good cover for discussing plans for dealing with Mr. Boaz and the gangster boss Mr. Sullivan. Rose had purchased a Yiddish newspaper in the street to see what they could learn about the factory and Mr. Boaz's behavior, and Little Ash had had the same thought and purchased a different Yiddish newspaper. Thus they sat with their heads together over their pot of coffee and a plate of knishes and two newspapers which largely disagreed with each other on the meaning of the news.

"The Shulmans are keeping watch to make sure no one sets the bookshop on fire," Little Ash told Rose. "And Isaak has promised Malke that he won't go anywhere alone. She made him swear that if he didn't look over his shoulder,

O Jerusalem, he'd lose his right hand. I didn't like her father much, but I don't mind her at all."

"That's very rude," said Uriel. "You shouldn't speak that way of the spirits in Gehinnom."

"I'll speak however I like about people who snub me," said Little Ash. "And after I took revenge for his murder, yet! Prejudice, that's all it is. This paper says that Mr. Boaz will have to cave to the strike, and this paper says he will never cave to the strike. Who do you suppose has the right of it?"

Rose and Uriel looked at each other. Neither of them felt they knew enough about strikes to answer the question. In fact, neither did Little Ash, but he had less shame about pretending.

"He mentioned he has a brother," Little Ash went on. "And he's trying to hide from him the finances. It says here the brother is the other owner of Boaz Brothers, but he lives in *Feeladelfie*."

"Do you suppose that's what your Essie is doing?" said Rose. "Didn't the girls say she was doing accounts for him?"

"*Cooking the books*," said Little Ash, savoring the English phrase Mr. Boaz had used the night before. "A greenhorn girl would have a hard time telling anyone about it, wouldn't she? Especially if she's in debt to him, and her family is from the smallest village in the whole world and has no money."

Uriel was frowning intently at Rose's newspaper. It was not used to reading Yiddish, so the task went slowly, but the necessity for deliberation caused it to notice details Little

Ash, skimming quickly back and forth in his usual fashion, had missed. "There is here an advertisement. The Jewish Women who helped Rose get from the island are inviting girls to attend a *banket*. What is that?"

"A feast," said Little Ash. "A simcha. Why?"

"Because this is Mr. Boaz's address," said the angel, pointing.

Rose grabbed for the newspaper. "A way to get into the house!"

The *banket*, or rather, *banquet*, was to take place on Tuesday evening, in celebration of the coming-of-age of Mr. Solomon Boaz's daughter Minnie. In a show of goodwill and charity toward the downtrodden Lower East Side greenhorns, Mr. Boaz was inviting a handful of immigrant girls to attend the event, girls to be selected by a representative from an uptown ladies' charity who would visit the Council House on Tuesday morning to assess the suitability of any young ladies who showed up. Rose, being a newcomer without a job, but respectable, would have a good chance of being chosen, according to Little Ash's confident assessment of the details in the advertisement.

In the meantime, there was a Sunday night strike meeting, where the garment workers would vote on whether they should refuse to labor at the Boaz Brothers factory beginning on Monday morning. Isaak Shulman would speak at the meeting, so Little Ash decided he and Uriel should go as well, to keep their eyes out for Mr. Sullivan or any other gangster interferers. Besides, all three of them were very fascinated to see what a strike meeting consisted of. Rose was particularly intrigued by the fact that Bluma and Freidy had mentioned some of their strike leaders were young girls like themselves.

"Typical that your Mr. Boaz didn't mention *those* names when he asked for the strike to be broken," she said to Little Ash, as they were discussing it in the cafe.

"Mr. Boaz didn't seem to me a deep thinker," said Little Ash. "Or maybe he thinks he is a gentleman, and wouldn't dare call out assassins on girls. Either way, it's good news for you, because you will be going into his house with intentions against him and only a pocketknife."

"Surely it is not so strange for girls to be dangerous," said Uriel. The more it saw of the world outside the study hall, the more it was realizing that it didn't understand the relations between men and women at all. "Does no one remember Judith and Ya'el?"

Little Ash laughed. "Mr. Boaz didn't seem to me like he studies much Torah either. Maybe you can give him a Mishnah when we see him face to face."

This reminded the angel that they were behind on their usual daily Talmud study, and it wanted to draw out a tractate at once, but when it tried, it found that the angelic magic of pulling holy books from nowhere was still not working. It had been using the rebbe's books on the ship, and had nearly forgotten about this consequence of its new name, but the books now were back at Malke's apartment.

"Are you very sure you don't want me to bury your papers?" said Little Ash, watching the odd little twitches of the angel's hands, which had, in the past, allowed it to snatch a text from empty air and now did nothing at all.

Uriel stilled its hands quickly. "Yes, I am very sure. I can use books like a person—there are many books in the world already."

"Or you can read the newspaper," said Little Ash, although in truth he missed the ritual of daily study. "Look, here is an advertisement for schmaltz made from vegetables, so you can cook it with meat."

Obedient, Uriel looked. There were many strange things in America.

"Let's go back to the bookshop," said Little Ash. "We never finished our Avodah Zarah, anyway."

So they went back to the bookshop, and Rose sat to write a letter to her family while Little Ash and Uriel borrowed once more the rebbe's tractates, to catch up on their lessons. Rose's letter was largely falsehood, or at least obscured the truth: she said that she had arrived safely in America, that Bluma was well, that she did not have a job yet but intended to have one soon, that she had made some friends on the ship. As in her previous letters, she did not mention that the friends weren't girls, lest her family get the wrong impression. She wrote, for Motl's benefit, the best account she could of the hustle and bustle of New York City, and how she saw boys his age everywhere playing stickball and running around in the street.

At the end of the letter, after a bit of hesitation, she added that she'd met Dinah's aunt, Malke, who was also doing well, but she was sorry to say that they'd learned Dinah's grandfather had gone on to the next world. Her last letter, written on the ship, had studiously avoided any mention of Dinah, but that no longer felt right. After all, she liked Dinah's aunt very much, and she had accepted hospitality from her. Her anger at Dinah felt rather distant now that there was an ocean between them and she'd seen some of the dangers of America. Dinah would have been hurt by the implication from the Ellis Island officials that there was something suspect about an unmarried girl alone—she would have felt it in a way Rose did not. Rose found that she was glad Dinah had been spared that hurt.

Dinah could come later. Her new husband could come with her, and keep her from suspicion. That didn't seem so bad. Rose even felt better disposed toward the rebbe's students. In fact, she realized, it no longer bothered her that her plans for America had changed. Things seemed to be going right, all the same. She'd even been to a dance hall!

Not that she'd put that in the letter to her parents. That, she'd save for when she felt ready to write Dinah directly.

thirty-one

THE STRIKE MEETING took place in a basement which was used at other times for wedding feasts and the crowds that could not fit into the little shop-front shuls at Yom Kippur, when even the secular people of the Lower East Side remembered that being Jewish included also religion. Someone had set up a stage at one end of this basement, a stage which was constructed from leftover materials and tended to sway a little at the motion of feet upon its surface, whether they were pacing back and forth to give speeches or playing in a Purim spiel. Since Isaak Shulman was pacing from one side of the stage to the other when Uriel, Little Ash, and Rose arrived, they got to see at once the effect this had, which was to make any speech seem like it was being delivered in the midst of the Flood of Noah, on board an ark that might sink at any moment into the crowd.

From this scaffold Isaak was prepared to make a speech that would, he and the other strike leaders hoped, stir the workers to vote for a stoppage, which would paralyze the Boaz Brothers factory and its profits until Mr. Boaz relented and stopped squeezing the workers for all they could give. The room was packed from wall to wall, most of the audience sitting in the same flimsy wooden chairs they would have used for High Holy Days and the rest standing wherever they found space. Isaak Shulman had something of a reputation as a speaker, and so did the young woman who would speak after him. There was almost a joyous atmosphere in the room as everyone anticipated hearing their concerns put into words.

Indeed, Isaak's speech wrapped around the crowd like a magic spell. The words mattered less than the spirit. He spoke like a prophet, in images: backs bent over machines; cotton scraps floating through the air and nestling in the lungs of young women until they choked on their own breath and could not climb to their second-floor apartments without gasping; needles that broke and stabbed hands, faces, blinded eyes; blood on white fabric; doors locked and pockets searched so that not a penny of stock could be stolen to buy a penny's worth of bread when the wages didn't stretch to feed an infant who lay home in its cradle and cried, for fourteen hours a day, because there was no one there to hold it in her arms.

Isaak brought all of these into the crowded basement room and painted them in the ink of his anger until they were as bright before everyone's eyes as the sun that shone from the sky outside—the sun they could not see in the factory and could not see in the room where they planned their strike. Uriel's heart was pounding in a way it had never noticed before, and it pressed its hands to its chest, trying to contain the feeling.

Rose, too, was transfixed. She wanted her parents and Motl there to hear the words, wanted Dinah there to hear them and understand that there were things more powerful than the respect one got from village boys who liked a pretty face. She felt herself trembling, and she almost thought she could have leapt up on that stage and given a passionate speech of her own, saying what she had seen since coming to America, and how many things she disagreed with, and how she would change them now that she saw that change was possible.

Little Ash, keeping his eyes open for danger and cataloging the sins of everyone in the room, was perhaps the only one left unmoved. As his friends sat watching with Bluma and Malke, he moved to a spot where he could keep his eyes on the door.

After Isaak, a girl as young as Rose took the stage, and in a clear, high voice she read from a sheet of paper the list of workers who had been injured or had fallen ill from their labor in the factory the Boaz brothers owned. The long hours sapped one's strength, the close work strained one's eyes. A young woman had collapsed from exhaustion because she had no time to drink water. A man's hand had been caught in a cutting blade, and his wages were docked for bleeding.

She had all of their names, and their ages, too: none over thirty, except for Mrs. Shulman, who had died of exhaustion. The workers were young, but it took effort for them to feel as young as they were. For all they did, they earned less than they deserved, and for every worker in the factory there was a family also. Elderly parents and little brothers and sisters who could not afford to be married or educated, and always the rent, and the bread, and the little set aside for steamship tickets for family they hadn't seen in years.

The girl's voice rose and fell like a cantor's, and Uriel listened as to a voice from Heaven, drinking in every word of the Yiddish that was starting to feel as familiar to it as a mother tongue. The words filled it up and soaked into its heart, and it thought to itself, all of this time I have been missing something, and I had no idea.

Its heart was heavier with the weight of the young worker's words. But should a heart not be heavy, in a world full of injustice? It looked down at its lap, twisting its tzitzis in its fingers. This was the world Essie lived in, and her family, and all of the people back in Shtetl, and it had never noticed. How many times had it said, *Listen, Israel,* and not been listening? Oh, it thought, I have been terrible, terrible. Uriel Federman needs to be someone who sees what is happening in the world around it. I must stay this way, this person, so that I won't forget.

This was why Torah was not for angels. Angels forget what humans can remember. Angels skip lightly over ground that needs plowing with rough hands and sharp blades.

Uriel had thought that it could not be doing wrong because it had no inclination for evil—but what *had* it been doing for hundreds of years? Studying, and forgetting that study should lead to action. It would never have left Shtetl without Little Ash, would never have known it was missing anything. But it had missed the most important purpose it could ever have, something bigger than an angel could ever be.

"Are you all right?" Rose whispered in its ear, drawing Uriel out from its own thoughts in time to see the young girl quit the stage.

"Hmm?"

Rose lifted a hand to Uriel's cheek, as she would have done for Motl, forgetting that she ought not to touch someone who was not related to herself and looked like a boy. "You're crying."

"Oh." It felt its cheeks, amazed. "Oh, no, I feel very good."

When the speeches were finished, every hand in the room went up in favor of moving to strike.

thirty-two

LITTLE ASH AND URIEL had been sleeping together on the quilt next to the stove in Isaak and Malke's apartment. That night, Little Ash waited until everyone else was asleep and then carefully disentangled himself from the blankets. Uriel, despite all the ways it had changed since leaving Shtetl, still slept like a rock, to his relief. In order not to risk waking the Shulman family by opening the door and leaving through the cluttered hallway, the demon climbed out the window, onto the fire escape, and took off barefoot in the direction of the Boaz Brothers factory, with his packet of needles and lockpicks in his pocket.

He was standing at the corner, in a patch of shadow between gas lamps, and waiting to make sure there was no night watchman patrolling the building when someone tapped him on the shoulder.

Little Ash had been keeping his eyes and ears open for anyone following him, in case one of Sullivan's men was watching the Shulman apartment. He had therefore thought he was quite alone, and he nearly leapt out of his skin. But it was only Uriel.

"What are you doing?!" Little Ash hissed, pressing a hand to his bruised ribs. His startle reflex had jarred them.

"What are you doing?" Uriel returned the question. "Why are we outside the factory?"

"I thought I'd look and see if Boaz keeps any of his accounts here, since he's trying to lie about his numbers. But I was going to do it *alone*."

"Why?" Uriel asked, reasonably. "You can look twice as fast with two sets of eyes. You left your shoes behind. Are your feet hurting you?"

"Yes, very much. Leave me alone."

"I will not," said Uriel. "Show me what you are planning."

"I didn't think you'd like to be sneaking around like a thief," said Little Ash. "Which part of your new name is that kept in? I didn't put a gimel for *gonif* in your papers."

"I told you, it isn't the papers. I liked the name, only. And it isn't that I want to be sneaking; I just think it is more sensible if we stay together. After all, what if another demon sees you with those bare feet and wants to kill you? I want to be close, so I can stop it."

This declaration touched Little Ash too closely for him to respond, and so he clamped his mouth shut and led the angel down the street to the factory's fire escape. It only reached down to the second floor, and Little Ash reluctantly had to admit that he didn't mind having a friend to help with the climb, given that using the muscles in his chest was causing him pain. Uriel made its hand into a step for him to jump up, and he then lay on the grating to pull the angel up after him. It was not used to clambering like an alley cat, and it took several minutes to figure out how to place its hooves against the brick wall for leverage, so that by the time it got onto the fire escape they were both out of breath, and Little Ash was laughing.

"You are not helping whatsoever," he said, cheerfully. "I'd be done by now without you. But never mind, it should say on my grave that I trained the first-ever Angel of Burglars. Come on."

He showed it the third-floor window through which he intended to break into the factory, and then had the angel sit watch while he dug into the window frame with his pocketknife. The window was locked on the inside, but the latch was cheap and snapped quite easily when he found the right angle.

Inside, the factory floor was cluttered with machines and tables, which appeared in the dark to be looming shapes, occasionally draped with ghostly fabric. Little Ash's cat eyes let him see perfectly well by the faint gaslight from the street, but Uriel's night vision was not as good, and it ran into the edges of two worktables before Little Ash took pity on it and took it by the arm.

"You're not a demon, anyway," he said. "I was starting to think you'd changed into one, somehow, with you seeing the creeping sins, but you've still got no eyes for the dark."

"I had not thought of that," Uriel admitted, feeling silly. "I thought I was a human."

Little Ash made a disgusted noise. "And you didn't want to bury your papers? Why would you *want* to be a human? I like humans very much, you understand, but I don't want to *be* one."

"I think it would be interesting. Humans move so fast."

"Humans get cholera and shrivel up and die. And you! You're bulletproof. I mean, you used to be. Why would you want to be weak when you could be invulnerable?"

Uriel considered this while Little Ash drew it on through the maze of sewing machines toward a row of small offices on the other side of the factory floor. It had not given much thought to weakness or invulnerability while it was making its choices. It had been chasing after something else. Something like the identity of Curiosity, which it had often had when it was with Little Ash, but bigger than Curiosity, and more permanent.

"It doesn't matter to me," it said at last. "Being an angel is not so nice, sometimes. It is very confining. I wanted to be something else. And now I am something else."

Now it was Little Ash's turn to be silent. For a moment Uriel wasn't sure he had even heard what it said, as he was testing the office doors. When they proved locked, he reached into his pocket for the roll of lockpicks.

"Wanting to be something else, I understand," he said. "Wanting not to be something, when that *something* is made of magic—that, I don't understand at all. You could do anything you liked."

"Only I couldn't," Uriel explained. "I could do things that fit, only. And sometimes it didn't feel like *I* fit. Like . . . like wearing a shirt with no sleeves."

"That makes no sense at all," said Little Ash, squinting at the lockpicks in the darkness.

"Do you like being a demon?" Uriel asked. It had always assumed that he did. He was out of sorts lately, but before that, at home, he had always seemed to be enjoying himself, no matter what was happening.

Little Ash did not look up. "I like being a demon all right. Except I hardly count as one, and that I don't like."

The lock clicked, and he wrenched the door open with a bit more force than it needed. This was a storeroom, full of bolts of fabric and shelves of bobbins. Little Ash shut the door again and moved on to the next.

"I don't understand," said Uriel.

"It's one thing in a little village," said Little Ash. "There weren't any other demons there, except the gentiles in the market towns, and I could forget about them if I wanted—they're just silly peasants, anyway, same as me, I suppose. They throw rocks at me and I throw rocks back; it's neighborly. Only I forgot it isn't like that, out in the world. Out in the world you're supposed to be able to *do* things, and I can't."

They had been whispering, but over the course of this speech his voice had grown louder, until he fumbled his lockpicks in frustration and dropped them, swearing.

"You have done a lot of things," said Uriel carefully. "You have brought us to America. And found out where Essie is. And now we are looking for these account books. And the rebbe got to Malke in time to hear his Kaddish—you did that."

"I did not. You did. I didn't even *like* him. I would have left him in Warsaw if I could."

"But I wouldn't have gone to Warsaw without you, so it turns out the same."

"Well, fine! It makes no difference." Little Ash shook out his hands and picked up his lockpicks again.

"You are talking about the shirt with no sleeves," said Uriel. "Only, Ashel, you don't need to be any different. I like you the way you are."

"*You* wanted to be different," said Little Ash. The lock clicked open, and this time the door opened to an office, with a sturdy wooden desk and all the trappings of a boss who wanted to look impressive, the relatively small room giving a sense of more space than the cluttered work-stations of the factory floor. "Keep an eye out, would you? There might be a night watchman. These places go up in flames in a breath, if anything happens, so if I were in charge I'd keep a watch on it at night."

Uriel dutifully took up its station on the threshold while Little Ash started opening drawers and rifling through their contents. "I only wanted to be different so that I could stay myself. You have a name already, and you can be Ashmedai always, no matter what happens. But if I didn't have my name, I wouldn't be the Angel of Shtetl anymore, and I want to be the Angel of Shtetl forever."

"Do you see the footprints, by the way?" said Little Ash. "They're all over. The dybbuk."

"I do not see them."

"Well, then, at least I still have better eyes. Hold on." He came over to it and repeated the charm he had used in Warsaw, dabbing his own tears into its lashes. When it blinked, it could see tarry little prints all over the room and ranging out onto the factory floor.

"I see them now," Uriel agreed. "It has been everywhere."

"It must not stick to Boaz, only. I wonder if it's someone who worked here." Little Ash went back to the desk and resumed his search. "Essie could be in danger, if she's living in a house with it."

"I don't like seeing this wickedness all over," said Uriel. "I don't know how you can ever be happy."

"Because I don't mind that the world is wicked. Damn it, there's nothing. He must have taken the account books away."

"The package he gave to his driver?" Uriel suggested.

"Everyone said they haven't seen Essie in a while. Maybe he's got her locked up with the books in his house. All the more reason to go to that banquet." He slammed shut the last desk drawer, then went around to the back of the desk to run his fingers over it, just in case of a secret panel.

Mr. Boaz had not seemed cunning enough for such a thing, but it never hurt to explore every angle. "Nothing. Sorry, little bird, you'll have to wait before we make you an Angel of Stealing."

Halfway back across the factory floor, they heard the tread of the night watchman on the stairs from below. Little Ash tugged at Uriel's elbow and they crouched under one of the cutting tables, among the piles of fabric scraps. Lying under the table, with its face so close to the floor, Uriel found itself inches from another set of the dybbuk's footprints, the tarry patches giving off a faint unpleasant scent. When it touched one with its finger, it came away smudged and tingling.

"Bad luck," Little Ash whispered in its ear. "Clean it off." He pushed a clean scrap of fabric under its nose, and it scrubbed its hand carefully, trying not to make a sound.

The watchman opened the main door from the stairs and waved his lamp perfunctorily from side to side. As Little Ash had guessed, his job was more to check for fire than anything else, and seeing no signs of it, the man turned back again. Little Ash kept his hand on Uriel's elbow for a count of twenty before pushing it out from under the table again.

"You see," Uriel whispered to him. "You've done all this tonight, with no magic, yet."

"Stop it," he said, giving it another little shove. "I don't need to be encouraged. You first, out the window."

Uriel climbed out and was turning back to offer Little Ash its hand when a sudden shout went up in the alley.

thirty-three

YOU! STOP WHERE YOU ARE!"

It was not the night watchman; he hadn't had time to get down the stairs and around the corner. Little Ash grabbed Uriel and yanked it back inside just as a gunshot rang out, the bullet ringing off the bricks just inches from where the angel's head had been.

"Run!" said Little Ash. "Don't go down. Up the stairs!"

They sprinted for the door as another shot echoed in the alleyway, and someone started shouting in the street. Uriel's eyes still had not adjusted well to the dark, and the cluttered factory floor slowed their progress so that when they reached the stairs they could hear someone already starting up from street level—two sets of feet. Little Ash dragged Uriel upward, the stairs a dizzying spiral in the dark, for another six stories. The door to the roof at the top was locked, and Little Ash spat curses as he pulled out the lockpicks again.

"Do you need light?" Uriel whispered.

Little Ash did not stop to ask what it meant. "Please."

Uriel placed its hand on the door over his head and sketched the only Holy Name the rebbe had been able to teach it on the ship: its own name. The letters lit with a soft, golden glow, and for a moment Little Ash stopped what he was doing to stare at them. Then there was a crash from the factory floor below them, and he blinked the surprise away and applied the picks again.

The voice of Mr. Sullivan, below, was raised in anger. "They must have gone up to the roof! You bastard idiots!"

Uriel glanced down the stairwell. "What do I do if they shoot at us again?"

"Don't get hit, I suppose," said Little Ash. A door slammed below them. The lock clicked open. "We should have brought Fishl's gun with us—only I don't know how to use one."

He threw the door wide and they dove out onto the roof, where at last Uriel found it could see, the full moon as bright as any streetlight after the gloom inside the building. What it saw, however, was not very encouraging. They'd have to jump a sizable gap to the next roof over, and it wasn't level, so the landing would be six feet or so below the takeoff.

"Are we really going to jump?" it said.

Little Ash grinned his wicked grin. His eyes were

shining as he reached for Uriel's hand, and it stopped in its tracks, its breath taken away by his face in the moonlight.

"Trust me," he said. "Don't hesitate and don't think, just trust me."

Uriel squeezed his hand. It wanted to tell him that the two of them being together, causing trouble together, was a miracle.

But there was no time. Little Ash pulled Uriel by the hand so that it had no choice but to run with him, and at the last second, afraid the jump would be too far, the angel shut its eyes and pretended it was in the dark again.

For an instant they were flying. It opened its eyes, sure they would hit the ground in the alleyway, and found the roof rushing toward them. Little Ash threw himself sideways so that the impact hit them off-balance, and they rolled to a stop on solid ground. Quick as a blink, the demon was on his feet again, picking up Uriel's embroidered cap, which had blown off in the fall. He placed it back on the angel's head as it sat up, then drew it to its feet by the elbow.

"Downstairs again," he gasped, fully out of breath as he pulled it across the roof. He was pressing a hand to his ribs, but he was still grinning. "A curse on America! All of America can bake bagels in hell."

Perhaps it was a lingering touch of angelic luck, but when Uriel tried the door to get into the new building, it was unlocked. The shouting of Sullivan and the night watchman faded behind them as they climbed down the stairs, more slowly this time, past another set of fabric factories and into the street. They were around the corner from the front entrance of Boaz's, so they would have another moment or two of a lead if the men came onto the street again. Little Ash, limping, led Uriel in the opposite direction it had been expecting, taking them to the north and west instead of southeast back to the Shulmans' apartment. A few blocks over, there was a little park barely the size of a single building, with only a handful of trees, but it had deep shadows. Little Ash climbed over the iron fence and threw himself to the ground under a bush. Uriel did the same, then sat beside him.

"So you see," he said after a moment, as if returning to their conversation inside the factory, "no respectable demon would have such troubles. Any of my brothers could open a lock with a word, *and* they have wings."

"I do not think I would like your brothers," said Uriel. "I have no wings, myself."

"You do," Little Ash protested. "You used to wear them all the time. Where are they, anyway?"

"Folded up in the rebbe's trunk. I did not want to look strange. So, all right, I have wings. But not wings for flying. They're wings for praying, only."

"Anyway, you've never met my brothers."

"I don't need to. I know what I need from a chevrusa, and I have it. So *you* see, we did not get shot, and tomorrow we will try again."

"To get shot?" said Little Ash, and laughed at his own joke. Then he curled up over his bruised ribs and sat silently catching his breath for a long time. The light of mischief had gone out of his eyes now that they were no longer being chased, and his body had remembered that it required rest.

"It is all right to need help," Uriel said, when they'd been sitting in silence for a while. "You should not be ashamed of it. Haven't you seen how the humans help each other? Ever since we left our shtetl, we've seen it. Even the wicked ones help each other to be more wicked."

Little Ash could think of no argument to contradict this wisdom.

thirty-four

IN THE GARMENT FACTORIES they had cutters, pressers, piecers, runners, finishers. All these roles between them brought the fabric from bolt to shirtwaist in a steady rhythm. On the picket line, the garment workers had a similar method, an unspoken division of roles and pattern of movement. The cutters were the Goliaths of the factory, men who took pride in the strength of their arms, and when the police moved toward the striking workers, the cutters moved toward the police. At the same time, certain other workers would draw back, these being the young ones, thirteen or fourteen or not yet b'nei mitzvah, and a handful of pregnant women with them. Along with this group would go a few of the young men whose job it was to make sure that when the vulnerable ones needed to run, they were protected.

On the picket line of the Boaz Brothers factory, Isaak Shulman stood in the middle with the cutters arrayed around him like the bodyguards of a king. Malke he had begged to stay at home, and she had stayed in exchange for his promise that he would not make foolish decisions without her. There was rarely trouble on the first day of a strike—the first day was a day for the boss to pretend he did not notice and did not care. But with Little Ash's warning about Mr. Sullivan on their minds, they were being cautious.

Little Ash, for his own caution, was not at the picket line himself. He, Rose, and Uriel instead had gone the few blocks north to Mr. Boaz's own neighborhood, hoping to take advantage of the distraction of the strike to spy on his home and get a glimpse of Essie if they could. In order that they should not appear like beggars or troublemakers in the street, the demon had borrowed the Belzer Rebbe's trunk, emptied it of books, and laid Malke's sewing tray over the top so that, when opened, it passed for a peddler's wares. Freidy had confirmed that greenhorn peddlers quite often went to the richer Jewish neighborhoods to try and get a bit of goodwill and have their awkward English understood. Indeed, she had cousins who had done it. She would have told them much more—she had been made to stay home with Malke and the little ones again, and felt out of sorts about it—but Little Ash pretended they were in a hurry to meet Rose, and so he cut off her narrative.

Rose was wearing her new dress again, and Bluma had done her hair for her so that the braids were prettier and more complicated than Rose was used to doing for herself. She felt quite sophisticated and cheerful as they walked uptown, and she didn't even mind much that she was missing the action of the strike. Finding Essie, after all, was a noble mission in itself, and one that was unlikely to repeat itself, whereas a strike, as Bluma had told her, could go on for months.

"I'll be the peddler," said Little Ash, taking charge as usual. "I've done it before; I know the technique. You two can be out for a stroll. You're in the neighborhood because your parents won't see you here, and you want to daydream about the pretty houses, maybe."

"Our parents?" said Rose. "Are we sweethearts?"

"What else should you be?"

"I don't know! Brother and sister!"

"You don't like Uriel?" said Little Ash. "You don't think it's pretty? It thinks you're very pretty, I'm sure."

"Only because Uriel is *nice*," said Rose. "Isn't that right?"

Uriel was quite confused and not sure what to say. Of course it thought Rose was pretty. Her face shone with the light of a righteous mind to its angel's eyes, unchanged by its new capacity for seeing traces of wickedness. It felt, however, that this was not really what was meant by the conversation. "But we are only pretending?"

"Of course it's pretending," said Rose, who could not even name for herself why she felt so offended. "But why should he cast me as a daydreaming young bride? I could be a peddler; I'm very persuasive."

"You can be sweethearts having a vicious argument, if

you'd prefer," said Little Ash. "I'm only thinking what fools believe when they look at you. The point is not to seem strange; that's the secret to lying."

Rose huffed an exasperated breath. "I wish you were a girl," she told Uriel. "Then I wouldn't feel so strange about it. I don't know how I'd talk to a boy who was courting me, but if Dinah were here . . ."

She could imagine all too well strolling arm in arm with Dinah through the wealthy square, pointing out details of the expensive brick houses, and how Dinah would describe things like curtains and carpets that she'd have if she lived in such a place. The rain had cleared out and today was sunny and cool, the perfect day for that sort of idleness. At home she had sometimes spent days like this with Dinah in the fields, knitting or doing accounts while they kept an eye on the goats.

"So pretend Uriel is Dinah," said Little Ash.

"I don't know how I would talk to a sweetheart either," said Uriel. "I don't even really know what that is."

Little Ash laughed his hyena laugh. "A perfect couple you are. Just keep an eye out for trouble and don't look suspicious."

He left the two of them at the corner and went ahead with his trunk full of fabric swatches. Committed to his act, he knocked first at the door of the house next to Mr. Boaz's, but moved on quickly when no one answered. Rose and Uriel walked slowly behind him, watching without being sure what they were watching for.

"I suppose it is men with guns," said Uriel. "One shot at us at the factory, before."

Rose supposed she should be troubled by this. She had hoped that there would not be men with guns in America as there were in Russia. However, there was something thrilling about being here to rescue Essie, like a princess in a fairy story, from the clutches of evil. "I don't see either men or guns. Don't you think it would be strange for them to be in a neighborhood like this? Everything is so clean."

Little Ash was dragging his trunk up the walk to the Boaz house, letting it make quite a noise on the bricks. If there were any guards or gangsters about, they would surely be alerted to the presence of a stranger. At the step he pounded on the door with rather more gusto than he'd used for the first house. He did it, however, with his sleeve pulled down over his hand, because, to his eyes, the door was dark and sticky with the bad luck spread by the dybbuk. He was almost reluctant to go into a house that so evidently had a curse upon it. Even the mezuzah on the doorpost was drowned in tarry misfortune and barely stirred itself to notice there was a demon knocking to come in.

After a moment, a middle-aged woman in a servant's uniform opened the door, giving Little Ash a suspicious look. To another set of eyes she would have appeared neatly put together and perfectly ordinary, but to Little Ash it was clear that she'd been in contact with the dybbuk: her starched white apron, perfectly clean to human eyes, was smudged invisibly with malevolent handprints.

"What do you want?" she said. "Don't you know that vendors use the back entrance?"

Little Ash knew this very well, but he put an expression of childish distress on his face and said, "The back?"

He said it with a very thick Yiddish accent, though he could have spoken English, as the woman did, with the flavor of an American. The accent was intended to show that his ignorance of manners was entirely innocent.

The housekeeper, meanwhile, was looking at the trunk and doing the simple mathematics. Peddlers didn't come often to the Boaz house these days. Although the housekeeper herself was not Jewish, but Irish, she'd heard the rumor passed around that they were on a sort of blacklist in the Jewish community for Mr. Boaz's offenses. Mr. Boaz, besides, had been acting more and more strangely, hardly ever leaving the house and never inviting guests, and not giving the servants their regular days off. His excuse was that they had to prepare for his daughter's banquet, but the housekeeper, whose name was Bonny, suspected the man was mad or drinking too much. She'd seen it before.

The fact was, the house was gloomy and too quiet, and Bonny missed the novelty and gossip that peddlers brought with them. Besides, this one was awfully young, and he looked like he could use a solid meal, thought the part of her that missed her sister's little ones back in Ireland.

"What is it you're selling, then?" she said.

"Ribbons and thread, fabric patches," said Little Ash. "If something for a little decoration you want."

Bonny had been having a terrible time lately with the

hems fraying on all of her dresses. She took great pride in her neat appearance, and this had been plaguing her. The bad luck of the house was good luck for Little Ash.

"All right," she said, with a sigh. "Next time, go around the back, but for now why don't you come to the kitchen and show us what you've brought? We'll have a cup of tea and a bun for you. You keep kosher, I suppose? This is a Jewish house; they keep it Jewish."

"Next time the back," Little Ash repeated obediently and stepped over the threshold.

Inside, every surface in the house was saturated in bad luck, so that to the demon's eyes it appeared everything had been thickly painted black. It stuck to his shoes with every step, and for once he was glad that he was wearing them. He thought of Essie as he remembered her in Shtetl, a clever and lively girl with shining eyes, always ready to answer the teasing questions the old men in the study hall would put to her. He hoped that living in this house had not poisoned her.

Bonny brought him to the kitchen, which was at the back of the house and at the lower level so that the windows were just over the soil of the garden, and the sun shone in through the stalks of herbs. It should have been gloomier here, underground, but to the contrary, there were only a few dybbuk footprints here, so the light was able to shine off the whitewashed walls and the clean-scrubbed table. What looked like all the servants of the house were gathered around that table, doing their work. Little Ash recognized

Mr. Boaz's driver first, and then, at the far end of the table and bent over a set of ledgers, there she was.

Essie.

Her dress was soaked in bad luck, the ledgers even more so, so that they seemed to bleed out like ink onto the part of the table where she'd placed them. She worked slowly, as if exhausted, holding her pen with stiff fingers like an old woman. The dybbuk was not in the room, but Little Ash knew by looking at Essie that, wherever the dybbuk spent its time, Essie had been trapped with it on more than one occasion.

"What's this?" said a housemaid who must have been a relative newcomer to the house, as she seemed in better spirits than the others. "We haven't had any peddlers come by in ages! What have you got for us, then?"

"Are you from the Lower East Side?" said the cook, taking in Little Ash's sidelocks and the tzitzis hanging at his hips. "I don't care what you've brought, if you've been on Hester Street lately. You can give me the gossip, only! Have you eaten?"

The table was crowded with people, everyone having brought whichever household tasks they could into the kitchen to avoid the puzzling, oppressive atmosphere of the rest of the house, the feeling of unease on the upper stories that they all felt but none were able to articulate. There was a shuffle as they made space for Little Ash and his trunk, and started to put together a plate for him.

He played the part of the greenhorn peddler almost automatically, keeping his real attention on Essie. At first she had seemed sunk so deeply in gloom that he was not sure she had even noticed the presence of a newcomer, but as he kept glancing over at her, he realized that from time to time she looked back. There was a sharpness in her eyes, behind her spectacles, that gave him hope. The dybbuk had not eaten her entirely. She could still be drawn out.

Little Ash waited for her to speak to him, but she never did, though the others had any number of questions to ask and wanted to see every fabric swatch and ribbon he'd brought from the Shulmans' apartment. More than anything, they were hungry for news, and he found himself explaining a great deal more about the Boaz Brothers factory strike than he'd expected them to want to hear. It seemed Mr. Boaz was not popular among his own servants, as none of them seemed upset at the thought that his factory might be shut down, even though this would presumably eat into the money they themselves were paid. He did his best to encourage them in this rebellious spirit, without dropping the affect of a baffled newcomer, asking questions of his own as if he did not know perfectly well what striking was.

He had been there for half an hour or more, and the cook had made him taste a bit of everything she was cooking, when a bell rang from upstairs. Everyone reacted as if they'd been caught out, suddenly ceasing conversation and looking around in apprehension.

"It's just Miss," said the housemaid, when the bell rang again. "I'd better see what she needs, then. These two ribbons, please."

The others hurried to settle their purchases as well, as if the ringing bell had irrevocably shattered the atmosphere and they'd all suddenly remembered that they were supposed to be working. As the housemaid went upstairs to see what Boaz's daughter needed, Bonny showed Little Ash, his pockets now full of nickels, to the back door.

As he went out, he glanced back and saw Essie shutting her ledger.

thirty-five

URIEL AND ROSE had settled themselves on the wall of the little park, far enough from the house for it not to be obvious that they were spying, but close enough so that they could see if anyone came to the door. Uriel became very anxious when Little Ash disappeared inside, thinking of every kind of trouble he could get into by himself, and it was deeply relieved when he appeared from the back, looking perfectly untouched.

When he came over to join them, however, he started scraping his shoes on the street with an expression of disgust. "That house is a curse! Mr. Boaz should count himself lucky he hasn't died already."

"What do you mean?" said Rose.

"The place is haunted by a dybbuk," said Little Ash. "And it's very, very angry with him. Not with everyone, I think, as it's more or less left the servants alone. But with the family certainly."

"And Essie?" said Uriel. "Did you see Essie?"

"Essie's up to her ears in bad luck, but she's alive." He laid the rebbe's trunk down on the cobbles and opened it up, as if he were showing his wares to the two of them, but instead he extracted a swatch of red cloth and laid it on the ground to clean his shoes. "In danger, though. That banquet they're preparing for—we should get her out then. It sounds like Boaz isn't letting anyone leave the house, but he'll be distracted with guests. Get Essie, get his account books, and get far away, that's what we should do. You can scarcely breathe in there."

He stepped off the cloth and carefully folded it up, using his fingertips only, and hopped over the wall into the park to bury it in the soil. As Rose watched him, perplexed, Uriel was the first to see Essie approaching, looking over her shoulder as she hurried toward them.

"Ashel." It prodded him in the shoulder to get his attention.

"Ah," said Little Ash, pleased. "I thought she had her eyes on me."

Essie stopped a few feet from them, eyeing them all suspiciously. They looked like what they were, a group of friends behaving somewhat oddly, rather than a peddler and customers. Essie was clever enough to see it.

At the same time, she was clever enough to feel the danger that followed her, even if she didn't recognize it as supernatural. "You said they're striking at Mr. Boaz's factory," she said to Little Ash. "Is that true?"

"I wouldn't lie," said Little Ash.

Essie searched all of their faces. "Did they send you?"

"Did who send us?" said Rose, entirely forgetting to pretend that they weren't together.

"The strikers. To spy on the house, maybe?"

"What an idea," said Little Ash. "Why would anyone want to spy on this house?"

"Yes," said Uriel, holding its hand out to quiet him. "Yes, we are here to spy on the house."

To Little Ash's surprise, Essie breathed a sigh of relief at this. "Malke Shulman sent you? I couldn't get word to her. Mr. Boaz hasn't allowed me to leave the house, but I hoped she'd think of something. You have to bring her a message, please. Mr. Boaz is going to try and stop them from striking, but they mustn't stop. They can win if they only hold on. I do his accounts, I know the truth. He's got nothing left."

"We'll tell her," Uriel promised. "But to tell the truth, we weren't from her at all. We're from your shtetl. We came on behalf of your father, because he misses your letters."

Essie looked them over again, a closer inspection. "From *Shtetl*? You can't be from Shtetl; I don't know you. And all right, I don't know the boys so well. But her, I'd remember."

She nodded at Rose, who felt unaccountably pleased to be so singled out.

"She's from Belz," said Little Ash. "And we are from

Shtetl. Shall we prove it? I can name everyone in your father's minyan."

Essie considered it. "Go ahead, then."

"There's your father, Samuel the Baker. Yakov Alter, and Yakov Yunger, who's eighty years old yet, may he live to a hundred and twenty. Abraham Krumer and Abraham Shtarker. And the cheesemaker, and the cantor, and all three Moshes. Abraham Krumer used to tease Abraham Shtarker by making you quote Mishnahs he couldn't."

"All right," said Essie slowly. "That's true. But then who are you?"

"We are angels," said Uriel, for the sake of simplicity. "The angels from your shtetl."

"I'm the evil angel," said Little Ash. "That's the good angel. But in any case we both came to help you, and not a moment too soon, because you're covered in bad luck already."

Essie glanced over her shoulder, checking the windows of the Boaz house for any spies, then leaned closer to them and whispered, "What do you mean, covered in bad luck?"

She said it not as if she thought they were talking non-sense, but as if the sudden supernatural turn of the conversation had confirmed some analysis of her own.

"The house has a dybbuk," said Little Ash, matter-of-factly. He reached into the rebbe's trunk and pulled out a length of red ribbon, which he held out to her. "I'd put this on before I went back in, if I were you. You're soaked in it."

Essie took the ribbon and rubbed it between her thumb and finger as she stood thinking. "A dybbuk, you said?"

"It rides on Mr. Boaz, but there's bad luck all over the house, and the ledgers are bleeding with it."

Essie nodded. "I've been dreaming of her. The old Mrs. Shulman. I told myself it was only silliness, that I'm only anxious, keeping secrets I don't even want to keep. But everyone else in the house seems to feel it too."

"We are going to get you out," Rose cut in. "At the banquet tomorrow. We'll be there, and while everyone's looking the other way, you can run off."

"Only, you have to bring the ledgers with you," said Little Ash. "That way we can prove Mr. Boaz has been lying, and ruin him forever. I don't think your old Mrs. Shulman would settle for less."

"Good," said Essie, decisively. "I won't settle for less than ruining him either."

Essie couldn't stay gossiping in the street for long, but they agreed that she and Rose would find each other at the banquet, and they would let Uriel and Little Ash into the house to look for the ledgers, which were kept locked up in Mr. Boaz's office when not in use. Essie had a key for the desk they were stored in, but not for the office door itself, which would surely be locked; Little Ash and his lockpicks could eliminate that obstacle. In the meantime, the three conspirators returned to the Lower East Side with Essie's message for the striking workers.

At the Shulmans' apartment, they found that the first day of the strike had not gone as expected. Malke and Freidy were sitting in the apartment alone, exhausted and disheveled, and none of the Shulman men were anywhere to be seen.

Ordinarily, the picket lines stayed peaceful for days or even weeks while bosses and workers waited for the other side to show its weakness, or the bosses tried to bring in scab workers. Contrary to this established tradition, today's first day of picketing had come to an abrupt end when, instead of being replaced by scab workers, the strikers were confronted with a gang of toughs from the Irish side of the Bowery, armed with blackjacks and in a terrible temper. As Malke wearily explained to Uriel and Little Ash, Isaak and his brothers had been arrested and taken to the Tombs, this ominous name referring to what was officially, and with some irony, called the Halls of Justice. The eldest Mr. Shulman, Malke's father-in-law, had gone to plead for his sons' release on the basis that it was not in fact a crime to stand in the street and cry out for mercy.

Little Ash and Uriel exchanged worried glances. They knew well that Mr. Boaz's gangster colleague had his eye on Isaak, and there was a chance that no amount of pleading would free him.

"We will go and see if we can get them back," said Uriel. "You need to say Kaddish for your father."

This it said with the thought in mind that though it had not seen Malke's father, the rebbe, in days, it could not be entirely certain that he hadn't become a dybbuk himself. Malke seemed indeed to be having a great deal of bad luck.

"That's kind of you," Malke started to say, clearly intending to tell them it wasn't their dangerous business to be involved in, but Uriel took Little Ash by the arm and dragged him out of the room before she could finish her sentence.

"What!" said Little Ash, nevertheless going along with his chevrusa as it led him down the stairs. "We'll go to the New York City jail and try to break out a man we know for certain is the target of assassins and villains of every kind? Is that the promise you just made that woman?"

"Her name is Malke," said Uriel. "And yes. Don't be angry with me; it is the right thing to do."

Little Ash was not angry in the least. He was, in fact, delighted. "The right thing to do? It sounds like making trouble, as far as I'm concerned."

"Very much like that," Uriel agreed. "Who else can help her?"

"I don't see how even *we* can help her," Little Ash admitted. "But don't let that upset you; if you're wanting to make trouble with me, then certainly I want to make trouble with you."

This being agreed, they went to see what they could make of the infamous jail.

thirty-six

THE TOMBS WAS SO NAMED both for the tendency of young men designated criminals to disappear inside the damp stone edifice forever, and for its resemblance to a slab of cemetery stone. In its own way, it was as close to the heart of New York City as Ellis Island was to the heart of America.

Uriel and Little Ash stood outside it that Monday night, looking at the grey stone façade crawling with sins and misfortune, and both felt overwhelmed by the size of it all. The Tombs held prisoner more people than lived in their own shtetl, and even the angel found it difficult to feel hopeful when faced with such a sight.

As they were waiting, they caught sight of the elder Mr. Shulman, Isaak's father. He was leaving the building, dejected and alone: his sons had not made bail.

"Reb Shulman!" Little Ash called out to him, and the

old man looked up. When he came over, the demon said, "Malke sent us to see if there's anything that can be done for Isaak."

Mr. Shulman sighed and shook his head. "There's nothing to be done for any of them—but Isaak isn't even here. They say he never came in, but his brothers insist that he was with them, and then he was taken away."

"Taken away?" Little Ash tilted his head, looking about as if he could catch sight of Isaak's trail somehow. "Who took him?"

"They didn't know him. Not a policeman. Some gentile. Mr. Salvan, he was called."

"Sullivan," said Little Ash. "Mr. Shulman, I know this man. He works for Mr. Boaz."

The old man was not surprised by this terrible news. The day had worn him down to the point where even knowing that this meant his son was in terrible danger could do nothing to stir his spirits. He merely shook his head and gazed at the cobbles.

"We will find him," said Uriel. It did not know how they would, but after all, they had found Essie. "You go home and rest. We will bring Isaak back."

Mr. Shulman did not question why the rebbe's greenhorn students would make such a promise. He merely shuffled away, back toward Hester Street, with his hands in the pockets of his capote.

Uriel turned to Little Ash to ask how they could find a man they knew by name only, but the sheyd was already pacing up and down the street, frowning at the ground with the air of a terrier after a rat. There was something uncanny about the way he moved, as if at any moment he might drop to all fours and scurry away.

"You can see something?" Uriel asked.

"I've seen that Sullivan before," said Little Ash. "I know his character, and I have a good reason to want vengeance on him. After all, he tried to shoot you."

Uriel could see the film of creeping sins that covered the ground here, but it could make no distinctions between them; they all blurred together in its sight into an indistinguishable mass, like a coating of mud. Little Ash, however, appeared to know precisely what he was looking at, and he suddenly took off toward the west, his eyes on the ground. Uriel had to hurry to keep up with him.

Even after dark, New York City was busy, with streets full of activity. Once in a while Little Ash would lose the trail in the crowd and have to double back, but he always found it again, following an instinct as strong as the one that told Uriel exactly when it was time for prayers. At the corner of Mulberry Street, Little Ash paused to tuck his tzitzis into his pockets, then offered his cap to Uriel.

"Hide your peyes." He tucked his own shorter sidelocks behind his ears as the angel fitted the cap onto its head. "We're in a gentile neighborhood. It's only for safety."

Having thus made themselves look as much like an inconspicuous pair of gentile messenger boys as their faces would allow, they continued down the street, moving more slowly now as Sullivan's trail crisscrossed itself.

"He lives near here, or does business here," Little Ash

explained to Uriel, who was keeping a lookout on their sur-roundings while he kept his eyes on the ground. This was a rougher neighborhood, and though the street was busy, they had caught more than one suspicious eye. If it had imagined Hester Street to resemble Krumer Street at first, it now saw what the true Krumer Street of New York City was. The trail of Mr. Sullivan led them in twists and turns past saloons and dingy theaters and gloomy tenement door-ways piled with trash.

"I do not like this," Uriel whispered when Little Ash paused at the mouth of a crooked alleyway.

"I like it very much," said Little Ash, with the contrary spirit of demons. In fact he did not like bringing his part-ner to such a place as this, especially now that it had a name and soul for the Angel of Death to grab onto. Yet at the same time there was something comforting about having it by his side. He liked that they were now partners not only in study, but also in the world—where he felt he had a bit more authority. "He's gone this way." There was one light visible down the alley, a rather sickly bar front with a few men loitering outside. "Sullivan. It reeks of him."

"So we will try to get shot today, like before."

Little Ash lifted his eyes for a second to grin at the joke, and Uriel saw that his pupils had gone wide, the hunter close to his prey. Isaak Shulman's captors might not know it yet, but they were in trouble.

✧ ✧ ✧

The bar was called the Irons, when it was called anything at all. Most didn't bother to speak of it. If you were not a regular sight at the Irons, you might prefer not to speak of it at all, for fear of drawing the wrong kind of attention.

Mr. Sullivan—the blackmailer, the kidnapper, and the gangster—*was* a regular sight. Tonight he had come in with a handful of his cronies, dragging with them the unconscious Isaak Shulman, whom they'd locked up in a back room to stew in pain while they refreshed themselves with a glass of caustic gin. Mr. Sullivan wouldn't mind getting his dollar from Boaz for stopping the strike, but working for Boaz was no longer his priority. His patience had run out.

He was, at the moment, composing in his head a new threat to send to the recalcitrant debtor. Boaz wanted the esteem of the uptown types; he was throwing his daughter a party to keep up the appearance of respectability. There would be any number of wealthy and influential people at the Boaz house for the banquet, Mr. Sullivan knew. It would make a fine stage to ruin Boaz's reputation forever; or else, it made for excellent leverage. No respectable person, for instance, would want it known that he'd hired kidnappers to break a strike at his place of business. Even less would he want the body of the kidnapped worker to appear in his own house on his own daughter's birthday.

Mr. Sullivan did not believe that Boaz was out of money. He did not believe that Jews were ever truly out of money. It seemed to him that they always lied and complained about it, trying to scrape for pity from the world instead of doing honest business. There would be a secret store of treasure: didn't the expense of the birthday banquet prove it? That money could have gone to Sullivan's pocket instead of advertising for charity girls from the ghetto. Sullivan felt his conscience quite clear about the prospect of extorting from another liar.

He was, in fact, feeling satisfied with his day's work, and quite relaxed in the familiar territory of the bar. He had not bothered to set any guards on the room where Isaak lay, nor at the bar's entrances. He had no reason to believe he had been followed, and indeed no reason to believe the striking workers had any recourse against him.

He had not counted on the Universe itself to send messages for him.

Neither Uriel nor Little Ash much fancied a direct confrontation with a bar full of dangerous gentiles, but there was a mere crack of an alley next to the building, barely wide enough to navigate without scraping one's elbows. It reeked heavily of urine, drink, and rotten food, but Little Ash led Uriel sideways through it to the rear of the bar, where they found a yard with outhouses, smelling even worse, and a back door that hung askew on its hinges.

Little Ash went up to it without hesitation. Uriel followed after, feeling some relief that they had not needed to scale another fire escape, even as they found themselves in a poorly lit and narrow hallway creeping with both natural and supernatural vermin.

"Look," Little Ash whispered, pointing to a spot on the floor that looked to Uriel exactly like every other filthy spot. "There's been a dybbuk here."

"From Mr. Sullivan?"

"Not sure." He knelt down, inspecting the floor more closely, and Uriel bit its lip to keep from dragging him upright again. It did not like even the tips of its hooves touching the sticky, spongy floorboards, and hated to think what Little Ash was breathing in by bending so close. "I didn't notice it before. But the streets were so busy, you miss things."

"I don't see anything. Is a dybbuk different from those creeping sins you told me about?"

"A dybbuk is full of resentment," said Little Ash. "It smells of the grave and it leaves a trail of bad luck everywhere."

Perhaps, Uriel thought, it could not pick out the traces because it did not know what the grave smelled like.

They passed a door that was open a crack, showing a storeroom full of broken furniture. A second door was closed, but opened easily when Little Ash tested the knob. There was a bed inside with a man snoring deeply, dead drunk. The next door was locked.

"Now, why would you lock a door in a place like this?" said Little Ash. "You'd never leave anything here worth stealing."

He said it as if he had experience with such places. Since there were none in Shtetl, Uriel had to assume that he had found them in the larger villages, on market days. It wished for the first time that it had accompanied him on more of his market-day wanderings. It did not like thinking of him creeping around such places by himself.

He would be offended if it said so. It kept the thought to itself and sketched its name on the doorframe for him, to shed light on the lock as he dug his picks from his pocket. This lock was tricky; rarely used, it had rusted a bit inside. But the door itself was loose in its frame, and Little Ash only needed to push the lock halfway open before he could shove the door open with his shoulder.

Isaak Shulman lay in a heap on the floor, disheveled and unconscious. A few stains on the floorboard, looking like old blood, suggested that he was not the first person to have been taken to this room for a beating. There was a sharp scent of fear in the air.

Uriel pushed past Little Ash and knelt at Isaak's side, forgetting its distaste for touching the floor. It felt his forehead, and then his chest, looking for a heartbeat and signs of breath. "He's alive. But he's bleeding."

Little Ash was taking a step forward to help it lift Isaak from the floor when, with a sudden jerk, he sat up on his own. Uriel, startled, fell backward. Isaak's eyes shone strangely in the dark room as he glared at them.

"Reb Shulman?" said Uriel. "We have come to help you."

"I need no help," said Isaak. "I will take care of this myself. Certainly from *you* I need no help!"

This was directed at Little Ash, who had stopped in his

tracks and was watching Isaak with suspiciously narrowed eyes.

"I don't see what position you're in to refuse my help," he said. "You're locked up in a neighborhood you don't know, surrounded by gentiles, and that body's covered in bruises."

Isaak leapt to his feet, as agile as if he had not just been lying knocked out in a heap. He seemed ready to attack Little Ash, but Uriel stepped between them at the last second, and Isaak's fist smacked it directly in the face.

For a second all three of them stood still and shocked. Then Little Ash pushed forward past the angel's shoulder and slapped Isaak in the face.

"Now look what you've done!" he shouted in the Holy Tongue.

Uriel had never been punched before. It lifted a hand to its face and found that its nose was bleeding. It stared at Isaak, and Isaak stared back in confusion.

"Rebbe?" said Uriel.

thirty-seven

THE DYBBUK OF MALKE'S FATHER, who had possessed her husband Isaak's body, turned his eyes away, as if he did not want to see what he'd done to Uriel. "I come to America and I find a daughter who can't mourn me, and a husband who can't support her. I come to America and I find demons and villains running wild! I will not let this pass."

"So what?" said Little Ash, folding his arms. "You'll tear them all to pieces with a pair of bare human hands? You'll drag your daughter's husband through the fire and let him die for your revenge?"

"He is no husband to her," the rebbe hissed. He stepped closer to Little Ash, leaning over him. Isaak might have been injured, but he was tall and well muscled, and the dybbuk felt no pain. "He puts her in danger with his troublemaking."

"So you'll make her a widow," said Little Ash, before

Uriel could open its mouth to tell him not to say anything provoking. "You'll orphan your grandchild?"

The rebbe let out a roar of anger and grabbed Little Ash by the front of his shirt, flinging him aside with inhuman strength. Little Ash crashed into the pile of furniture in the corner of the room and lay there stunned as the rebbe shoved past Uriel and out of the room.

"Why did you provoke him?" the angel cried, frustrated.

"I was telling him the truth!" snapped Little Ash. He pushed himself upright with difficulty. He'd hit his head in the fall and felt dizzy.

"He didn't need to *hear* the truth." Uriel didn't wait for the demon to find his feet; it could already hear shouting from the front of the bar. The rebbe was out of his senses, and Isaak was in danger. So was everyone else in the building, and though it seemed likely not many of them deserved redemption, Uriel could not rest on such assumptions. It quickly wiped the blood from its face and ran after the dybbuk.

The bar was smoky and crowded, already chaotic even when no one was fighting. Yet the appearance of Isaak Shulman, bruised and bleeding and enraged, was enough to draw attention. The presence of the dybbuk made the air feel closer, somehow charged with energy as if there were a storm approaching. Men had lifted their heads from their card games and their drinks and felt, suddenly, that they ought to have chosen another place to be tonight.

Mr. Sullivan, sitting with a group of his cronies in a

corner with a good view of both doors, had been the first to recognize Isaak, and he leapt to his feet with a yell, reaching into his coat for his gun. Before he had even gotten it out of his pocket, the dybbuk, moving quick as lightning, had grabbed a bottle of whiskey and smashed it across the bar, scattering nearby drinkers. He was about to lunge forward with the improvised weapon when Uriel skidded through the doorway behind him, its hooves slipping on the wet floor.

"Rebbe, stop!" it cried. "This isn't right!"

"Do you know what is right?" the rebbe snarled, pausing for a moment. "You betrayed me. You promised you would bring me to my daughter in time."

"But I did," Uriel protested. "I did!"

"Not in time!" the rebbe shouted. He lifted the broken bottle, seeming for a moment as if he would hit Uriel with it—but a shot rang out from behind him, and he had to duck aside as the bullet hit the wall of bottles behind the bar, shattered glass flying everywhere. Mr. Sullivan did not care to wait and see how an argument between Isaak Shulman and his accomplice would go: he intended to shoot them both and be done with it.

The rebbe caught Uriel by the collar of its sweater, pulling it close. "Not in time," he repeated. "For a demon you betrayed me. You stopped to wait for word from him, and my time ran out. What is he to the world? What is he that my daughter should not say Kaddish for me?"

Uriel blinked at him, confused. It had known the rebbe

mistrusted and disliked Little Ash—but it had not thought this was so important. "He is my chevrusa."

The rebbe growled and shoved it away. "Do not tell me what is right. I will see this Mr. Sullivan dead."

Sullivan was trying to get another clear shot at them through the crowd of men, some of whom were trying to leave through the narrow doors, while others, angry on their own behalf to have their night of entertainment interrupted, were brandishing blackjacks and guns of their own, looking for the source of the trouble. Uriel could see that soon enough it would be all of the barflies versus the two interlopers, the two obvious Jews at the back door. If the rebbe could not see it, it was because his rage had blinded him to everything else. But not even the wild strength of the dybbuk would be enough.

The rebbe was shoving through the crowd to get to Sullivan, who had his gun raised and pointed in their direction, squinting one eye to get his aim. His companions, a pair as rough-looking as himself—indeed, one might have been his brother—were stalking forward with their fists at the ready to grab the dybbuk-Isaak and hold him still.

Little Ash came up behind Uriel and tapped it on the shoulder. "We have to go. Leave him, he won't listen. If we stay, we'll be shot to pieces."

"We can't leave him," Uriel objected. "We can't let Isaak die, and the rebbe—we can't just let him forget himself."

"He's forgotten himself already!" Little Ash stamped his foot. "All but the worst parts of himself! You don't have any obligation to him; he's nothing but an angry old man."

"Ashel . . ."

"Ashel, nothing! I'm not helping the bastard."

Uriel looked from Little Ash back to the rebbe. He'd smashed a man—a stranger, not even one of Sullivan's circle—over the head with the whiskey bottle and three others were trying to wrestle him to the floor. One or two of the bystanders were calling encouragement, not wanting to get involved with the pain-crazed and apparently invulnerable Isaak, but wanting to see blood all the same. For now, the spectacle of the rebbe's strength had kept all eyes on him, no one really noticing the two by the door.

Little Ash caught hold of the back of Uriel's sweater and gave it a tug. "If we get any closer, he'll just hit us too. He's done listening. Just leave him."

Uriel planted its hooves and shook its head, resisting. Malke had suffered enough grief. The angel could not watch her father drag her husband's body into death with him.

It pulled away from Little Ash, ignoring his shout of protest, and reached over to the bar. This end of the room was soaked in spilled alcohol, the bar top slick with it. Uriel dipped its finger in the liquid and sketched, quickly, the letters of the Name the rebbe had taught it—alef, vav, resh— and with a whoosh of air, the puddle of whiskey on the bar burst into flames.

"What are you *doing*?!" screamed Little Ash, dragging Uriel backward. It felt the flames lick at its fingers and snatched its hand back instinctively. All around them, men were ducking their heads, expecting another gunshot—and then the sounds of the fight gave way to shouts of "Fire! Fire!" and suddenly everyone who was still in the room was pushing for the doors.

Little Ash was already pulling Uriel toward the back of the building, and now the crowd pushed them on, so that the angel could no longer resist him. The fire climbed toward the ceiling at shocking speed: by the time they turned the corner into the back hallway, the room seemed eaten up by the flames. Uriel lost sight of the rebbe in the jostle of the crowd, almost fell, and was forced to turn away to watch where it was going. Little Ash had both hands wrapped around its arm, pulling with all his strength.

Something exploded behind them. A gunshot? Or the last unbroken bottles? They were out in the air now, in the small backyard. Little Ash was quicker on his feet than most of the men around them; Uriel now let him lead, no longer resisting, as they ran out of the yard and into an alley, another alley, twists and turns until the city spat them out onto a busy street still crowded with nighttime revelers.

"What was that!" gasped Little Ash, slowing at last. "What sort of madness was that?!" He let go of Uriel's arm so that he could lean on the wall of a building, coughing up soot and taking some of the weight off his feet. "You could have killed all of us!"

Uriel had no answer for him. It had only meant to

create a distinction. It had not known the fire would spread so quickly.

Little Ash took a moment to catch his breath, then looked up at Uriel, who was standing next to him in silence, frowning at nothing. There were cuts on its face from the bottles shattered by Sullivan's gunshot.

"Well," said the demon. "I suppose it's no great loss for the world if you burned down a bar full of murderers."

"No," said Uriel, blinking the faraway look from its eyes. "No, it isn't right—I didn't mean to. Others could be hurt . . . and we didn't get Isaak back."

Little Ash snorted. "We were never going to get Isaak back. Hold still, you're bleeding."

He untucked his tallis katan from under his dirt-and-soot-smudged shirt and tore off a corner of the fabric to dab the cuts on Uriel's face. The angel was now wringing its hands, oblivious to the blisters beginning to rise on the one it had used to sketch the Holy Name that started the fire.

"I don't know what I am doing," it said at last. "Ashel, I don't know what I'm doing."

"Hmm?"

"I thought it was good, having a name, and doing what I like. But look what I did! Look what a terrible thing I did, because I wasn't thinking, and no one told me not to do it."

"I did tell you," said Little Ash, licking a finger and swiping away a smudge of soot from over the angel's eyebrow. "I told you the rebbe wouldn't listen and we should leave."

"But you're *always* telling me things!" Uriel wailed. "And you—you don't always know what is the right thing. You don't even always know what is the thing that will keep us from getting killed, so don't tell me that's why I should listen to you! You made me get shot in Warsaw. You almost made me get shot at the factory. You almost let that doctor on the island kill you!"

Little Ash dropped his hand from its face and took a step back. "I didn't *let* any of those things happen."

"Oh Ashel!" Uriel dropped its head into its hands and burst into tears. "What are we doing here?"

Little Ash shoved his hands in his pockets to keep from reaching out to it again, and turned away. "We're rescuing Essie. So we'd best go back to Hester Street, and you'd best sleep, so we can do what we planned tomorrow. Unless you'd rather not follow that plan, since *I* made it, and I don't know what the 'right thing' is?"

"Please don't be cruel." Uriel sniffed. "Of course we should rescue Essie, but we've killed Isaak—I killed Isaak."

"The rebbe killed Isaak," said Little Ash curtly. "Come on. We should go to the baths before we get to Malke's apartment. Then we can say we don't know where Isaak is, and if we visit the mikveh, we'll get the bad luck off from the dybbuk."

Uriel wiped its face on the sleeve of its sweater and shook its head. "We shouldn't lie to her."

"It isn't a lie. We don't know where he is. *I'll* tell her, if you hate it so much. She doesn't want to hear that her husband's been kidnapped and burnt to a crisp."

Uriel wished it could find the words to tell him he didn't need to act so heartless, but he was looking away down the street, and the tense line of his shoulders shut it out.

"All right," it said, resigned. "All right. Tell her we could not find him."

thirty-eight

THE NEXT MORNING SAW ROSE, dressed sharply in her new dress and with her hair again done carefully by Bluma, waiting with a handful of other girls at the Council House to see if they would be accepted as guests for Mr. Boaz's daughter's birthday party. An intimidating older woman from uptown had given each of them a short interview, in which she tried to determine, mainly by staring them in the face from behind her spectacles, whether they were virtuous and industrious, or simply looking for a free meal. She spoke Yiddish like a German, with strange, mushy consonants. A few of the girls had been entirely baffled by her, but Rose was beginning to feel that nothing could faze her anymore.

Rose had impressed the lady, whose name was Mrs. Ficksman, very much. She had told the tale of straightening up her father's accounts and supporting her friend's impoverished but pious family. Mrs. Ficksman had as good as told her she would have a spot, giving her the encouragement that "Those girls we invite to the party will have a ride in an automobile, you know—it's quite a treat!"

Once she had finished interviewing each girl, Mrs. Ficksman went out of the room for a few minutes of deliberation with the Council nurse, perhaps to see if the latter knew any rumors about them from working in the neighborhood, and then came back with her choices: Rose and two other girls. They would be picked up from the Council House that evening, would attend Minnie's birthday dinner, and would be able to speak through Mrs. Ficksman and her odd Yiddish with the other guests, perhaps impressing them and finding good jobs or a bit of charity from the uptowners.

Rose had already been more or less aware of these details from Essie, who had heard them already in the course of the household's plans. The two of them would find each other while the rest of the party guests were having their pre-dinner conversations, and they would let Little Ash and Uriel into the house by a back way, so that with the help of Essie's keys, they could get into Mr. Boaz's office and search for his ledgers. Rose felt in a way that this illicit activity would be easier than making conversation with people who saw her as an object of charity and did not speak Yiddish. She didn't like the thought of merely smiling and nodding and behaving pleasantly while unable to speak her mind to anyone.

The automobile was not a bad bonus, on top of it. She felt bad for enjoying herself when Bluma was once again on the picket line and the strikers were worried they'd be attacked by strikebreakers again, but as the sun began to set and the automobile pulled up outside the Council House, Rose couldn't help feeling a bit of a thrill. Here she was, far from Belz, on her way to bring a wicked man to justice, and riding in a sleek metal machine that zipped along the city streets like a swift fish against the current of the crowds. The wind in her hair felt like a promising omen.

The last time she had seen the Boaz house, it had seemed very gloomy from the outside, with all the curtains shut and an oppressive silence around it. Today an effort had been made to give it a cheerful appearance, with fresh flowers in the window boxes and extra lamps burning against the evening shadows. The downtown girls were delivered to the front door, like regular guests, which set the other two to delighted laughter. Rose joined in with them for appearances, but as soon as she crossed the threshold she cast her eyes about for Essie.

It was not as easy as she'd thought to spot her. After all, the party was intended for Mr. Boaz's daughter, who was about Rose's own age. In addition to the charity girls, Minnie had invited her schoolmates, and the house was full of girls in their prettiest dresses. There were other guests as well: the well-dressed adults whom, according to rumor, Mr. Boaz was trying to impress with his respectability. Although Rose did not know him, one was Rabbi Wolf, who had refused to help Uriel get Little Ash off Ellis Island. Mr. Boaz himself was moving about the front drawing room and hallway with a nervous energy, trying to pay attention to every important guest at once.

At the bottom of the main staircase stood a manservant with a dark expression, whom Rose immediately suspected of not being a real manservant, but one of the strikebreaking gangsters. She made note of him to mention to Little Ash and Uriel, and looked around again for Essie.

Mrs. Ficksman swept Rose and the other charity girls into the drawing room and introduced them to Minnie—a pretty, curly-haired girl in lots of lace and ruffles, who looked a bit uncomfortable with all the attention. The other schoolgirls gravitated toward them, fascinated by the idea of girls their own age who lived away from their families, and worked, and did all sorts of daring and dangerous things like going to dance halls.

Essie had expected to be helping serve drinks and little appetizers to the guests. She'd told Rose this was where she would be. There were other servants circulating, and Rose couldn't resist the temptation to try a small pastry from one of their trays, but she didn't see Essie among the household staff.

After a few minutes, she decided there was nothing else for it. She would have to move to the next step of the plan herself.

When Mrs. Ficksman's attention was elsewhere, Rose quickly slipped away. She passed by Mr. Boaz talking to the rabbi, and went out into the hall. If anyone asked in English where she was going, she wouldn't understand them and would not have to pretend; if they asked in Yiddish, she was prepared to tell them without shame that she was on her way to the bathroom. In fact, she was beginning to feel a bit queasy, more so as she hurried past the glowering man at the foot of the stairs. She might really need to be sick if anything else went amiss.

Once out of sight of the guard on the stairway, she tested a door and found herself in a library—a grand room with shelves of books to the ceiling and big armchairs arranged around the fireplace. Her father would have been overjoyed to find himself in such a room, and for a moment she wished she could stop and inspect the books. But Little Ash and Uriel were waiting.

There were tall windows overlooking the garden, and Rose hastily went over and pushed one open. Little Ash and Uriel were meant to be outside, but Rose worried there might have been guards on the drive and they'd been stopped.

They hadn't. They were just where they were meant to be, concealed in the bushes outside.

"Took you long enough," said Little Ash when they'd climbed into the library. He was in a terrible mood because his legs had gone stiff from crouching under a rhododendron and he and Uriel had slept poorly the night before, each of them miserably keeping to their own side of the quilt they shared on the floor of the Shulmans' apartment. Besides that, he was keenly aware of the ominous atmosphere in the

Boaz house, and having been thrown across a room by the rebbe's dybbuk, he had no desire to see another dybbuk again so soon.

"It took me exactly as long as it needed to take!" snapped Rose. "I couldn't find Essie, so I don't have the keys. You'll have to get into his office by yourselves."

Little Ash swore under his breath.

"I'm going to check the servants' quarters and see if I can find her," Rose went on. "No one will think it's terribly strange for me to be lost in the house, because I'm supposed to be here, and I'm a silly greenhorn girl. I can pretend to be dazzled by the richness of everything if anyone asks. You two have to stay out of sight—and there's a very suspicious man at the bottom of the stairs, so don't do anything obvious."

Little Ash had made note of the servants' staircase on his visit the day before, so he was able to lead them in the right direction as they left the library, glancing over their shoulders to be sure the man at the front stairs was not watching. They climbed to the second floor on quick feet, ready each second for someone coming down from above to shout an alarm, but there was no one.

At the second floor, Little Ash and Uriel crept out into the hall while Rose continued upward to check the servants' attic for Essie. The second-floor hallway was carpeted, which helped silence their steps, and Little Ash could see a second carpet of the dybbuk's prints, coating the floor and the walls. It was clear enough which room was Boaz's office. Bad luck had spilled out into the hallway from under the door, thick as ink.

"You keep watch," he whispered to Uriel as he took out his lockpicks. "Once we have the ledgers we go find Rose and Essie, and run."

Uriel stood behind him, listening carefully in the direction of the main stairs. The sounds of cheerful conversation from below made it difficult to hear if anyone were coming up, but at least that would also keep the guard from hearing any sound Little Ash made in the course of his break-in.

This lock opened easily, as if it had been greased. Little Ash pushed the door open carefully, ready for anything inside.

"She's here," he whispered.

"What?" Uriel turned its head.

"The dybbuk." Little Ash pointed to the desk. Even Uriel could see her, a dark figure crouched on top of Mr. Boaz's desk. She was larger than the rebbe had been in his ghostly form, but still smaller than she would have been in life. She'd pulled herself together enough to have a nearly human shape, but the proportions were off, and when she grinned at them her teeth were long and sharp.

"I have been waiting for you," she said in a painful whisper of a voice, wet and raspy at once.

thirty-nine

MRS. SHULMAN," SAID LITTLE ASH, stepping over the threshold. Uriel followed him, though it did not like the way Mrs. Shulman looked at them; it, too, remembered the rebbe's anger the night before, and his unwillingness to listen to reason.

Little Ash hesitated, glancing into the hall, and reluctantly drew the door closed behind them.

"You have come to kill Mr. Boaz," Mrs. Shulman said.

"We came for his ledgers, only," said Uriel. "Not to kill him. We want him to pay his debts and do teshuvah."

The dybbuk hissed in anger. "*Teshuvah!* It is too late for that. I will drink his blood, and if you try to stop me, I will drink yours."

"I don't mind you killing him," said Little Ash. "But we do need the ledgers, Mrs. Shulman. Your family's debts are in there, and our Essie's."

"Essie, too, I will eat," said Mrs. Shulman. "Essie has been helping him! Essie is a wicked girl, and you are a wicked, wicked creature." She leaned forward over the edge of the desk and drew in a deep breath. "I smell blood on your hands. You have no standing to lecture me."

"I told you, I'm all right with you taking your vengeance," Little Ash repeated. "Your vengeance on Mr. Boaz, only. On his comrade Mr. Sullivan, if you like. Not Essie. You don't touch her."

"Please, Mrs. Shulman," said Uriel, holding out its hands in supplication. "Your family has had enough grief. Let us only take the ledgers and have no more violence, so that they can rest and say Kaddish for you. You deserve to rest, yourself. You do not need to kill anyone. We will fix everything. Essie had no choice but to help him; she is in debt along with everyone else. She is helping us to destroy him."

"Give us today, from now until sunset tomorrow," said Little Ash. "If we haven't given your family their vengeance by then, you can kill anyone you like."

Uriel looked around at him, alarmed, and Little Ash shook his head at it, as if to say, Don't ruin it. The dybbuk of Mrs. Shulman, indeed, was giving it some thought, sitting back with her eyes narrowed.

"Mr. Boaz has a gentile accomplice, Mr. Sullivan," said Little Ash. "That's the one who arrested your sons yesterday— did you know about that? Uriel may have destroyed Mr. Sullivan already."

Uriel wished he wouldn't mention it. If it had destroyed Mr. Sullivan, equally it had destroyed Isaak, one of the same

Shulman sons—but the dybbuk held out her hand to Little Ash, smiling. The smile was full of fangs, and difficult to distinguish from a threat. But Little Ash nodded, and shook with her on the deal.

"Very well," she said. "I will rely upon you, only because I wish to be a blessing for my little grandson, who will soon be born. And if you have not delivered my justice by sunset tomorrow, I will eat you both along with Essie and Boaz and everyone I can find."

"Of course," said Little Ash, as if this did not worry him at all. He nudged Uriel with his elbow, and Uriel reluctantly added its own promise.

As it did so, Mrs. Shulman's solid form melted away, and if she remained in the room it was only as a thickening in the shadows at the tops of the walls.

"It's hard work, being a dybbuk," said Little Ash. "Not so easy to work without a body. She's been running all over this house, spying on everyone; she'll be exhausted. I knew she'd agree."

"I wish you had not promised she could kill people," said Uriel. "Even if you knew she would agree to it. You should have asked me first."

"What, so you could say no? Waste of time." Little Ash was already casting his eyes around the room, checking the spines of the books on the shelves that lined the walls. He'd seen Essie's ledger before, and he thought he would recognize it. But Mr. Boaz had bound all of his personal library in the same dark leather covers, stamped in gold. The effect was imposing, but his shelves were disordered, as if he had taken books down and shoved them back in any spot without making certain they were organized. The dybbuk's handprints were on all of the spines; there was no way to tell which she'd handled.

"If I understood why it was needed, I would not say no," said Uriel, under its breath. It took the other side of the room from Little Ash, scanning the shelves. "I just don't like you rush-rushing everywhere without telling me."

"This is not the time," Little Ash snapped. "Who's rush-rushing? I'm not the arsonist here! I'm following the same plan we've had the whole time, since we left Shtetl. If you don't like it you should have told me the hundred times we've talked before. In Warsaw or Hamburg or on the ship already you could have told me."

"Why are you so angry?" Uriel turned to look at him. "You have been angry the whole time. 'Since we left Shtetl,' that's how long you've been acting like this."

"It is not."

"Then maybe the ship. You pushed and pushed and pushed for me to come with you, and as soon as we weren't at home you don't want me around anymore? You don't like looking after me, maybe? Or you think the world is too hard for me. You think I can't be trusted to take care of myself, and you have to make all the decisions because you know what is going on and I don't? I'm not stupid, Ashel. Just because I am nicer than you, it doesn't make me stupid."

Little Ash had been glaring determinedly at the shelves, but now he, too, turned around, staring at the angel in shock. "What are you talking about? You're the one who'd rather talk to a ghost you met three weeks ago than to me, after hundreds of years we've known each other. You've been talking loshn horeh with him behind my back! You let him give you a name!"

"He didn't give me a name," said Uriel. "You gave me the name. I wanted a name so I could stay with *you*. It was only lucky the rebbe needed me to have it."

Little Ash opened his mouth to answer, but before any words could come out, there was a sound in the hall outside: the sound of heavy footsteps on the stairs.

Whatever the sheyd had intended to say was replaced with a whispered curse.

"All right," he said, waving a hand as if to dispel the conversation. "All right, never mind. Listen. I'll go out and distract them; you keep looking for the ledgers. Break into the desk if you have to. I'm the better at talking; I have more excuses. Take the lockpicks—you can lever a drawer open at least, even if the locks won't come."

He said all of this in a single breath, and held out the tools to Uriel across the desk.

"It's teamwork," he added. "Playing to our strengths. It isn't that I look down on you."

Uriel reached over and took the picks from his hand. It still did not understand how he intended it to use them, but it saw that this was Little Ash's hasty attempt at an apology. He was already balanced on his toes, ready to bolt, and as soon as it took the picks from him, he leapt for the door.

"Lock it behind me," he whispered, and then he was gone.

forty

ROSE STOPPED AT THE TOP of the stairs to catch her breath, checking her pockets to make sure she still had Little Ash's knife, just in case. She was in a narrow hallway that had shabbier carpet than the main section of the house and peeling paint, as if all the money for upkeep had gone into the public rooms. There were a few closed doors on either side, and the air felt still and heavy the way it does in empty houses. She guessed that all the servants were downstairs attending to the banquet; this would be a blessing, as her excuses would seem rather thin now that she'd strayed so far from the drawing room.

Edging forward along the hall, she checked the first door and found an empty bedroom with two narrow, neatly made beds and a few personal effects scattered about. The next two doors were similar, but the one after that was locked.

"Essie?" said Rose in a loud whisper, rattling the knob. "Essie, are you there? It's Rose."

There was a scramble of motion inside. She could almost see Essie through the door, mirroring her, even before the other girl spoke.

"Mr. Boaz didn't want me talking to the guests," she whispered back. "He's worried someone will find out about his gambling debts. The door's locked. Is everything all right downstairs? Did you find the ledgers?"

"Ash and Uriel are looking," said Rose, checking the knob again and then bending down to look at the lock. It didn't seem *so* different from the one on the rebbe's trunk. Little Ash had shown her how to lock and unlock that one about a hundred times on the ship, but she didn't have his tools. "Do you have hatpins? Or maybe one of the other maids does?"

"Try the room on the left of this one," Essie whispered back. "That's Minnie's lady's maid; she spends all of her pocket money on hats and such. What are you planning?"

"I might be able to pick the lock," said Rose. "I'll be right back."

She ran to the room next door. There was a single bed in this one, and the room was more prettily decorated than the others: perhaps Minnie Boaz was generous with her hand-me-downs or tips. There was a battered little vanity under the window, and a quick search through its drawers turned up an assortment of pins. Rose swept them all up and returned to Essie's door.

"If I can't unlock it," she whispered as she knelt by the keyhole, "then I'll have to kick it down. But I've still got shtetl boots on—that's what my cousin called them! Boots like a peasant who has to walk through the mud all day! They're sturdy enough."

Essie laughed, a pleasant, musical sound that lit a little glow in Rose's chest. From the sound of her voice, she must have been sitting just on the other side of the door. "I look forward to seeing your shtetl boots knock down my door," she said. "Unless you *can* unlock it with a hatpin, in which case I look forward to hearing the story of how you learned to do that."

"It's no story," said Rose, inserting the first pin as Little Ash had shown her. "It's just something Ash showed me when we were bored on the ship—you know how it is in steerage. You get tired of doing ordinary things."

"I didn't mind it, to tell you the truth," said Essie. "I was on my own, and my father let me take a couple of his books. It was the first time in my life I had nothing better to do than read."

"Really? Do you like reading? I like to read the newspapers."

"I used to be a regular scholar," said Essie, "reading Torah with my father. But you can't do that as a woman, can you? So now I read revolutionary books. We didn't have those in my village. It's so small; everyone lives like it's the eighteenth century."

Rose was trying to remember precisely the sequence of movements she needed with her two pins, and she was wondering if perhaps there was a secret to Little Ash's picks that he hadn't explained, which would render the hatpins useless. She very much wanted to impress Essie with this exotic skill, so for a moment she bit her tongue.

Essie didn't seem to mind. "Did you come to America by yourself too?"

"That's right. I have a little brother, in Belz, and my parents. I want to earn money for their tickets, so Motl doesn't have to go in the army."

"I have younger sisters," said Essie. "And I want to get them somewhere where they can have an education. There's no school in our shtetl. There's hardly anything at all, really. Just goats. I thought I'd be saving money by now, but Mr. Boaz and Reb Fishl back in Warsaw have eaten all my wages."

"Don't worry," Rose assured her. "We're going to make Mr. Boaz vomit them all back up."

Essie laughed again. "Even if he didn't, I'd be glad only to be out of this house. I thought it was good money, doing the numbers for him, but I'd rather work at the factory only to see other people every day."

"We'll get you out," said Rose. "And then you can do anything you like."

As if to underline her promise, the lock clicked open.

As Little Ash had expected, the footsteps did not belong to Mr. Boaz or any of his upper-class guests. He was not even surprised to see that one of the two new arrivals was

Mr. Sullivan, although, to the sheyd's delight, the man was sporting a new collection of cuts and bruises. He had not died in the bar the night before, but neither had he escaped untouched.

Little Ash strode forward, approaching the men at speed and with the illusion of confidence. If he distracted them enough, they might not even recognize that he had come from Boaz's office.

"You!" he shouted at them, in the Yiddish-accented English he'd used for his peddler character. "Where is my sister?"

Sullivan and his colleague—the man who'd been guarding the stairs—halted for a second.

"What's this?" Sullivan was annoyed at the interruption. He was in this part of the house on shaky ground himself. He'd had a conversation with Mr. Boaz earlier, and Boaz had assured Sullivan that he'd send the first payment as promised by the end of the night, but he'd also threatened to call the police if Sullivan did anything but stand in the back garden and make sure none of the striking workers showed up to make trouble.

Sullivan didn't believe that he really would—Boaz was a coward and as much of a criminal as anyone else—but it would be simpler to break into the office, take all the cash himself, and wash his hands of the whole affair. The freak appearance of Isaak Shulman the night before had rattled him. Isaak had killed at least two of his cronies in the brawl, while Sullivan himself had stood frozen in shock that the strike leader could even hold himself upright.

Freezing like that had been beneath him. The sort of thing that happened to green kids who'd never been in a real fight before. Not career men with guns in their hands. The embarrassment made him angrier than ever. He could practically taste the money, and now here was another obstacle out of nowhere.

"My sister!" said Little Ash. "You work for Mr. Boaz, isn't it? What has he done with my sister? Esther Singer! She works for him and no one has seen her."

"Not my affair," Sullivan growled.

"She's supposed to be here." Little Ash had kept moving toward the two men as they spoke, and now he caught at Sullivan's jacket. "Please, mister, that Boaz told me to go away and he won't talk to me. I looked for her everywhere. Haven't you seen her?"

"Get off," said Sullivan's companion. He grabbed Little Ash by the collar and dragged him away before his hands could find the gun inside the jacket pocket.

Sullivan had stopped and was frowning at Little Ash. He had been tempted to brush the interruption away with a simple dismissal: how was he supposed to keep track of one Jew girl among the half-starved, tattered mass of them? But when he actually looked at Little Ash, there was something familiar about the face.

"You," he said. "You work at the factory, do you?"

"Yes," Little Ash lied. Sullivan's companion still had him by the collar, and now pinned his right arm with the other hand. The demon declined to struggle. He was still trying to buy time for Uriel in the room behind him.

Sullivan was not a fool. Something about Little Ash bothered him. He took in the sharp, catlike features and the expression of greenhorn innocence that didn't sit quite right on them. Sometimes a liar recognizes another liar, not from any flaw in the lie, but from his own instincts, a prickling in the back of the mind.

"I've seen you before," he said. "You work for Isaak Shulman. Twice I've seen you. You spied on us at the dance hall, didn't you? And you were at the Irons. You let Shulman out, I guess. Where's your little friend?"

"What?" said Little Ash. The hand restraining his arm tightened as Sullivan's man waited for orders. "I don't know what you're talking about. I'm looking for my sister."

Sullivan was now peering around the hall, frowning as if he expected Uriel to materialize from the wood paneling. "Like hell you are. I saw you on the fire escape, you little sneak bastard, and you set the fire last night and nearly killed me. Keep ahold of him, Jamie. Next time Isaak Shulman tries to mess with me I'd like to serve him the kid's liver on a plate."

This struck Little Ash as an odd thing to say. Odd enough that, given that he was already discovered, he gave up his pretense entirely. "What do you mean, next time? You didn't kill Isaak already?"

"Bloody bastard beat a man over the head with a chair," said Jamie. "You won't be seeing him again."

This did not entirely answer the question, Little Ash noticed.

"Stop talking," Sullivan snapped. "Hurry up."

He did not say what he was thinking, which was that the Boaz house gave him a creepy feeling, as if someone were always watching over his shoulder. He beckoned to Jamie to follow him, dragging Little Ash along. To the demon, Sullivan added, "Don't think of calling for help, or I'll tell Boaz you're breaking into his house, and you'll be locked in the Tombs until you rot."

Little Ash was in fact not thinking of calling for help. He was trying to think how to stop them from opening Boaz's office door without getting himself shot in the head. The only way Uriel could leave the room without being seen was to jump out the window, and Little Ash was not sure it would think of that.

Sullivan rattled the knob and found the office door was locked. This at least would give Uriel some warning, but Sullivan was not in the mood for finesse, and rather than trying to unlock it, he simply took a knife from his pocket and started to hack at the doorframe. Had Mr. Boaz not spent his money poorly, this plan might have come to nothing, thwarted by high-quality hardwood. But he *had* spent it poorly, and the wood came off in big splinters, allowing Sullivan to wrench open the door before Little Ash could think of a plan.

forty-one

ROSE AND ESSIE, carrying Essie's worldly belongings wrapped up in a pair of bedsheets, stopped on the second floor, hoping to find Little Ash and Uriel with the ledgers, ready to run. Instead they saw the confrontation between Little Ash and the two men, and Uriel nowhere in sight.

"I know them," Essie whispered. "That's Mr. Sullivan and his brother. They're gangsters, from the Five Points—Mr. Boaz hired them to scare people out of striking, and to collect debts for him."

"I've seen Mr. Sullivan before too," said Rose. "We spied on him at a dance hall. He was meeting Mr. Boaz there; that's how we found this house at first."

Essie looked impressed. "How clever! But very dangerous. I don't know that I would have dared. I've been hiding away here like a little mouse."

"You're no mouse," Rose assured her. "You're . . . I don't know. A clever, patient serpent."

Essie smiled, but the look was strained, most of her attention still on the scene in the hallway. "Should we help? Can we help? Mr. Sullivan has a gun; I've seen it. Everyone in the house is afraid of him, even Mr. Boaz and the family—I don't think he's even supposed to be upstairs, though perhaps it matters less when Minnie is down in the public rooms."

"Did he say he was looking for money?" Rose asked. Essie had whispered a quick translation for her as the men were talking. "Is there a way you could find some for him? Bargain for him to let Ash go? At least so we can keep looking for the ledgers without worrying about getting shot?"

Essie thought about it. "It isn't a bad idea. I know where Mr. Boaz's safe is hidden. But of course I don't have a key, and there's a risk of making Sullivan angrier if I say so."

"The house is full of people," said Rose. "What if we called for help? I'll scream. You go outside, so you can run away if you have to, and so Mr. Boaz can't lock you up again. No one knows who I am; I can get away with it."

Essie hesitated, biting her lip. "I'll be leaving you in danger, if it goes wrong."

"It's all right," said Rose. "I don't mind. It's like an adventure. Besides, I came all the way from the Pale of Settlement by myself! Can this be more dangerous?"

Essie nodded, but she hesitated a moment longer. At last

she gave Rose an awkward pat on the shoulder and retreated down the stairs with her bundles.

Rose drew in her deepest breath.

As the office door opened, Little Ash threw himself sideways out of Jamie's grip, leaving the man holding his empty coat. Jamie swore and dove after him, but Sullivan was not distracted: he saw exactly what Little Ash had not wanted him to see, Uriel standing behind Mr. Boaz's desk with its hands up like a criminal caught in the act.

"There you are," said Sullivan. "I thought you'd be somewhere. Stealing, are we?"

Jamie grabbed for Little Ash again and missed, and, determined not to lose his grip a third time, tackled him to the ground. Little Ash twisted around and sank his teeth into the man's hand, and Jamie roared in pain. Uriel didn't care what Sullivan was saying: it leapt forward to try and intervene as Jamie punched Little Ash in the side of the head, but Sullivan caught its arm as it went past, and he slammed it into the wall.

This was the moment at which Rose started screaming, "Help! Help! Thieves!"

"Damn it!" Sullivan shouted, as sounds of alarm rose from the first floor. "Damn it."

Jamie had pinned Little Ash to the floor, holding both of his arms now twisted behind his back so that if he tried to free himself they'd be pulled out of joint. Uriel, less used to fighting, had hit its head on the wall and was trying to blink the dizziness out of its eyes.

"What now, boss?" said Jamie.

Sullivan responded with a string of curses, then shook his head to clear it. "Brazen it out. These are Isaak Shulman's boys. We'll take them down to the river, tell Boaz they were breaking in. Get rid of all three for him, and he's in our debt forever."

Rose's shouting had brought the guests out of the dining room downstairs, Mr. Boaz trying to keep ahead of them and pretend he wasn't equally alarmed. Sweaty and feverish, he was mumbling excuses at the bottom of the stairs.

Sullivan gave Uriel a shake and hissed in its face, "Try anything, and we'll shoot your friend."

Uriel looked at Little Ash, whom Jamie was now hauling to his feet. He shook his head in a way it hoped meant that he would prefer not to be shot; in any case, it did not know what sorts of things it could try without putting everyone else in the house in danger.

Sullivan gestured to Jamie to take hold of both of them. When he was satisfied that they didn't intend to make any more trouble, he straightened his jacket and quickly finger-combed his hair to make himself more respectable. It was difficult to look like a gentleman with the bruises from his encounter with the dybbuk, but he liked to put his best foot forward and tell his lies with authority.

At the top of the stairs, he gave his best reassuring smile

to the baffled dinner guests. "Do forgive us, Mr. Boaz. Everyone. My name is Peter Sullivan—I've been employed as security for Mr. Boaz's factory. You may have heard of your good host's recent troubles. Immigrants and radicals, you know. These boys have been trying to break in on your celebration, but don't worry. Everything is under control."

This speech did not do much to calm the dinner guests, or Boaz himself, but the factory owner, feverish from Mrs. Shulman clinging to his back, and unable to question the story without admitting that he had more than honest mishaps to worry about, quickly turned to shepherd them back into the dining room. "Please, everyone. Don't be alarmed. It's only a little interruption. Mr. Sullivan will take care of everything."

This was enough to convince a couple of the guests, but most hesitated in the doorway. They'd all heard of the radicals and anarchists who lurked in every corner of the immigrant neighborhoods, looking for honest businessmen whose beds they could put bombs under, but Mr. Sullivan did not have a trustworthy affect, and neither Little Ash nor Uriel looked terribly dangerous. Rabbi Wolf, among the crowd, met Uriel's eyes, recognized it as the young Hasid who had visited him the week before looking for charity, and stopped where he was, feeling distinctly unsettled.

There was thus a large audience as Jamie and Sullivan hauled their prisoners down the stairs—an uncomfortable audience, murmuring to one another in uncertainty. Minnie Boaz, who'd never liked Mr. Sullivan, thought the radical immigrants looked rather young and tragic, and blinked tears from her eyes as they went out the door.

"Who was that screaming?" someone asked, as the door closed behind the little group.

No one knew the answer.

There was a police wagon parked outside, a modern, motorized one with a steel cell in back. It belonged not to the police, but to the Sullivan gang, who had purchased it from a friend in exchange for a cut of the profits they made from smuggling. Jamie threw Little Ash in the back first, and was about to shove Uriel after him when Rose and Essie came running from the rear of the house. Rose swung the bundle of clothing and books she was carrying at Mr. Sullivan's head, drawing another outburst of cursing. Mr. Sullivan by now was thoroughly tired of these Jews, and said some things that would have burned the ears off his own mother, had she been there to hear them.

Essie ran at Jamie and was trying to help Uriel wrestle itself from his grip.

"Shoot them!" Sullivan yelled, grabbing the bundle as Rose swung it a second time. He wrenched it toward himself, pulling her off-balance.

"It's just girls," Jamie objected. "We can't shoot some girls in the street."

Sullivan threw the bundle of books aside and grabbed

Rose in a headlock. She scratched at his arm and stamped on him with the wooden heel of her boot, but all of her fighting experience came from wrestling with Motl, and while, as the elder sibling, she always won those fights, she wasn't able to pull free from a larger opponent. Jamie still had ahold of Uriel's arm and was fending off blows from Essie with the air of a confused behemoth attacked by small birds.

Sullivan took out his gun and held it to Rose's head. At the cold click of metal, Essie stopped her assault and stepped back.

"My brother doesn't want to shoot girls in the street," said Sullivan. "But I don't mind it. I've had enough. All four of you get in the wagon. Or I will shoot."

Essie held up her hands in surrender.

forty-two

IN THE BACK of the police wagon, Little Ash was rather subdued. He'd been defensive of his plan while it was working, but now that it had gone wrong it suddenly seemed to him to have been a terrible plan all along, and entirely his fault that the four of them were locked up in a steel cage, being taken who knows where.

"You did not need to help us," Uriel was saying to Essie and Rose. "It would have been safer to run away."

"Who needs safer?" said Rose, with a confidence she didn't feel at all. The little click of Sullivan's pistol was still echoing around the inside of her skull, and she found herself trembling. She wrapped her arms around her knees, feeling suddenly very cold.

"You did all this to help me," said Essie. "What sort of person would I be if I didn't try to help you in return?"

"It was very kind of you," said Uriel, graciously.

Little Ash had been lying on the floor where he'd landed when Jamie tossed him unceremoniously into the back of the wagon. He now sat up and said, "I don't have a plan for this."

They all looked at him. Rose was very pale, but her eyes were burning brightly, as they always were. Essie's expression was thoughtful. Uriel's eyes were deep and dark, and looking into them, Little Ash felt very small and very stupid, and very sorry. He had brought all of them here, but Uriel he'd brought all the way from Shtetl, and he'd treated it unfairly all the way.

"I'm sorry," he said. "For being so angry about the rebbe."

Uriel shook its head. "I am sorry I let him be rude to you. I have something to show you."

The angel put a hand inside its vest, and drew out a little leather-bound book. Everyone leaned in closer, squinting to see the pages in the dark, and with the car jostling on the cobblestones.

"I couldn't find the big ledger," said Uriel. "I think it was hidden away somewhere. But I found this book. It is a sort of diary. It has a list of people whose tickets Mr. Boaz arranged with Reb Fishl, see? He has been collecting money and sending it to Poland."

Little Ash took the book and flipped through the pages, then handed it to Essie, who'd been looking over his shoulder.

"It's almost as good as the ledger," said Essie. "This is illegal—bringing people over to work for you. Not that it always stops people, showing the world they've done something illegal, but Mr. Boaz cares very much about his reputation."

"And that rabbi," said Uriel. "The uptown rabbi, I saw him at the party. I talked to him before, and he said it is terrible for the Jews in America if any of us behave badly."

"Rabbi Wolf!" Essie exclaimed. "He's very respectable; if we show him this, he could help us."

"Right," said Little Ash. "If we show him, which means first we have to get out of this cage and away from two men with guns."

"I have your lockpicks," said Uriel.

"I have your knife," said Rose. "And a handful of hatpins. We picked a lock to get Essie out of the house! It really works."

Little Ash tilted his head at her, interested despite his despairing mood. "Really? That's very good work."

"It was amazing!" Essie agreed, the compliment bringing a little glow that chased some of the chill out of Rose's soul. "I was sure I would have to climb out the window on a rope of bedsheets, but she broke me out like a regular revolutionary."

She squeezed Rose's hand as she said it, and the glow spread further. Rose squeezed back, fighting a silly smile that she couldn't quite explain.

"So we have a book, and a knife, and some hatpins," said

Little Ash. "All I have in my pocket is a spool of thread. It isn't nothing, I suppose."

Mr. Sullivan's gang had a headquarters of sorts on the bank of the East River, in a building with damp timbers and a sagging brick façade that smelled strongly of the brackish water. Throughout its life the building had been used to store smuggled goods and smuggled people, and its cellar, a floor below the level of the riverbank outside, had much stronger locks than the little room in the back of the bar where Isaak Shulman had been kept.

Sullivan and Jamie, along with a third man who'd been smoking a cigar outside the building, marched their four prisoners to the cellar at gunpoint and locked them in. Sullivan gave no indication of when he intended to come back, and he'd left them without a light. Rose and Essie instinctively linked arms in the dark, and Uriel reached for Little Ash, hooking its hand through the back of his suspenders so as not to lose track of him.

"He's either going to leave us in here forever," said the sheyd, "or he's going to come back and kill us. Either way it's better if we get out beforehand."

"Keynehore," said Uriel. "Please don't say such things; you'll tempt the evil eye."

Little Ash scoffed and took a step forward into the dark, pulling the angel with him. He'd seen something in the corner, by the opposite wall. A dark heap of something soft, like a body.

"Can you make a light?" Little Ash asked Uriel. "Like you did in the factory, please."

He unhooked its hand from his suspenders and guided Uriel to the wall. It traced the letters of the Holy Name on the slimy brick, and the room lit with a gentle, golden glow.

Isaak Shulman was lying at the base of the wall, unconscious and handcuffed.

"Oh!" Rose gasped from behind them. She dashed forward and pushed past Little Ash to check Isaak's pulse and temperature. "He's feverish."

"They beat him yesterday," said Little Ash. "And he's been in more fights since then. But the real problem is that there's an angry dybbuk riding him."

Rose only half heard him. She'd taken the knife out of her pocket and was cutting a square from one of her petticoats. There was no clean water to be found, but the floor they stood on was dotted with puddles. She was sure she was introducing terrible diseases as she did it, but Rivke had told her there was nothing more dangerous than fever, and Isaak was burning hot, so she quashed her doubts and dipped the makeshift bandage in one of the puddles.

Little Ash watched Isaak's shallow breathing. The rebbe had been holding onto him for days now, and the exertion of the night before would probably have killed him if he'd been any less strong.

"This Isaak Shulman must have a very determined

spirit," the demon remarked to Uriel. "But if the rebbe wakes up again, he'll kill him."

"Is there anything we can do?" Uriel asked.

"We'd best get the dybbuk out," said Little Ash. "He'll burn Isaak's heart out, otherwise."

"How does one get a dybbuk out of a man?" said Essie, who at Rose's quiet request was soaking another rag in the least disreputable puddle she could find. Rose held one of Isaak's hands against the cool bricks of the wall, in hopes that she could bring some of the heat out of his blood that way.

Little Ash heaved a sigh. He was reluctant to speak to the rebbe again, after being thrown across the room, but he could see that Isaak had very little time left, and he could feel Uriel's worried gaze on his face. The easiest way would be to draw the rebbe's soul out from Isaak's eyes and devour him—if he didn't fall to pieces on his own. But Uriel would want him to save both Isaak and the rebbe, if it could be done.

There was nowhere else for the rebbe to go once he was extracted from Isaak's body.

Little Ash knelt next to Rose and took the spool of red thread from his pocket. He broke off a length and made four loops of it, which he tied around each of Isaak's wrists and ankles. He then held out a hand to Rose. "You said you have a hatpin?"

Rose checked her pockets and handed over one of the pins, a little silver one with a pretty floral headpiece. Little

Ash tested the point on his own thumb and nodded, satisfied.

He then took a breath and recited, "Menachem ben Yakov. Do you hear me?"

Isaak drew in a rattling breath, making Rose jump. The sound was unsettling, like the gasp of a dying man. His eyes opened only a little, showing bloodshot whites and fever-bright irises. "What do you want from me, Ashmedai?" he said in a harsh whisper.

Essie narrowed her eyes, listening.

"You're killing your daughter's husband," said Little Ash. "I told you that you would."

"Ashel," murmured Uriel, over his shoulder.

"You have something I want," Little Ash went on. "And I have what you need. If you'll make a deal with me, we can all leave this place alive, and get revenge for your murder on top of it. What do you say?"

For a moment Isaak lay silent but for the loud, echoing breaths. His eyes closed and then opened again. "What is it you think you can give me?"

Little Ash glanced at Uriel, then laid a hand flat over his own heart. "I have a body and a soul for you to cling to. One that isn't dying."

forty-three

WHAT?" SAID URIEL, STARTLED. "But you kept telling me that it wasn't safe."

The rebbe seemed to be thinking the same. His eyes sharpened, scanning Little Ash's face. "It will hurt you, selfish creature. Are you really willing?"

Little Ash brushed them off. "What, am I not allowed to care about the fate of my kehilleh? Rebbe, did you forget about Josef, who sat in the study halls, and ben Temaylon, who helped redeem the Jewish People from the Romans? It seems to me that there are humans as selfish as I am and as long as you're sitting on Reb Shulman's heart and crushing it, you're one of them."

Uriel tensed, expecting the rebbe to lash out at him, but he did not. Instead, he began to laugh. The sound had a quality to it that did not belong in the cramped cellar space, as if the rebbe were laughing at them not with the air from Isaak's lungs, but from some vast, dark cavern full of stone. Rose and Essie both shivered, feeling as if they were standing at the edge of a precipice with cold water rushing below.

But the rebbe did not mean the laugh to be malicious. He lifted Isaak's hand and patted Little Ash on the knee, as one might praise a clever student in cheder. "Very well. If you'll make the sacrifice, I will accept it."

Little Ash nodded and took a deep breath.

"Then for the sake of your children and your children's children, I adjure you to leave this man, only by the path I show you, that you not harm him, and if you do as I say, I promise in the name of my father and in the name of my mother, by Ashmedai, the king of demons, and Kapkafuni, the queen, that I, Ashmedai ben Ashmedai v'Kapkafuni, will carry you and carry out your revenge."

At the end of the adjuration, he pricked Isaak's foot with the pin, drawing a drop of blood, and pressed his own thumb to the spot.

For a moment they all held their breaths, watching Isaak's face. He lay as limp as ever for a few seconds, then suddenly his limbs jerked, and he gave another great gasping breath, and Little Ash fell backward as if someone had struck him.

Uriel rushed to his side, grabbing his shoulders and looking into his eyes. "Are you all right?"

Little Ash gasped, an echo of Isaak, and coughed as if something were stuck in his throat. Pressing the heel of his hand into one eye, he said, "I'm fine!" in a tone that made it clear he was not.

Rose had caught Isaak's head as he flailed, to keep him from hitting it on the wall or the floor. Now he opened his eyes and blinked up at her.

"Malke?" he said, his voice still a hoarse whisper, but without the chill echo of the rebbe's. "Malkele?"

"It's not Malke," said Rose. "I'm sorry."

"Is that you, Reb Shulman?" Uriel asked.

Little Ash dropped the hatpin and rubbed his hands up his arms, as if trying to brush something off his skin. Uriel and Essie exchanged wide-eyed looks, but Rose was preoccupied with the delirious Isaak. "We need to get Reb Shulman to a doctor. He's very weak."

Little Ash coughed again, and then spoke in a voice quite different from his own, in the rebbe's southern Yiddish accent. "I know Holy Names, but to speak them will burn this one's tongue."

"Isn't there anything else we can do?" said Uriel, worried. It was still holding Little Ash by the shoulder, steadying him, and it could feel him trembling. "Couldn't you borrow my body instead?"

"No!" exclaimed Little Ash, in his own voice. "No. You don't want to kill Mr. Sullivan."

"We need a plan," said Essie. "If we get out, Rose and I can get Mr. Shulman to the doctor. But how do we get out without all being shot?"

Little Ash broke away from Uriel's hand with an odd,

jerking step and started pacing. "The rebbe says he can unlock the door. We'll find Mr. Sullivan and his men. You three take Reb Shulman and run."

"Two," Uriel corrected him. "I will stay with you."

Little Ash stopped and looked it in the face. Its expression was determined, and he found his objections dying on his tongue. He did not like the feeling of the dybbuk curled along his spine, drinking from his soul, and though he wouldn't have admitted it aloud, he'd been frightened of being left alone with the rebbe.

"Fine," he said. "Then Essie should take the ledger, and the girls should run. Can you carry Reb Shulman between you?"

There was a bit of shuffling as Rose and Essie each took one of Isaak's arms and lifted him from the floor. He was a tall man, and Essie was shorter than Rose, so it was awkward to carry him together, but they could at least move him even if his feet dragged behind him.

They knew only the part of the building they'd come in through, but that was at least enough to know that outside the locked door was a staircase leading up to the hallway. From there, on one side was the door to the building, and on the other were unknown rooms with an unknown number of men in them. It was late; the men might be sleeping. But none of them wanted to count on it.

Once Boaz's account book was safely hidden in Essie's pocket, and she and Rose, with Isaak over their shoulders, were ready to run, Little Ash put his hand on the door and the rebbe spoke a series of Names. The words smoked on Little Ash's tongue and sent him into another fit of coughing. As he stood there, the wood around his hand began to darken and shrink away, until suddenly the door fell from its hinges in a pile of rot.

The demon swallowed his coughs and jumped over the pile of debris, running ahead of the others up the stairs with Uriel barely on his heels. There was a guard at the top of the staircase who'd turned at the sound of something falling, but Little Ash hit him at full force before he could so much as shout an alarm. They fell to the ground together, and for a moment Little Ash and the rebbe wrestled for control of their shared left arm, Little Ash trying to grab the man's face and the rebbe trying to squeeze his throat. Then Little Ash pushed past the resistance and plucked the man's soul out from behind his eyes.

The crash of bodies hitting the ground, however, had alerted the other men in the house. Before Little Ash could get to his feet, another door burst open and Jamie ran into the hallway, brandishing his pistol.

Uriel jumped between him and the slower-moving Rose and Essie just as the gun went off. The bullet hit its shoulder, spinning it around and knocking it to the ground at Little Ash's side. At the sight of blood, Little Ash froze, but the rebbe, less sensitive, shouted another Holy Name and Jamie leapt back, dropping his gun as if it had burned his hand and crashing into Sullivan, who was trying to get through the doorway behind him.

"Peter Sullivan!" the rebbe shouted, his voice hoarse in Little Ash's throat. "Did you think you had killed me?!"

Jamie and Sullivan, tangled in the doorway, looked at him and saw not Little Ash, and not even the frightful vision of the insensible Isaak Shulman who had attacked them in the bar the night before, but something larger, darker, sharper. Something they'd never seen before with their waking eyes, a thing that visited them on long nights when there wasn't enough whiskey in the world to soothe their consciences.

Jamie was the weaker soul. He fell to his knees, sobbing, and began to scramble away, not even reaching for the gun he'd dropped. Sullivan merely stood for a moment, rooted to the spot.

Rose and Essie hovered on the cellar stairs. Little Ash and the rebbe, for a moment thinking the same thought, both pushed their body upright, moving toward Sullivan and away from the stairs to give the girls more room. Sullivan lifted his gun with a trembling hand, then suddenly turned and ran.

Little Ash leapt after him, and Uriel, one arm hanging limp, got to its feet and followed.

Sullivan had fled out a back door, with the rebbe and Little Ash pursuing him. The house was suddenly dead silent, a large, empty quiet like the moment after a clap of thunder.

Rose shook her head to clear it and nudged Essie's ankle with the toe of her own boot. "Come on. We should go, in case there's anyone else. How will we get back to Hester Street?"

"I have an idea," said Essie. "The motorcar. I've watched Mr. Boaz's driver operate one—I think I can work it out."

The Sullivans' police wagon was just outside, sitting empty but for Essie's bundle of belongings, which had been left in the front seat. Rose was reluctant to lay Isaak on the floor of the steel cell, but there was no room for him in the front. As Essie inspected the front of the vehicle, Rose laid him down and then took the risk of ducking back into the building. There was a staircase leading upward, and at the top, as she had hoped, she found a few dingy bedrooms. The blankets she was able to bring back were filthy and moth-eaten, but they'd at least keep Isaak from being jostled too badly.

Rose found Essie standing by the running board at the front of the vehicle. "I need you and your hatpins," she said.

Following Essie's direction, Rose got in the cab and stuck her hatpin into the ignition, standing at the ready as Essie turned a crank outside, then wriggled the pin when Essie gave the word.

Nothing happened.

"Damn it!" said Essie, to Rose's surprise and delight— she hadn't heard a girl swear before. "All right. Again. We can hardly walk back to the Lower East Side."

She turned the crank again, throwing her whole weight

into it, while Rose frantically pushed the pin back and forth. Suddenly, with a cough, the engine came to life, and the wagon gave a shudder.

With a shriek of delight, Essie leapt up into the driver's seat. It seemed to Rose that they were hurtling straight for the river, but then Essie threw the wheel around and they turned, both girls now screaming in a mixture of terror and excitement.

The wagon plunged forward into the night as the sound of gunshots rang out behind them.

forty-four

M<small>R. SULLIVAN HAD RUN</small> from the building as if a hellhound were snapping at his heels, but a block away, standing at the edge of the dark water of the river and with the familiar sounds and smells of his city around him, he slowed. What was he afraid of? It had not been a rational reaction that caused him to flee, but some animal instinct. When he thought back to that moment in the hallway, what had frightened him? Only the same young Jew pests from Boaz's house.

He stopped and tucked his gun back into his jacket, drawing out a pack of cigarettes instead, disgusted at how his hands shook. He considered himself a sophisticated man, above the irrational vices that plagued many lesser gang leaders. He did not gamble away the money he earned, he never drank until he lost his mind, and when he killed he killed with purpose. He'd broken strikes before.

He was not afraid of ghosts.

And yet. Something was not right.

"Jesus, Mary, and Joseph," he swore, as a match snapped in his hand without lighting. He'd meant to go back to Boaz's house in the morning to inform him that the troublemaker Isaak Shulman was locked up in a cellar and that Sullivan would accept another $500 to make him disappear entirely. Now he wondered if he didn't need a break. Maybe go upstate in the middle of nowhere, and visit the boys who brought goods in from Canada. Get some fresh air. Look at a cow and remember why he'd left the farm in the first place.

A match caught at last, and he paced up and down the dock, drawing the smoke into his lungs. Where the hell was Jamie? Jamie was always taking fright at nothing. Wouldn't shoot a girl. Coward. You should never go into business with family.

The East River docks were stacked with crates, and in the shadows behind Mr. Sullivan, Little Ash now crouched next to one of those stacks, untying his boots. The rebbe was shouting at him, inside his head, to simply run up and tear the man to pieces, but Little Ash had less confidence in his own fists than the rebbe had. As he tucked his socks into his boots, Uriel arrived and knelt beside him. It was holding its left shoulder tightly with the other hand, blood spilling over its fingers.

"What are we going to do?" it whispered to Little Ash. It could see Mr. Sullivan as a silhouette on the edge of the river, his face lit by the cigarette whenever he lifted it.

Little Ash looked at its shoulder. Without answering the question, he pried Uriel's right hand away to inspect the wound, and he did not like what he found. There was quite a lot of blood soaked into its sweater, and there was a glassiness in its eyes.

"Doesn't that hurt?" he asked, unhooking his suspenders so he could wriggle out of his tallis katan. "Keep an eye on Sullivan and shout if he starts to leave."

Uriel pressed its shoulder again and nodded, looking over at Sullivan as Little Ash tore up his undershirt and bandaged the wound as best he could. Sullivan was still pacing.

"He will shoot us again," it murmured.

"Six bullets," said Little Ash. "One hit you. I heard one hit a wall. Four left."

He couldn't be confident that Sullivan hadn't reloaded. He wasn't going to tell his injured partner that. He felt the rebbe notice the deception and choose to let it pass.

"Distraction," said Uriel, in the dreamy tone of someone who might pass out at any moment.

"Look how he's moving," said Little Ash. "Like a bad puppet. He's nervous, you see? Nervous people do things that are stupid."

Satisfied that Uriel's shoulder was as well wrapped as it could be, he looked around, taking in their surroundings. Little Ash knew Sullivan would not be able to see as well as he could, with his cat's vision.

"Enough delay," rasped the rebbe, through Little Ash's lips. His voice tasted caustic on the demon's tongue.

"We are making a plan," said Uriel. "Ashel has done all of this before—let him think."

Little Ash glanced around at it, and it gave him a confident nod. He swallowed an unaccustomed surge of nerves. He had *not* done this before: he'd never put his partner in this much danger.

But it believed in him. Even the rebbe's scorn, searing at him from within, could not eclipse that.

He took a deep breath and rose to his feet. Just as Sullivan turned to leave the dock, Little Ash threw one of his boots into the river. Startled by the sound, Sullivan looked around, his hand going to his pocket to draw out the gun again. Little Ash threw the other boot directly toward him.

The gun went off, the bullets wild as Sullivan fired twice at what, to the eyes of a man walking half in a nightmare, seemed like some creature flying at his head. Little Ash threw himself sideways, knocking over the pile of crates between them. Sullivan leapt backward as the crates crashed to the ground, but he'd regained enough control that he didn't shoot. Little Ash started to run as the crates fell. Sullivan's third shot shrieked past his ear and slammed into another stack of crates.

Little Ash collided with Sullivan at full speed, grabbing for his gun arm. Sullivan stumbled and regained his balance, and for a moment they wrestled for control. The rebbe's inhuman strength made Little Ash's grip into iron, and Sullivan could not free his arm. He drew a knife from his pocket left-handed, and stabbed at Little Ash half blindly, slashing at his wrist, but Little Ash let go of Sullivan's arm for a moment and grabbed instead for the gun itself. The movement threw Sullivan's weight off-balance, and he slipped on the edge of the dock.

The final gunshot went off just as they both plunged into the rushing water.

Uriel scrambled forward as they went over the edge. For a moment it could see the stir of the water where they'd hit the surface, and then the current snatched at the movement and dragged it away.

Kneeling on the edge of the dock, it desperately scanned downriver, but nothing broke the surface.

forty-five

Rose thought that Essie would crash the police wagon five times before they reached Hester Street, but rattled as the girls were, they were all in one piece when Essie braked in front of the Shulmans' bookshop and wrestled with the controls until the engine stopped coughing.

"Run to the Women's Council House and get the doctor," said Rose, leaping out of the cab. "It's down that way on the corner. I'll wake everyone and tell them about Isaak!"

She didn't wait for Essie's response. The two girls ran in opposite directions, Rose up the stairs to the Shulman family's apartment and Essie down the street.

Soon the bookshop was brightly lit and crowded not only with the Shulman family, but with other strikers who'd heard the motorcar and come out to see what was going on. Isaak's brothers brought a mattress down from the apartment and laid him on it, and Malke sat next to him holding his hand while the doctor from the Women's Council looked him over, cleaning his cuts and bruises and spooning medicine down his throat.

After a few minutes' inspection, the doctor declared that she could see no reason Isaak would not be better in the morning—his heart was beating strongly, his breaths were even, and the fever was coming down already. Hearing this good news, the assembled company broke out into cheers until Malke sternly shushed them.

Not wanting to intrude on the family reunion, Rose nudged Essie and pointed toward the stairs. Essie, to her surprise, took her hand, and linked together they went up to the apartment and climbed out onto the fire escape, where the night air felt somehow warm and soft, and the moon shone down on them with a reassuring light.

"Thank you," said Essie, after a few minutes of sitting in silence.

"For what?" said Rose. Essie had not let go of her hand, and the warmth from where their arms were pressed together seemed to be spreading throughout her body, chasing away the chill that had clung to her since Mr. Sullivan had held his gun to her head.

"For what!" Essie laughed. "Silly girl, for rescuing me. For being brave, and helping Isaak, and getting us here with the ledger—we'll be able to stop Mr. Boaz from threatening everyone now. He won't be able to hold our debts over us anymore. You might have changed the lives of half of Hester Street tonight."

"It was only the right thing to do," said Rose, embarrassed. "I couldn't sit aside and let those men hold you hostage."

"Don't be modest," said Essie. She leaned closer, her eyes shining in the moonlight, and suddenly Rose felt as if she understood something that had plagued her forever.

Why she had felt so betrayed when Dinah got married. Why she had run all the way to America to get away from that feeling.

The revelation knocked the breath out of her. She felt like she was standing at Sinai, receiving the word of Heaven, a responsibility so huge that one could hardly imagine it. What did one do with a thought like this? What did one do with a girl whose dark braids and bright green eyes held in them all the secrets of the Universe?

She did not have to find the answer.

Essie kissed her first.

Uriel had watched for several long minutes at the edge of the water, then dragged itself downstream, looking for anyone washed up on the banks, and found nothing. At last, feeling light-headed and despairing, it returned to Sullivan's empty headquarters and sat on the step with its head in its hands. There it stayed until the sky began to lighten over the river, and a little voice whispered somewhere deep inside itself, *Shacharit.*

It scarcely noticed the return of the angelic direction.

It could not pray Shacharit without Little Ash. What blessings could be worth saying?

Besides, its arm hurt so much. It wanted only to sleep. Perhaps it might lie down on the ground, and become dust.

Uriel had its eyes closed, lost in misery, when it heard footsteps in the street, a familiar uneven rhythm. Its heart leapt, and there was Little Ash, soaking wet and looking rather small and fragile, his shirt stained with blood. He was holding a gun. He was not dead.

"What happened?" said Uriel. "Oh, Ashel. Ashmedai, I thought you were gone."

It tried to get up, but Little Ash dropped onto the step beside Uriel first, and leaned against its good shoulder. "Mr. Sullivan is drowned. The rebbe went with him. I suppose they're at the bottom of the ocean now."

He laid his head on the angel's shoulder, and dropped the gun onto the cobbles. He closed his eyes and sighed. "I thought you would have bled to death without me. Why did you have to go and take a human name, you wretched creature?"

"I don't know," said Uriel. "I don't know. For the same reason you needed me to come to America with you, I think."

"What reason?" said Little Ash, without opening his eyes.

"Because," said Uriel. "You are the friend of my soul. I needed a name so I could stay with you. I have decided something. If you are going to get yourself in trouble, you need to bring me with you. It feels right, like a mitzvah. You don't have to protect me. I'll protect you, if you like."

Little Ash was quiet for some time. He couldn't think of anything he could say that would mean as much as those three words, *like a mitzvah*, from the mouth of an angel. He loved his chevrusa with all of his heart: he'd known it by a hundred names, and he'd loved it always. He could not ask it to give up a name it liked having, not even to keep it safe.

"All right," he said. He laced their fingers together and lifted its hand to his lips, kissing its bruised knuckles. "All right. You can be Uriel forever, and save a hundred rebbes. Be an angel or a demon or anything you like. Just don't leave me."

"I won't," it said, and for a while they were quiet, counting each other's slow breaths.

Finally Little Ash said, "I suppose we should tell Mr. Boaz that we've killed his enforcer. So Mrs. Shulman can rest, and not devour Essie's soul."

"Essie!" Uriel exclaimed, sitting up. "What happened to her and Rose? They aren't here; there is no one here at all."

Little Ash pushed himself to his feet. "Best find out. But first I need to stitch us both up—you're still bleeding, and Sullivan almost carved out my kidneys."

There was a kitchen in Sullivan's headquarters, and Little Ash made Uriel sit at the table while he searched out a bottle of whiskey, some clean linen, and a needle. While he was looking, he found also a pile of dollar notes in an iron kettle behind the stove—a small fortune in paper. This he placed next to the whiskey and linen on the table, and he sat across from Uriel while they waited for a pot of water to boil.

"If only you could pull out a tractate," he said, kicking his heels. "It's been so long since we've studied anything."

At this, Uriel remembered the little whisper that had told it the dawn was approaching. Curious, it closed its eyes and reached out its hand, the way it always used to do, simply expecting to find a book there.

And there it was: a clean little volume of Eruvin, bound in sheep's leather.

Little Ash blinked at the book. "But I thought your magic wasn't working? The name?"

"I think it was the rebbe, only," said Uriel. "My soul feels lighter without him. I suppose it was his evil impulse, or being so close to death?"

It spoke the words as a question, hoping Little Ash would have heard of something to explain it, but he hadn't. He shrugged, wincing as the movement pulled on the place where Sullivan had stabbed him, and got up to retrieve the steaming pot. He soaked a rag in the boiled water and sat next to Uriel, untying the makeshift bandage from its shoulder with careful fingers.

"Read me a Mishnah," he said. "And don't scream when I touch you. I need to make sure the bullet is out."

Uriel read him a Mishnah, and then the commentary, and they were onto the second Mishnah by the time he'd stitched up its shoulder with his lucky red thread and cleaned out his own wounds. The one on his torso was in truth not so deep, and when Little Ash touched it he could feel a lingering strangeness like the feeling of the Holy Names the rebbe had pronounced with his tongue: it seemed the old man had left him a refuah, a healing, as a gift.

forty-six

SOLOMON BOAZ, TORMENTED by guilt and the promise of bad dreams, had not slept a wink. Just before dawn, he left his bed and went into his office, where he lit all of the lamps and sat down to write a letter to his brother, confessing that he had squandered his share of the company's profits on gambling, fallen into bad company, and lost sight of his way so terribly that he had hired thieves and murderers to solve his problems for him. He had left widowers and orphans in his wake. And he had, by all of these actions, placed his beloved daughter Minnie into danger.

The writing occupied him well into the morning, interrupted by long pauses during which he simply sat and stared at the wall, murmuring incoherent speeches of remorse to an invisible interlocutor. He was still thus engaged when someone knocked at the office door.

"Come in!" he called, out of habit, and then realized he was in his nightclothes, disheveled, and scarcely knew what was happening.

The housekeeper opened the door and said, "Rabbi Wolf is here to see you, with some people."

She sounded perplexed. This was because one of the visitors was the young peddler from whom she'd purchased a spool or two of thread a few days earlier.

"Rabbi Wolf?" said Mr. Boaz, shaking his head in an attempt to clear it. "Oh. Rabbi Wolf! At this time of the morning? Please, send him in."

Rabbi Wolf came into the office, with Uriel and Little Ash behind him. The rabbi took in Mr. Boaz's appearance and sighed. This morning, on his own sunrise ramble about Central Park, he had found Little Ash and Uriel waiting for him on the path, as if they'd somehow known exactly where to find him. They had shown him Mr. Boaz's ledger, and explained that not only the Boaz family but the whole Jewish community could be in danger if something was not done, and then Uriel, honest as always, had informed him that the danger was a dybbuk.

Rabbi Wolf had not thought he believed in dybbuks. But he had felt something in the Boaz house that he could not explain, and after the strange party he had gone home, read some newspapers, and discovered that a worker in Boaz's factory had died, and he had remembered the old wives' tales his family's cook used to tell him, in her Eastern Jewish accent, while she fed him rugelach and chunks of kugel.

He therefore had agreed to bring the message to Mr. Boaz, and so here they were.

"Solomon," said the rabbi, "on behalf of the community, I am very concerned for you."

He did not even need to relay the rest of his message. Mr. Boaz broke down sobbing and pushed his letter across the desk. "Please, rabbi. Help me make amends! I have been consorting with the worst kind of criminals."

Little Ash and Uriel saw Mrs. Shulman perched on the back of his chair. She met their eyes and nodded, a smile growing across her face that was much warmer, and less full of teeth, than the smile she had given them before.

The bad luck was sinking into the floorboards with every word Mr. Boaz said. He had the idea that he might sell the factory to the workers—that he would sell his house and take his family upstate for the air, that he was going to tell the police about Mr. Sullivan, and on and on.

The two angels, the good angel and the wicked, left the house together hand in hand, leaning on each other when they grew tired, and walked back to the Lower East Side carrying only good news.

epilogue

Rose sat next to Essie at a table in the Cafe Krakow, writing a letter to Dinah. They'd gone out dancing the night before, and she would tell Dinah about that at the end of the letter, but first she had to explain the whole story of how she'd helped Dinah's aunt and uncle-in-law take over a factory and overturn so many debts that Hester Street might have been celebrating its own Jubilee year.

She did not write *I forgive you for marrying Saul*, but she hoped that Dinah would understand it all the same. She felt she had been very unfair to Dinah. If Dinah saw in Saul's eyes what Rose saw in Essie's, how could she have done anything but fall into his arms? Dinah was not made for adventures, and neither was Saul. Rose was made for adventures.

"You'd better finish writing," said Essie. "Otherwise

you'll have to explain to her that you missed her cousins' bris."

Malke's twins had come, with the impeccable timing of babies, just as work was about to begin again at the reopened factory. Menachem and Dovid, they were called, one for his grandfather and the other for his grandmother Dvorah.

Little Ash and Uriel had been asked to hold the babies for the bris, not only as the rebbe's supposed students, but also because Essie had spread around the whisper of their real identities. She'd heard the rebbe's dybbuk call Little Ash by his full name, and she recalled the story that was always passed around the children of Shtetl, that their synagogue was haunted by an angel and a demon, and depending on how good or wicked you were, one or the other of them might leave their studies to interfere with your life. Neither of the two had denied it when she asked them to their faces, and besides, if she squinted sideways, she could see their feet.

The events of the strike had been so strange that no one disbelieved the story, especially once Isaak Shulman backed it up with his account of waking from a dream that his father-in-law's vengeful ghost had dragged him around the city, chasing down the evildoers and scaring Mr. Boaz into doing his teshuvah.

Rose folded up her letter, and Essie tucked away the pages of a letter she'd been working on herself, to send back to Shtetl and let everyone know that she was safe. There would be a generous portion of dollar bills included in the letter:

Little Ash had given her nearly all of the money from Mr. Sullivan's kettle. She'd added, in a postscript, that their local angel and demon were now to be found in America, in case anyone had noticed an empty spot in the synagogue.

The angel and the demon, at that moment, were sitting in a corner of the Shulman bookshop, their heads together over a volume of Talmud. They'd left the complexity of Eruvin behind for something more restful, and were studying the Laws of Blessing instead. They were in their accustomed spot, as if the bookshop were a study hall, with their backs to the door, both of them wrapped in Uriel's tallis to keep off the draft.

"It can't go by the word of Rav," said Little Ash, slapping the table. "Rav's word makes no sense at all. The logic doesn't follow!"

Uriel looked sideways at him as he again slapped the table to emphasize his point. "It *has* to go by the word of Rav," it said. "You don't understand the logic, only."

It was very pleasant to have such an argument. They fully intended to stay that way forever.

Next time you're in shul, or in a bookshop, look over your shoulder to the back corner, far from the stove and close to the door. You'll see them, maybe.

The End

glossary

THE CHARACTERS IN THIS STORY speak in four distinct languages: English, Yiddish, Hebrew, and Aramaic. For those not familiar with any of those words, I offer this glossary with my own understanding of the words' meanings, recognizing that translation is not an exact science! Context always suggests shades of meaning.

Many of the words are "loshn koydesh": words that are borrowed from Hebrew but spelled and used as Yiddish. The Yiddish transliteration mostly follows the YIVO (Institute for Jewish Research) standard, but with some words spelled as they are more commonly seen in English.

ACH! (YIDDISH): an exclamation meaning "Oh!" or "Yes!" or "Darn!" depending on context

ADONAI (HEBREW): one of the most common euphemisms for the unpronounceable Name of God, literally "my Lord"

ALEF (HEBREW): the first letter of the Hebrew alphabet

ALEICHEM SHALOM (HEBREW): "unto you peace"; often said in response to the greeting *shalom aleichem/sholem aleichem*

ALEINU (HEBREW):   the concluding prayer in a Jewish service

ASHAMNU (HEBREW):   a penitential prayer consisting of an alphabetical list of sins, usually recited while pounding the chest with a fist

AVODAH ZARAH (HEBREW):   a section of the Talmud dealing with the religious practices of non-Jews; historically often banned by Christian authorities who thought it contained slander against their religion

AYIN (HEBREW/YIDDISH):   the sixteenth letter of the Hebrew alphabet; eye, in Yiddish

AYIN HOREH (YIDDISH):   the evil eye

BAR/BAT/B'NEI MITZVAH (HEBREW):   variations of a term meaning "child of the commandments"; a celebration of a child reaching adulthood in the eyes of the Jewish community (bar: son of; bat: daughter of; b'nei: children of, not gender-specific)

BEYS-MIDRASH (YIDDISH):   a school; a house of learning

B'NEI ELOHIM (HEBREW):   literally children of God, refers to angels and sometimes demons

BRIS (HEBREW): the Jewish ritual of circumcision performed on the eighth day of a boy's life

CANTOR (ENGLISH): a person who leads the congregation in prayer; see also *chazzan*

CHAZZAN (HEBREW): a person with training in the vocal arts who helps lead the congregation in prayer

CHEDER (YIDDISH): an elementary school for Jewish children in which Hebrew and religious knowledge are taught

CHEVRUSA (HEBREW / YIDDISH): a study partner

CHUMASH (HEBREW): a prayerbook consisting of the Five Books of Moses (aka the Torah)

DAVEN, DAVENING (HEBREW): pray, praying

DYBBUK (ENGLISH): from the Yiddish *dibek*; a malevolent supernatural being created when a deceased person's soul stays behind among the living to complete unfinished business instead of passing on to the afterlife

EISHET CHAYIL (HEBREW): literally "woman of valor," a woman who exemplifies the best of her gender

ERUVIN (ARAMAIC): a notoriously difficult section of the Talmud dealing with every possible permutation of the difference between private and public space

FALSE MESSIAH, THE (ENGLISH): generally, anyone who falsely claims to *be* the messiah and is not; most famously Shabbatai Tzvi

GEHINNOM (HEBREW): the place where souls go to be purified after death, but also metaphorically a place of torment

GEMARA (HEBREW): rabbinic commentary on the Mishnah; Mishnah and Gemara together make up the Talmud

GIMEL: the third letter in the Hebrew alphabet

GONIF (YIDDISH): a thief

GOYISH (YIDDISH): having the quality of being non-Jewish

HEYMISH (YIDDISH): down-to-earth; possessing a warm, homey quality

IBBUR (HEBREW/YIDDISH): a benevolent possession; an invited spirit

KABBALIST (ENGLISH): someone who knows the secrets of Kabbalah (Jewish mysticism); Little Ash worries that they know how to banish demons

KAPORES (HEBREW/YIDDISH): a ritual traditionally performed before Yom Kippur in which a person symbolically transfers sins to a live chicken, which they wave over their head three times. More modern versions of the ritual consign transgressions to money, to the bills and coins gathered in one's hand instead. The Yiddish idiom "a kapores on something" more or less translates to the English expression "to hell with it."

KEHILLEH (HEBREW): congregation; in Eastern Europe, also referred to a structure of semi-autonomous Jewish lay leadership which oversaw the maintenance of religious law and community standards from the sixteenth to the mid-nineteenth centuries

KEYNEHORE (YIDDISH): literally, "no evil eye"; an expression uttered to prevent the evil eye from noticing your good fortune and taking it away

KOSHER (ENGLISH): following the laws of Judaism; most commonly refers to food, but can apply to any thing or action

*LAI-LAI-LAI*ED: "lai-lai-lai" is a rendering of the syllables sung to a prayer or tune (the equivalent of "la-la-la" in

English); "*laied*" is a made-up construction to form a verb of the activity of singing this way

LAWS OF BLESSING (ENGLISH): tractate Berakhot, the first section of the Talmud

LOSHN HOREH (YIDDISH): literally, "evil talk"; refers to malicious gossip

LOSHN KOYDESH (YIDDISH): the holy language

MAARIV (HEBREW): traditional Judaism has three daily prayers; Maariv is the evening prayer

MACHER (YIDDISH): a big shot; someone who likes to have their hand in all the goings-on

MECHITZEH (YIDDISH): a barrier put up to divide men from women, usually in an Orthodox synagogue

MELAMED (HEBREW): one who teaches Hebrew to small children

MENSCH (YIDDISH): literally, "man"; refers to anyone who is a good person

MEZUZAH (HEBREW): a decorative container that holds the text of the She'ma, a foundational prayer in Hebrew proclaiming that there is one God, put up on the doorframes of observant Jews to fulfill an obligation detailed in that prayer

MIKVEH (HEBREW / YIDDISH): a ritual bath

MINYAN (HEBREW): a quorum; a gathering of people large enough to form an "official" prayer group

MISHNAH (HEBREW): the core text of the Talmud, on which the Gemara is a commentary

MITZVAH (HEBREW): a commandment in Judaism, something we are obligated to do (or not do); can also mean "a good deed"

OLOV HASHOLEM (HEBREW / YIDDISH): "may he rest in peace"

PALE OF SETTLEMENT, THE (ENGLISH): a western region of the Russian Empire with varying borders (now parts of what is Belarus, Lithuania, Moldova, Ukraine, Poland, Latvia, and Russia) that existed from 1791 to 1917, inside which permanent residency by Jews was allowed and beyond which Jewish residency, permanent or temporary, was mostly forbidden

PEYOT / PEYES (HEBREW / YIDDISH): the curled locks of hair that fall in front of the ears, worn by some Jewish men

PIKUACH NEFESH (HEBREW): the primacy of saving lives; an indication that this value surpasses all other values in terms of Jewish law

POGROM (YIDDISH): from the Russian *pogrom*; devastation or destruction; refers to officially sanctioned massacres, leveled against the Jews of Russia and Eastern Europe

PSALMS (ENGLISH): songs found in the first book of the Ketuvim ("Writings"), the third section of the Tanakh (the three volumes that make up holy Hebrew scripture); traditionally ascribed to King David

RABBI / REBBE (HEBREW / YIDDISH): the official head of a Jewish congregation, or a respectful way of addressing a particularly learned person; as used in this story, a rebbe is specifically the leader of a Hasidic Jewish sect

REB (YIDDISH): approximately translates to "Mr."

REFUAH (HEBREW): a healing

RESH (HEBREW): the twentieth letter of the Hebrew alphabet

RUGELACH (YIDDISH): a delicious baked treat originating in Poland, made up of a crescent pastry wrapped around a filling of cinnamon, chocolate, etc.

SCHMALTZ (YIDDISH):   fat; colloquially, can mean "corny"

SCHNORRER (YIDDISH):   a beggar

SHABBAT / SHABBES (HEBREW / YIDDISH):   the holy seventh day of the week, meant to be free of work

SHACHARIT (HEBREW):   the morning prayers

SHALOM ALEICHEM / SHOLEM ALEICHEM (HEBREW / YIDDISH):   a greeting meaning "peace be with you"

SHEMONEH ESREH (HEBREW):   literally, "eighteen"; one of the most important prayers in Judaism, also called the Amidah or "standing prayer," made up of eighteen blessings

SHEYD, SHEYDIM (YIDDISH):   mischievous spirits of the earth

SHEYFELE (YIDDISH):   "little lamb"; a term of endearment

SHTETL (YIDDISH):   a small town

SHUL (YIDDISH):   a place of prayer and study; a synagogue

SIMCHA (HEBREW):   literally, "gladness" or "joy"; refers to a celebration or a reason to celebrate

SPIEL (YIDDISH): a long and fast talk, speech, or harangue, usually used in persuading or selling; in a literal sense, refers to a play, as in a Purim spiel

TALLIS / TALLIS KATAN (YIDDISH): a Jewish prayer shawl/ small Jewish prayer shawl, worn under a shirt

TALMUD (HEBREW): literally, "study" or "learning"; commonly refers to a compilation of ancient teachings regarded as sacred and normative by Jews from the time it was compiled until modern times, and is still so regarded by traditional religious Jews

TATE (YIDDISH): father

TESHUVAH (HEBREW): repentance

TFILLIN (HEBREW): a set of small black leather boxes with leather straps containing scrolls of parchment inscribed with verses from the Torah; tfillin are worn by adult Jews during weekday morning prayers

TRACTATE (ENGLISH): one of the sixty-three parts of the Talmud; the Talmud is roughly divided by subject, with each tractate centered on a different topic, although they often overlap

TZEDOKE (HEBREW / YIDDISH): charity

TZITZIS (HEBREW/YIDDISH): specially knotted ritual fringes, or tassels, found at the ends of a tallis

URI, URI, SHIR DABEIRI, K'VOD ADONAI ALAYICH NIGLAH (HEBREW): a line of the traditional prayer Lecha Dodi, sung to welcome the Sabbath: "Awake and sing: the Eternal's glory dawns upon you"

VAV (HEBREW): the sixth letter of the Hebrew alphabet; also means "hook"

YESHIVA (HEBREW): a traditional school for Jewish learning

YESHIVA-BOKHER (YIDDISH): a student at a traditional school for Jewish learning

YETZER HARA/YETZER HOREH (HEBREW/YIDDISH): the evil inclination

YETZER TOV (HEBREW/YIDDISH): the inclination for good

acknowledgments

I'M SO EXCITED to see this story become a real book and thankful to everyone who has helped it, and me, along the way.

My agent, Rena Rossner, is tireless and responds to emails at mind-boggling speed. Thank you for liking my pitch tweet and thank you for always going beyond the call of duty for your clients.

The Levine Querido team. Thanks to Arthur for believing in the "classic Yiddish novel, but it's queer" idea and understanding the direction I wanted the story to go. Thanks to Maddie for edits (and making me put some of the cutest parts back in) and Anamika for wrestling with over 300 pages of Yiddish and Hebrew romanizations. Thanks Irene for your publicity efforts. Thank you to everyone who had a hand in taking the book from text document to physical object, including, of course, Will Staehle for the amazing cover!

Thanks to the sensitivity readers for your perspectives—it always helps to have an extra pair of eyes. I would like to thank Rebecca Levithan, Madison Werthmann, and Irene Vázquez for their helpful feedback.

Although my 2020 residency at Porter Square Books

got cut short by the pandemic, I was still so thrilled to receive it. Love you, PSB!

Thanks to Emily Danforth for selecting me as a Lambda Literary Fellow in 2018. Your guidance helped me see how I could turn a "story" into a "book," even if I thought a different story would get there first. The support and companionship of the 2018 YA cohort is unparalleled—thank you especially to jd, Kirt, Jen, Lin, Jas, Avery, and Octavia, the daily groupchatters, but thanks also to Caitlin, Amal, Amos, Tia, and Kate. Someday we'll all be on a shelf together!

Birdchat, thanks for talking me through crises and appreciating dog photos. Thank you, farm family—Pip, Fer, Cyril, dogs, goats, and sheep. Sometimes the solution to a plot problem is to go fix a fence. Thanks, Anzu; even though you made me sit in the rat barn to do line edits, you are still cute and I appreciate you making me wake up in the morning.

Finally, thank you to my parents for always encouraging us to follow our obsessions. Your support means a lot and I wouldn't have gotten here without it.

SOME NOTES ON THIS BOOK'S PRODUCTION

The display type was set in Brandon Grotesque, a sans serif designed by Hannes von Döhren in 2010 and influenced by geometric-style faces popular in the 1920s and 30s. The text was set in Mrs. Eaves OT, a typeface designed by Zuzana Licko in 1996, itself inspired by John Baskerville's work (and named after his wife, Sarah Eaves). It was composed by Westchester Publishing Services in Danbury, CT. The book was printed on 55 lb Enviro Book Natural paper and bound in Canada.

Production was supervised by Freesia Blizard
Jacket design by Will Staehle
Interior design by Sheila Smallwood
Edited by Arthur A. Levine

LEVINE QUERIDO